SOURCE
ISSLEWOOD BINDING

KIM SEVERE

Published by Hahlya L.L.C
P.O. Box 615, Clearfield, Utah, 84089
Manufactured in the United States of America

ISBN 979-8-9894059-0-9 (Hardback)
ISBN 979-8-9894059-1-6 (Paperback)

To a certain son. A tragedy inspired a dream!

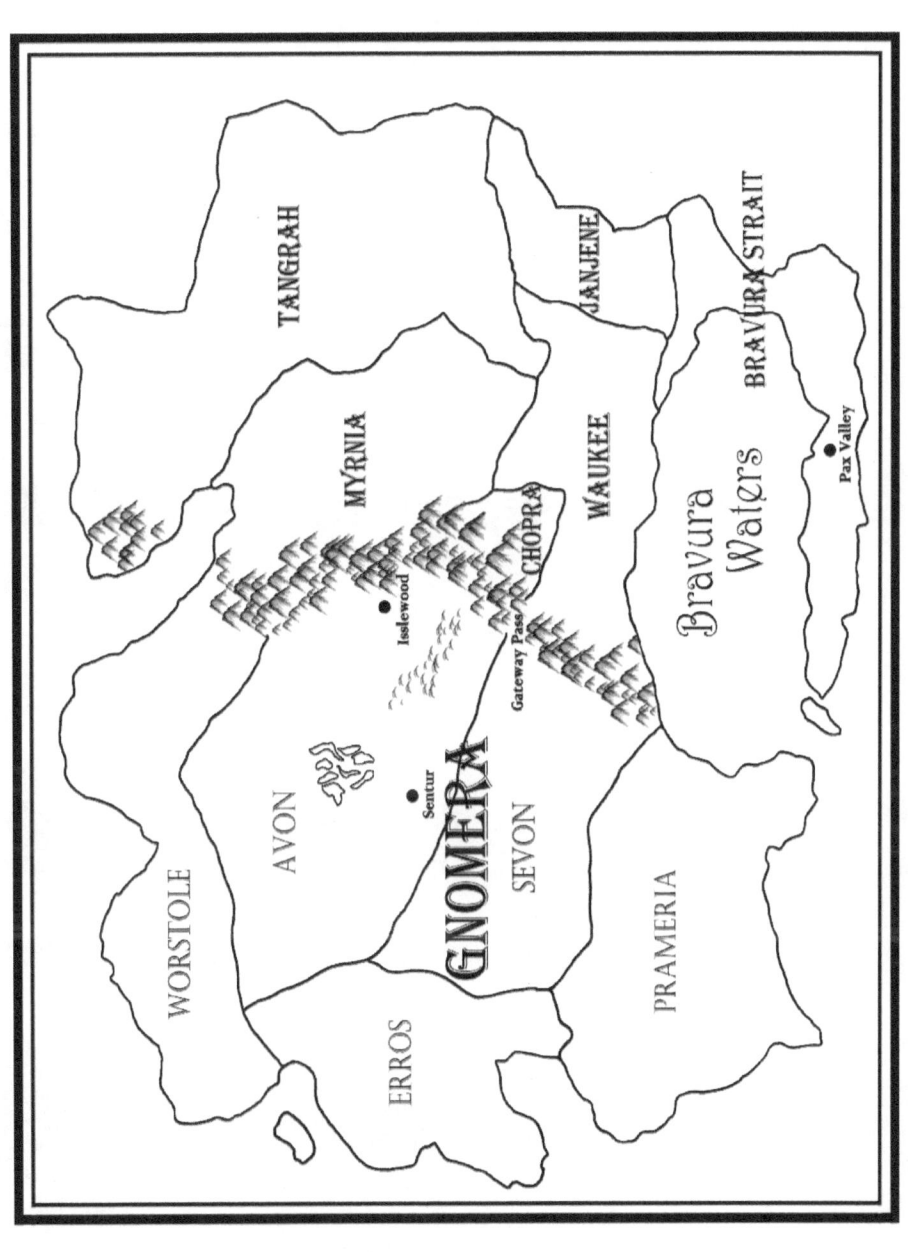

SOURCE

ISSLEWOOD BINDING

PROLOGUE

A thousand seasons cycles had passed before the Source had faded from truth to legend, and from legend to myth. Eventually, it was nothing more than campfire tales, but those who sought power continued to believe and diligently searched.

Long black hair slick with sweat hung to a narrow set of shoulders and a dribble of drink slid down a dark goatee. Dark eyes squinted across the table as they considered the preposterous words the stranger had shared. "We all grew up with those myths," the man smirked. "They are nothing more ... and you sound like you've lost your head."

A low raspy voice rumbled within the depths of a dark oversized hood. "Take care who you insult. I am the one willing to pay for service, and I know who you are, Viktus."

The man sat up straight in his chair with wide eyes. "How did you know my ...?"

The hooded man waved him off. "I have my ways."

There was no fear of being overheard. The gathering house was full of men who had assembled for a night of entertainment to escape their toils of a long day's work. They craved a good time. Two strangers huddled in dull conversation were beyond their notice.

A roll of laughter shook the walls on the other side of the

spacious chamber. A boisterous group of men eagerly shared their jokes and guzzled their brew, letting it drip down their beards as they gulped. All competed for attention, each shouting louder than the next. The smell of sweat and dirt and strong drink clung to the air in which the cloaked man breathed.

"It stinks in here," he complained.

"What do you expect?" asked Viktus as he looked around the chamber. "It is a gathering house after all! Are you of such rank that these places are beneath you?"

The hooded man ignored him and lifted his mug. After several large swallows, he slammed the empty mug on the table. "The Source is real," he said with authority. "The power is real. I will not beg – do I have your service or not?"

Viktus shook his head. "I am tempted by the payment you offer, but … I cannot believe what you say. I grew up with tales of the Source. I heard that whoever possessed it would have powers at their fingertips. Now you tell me those stories are true, that the Source is not a myth …" his words fell away.

The hood nodded.

A barmaid sashayed up to the two isolated men. "Hey, you two, this is your last chance for some stew," she said while suspiciously eyeing the hooded man. She ducked her head to peer into the shadows of the cloak, but the man drew back, clearly not liking her attempt to see his face. She wondered how he could bear the heat. There were a hundred oversized male bodies sweating up the place, radiating heat from every pore. If the hooded man was covering up, then he had something to hide.

"Why is your hood up?" the heavily curved woman inquired with narrowed eyes. "I don't trust a man that refuses to show his face."

She wiped away beads of sweat etching a path down the side of her cheek and resisted the urge to do the same with the perspiration leaving a big wet stain on her shapely chest. The gathering house was unbearably hot, and she would have removed her own dress if the men could keep their hands to themselves. This man had to have been drenched under his thick cloak.

Upon studying him further, she decided that he might have been hiding a deformity. If that was the case, she was glad he kept his hood in place. She had no interest to see anything ugly.

"Pass along, missy," Viktus piped up. "We are not interested in stew that will undoubtedly make us sick. We are only interested in drink and privacy. Keep us full and keep away."

The woman swept her eyes over him noticing his well-groomed goatee and dark, close-set eyes. A quick chill made her shiver.

"As you wish," she sniffed with a slight scowl. "I only aim to please." She filled their mugs then sauntered away.

After a glance around the stuffy room, Viktus turned back to the cloaked stranger. "I cannot believe I am thinking seriously of doing this. You are insane!" He paused a moment and added, "I am insane for considering it!"

A snapped retort came from under the hood. "What does it matter?! Why do you care if I'm mad as long as you have your reward?"

Viktus watched him lean back in his chair and for an instant, a flash of a smile appeared within the shadows of his hood. Then there was only darkness.

Viktus hunched over the table and rubbed a hand over his face. "You are right. It should not matter as long as I am compensated generously." He swallowed hard. "Can you describe this *Source* so that I know what I am charged to find?"

"No," came the curt reply.

His eyes widened. "You expect me to find something you cannot describe?" A snort escaped him. "That doesn't bode well for a successful outcome, does it?" Viktus stroked his goatee while staring into the shadows of the hood. He heaved an exasperated sigh. "Fine. Let us say I believe you. If I find this Source for you, what will you do with all that supposed power?"

There was silence within the shadows of the hood, then an irritated answer, "I'd rule the world, of course." After a moment, a hand reached across the table. "Then we have an agreement?" the gravelly voice asked.

Viktus eyed it for a long moment before grasping the hand in a shake. The grip was strong. "I'll do it! I will assemble a team." His voice was a rumble of amusement. "But I warn you, the compensation will be staggering. Me and my men will require top payment."

"You will have your compensation." The cloaked one produced a piece of writing. "This will lead you to half payment. You will receive the other half when I have the Source. Concentrate your search in Gnomera."

Brown eyes scrutinized the piece of writing. "Why Gnomera? And how shall I find you again when I …" Viktus's words hung in the stale air. The seat across from him was empty. He looked around searching the bodies close and far. How had the man left so quickly without him knowing?

A low gruff voice sounded across from him. "I will find you," the low growl came from the empty chair. "And Viktus, if you cross me, you will regret it, because I will find you and you will never see me coming." Then the quiet sound of footsteps retreated into the crowd.

Viktus drooped back in his chair, the wood creaking with the press of his weight. A tingle ran up his spine. Had his eyes played tricks on him? He dared not believe what he had seen, or rather, what he had *not* seen.

He had heard rumors of Talents but had never encountered one. It was said that Talents were somehow linked to the Source. He stared at the empty chair and had a suspicion that he had just bargained with a Shade. If he was right, perhaps the legend of the Source was true after all.

ONE

It was too dark for normal eyes to see. The evening shadows effectively concealed the target among elongated images which stretched and twisted across the forest ground. With frozen breath, the young hunter closed his eyes so he could view his target as clearly as if it were midday.

It was over almost before it began, the long blade spun from his hand and rotated silently toward the vivid grey form.

Rixs did not know how he could do it – how he could *see* with his eyes closed. He jerked his head to the side, needing to clear the hair from his eyes, and walked to the lifeless deer. It was a quick end for the animal.

The smile that spanned his face exposed dimples deep in his cheeks. *The crew would eat well tonight!*

It had been a season since the young man last kissed his mother's cheek and slapped his brother on the back, bidding them farewell and taking up with the crew. He might have remained in Pax Valley had the township council left him alone, but no. They required him to marry the girl they had picked for him when he was a mere thirteen winters. She had been only ten autumns.

Cliessa. The thought of her tears made him frown. Instead of marrying her as the law demanded, Rixsander of Pax Valley left his home and the only life he had ever known with little more than his clashing vest and rare collection of blades.

A thick, wet slurp sliced the silent night air as Rixs plucked the blade from the fallen deer. He wiped it clean on the leg of his pants then held it up to the moonlight. The black metal shimmered under the full moon and satisfaction fell over him. The Bravura Strait and Pax Valley was far behind him. A new adventure awaited.

Without needing eyes to guide him, he slipped the blade back into its pocket inside the left front panel of his clashing vest. The vest had been specially made for him and held all twenty-eight of his unique blades. There were two medium blades inside each front panel, four short blades, in two rows of two, on the outside of his vest at the side seams, just under his arms. His long blades, the length of short swords, crisscrossed his back, their grips easily accessible at his shoulders. The final touch was fourteen throwing sticks that lined the hem of his vest. With seven on each front panel, they looked more like decorative adornments than the lethal weapons they were.

No sooner had Rixs sheathed the medium blade than he perceived movement ahead. His eyes saw nothing in the darkness, but The Powers had bestowed a special ability on him that allowed him to distinguish the space that was no longer empty. It was the grey shape of a man meandering through the trees.

Ordinary vision was limited. The sun could be too bright making it difficult to see. The absence of light could be too dark making it difficult to see. Sometimes the eyes could play tricks on the mind – make a person see something that was never there or miss something that was always there. But Rixs had a second sight, and it never failed him nor fooled him.

This colorless view of the world lived in hues of grey. Empty spaces appeared in the lightest of greys and the darker shades of grey identified the object that filled the space. The darker the grey, the thicker, more solid, was the object. Not only could Rixs see the objects directly in front of him, he could see objects behind objects, behind objects. He saw everything – discerned everything, and it allowed him to comprehend the world around him such as no one else could.

Rixs focused on the form. It lacked the fine detail and color that defined the features of a person's identity, but features were not needed to recognize this man. His colossal size was evidence enough of the man approaching.

Skin that blended with the night, Rhages was a mountain of a man with hair that sprung out wickedly in all directions as though lightning had struck his head. Though he claimed to hate everyone, he had seemed to take a liking to Rixs, and it was he who had convinced the crew that the young adventurer should be allowed to tag along.

A large bundle of wood was held captive in his oversized arms as Rhages made his way back to camp, unaware that Rixs was only steps away. The deer slung across Rixs's shoulders created a horrifying figure in the moonlight. He snorted then stomped toward Rhages.

"Ah! By The Powers!" Rhages yelled. He jumped backward and grabbed his chest, the wood falling to the ground.

The skilled hunter grinned to himself. "Grrrrargh," he growled, jumping forward.

"Get hence, demon!" Rhages cried while yanking a hatchet from his belt.

A raucous laugh pierced and reverberated in the night air. "So! The fearless Rhages is not so fearless after all!" Rixs dropped the deer from his shoulders as rolls of laughter continued to shake his body. He could scarcely catch his breath.

"Kid! Is that you?" Rhages yelled. "By The Powers! What ya think ya be doing?" His breath raced his heart. "Ya know how close ya come to death? Nitwit! Startling the mighty Rhages!" He lowered his hatchet.

"Come clean, friend. You were not startled, you were scared! Shaking out of your …"

"I should wring yer scrawny neck!" Rhages interrupted and stomped forward. "And I ain't yer friend!"

Rixs held up his hands. "Forgive me…" he tried to hold his snicker. "But in truth, even you must admit the mighty Rhages appeared to be mighty terrified!" He laughed some more.

The first time Rixs laid eyes on Rhages he had to force himself not to stare. People of color were rare in the isolated community of Pax Valley where everyone looked like they had birthed from the same pedigree.

Harsh in demeanor, Rhages hailed from a township known for its rude customs and wild indulgences. The women were big, rough, and mean-looking, and the men were bigger, rougher, and just plain ugly. It was a place where people preferred to spit on you than shake your hand.

"Yeah, ya may be laughing, but ya best remember," Rhages barked. "I can beat the snot out of ya with one hand tied behind me back! Strikes! Make that with both hands tied behind me back!" After a beat he turned to the shadowed lump on the ground. "What's that?"

"Our night's meal!" Rixs responded with a wide toothy grin, dimples on display though it was too dark to see. "You hungry?"

The giant walked closer to get a better look. "You know it, kid! No meat for days and my belly has fussed over it!" He paused then mused, "I wonder how ya hit a deer this time o' night ... Kinda hard to hunt in the dark."

It was an observation Rixs expected. He was able to do things nobody else could do, and though he tried to hide his abilities, someone always noticed. He was the best hunter in the crew, able to find meat when nobody else could. Rhages was always poking around with his nose in the young man's personals.

"Just lucky," Rixs smiled. "The Powers took pity on your empty gut and sent a deer my way."

"Heh, heh; there be truth in that, kid." Rhages agreed then added, "Still had to be awful hard to hunt this time of night."

Rixs shrugged. "Like I said, just luck."

Rhages let it drop though something in his voice hinted he suspected Rixs was hiding something. "Well, luck or no, I'll not complain a meal falling into our laps!"

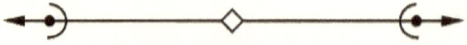

Early morning dew dampened the blanket Rixs cocooned

himself in after the hearty meal he had gluttoned himself on the night before. The sun had yet to make its debut for the still sleeping world, so the muted light appeared just as dull as the shadows that niggled in the far corners of Rixs's awareness.

Something was wrong. Muscles twitched and reflexes jerked until Rixs gasped awake, his eyes wide and blinking. There was nothing to see but trees and rock, yet he could make out the grey forms filling space and edging closer to camp, while the snoring forms of the crew dotted the ground nearby. It took no time to fling his vest over his shoulders and grab his quiver and bow.

Within a heartbeat, Rixs was over Rhages, shaking him. "Wake up, Rhages! We have company!" he whispered quickly.

Quicker than a snake's strike, a thick hand grabbed for Rixs's throat. Still quicker, Rixs knocked Rhages's hand away and slapped his own hand over Rhages's mouth.

"Shhh. It's only me."

Rhages batted Rixs's hand away. "Boy!" he whispered with a growl. "That be the second time ya nearly come to death! Don't be scaring Rhages if ya want to live!"

"Rhages, listen to me! We need to wake the crew! A large group is coming this way! They are armed!" Rixs's words were fast and frantic.

"How do you know they be armed?"

Emerald eyes stared at Rhages. No words were necessary. Rhages had already suspected that Rixs was more than what he seemed, but Rixs said it anyway.

"You already know how I know. You need to believe me now," he said then added with unmistakable urgency, "And get moving!"

Rhages digested the meaning. A quick nod and he was off to get his hatchet and daggers, kicking at bodies as he moved. Groans and threats on his life were mumbled with each body he booted.

"You wanna die, Rhages? Kick me again!" Bronan growled, just as the first arrow flew past his head.

"By The Powers!" Fogle yelled. "What's happening?"

The entire crew was up, confused but scrambling to snatch their weapons. A wave of arrows hissed through the air as the men ducked behind whatever protection they could find. A pained cry announced that one of the arrows had found its mark.

"Rayfe!" Rhages cried, running to his kinsman's aide.

Rixs took cover behind a large rock jutting out of the ground, knowing he did not need his eyes to see beyond it. The landscape was vivid in tones of grey, each shape clearly defined, including the intruders. There were so many.

There were twenty-four arrows in his quiver. Rixs pulled an arrow, taking notice of the position of each attacker, and realizing there were more of them than there were arrows. He would have to make each arrow count.

Before taking aim, he quickly slipped a leather thumb sleeve onto his right thumb. Unlike most archers, Rixs used his thumb to draw the bow string. The sleeve protected it.

Again, arrows rained around the crew, piercing the ground and trees. Still crouched behind the bolder, Rixs held his breath and waited for a cry of pain to indicate that an arrow had found a target. When no cry came, he sighed in relief.

He knew where each body stood and had already tagged his target. He raised the nocked arrow, drawing the bow string with his thumb, all in a single fluid motion while standing at the same time. When he released the arrow, there was no doubt of the outcome. Immediately, Rixs dropped behind the rock, grabbed his next arrow and with near inhuman speed had it sailing toward his next victim.

One by one the attackers dropped. Bronan, Fogle, Rhages, and other members of the crew watched the archer with stunned faces. Again, and again the arrows flew, seemingly without the young man eyeing his target.

"How does he do that?" Fogle asked no one in particular.

Rhages grunted in satisfaction. "I told you he's got Talent."

Bronan stared and might have questioned Rixs, but the attackers surged on them and the men raised their weapons to defend themselves.

Two axes swung savagely as Rhages faced three men that descended on him. The fire-headed Fogle released a war cry as he slashed his sword back and forth.

Though Rixs could not see with his eyes because the rock blocked his view, he saw with his gifted sight the bodies closing in and filling the space around him and the crew. He would have closed his eyes to eliminate the clutter of having both sights filling his head and confusing his focus, but he dared not. He needed his eyes to add color and definition to the grey shapes of his second sight, otherwise he might accidentally kill someone on his own side.

By The Powers! There are too many!

Rixs needed an idea to give them an edge. Something that would give the crew a fighting chance to escape. Without looking at his quiver, Rixs shot off another arrow, eliminating the body closest to him, then took aim at forms closest to his friends, dropping them one after another.

"Forget the others! Get the archer!" a powerful voice roared.

It had worked. All the bodies shifted in his direction and as they moved toward Rixs, the crew retreated and began disappearing into the trees. There were only a few arrows left compared to many more assailants, and though he had his blades, Rixs was not desperate enough to use them. His blades meant too much to him.

The only option left was obvious – he had to run. The thought made him cringe. Rixs had never run from anyone, or anything.

Hastily snatching his last three arrows, Rixs nocked all of them at the same time and drew back the string with his thumb. He did not care if they hit anything – he needed a distraction, something that would allow him to run. With eyes closed, he let them fly – then took off in a sprint.

Rixs was a fast runner. Many who knew him had commented at the speed his legs could move. Behind him, two grey forms dropped.

"Woo hoo!" he yelled. *Thank The Powers! I hit two!*

There was no time to celebrate. Bodies raced after him, and they were fast. The young rescuer had to be faster. Running in the opposite direction the crew had gone, he ran for his life, willing his legs to pick up speed.

Rixs closed his eyes as he ran, needing to shut out the additional hues and tones of his normal sight. He pushed his muscles until they ached, navigating him through a world devoid of color, but with enough detail to easily avoid obstacles that could trip him up. The darkest shades of black were thick solid forms like stone. The lighter shades of grey identified forms less solid.

The shape of an arrow speedily approached from behind, cutting through the air at great speed. Rixs could see it, because of his ability, and adjusted his steps to the right. The arrow zipped past to his left.

Another arrow soon followed. Thank The Powers that he had the ability to see things no one else could. Because of the way the shaft filled and emptied the air as it hummed toward him, he was able to know its specific path and where he was at risk of getting hit. This time he ducked as he ran. It whistled by just above his left ear. He shuddered. *Too close!*

More arrows came at him challenging his speed and skill. It was difficult to evade so many, but he shifted this way, then that way. He ducked and veered, each time, meeting success.

If his counting of the grey forms was accurate, fifteen bodies chased after him. His muscles begged for rest, but he sprinted faster than he knew he could, gulping ragged breaths of air that felt like rocks going down his windpipe even as he forced himself to maintain keen awareness of his legs. They were rotating faster than they ever had, and he was gaining distance, but with the task of looking ahead of him for an escape route while simultaneously keeping track of the activity behind him, Rixs's head began to throb.

The ambushers adjusted their strategy. This time, a cluster of five arrows sped from behind, nipping at his back. Judging their distance, formation, and speed, he knew he was sure to be hit and frantically tried to think of a countermove. Instinctively, he dropped to the ground. The arrows whizzed just barely overhead. He immediately popped up again and ran, knowing he had lost a little distance. His attackers had gained some ground.

Another batch of arrows flew his way. They were grouped high, and low, and wide. This time veering out of the way or dropping to the ground would not be an option. It was inevitable – Rixs had no choice but to take an arrow somewhere in his body. The best he could do was determine where to take the hit. He was right-handed, so he cut sharply to the right, leaving his left shoulder vulnerable.

Still running at full speed, Rixs prepared himself for the agony about to come.

A hard thud thrust his body forward just as searing pain blasted through his left shoulder. Making an earnest effort at stifling a cry, he staggered on for a few steps then tumbled to the ground.

He wondered who these people were and why they would attack the crew without any provocation. Their earnest intent to kill the crew left him baffled and seeking answers in the dirt where his face was smashed against a clump of grass. He wondered if the attack had anything to do with the reason the crew had come to Gnomera. It was in search of the mysterious Source. The object that no one could describe or had ever seen. How anyone was expected to find it was another wonder.

There was no time to lay idle. With great effort and muffled groans, Rixs pushed off the ground and willed himself to run, the arrow protruding through his shoulder. Through clenched teeth he ignored the fire radiating down his arm and focused ahead.

A river churned its way toward a ridge where it tumbled over a ledge. *A waterfall!* Rixs realized it might be a way out of his crisis. He closed his eyes and tried to see how far it dropped, but it dropped a long, long way and he was unable to perceive the bottom. He held his arm close to his side to restrict its movement, and the injured Rixs raced toward the cliff.

Rhages and the crew had been able to escape thanks to his actions. He had successfully distracted their attackers. He hoped they appreciated his sacrifice because it had placed him in a predicament. Beads of sweat dotted his pain-creased forehead as he wondered how to remove the arrow lodged in his shoulder.

The cliff was close now and Rixs knew what he had to do if he wanted the chance of living another day. Efforts to see below the falls had been in vain. The intense throbbing in his shoulder was too much of a distraction.

"Well, Rixs," he panted to himself. "You wanted an adventure. You found one." His chest heaved with every deep intake of breath and forced exhale. "Unfortunately, your first adventure just might be your last. I hope it's been worth it!"

The waterfall was close now. He stopped, sucking in precious gulps of air. Groaning in agony, he bent his elbow so that he could raise his left hand to brace the front portion of the arrow protruding to his front. With his right hand, he reached over his left shoulder, grabbed the portion of the arrow that stuck out from behind, and snapped it with a swift, hard yank.

An ear-splitting shriek shook the leaves on the trees. He thanked The Powers that the arrow had embedded high, just under his shoulder bones. With the arrow snapped, he was able to pull out the remaining piece without causing additional damage. He cried out again.

A huff of defeat blew through his lips when yet more shadowed arrows sailed behind him. Legs that wobbled to keep going struggled under his weight, but Rixs closed his eyes as he ran, reaching deep within and summoning the strength to keep his legs moving. He nearly cried when the seven arrows, spread out in such a way to ensure hitting their target, zipped past to his right.

There was no time to dress or wrap the bleeding wound. Rixs pushed his gift again to see what waited for him over the cliff but detected nothing that caused him great concern, so he increased his speed. Just as he reached the edge, Rixs closed his eyes, beseeching The Powers to have mercy on him. And jumped.

TWO

Blue eyes concealed under a hood of yellow stared at the shivering body curled upon itself atop a pile of straw. Neither of them knew that the legend of the Source had pulled them together. Nor could they have known the roles they would play to bring the legend back to life.

Without thought for the heartache yet to come, two delicate hands clasped the cell bars tightly. One hand pulled away. A thumb and middle finger raised high into the air – and snapped.

"Lady Syersi?" A guard hurried over.

A melodic voice floated out from under the hood. "The stranger shivers. Fetch a cover."

His words hesitated slightly, "Lady, the prison don't do covers."

"Well, you will *do* one for him!" There was nothing doubting in her voice.

"But …" the guard began, then stopped when the yellow cloak pivoted in his direction. With head lowered until his chin pressed against his chest, he amended his words. "As you wish, Lady." He promptly left, echoes of footfalls following him out.

Shifting her gaze back to the broken body, Syersi pressed her forehead against the bars. It was a miracle he was still alive. Covered in deep gashes and bruises, the man labored through his breathing and mumbled something incoherent every now and then. Bright red skin surrounded a wound oozing puss on his left shoulder. It hinted that his body fought a raging infection – and it was losing.

A pang of sympathy might have swelled within Syersi's chest, had the Lady not quickly brushed it off. When she was a little girl and had taken pity on a soldier who had been mortally wounded, the Absolute of the Gnomeran Armies told her that sympathy was for the weak and unworthy. Rangus had said those who had sympathy could be manipulated, and he had no time for big hearts. Since that day, and especially after her mother was murdered and her father abandoned his empire, and her, Syersi was determined to be cold and unfeeling like the Sanguinary who made sure Gnomera remained the most powerful land realm in the world.

Gritting her teeth, she squashed the compassion that threatened to make her soft. She might have succeeded had she abandoned the stranger after placing him in the cell. But curiosity begged her to stay.

Brown hair, the hue of aged honey, stuck to an ashen forehead. Numerous cuts marred the young man's swollen and dirt-smudged skin, yet the straight nose and rigid jawline hinted that a captivating face awaited discovery. Syersi wondered about the color of his eyes.

The exhilarating chase had ended at the base of the breathtaking Trifalls, the place where three separate waterfalls fell in succession, each tumbling into the next. The first cascade of water roared over a high cliff. It dropped into a pool where it churned and thrashed, overflowing into the next cascade. Again, the water was caught in a deep pool that deluged over the edge into a third mighty waterfall. The result that crashed into the river far, far, below was a torrent of violent spray and rapids so loud, it rivaled the storms of a dark and angry sea.

When the young lady had stumbled upon the place, she was awed by its lofty cliffs, and the rainbow of spring colors that blanketed the ground and swayed in the trees. It inspired her to dismount her horse and walk along the river's edge, letting the spray from the falls soak her through. She might have missed the partially submerged body had it not moved and groaned.

"What are you doing here?" a deep voice startled her. "I would have guessed you to be chest deep in your soaking font."

The voice was well known to everyone. Orris, the Commandant of the Lothorian Guard. The soldiers who had the misfortune of chasing her down would have had to report to him after dragging her back. Orris was responsible for the protection of Isslewood, and all who lived within its walls.

She ignored him, but he was not dissuaded. "Why is your hood up? Is this your attempt at concealing your identity?"

"Orris," she said with a deep inhale. "Have the wamps tattled on me? I knew their britches would itch to find you as soon as we returned, the tattletales that they are. If they knew what was good for them, they would learn to respect my privacy."

He stepped toward her until he was so close, heat radiated off him to warm her back. He inhaled. The hint of lilac wafted into his nose before his deep voice vibrated through the fabric of her hood, tickling her ear as he spoke.

"After that stunt you pulled today, you can be sure you'll have no privacy. From this moment on, Lady, if the guards do not alert me to every single sneeze from that pretty nose of yours, I'll have their heads impaled and speared into the ground along the gardens to scare away the crows."

His threat made her laugh. Her laugh made Orris grimace. It grated his pride when Syersi chose not to take him seriously.

Her voice was flat and monotoned. "I am so scared." Few things frightened the young lady. Orris was not one of them. "But, if I had not pulled my stunt, I would have never found this souvenir." A graceful hand waved toward the prone, shivering body. "And that would have been a tragedy."

Orris grunted, already feeling the need to compete with the sickly stranger. "Why are you interested in a dead man?"

"He is hardly dead." she snorted, the hood nodding in the stranger's direction. "He breathes. And he is interesting because we do not know who he is or how he came to be at the bottom of Trifalls."

It was the stranger's good fortune that Syersi had escaped through Isslewood's Tower Wall. Since the day of her birth, the imposing wall that surrounded the sprawling grounds of her palace home had symbolized the shackles that kept her from freedom. No one could have been more surprised than she when the sentries failed to stop her as she slipped past the gate, riding her beloved Juju fast and furious.

Syersi was out of their reach before they realized what she had done. What ensued was a chase across the Gnomeran countryside, along the base of the majestic and glittering Gneiss Curtain. For the young lady, suffocated by those who desired to protect her, there was something dangerously exciting about being hunted.

The Commandant tried to make her understand the danger outside of Isslewood. "There are rumors that a search for the Source has gained a great following," he declared. "We cannot take that risk with your safety." Nodding to the stranger, he added, "He could be one of them."

A giggle resonated beneath her hood. "And we know they waste their time. The Source is nothing more than a childhood tale meant for campfires late at night. Besides, it has nothing to do with me."

Orris responded quickly, "It still poses a danger. The type of people searching for the Source will bring crime to Gnomera. *That* poses a danger to you."

A welcoming voice resonated down the corridor to interrupt them. "What is all this fuss?" A lithe man rounded the corner and stopped short. "Oh! I apologize for intruding on you and your lady friend, Commandant. Um ..." The man paused and narrowed his eyes at the petite figure cloaked in yellow. He opened his mouth to say something but hesitated.

Orris perceived his hunch and enlightened him. "Your assumption is correct, Hobb. It is Lady Syersi."

Hobb's eyes popped wide. "What are you doing here?" he questioned. Then his forehead furrowed. "And why are you wearing that hood?"

"I asked her the same thing," Orris muttered.

If the Imperial Physician was expecting an answer, he would be just as disappointed as the Commandant. Syersi was not one to explain herself to anyone.

"Hobb!" she cried. "You have kept me waiting for an eternity! I was forced to listen to *him*!" Fingers waggled at the Commandant. "You have no idea how boring he is!"

The Physician cast a sympathetic shrug in Orris's direction. Syersi's petulance was no stranger to either of them. He stepped next to her and peered at the large motionless lump inside the cell. His features wrinkled. "What is that?"

"Do not be a dimwit," she retorted. "*That* is a man, of course. I found him, but he is nearly dead. One of the healers declared he was beyond hope."

Hobb scratched his forehead. "Then there is nothing more to do."

There was much that Hobb could do. He was the Imperial Physician. He was a Sanicle, a Talent that possessed the extraordinary gift to heal. He could make the stranger whole again.

Talents were rare, and Hobb was one of them. It was why he owned the prestigious title of Imperial Physician. He hadn't obtained that status because he was useless. It was also why he was a key member of the imperial inner circle known as the Intimus. There were four of them, each with a special ability that made them invaluable to Gnomera's strength.

A low moan coaxed Syersi closer. "I think he is waking," she whispered, while unsuccessfully yanking at the cell door. It didn't budge. Fingers snapped demanding that someone read her mind.

"You might ask," the Commandant offered in a growl.

He unlocked the door and pushed it wide, but just before the Lady could enter, he cut in front of her. It was a move intended to annoy. He smiled when she bumped into his backside then huffed under her hood. She grabbed Hobb's tunic and dragged him into the cell behind her.

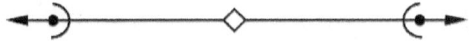

Few men were brave enough to throw themselves off a cliff to save their friends. Rixs had thrown himself off a cliff for men he hardly knew. He wondered what that made him. *Stupid!* he thought. Death was never an ideal choice if one wanted to be a hero. It was preferable to be alive when people sang praises to one's name.

A searing burn had greeted him when the haze of unconsciousness slowly lifted. It was severe enough to convince him that he had died and passed into the life beyond. Muscles quivered, and uncontrolled groans hinted of his suffering. The heavy pulse in his temples made it impossible to open his eyes, but even so, he knew three grey figures hovered close by.

During situations such as the one in which Rixs found himself, his gift was very convenient. Though he had no idea where he was or how he got there, he was able to study his surroundings and the strangers in front of him without them knowing. Their unsuspecting forms moved closer but one shapely outline captured his notice – a female.

A woman's body had a very distinguishable way in which it filled the measure of its space. The shape was just as pleasing in his world of grey as it was in his world of color. The only disadvantage was the absence of the intricate details that only his eyesight could provide. Surrendering to curiosity he struggled to blink his eyes open.

A figure of color had barely begun to take focus before a tickle seized Rixs's throat. A cough erupted. He coughed again. Then again. A thousand bone fragments clawed his chest raw. Each movement caused fire to wage war throughout his body.

The woman moved forward but a larger, bulky male held her back. There was a growl in his voice. "No! He could be contagious. Rangus would have my hide if something happened to you!"

A chuckle came from the skinny male before he murmured, "The Absolute is more likely to rip out your throat with his teeth than take your hide." He squatted next to the young man and began gliding long fingers over him. They hovered just above the skin yet never touched.

A festering wound on the prisoner's shoulder caught his gaze. It oozed yellow mucus that smelled of rotting meat and the skin was swollen with a red angry tinge.

"The infection is severe," the skinny man said. He let out a low whistle. "Now that one hurts for sure!" His cautious fingers slid over the right leg where it twisted in an awkward position.

Emerald orbs squinted at the man kneeling before him then flitted around the cell absorbing details about his surroundings. The thin man was unremarkable – a person who could blend in a crowd without notice. The stalky man was dressed like a soldier and stood straight as a board. He had impeccable posture. But it was the curvy figure wrapped in a cape of bright yellow that enslaved Rixs's green stare. Her face was shrouded under a hood.

"Where …?" he began then stopped and coughed. It was as if he had swallowed an entire riverbed of sand.

The skinny one had a voice that was kind and smooth. "Shhh, you must not talk. You are safe enough. I am Hobb, the Imperial Physician. That," he nodded toward the muscled and rigid man, "is Orris, the Commandant of the Lothorian Guard."

Rixs smiled weakly, but it was more a quiver on his lips. "I am Rixsander of Pax Valley, but you can call me Rixs."

The woman caped in yellow stepped forward and elegant hands reached up to push back the hood from her head.

Rixs had never seen eyes so blue. Even Cliessa's bright blue eyes were dull in comparison. He blinked hard and wondered if he was hallucinating, but the woman was still there. Long ebony hair framed an oval face. Light pink lips that hinted a smile ornamented a complexion that looked as velvety as a white rose.

"And this is Lady Syersi," Hobb announced. "The First Daughter of the Emperor Lothorius, and Empress Heir to Gnomera!"

The who of what? Ringing in Rixs's ears made everything impossible to comprehend. Had he heard right? He had no idea names could be so long, and he wanted to ask the man to repeat it, but his throat was on fire. He was sure someone had poured a mug of thorns down his gullet.

He managed to scratch out, "That … is a big name." Then his head lulled to the side and with eyes closed, he became still.

Hobb blinked up at Syersi. "Well, apparently, your name did him in."

Syersi smoldered at him. "I have that effect."

Orris rolled his eyes.

THREE

The attendants scrubbed Syersi's skin squeaky clean and left her to relax in the soaking font. The hot water lapped around her worn and sore muscles. Being chased through the countryside was exhausting.

The imperial bathing chamber was one of Syersi's favorite places. She had relaxed in a small circular font while attendants scrubbed her body until her skin was a glowing pink. The large dipping font provided a tepid rinse and room to swish through the water. But her favorite was the font sculpted for comfort and relaxation. It was a little larger than the small scrubbing font and was filled to the brim with water hot enough to purge troubles from every pore.

Heavy lids blinked open adjusting to the torchlight's dancing shadows flickering against the chamber walls. Someone was shouting. Syersi's narrowed eyes searched for the one foolish enough to interrupt her tranquility.

A large man, as dark as midnight, came to a stop within the entrance of the chamber. She ducked a little, sinking into the water. Trouble had found her.

"Syersi!" the man raged at her. Ebony muscles, twice the size of Orris's, bulged in irritation. His voice was thunder and she watched him, wide-eyed, as he stopped short of entering the bathing chamber.

"Remove yourself this instant or I shall pull you out myself!"

Feigning ignorance, she blinked at him and called. "Hello, Chadgerwin, is something wrong?"

His dark features darkened further. He was a storm ready to deluge the bathing chamber. Glaring at the attendants, they scampered away. "Do not play games with me, child! You violated my trust and left Isslewood. We had to chase you across the territory to retrieve you. Then you deliberately ignored my demand to see you as soon as you returned!"

Her temper ignited. "Can this wait? I am bathing! Who do you think you are?"

Chadgerwin breathed heavily, the scars on his face twisting into a web of boiling indignation, and the speech perched on his lips itched to be delivered. "Stop it! I have no wish to gawk at you, little girl. I helped Hobb during your birth, and *that* is a sight that will haunt me the remaining days of my life!"

He remembered the day well. Lothorius had anxiously paced. Mazzlin had nervously chatted everyone's ears into a stupor. It had the same effect as a rusty door screeching. And Rangus had left the great house because the smell of blood was so strong. Nonetheless, it had been a glorious day. An heir to Gnomera after eighteen seasons cycles and numerous failed births had finally graced the imperial family.

"And let me remind you who I am, child!" Chadgerwin thrust a thumb into his own muscular, scar-riddled chest that he kept proudly displayed for all to see. "I am the First Counselor of Gnomera, and I rule everything in it!"

Syersi eyed Chadgerwin's twitching muscles. Tall, ebony-skinned, and bald. He had fought alongside her father in numerous wars, evident by the scars that webbed his entire body. He wore them like a badge of honor.

A wide scar ran across his right cheekbone, and another one marred deep on the left side of his face, from temple to chin. But those were nothing compared to the most prominent scar that made Syersi shiver each time she noticed it. A long crater sliced the back of his head. It began at the top left of his crown, dragged down across his skull, and ended at the base of his right ear. By the look of him, he should have been dead, several times over, and those were only the scars on his head.

When Chadgerwin was still a wamp of seventeen seasons cycles, he had fought in the armies of Gnomera under Emperor Garvier, Syersi's grandfather. Chadgerwin had met Lothorius, Syersi's father, during a violent battle to expand the borders of Gnomera from the Gneiss Curtain all the way to the western seas. Her father, not much older than Chadgerwin, had taken a lethal wound that would have claimed his life had Chadgerwin not been there to render aid, stopping the blood loss and pulling him away from the fighting. At the time, the young warrior couldn't have known that he had just rescued the Emperor's last remaining son and heir, but from that moment forward, there was a friendship between them that grew into a brotherly bond. When Lothorius became Emperor, he appointed Chadgerwin as his First Counselor, an honored and important position.

The Counselor was an intimidating man to everyone around him, except for the girl huddled, her bare skin scraping against the side of the font. She thundered at him, "If I had clothes on, I would …"

"My patience is spent! Get out!" His thunder was superior to hers.

Apprehension shown on the guards' faces, standing just outside the doorway. The First Counselor never lost his temper with the First Daughter in such a manner. He never berated her in front of people, which was why the guards were hesitant to leave Syersi alone and naked with the furious Counselor.

"You did a reckless and dangerous thing today!" he yelled. "You snubbed your nose at the Intimus and everyone else who sees to your safety! I have a mind to take a switch to you!"

Syersi narrowed her brows at him. "You would not dare!" she cried, and in a pathetic attempt to tune him out, the Princess plugged her ears. "And I will not listen to you anymore!"

A pair of short legs bounded through the palace halls as fast as they could move, a generous chest bouncing with every step.

Mazzlin's flushed face rushed up to Chadgerwin and dimpled hands pressed forcefully against his chest.

"What is going on here?" she cried.

"Mazzlin!" he growled. "This does not concern you!"

"Of course, it concerns me!" she yelled in her high chirping voice. "I am the Guardian! Look at her!" She pointed with discontent. "The child is in a bath with no clothes!"

It was her Talent that had motivated her to leave the family hall where she had been relaxing and hurry to the bath chamber with the image of Chadgerwin's fury etched in her vision. As a Seer, the plumpish woman possessed the ability to look through the eyes of another, and she frequently targeted Syersi's eyes in which to peek from as a means of keeping tabs on the young lady destined to become Empress of Gnomera. It was her responsibility to keep the Empress Heir from mischief, which was why Emperor Lothorius appointed her as Guardian.

With a voice deadly quiet, the Counselor ordered, "Syersi, you will remove yourself from the font and join the Intimus in the dining hall. We will discuss your behavior today, and its consequences!"

Syersi released a relieved breath when her eyes landed on Mazzlin. Pleading innocent eyes turned to the Guardian. "Mazzy, make him leave!"

The Empress Heir, aged nearly eighteen springs, had grown up with the Intimus, her father's inner circle. Chadgerwin, Hobb, Mazzlin, and the dreaded Rangus, made up the foursome that the Emperor had trusted. However, none of them had intimidated her – not Chadgerwin, the scar-covered Soothe who had stepped up to lead Gnomera when Lady Saudria was murdered and Lothorius disappeared. Even Rangus, the Sanguinary, with his eyes of blood who frightened everyone, even he did not cause her to cower.

The First Counselor was locked in a battle of stares, and though the Intimus all shared in the responsibility of caring and protecting the First Daughter, it was his primary burden to train up the next ruler of an empire. He calmed his breathing and focused on Syersi's energy. His heartbeat slowed and with a mellowed gaze he captured Syersi's eyes and held them. The air shifted and pulsed with the soft rhythm of the Counselor's breaths. Syersi's own body obediently followed.

An encouraging smile curved Chadgerwin's lips and he held out his hand. "Come, join the Intimus for the evening meal," he said gently.

Her will to fight melted, Syersi shifted in the font to get out, the water sloshing over the sides and onto the floor. The sound echoed as though she were far away, and it was as if she looked through a white mist. It was a familiar feeling and suddenly her bright blue eyes narrowed to his influence.

"Do not use your Talent on me, old man!" she hissed.

Chadgerwin inhaled sharply. Mazzlin froze. Syersi was in rare form.

There was a silent understanding in Gnomera that Talents existed. In Isslewood, Syersi's palace home, it was knowledge. One only needed to look at the Absolute, the Commander of the Gnomeran armies, to know he was Sanguinary. Unlike the other Talents, Rangus could not conceal his. Even so, Talent and those who were gifted with it were never discussed openly.

Syersi knew better than to speak of it so callously around the servants. There were dangers associated with people knowing about the Intimus and their gifts.

Mazzlin pushed her palms into Chadgerwin's chest as she cautioned in a hushed voice, "Keep control, Counselor. She purposely taunts you."

His reply to her was barely a whisper, "Be silent or leave, Mazzlin. This is for me to handle." Chadgerwin's scars shimmered in the torchlight. "Syersi, I will give you to the count of three to come willingly or I shall pull you out by your hair."

Water splashed in Syersi's mouth as she yelled, "I'd like to see you try!" She took comfort in the fact that she was the only child of Saudria and Lothorius. She would soon rule Gnomera. And he would never dare to make such a spectacle in front of the servants!

"One," he began. "Two."

Her breath quickened. This was a battle she intended to win.

"Three," he finished. "Very well."

Without pause, Chadgerwin moved forward into the chamber, but one of the guards took a cautious step forward. "Counselor," he pleaded, his voice trembling and his wary eyes shifting as he confronted the most powerful man in Gnomera. Chadgerwin threw him a dangerous scowl which sufficiently motivated the guard to retreat, allowing the Counselor to proceed, his long strides determined and powerful.

He would not dare! Syersi watched nervously as the Counselor approached. Mazzlin hurried behind him and grabbed his arm, but he easily jerked it from her grasp.

"All right!" Syersi screeched, pressing herself against the side of the font. "I shall come!" She ducked as low as she could without submerging her head and cursed under her breath then threatened him out loud. "Mark my words, Chadgerwin! You will be sorry for this! I will make your life miserable!"

The Counselor stopped, a grin hinted discretely at the corners of his mouth, "You already do, child. You already do." Turning on his heels, he exited the bathing chamber, leaving Syersi to her own fumes of anger, but called over his shoulder, "Do not keep me waiting."

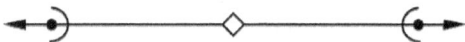

He ran like the wind, approaching the cliff and knowing his best chance of living another day was to jump. Efforts to see beyond and below the falls were in vain. The drop was too far for his ability to reach and the intense throbbing of his shoulder was too much of a distraction.

The waterfall was close. He stopped and tried to control his heaving chest as it fought for precious gulps of air. Groaning in agony, he raised his left hand to brace the front portion of the arrow that protruded from just under his left shoulder. With his right hand, he reached over his shoulder and grabbed the portion of the arrow just in front of the fletching then mustering courage, he snapped it with a swift, hard yank.

A loud cry vibrated through the air and shook the leaves on the trees. He thanked The Powers that the arrow had embedded itself in a place where he could snap it. He had to pull it out before he could jump, not wanting to risk any additional damage from the fall. He yelled again as he jerked the arrow out and threw the shaft on the ground.

Voices were closing in. More arrows were on the way. There was no time to dress the bleeding wound. He ran to build up speed. Just as he approached the drop, he closed his eyes. "Have mercy on me!"

The distinct feeling of falling and falling, tumbling, and tumbling, again and again jolted Rixs awake. His face tightened as memories of his tragic journey to the bottom of the waterfall, and the bones he felt snapping, replayed in his mind.

A quick shake of his head shifted the hair that hung just over his eyes and allowed him to look around his surroundings. He tried to remember where he was. Nothing seemed familiar in the confines of the cold stone cell. The murky memories in his head were no help. A headache had made it impossible to concentrate, and his body felt as if it had been used for a battering ram, but the worst irritant to his ability to think was a piece of straw digging into his side. He shifted on his pile of hay.

Rixs had realized too late when he hurled himself off the cliff, that there was not one waterfall, as he had thought. There were three. His body splashed from fall to fall at the mercy of the raging torrent until he violently crashed into the roiling rapids of the river far below from the place he had jumped.

Drowning seemed inevitable. The churning white water pummeled and tossed him until he lost all sense of direction, while the weight of his clashing vest made it impossible to stay afloat. Then everything became dark.

Stretching out on his prickly bed of straw, Rixs realized he felt strangely whole even if he was sore. He remembered his shoulder. Wide eyes looked at the area where a pink patch of skin covered the area where his arrow wound had been. He moved his arm, and found it surprisingly easy, if not terribly sore.

He remembered his leg had snapped at some point during his fall. There were no words to describe that pain. He groped along his thigh and winced. His leg hurt something fierce, but the bones and muscles felt whole.

With fisted hand, Rixs tapped his knuckles lightly against his forehead and willed himself to remember. There were no memories of how he came to be in his prison cell. As he grasped for something to ground him, only one thing came to mind – a hazy yellow image and penetrating blue eyes.

FOUR

Three pairs of eyes stared as a bowl flew across the dining hall smashing into the far wall, its contents splashing everything in its vicinity. Syersi ignored the Intimus and reached elegantly in front of Chadgerwin for bread. After a quick sniff, she shoved the entire chunk of bread into her mouth and began to chew as politely as she could with both cheeks bulging to capacity. A moment later, a mouthful of soggy bread landed on her plate.

Mazzlin's eyebrows shot up in disapproval as servants scrambled to clean up the bowl of soup and remove the plate of half chewed bread. "You forget yourself, Syersi," the Guardian chastised.

A melodic and ethereal voice so lovely that it had to have been blessed by The Powers responded, "What do you expect? The broth is sour. As for the bread, I might as well have eaten an armful of dried twigs! Honestly, I am better off eating straw."

"That can be arranged," snarled Rangus. "It would amuse me greatly to pasture you with the cows."

Syersi blew him a kiss causing the Absolute to snarl.

Mazzlin swallowed her mouthful and said, "Child, why do you provoke? Throwing bowls and spitting food does nothing to improve the cook." She chuckled then continued. "I doubt the cook even knows you dislike the meals. If you are dissatisfied, you must seek out the cook and throw your contempt there. But you know what they say – it is easier to catch more flies with honey."

"You mistake me, Mazzy. I do not wish to catch flies. I wish to catch a good meal."

A high-pitched chuckle sounded and Mazzlin's eyes danced. "Yes, of course," she laughed.

Chadgerwin swept his eyes around the dining hall. He, Rangus and Mazzlin sat at the table, along with the First Daughter. Only Hobb was missing. He brushed his hands together and signaled the servants to leave. They had hardly left the room before Rangus stood, knocking back his chair.

"I speak first!" he growled. "Syersi, you have a head on your shoulders! I want to see you use it!" Then he turned to the Counselor, pointing a finger at him. "*You* coddle the girl! The *real* world will not indulge her like you, Chadgerwin!"

Syersi interrupted before the Counselor could speak. "You are wrong, Rangus. They will indulge an Empress." Syersi flipped her hand into the air.

"Come here," Rangus growled, his eyes flashing bright red for a quick moment. "I want to choke some sense into you!"

No other Talent was like that of a Sanguinary. They possessed no patience, nor did they have feelings of guilt or compassion. Their sense of right and wrong was driven only by loyalty. Decisions were never wrong when they achieved a desired outcome. This made Sanguinary excellent fighters – the absolute warriors. It was also the only Talent that could not be hidden. Their bodies were larger, stronger, and faster, their senses keener, but it was the Talent's defining trait that gave them the advantage in any fight – it was bloodlust, manifested in eyes the color of blood.

It was why Rangus led the Gnomeran armies, one hundred thousand strong. And it was the warrior in him that wanted to squeeze Syersi's neck just enough to make her eyes bug out. A good choking might do wonders for her defiant attitude.

"It's time she knows!" he continued his rant. "If Syersi wants to be an idiot, she can do so with the full knowledge that she is being one!"

Mazzlin gagged then spewed drink onto the table as she

coughed. The Talent had guts to lead them down this path.

Chadgerwin glared at the Absolute. "That will do, Rangus!"

The man was not to be silenced. "Our Empress Heir interrupted targeting practice for the new recruits."

"Absolute …" Chadgerwin warned.

Rangus held up his hand. "Hear me out, Soothe. As I was saying, the wamps were in the middle of their first archery lesson. *She*," a big accusing finger pointed at Syersi, "purposely distracted them! You know how wamps are, Chadgerwin. Little more than pups with tongues wagging, and not as smart, mind you!"

Chadgerwin nodded, remembering his own early soldiering days.

"Half of them get eliminated within the first ten days of training! They are nervous and stupid. Now throw a beautiful woman at them!"

Syersi's eyes brightened. "You think me beautiful, Rangus?" She smiled seductively then blew him another kiss.

"It was not given as a compliment, squirt!" His dull, rust eyes flamed to bright red. "And stop flinging kisses at me!"

"So sensitive," she pouted.

Dark fingers sifted through long strands of his goatee as Chadgerwin realized he had lost control. He settled back in his chair knowing where Rangus was headed. The Counselor had heard all this before – Syersi's involvement in the archery master's injury had been the talk of Isslewood for several seasons.

"I know what you are going to say, my friend," the Counselor cut in. "You can skip this part and get to your point." He threw a warning glance at Syersi to keep her taunts to herself.

Rangus and Chadgerwin had served Emperor Lothorius loyally for many seasons cycles. Both had fought together in battles too numerous to count, and Chadgerwin knew the damage a Sanguinary could leave in his wake. He dared not attempt to Soothe him into compliance. The one time the Counselor had attempted it, he was left with a huge scar to remind him never to try again. An excited Absolute was something they needed only during war.

"Calm yourself, Rangus. Your eyes are glowing."

Rangus pressed on. "We all know what happened! One wamp,

preoccupied with the *Lady*," he nodded crimson eyes at Syersi, "and not giving attention to his training, released his arrow right into the archer master's thigh! He nearly lost his leg!"

Mazzlin piped up, "And Hobb had to heal the poor master!"

Feigning humility, Syersi spoke softly, "And Chadgerwin had to Soothe the wamp because Rangus nearly tore out his throat with his teeth and the poor boy almost went mad! We know this already." She lowered her eyes and fluttered her eyelashes. "I said I was sorry." Her words were almost a whisper.

Chadgerwin's head snapped up and he glanced around the table. There was a voice missing. "Where is Hobb?"

Mazzlin and Rangus looked around them.

Blinking repeatedly, Syersi gasped. "Oh! I forgot. He is most likely recuperating after healing the prisoner."

The goblet froze halfway to the Counselor's lips. "What prisoner?"

Rangus growled. "What prisoner?"

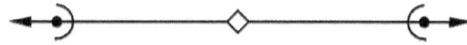

A quick swipe caught the little creature hiding in his bed of straw, but an instantaneous sharp prick with tiny teeth startled Rixs enough to throw it across the cell.

"Strikes," he cried.

The mouse scurried through the cell bars. Rixs might have tried to catch it again so that he had something to do, but he was healing from his injuries, so his normally quick reflexes were slow and swift movement brought him discomfort.

No one had been to see him since he woke to find his injuries had been healed. He tossed his hair out of his eyes, not because it blocked his vision, but because it itched his eyes, then he laid back on his dreary pile of hay and tried to get comfortable.

After an unknown amount of time, when Rixs was about to dose off, three bodies of grey became known to him. His ability to see past the walls and down the corridor revealed space filling and emptying in shadowed movement headed in his direction. Eager to finally speak to someone, he sat up and waited for the three men to come into view of his eyes.

When they appeared, one man stood out, but it was not because his skin was dark like the night. It was because he carried himself like someone of importance, refined as polished onyx with the bearing of a king. His own friend, Rhages, was also black as night, but was as refined as a pit of rocks, and had a physique that was more chunk than bulk. This man reeked of muscle – and scars. The open and sleeveless cloak he wore showed off his arms and chest. He was webbed in scars, even on his bald head.

It became obvious to Rixs that the man of scars was not threatened by him, as he dismissed the two guards. They thumped their right fists against their chests then flung a threatening glare at Rixs as they left.

Emerald green eyes flicked over the vest which the man of scars held tightly in his grip. One glance was all Rixs needed to know that every blade occupied its appropriate sleeve – all twenty and eight of them.

"I presume this is yours?" the man asked. His voice was deep and authoritative.

Before answering, Rixs silently thanked The Powers that the vest was not at the bottom of the river. "Yes," was all he said. Fingers itched to reach for it, but he fisted them into the bed of hay.

Cool grey eyes studied the young stranger before the man of scars spoke again. "Allow me to introduce myself. I am Chadgerwin, First Counselor of Gnomera."

The news that Lady Syersi had returned from her roguery with a mangled body without anyone telling him had instantly claimed Chadgerwin's fury, as if the First Counselor had not already been furious enough with the Empress Heir. He immediately left the dining hall in search of the Physician who had spent the day healing the stranger.

Hobb had looked terrible, which revealed a great deal about the condition of the stranger he had healed. If the Sanicle had exhausted himself to the point of being too ill to attend the evening meal, then it was most likely that the stranger would not have lasted another day without the Physician's healing Talent.

Chadgerwin awaited the stranger's reply and took note that Hobb had done well. The young man appeared healthy.

"I am Rixsander, from Pax Valley, in the Bravura Strait," Rixs replied, then cleared his throat. "Um … my friends call me Rixs."

Chadgerwin smiled, showing off a mouthful of white teeth. "Ah then, shall we be friends?"

Rixs skirted his eyes around the stone walls of the prison cell. "If I say *yes*, will it get me out of here?"

A chuckle bubbled from Chadgerwin's throat. A good first impression. "And how did you come to be here, *Rixs?*"

Rixs grinned at the sound of his name. "Have no idea. I jumped off a cliff, and here I am."

One scarred eyebrow arched high on Chadgerwin's forehead. "This, I have to hear."

Opening the cell door, the Counselor pushed through, shut it again, then made himself comfortable on the floor. An eager stare greeted Rixs. "My ears are burning. Please continue," he urged.

There was nothing to hide so Rixs recounted his story of how he had traveled into Gnomera with the crew. He had left his home in Pax Valley to purposely delay his marriage to the girl the township council had selected for him. He had not chosen to be husband to Cliessa, but the township council planned out his life for him anyway. So, he left and thought he would take in a great adventure.

Chadgerwin smiled. Adventure, indeed.

The story evolved from Cliessa, his betrothed, to Rhages, the giant who had befriended him. Rixs's expression changed from a near frown when speaking of his betrothed, to a relaxed grin when the name *Rhages* passed through his lips. There was adoration in the description of the friend he referred to as a wild beast and recounted how the man had defended Rixs and convinced the crew to let him join their ranks. The beast of a man always seemed to have his back.

When they had been ambushed, it was Rhages that Rixs had mostly worried for and had thrown himself off a cliff in hopes his friend would have a chance to live another day. No one knew why they were attacked, or by whom. The fighting had been fierce, and when so many had fallen, Rixs knew he was the only one capable of doing something to help Rhages and the others get away. So, he used himself as a decoy to draw away the enemy arrows, keeping their attackers focused on him.

Absorbed by the story, Chadgerwin sat quietly, absorbing every word. He would have been even more absorbed had Rixs shared that his unique ability allowed him to single-handedly take down most of their attackers. The Powers had blessed him with a gift that no one else had which made him a deadly aim, and so many had fallen by his hand. So many that the leader had ordered his men to focus their efforts on eliminating him.

When Rixs finally stopped speaking, Chadgerwin stroked his goatee thoughtfully. He believed the boy's story, but something was missing. He held up the unique vest laden with blades of superior workmanship. There were fourteen sleek black blades of various sizes tucked in sleeves both inside and outside the vest, and an additional fourteen sharp ornaments hemming the bottom of the vest. Chadgerwin suspected these were weapons as well, but only someone of exceptional skill would dare wear a garment so bold, yet the young stranger had made no mention of any abilities.

Then unknowingly, Rixs opened himself up to additional scrutiny when he became distracted watching the stone wall on the other side of his cell bars. His eyes appeared to follow something that the Counselor could not see. Chadgerwin flitted his gaze back and forth from Rixs to the hall wall.

Moments later a giant man rounded the corner, coming into view, and Chadgerwin suddenly had a hunch. Their young guest had a Talent.

Rixs stared at a massive head of long and chunky curly locks that had clearly been struck by lightning, for it stuck out and frizzed in all directions. A matching bushy beard hid most of a large, stern face, except for the one feature that distinguished the mammoth in one word, *savage*. Blood red eyes stared back at Rixs. The beast of a man dwarfed Chadgerwin by a head.

The Counselor smiled wide and said, "Rixsander of Pax Valley, I introduce to you, Rangus of Gendell, the Absolute Commander of the Gnomeran Armies. Rangus, this is…"

"Close your mouth, boy!" the beast cut in.

But Rixs was helpless to close his mouth. It hung wide open while words froze on his tongue. The man was scary big, and something about the way he looked at him made Rixs feel like he was about to be the next meal.

A face-splitting smile proclaimed Chadgerwin's amusement at Rixs's reaction. "I take it, Rixs, you have just seen your first Sanguinary!"

FIVE

The First Counselor was a skillful interrogator. Because of his Soothe, he could coax food from a starving man's fingers. Patience was a virtue, and Chadgerwin had oodles of it. He could have easily had his answers quickly if he wanted but coaxing them slowly told him much more about a person.

Many times, over the seasons cycles, Chadgerwin had used his Talent to buoy up the courage of young wamps in their first campaign as soldiers. It helped to build their confidence and gave them hope to survive. He had extracted valuable information from prisoners and spies who were unable to resist his Soothe. More significant, it was the Counselor who had stroked Gnomera's way to diplomacy, using his Talent to build alliances with other kingdoms and land realms through peace.

Rixs would be helpless to keep his secrets if the Counselor wanted them. Chadgerwin always succeeded. Even the Sanguinary was no match for the Soothe when he wanted information. Once, he tested his Talent on Rangus, who had worked himself into a bloodlust and nearly killed the Counselor, trying to resist his Soothe. In the end, Chadgerwin still succeeded though he vowed he would never Soothe a Sanguinary again.

The three of them sat on the cell floor. Each time Chadgerwin posed a question and Rixs held back, Chadgerwin would help him along. He began with the exact number of blades the vest held – twenty-eight. There were two long blades, four medium, eight short, and fourteen throwing stix. Of course, Chadgerwin already knew the correct number of blades, he had counted them. What he wanted to know was how they were used.

As if surrounded by a lightning storm, the hair on Rixs's skin flared on end. Reflexively he rubbed his bare arms and chest. Then he stretched his neck and rotated his shoulders before landing his emerald gaze on the Counselor with a suspicious tilt of his head.

A silent and unseen predator, Soothe misted over its target then gently seeped into the skin to impose Chadgerwin's will on those he chose to influence. Its effect served to erode fears, calm anger, and massage emotions, so that secrets were likely to roll off his tongue. And they did.

After Rixs confessed that he had only used his blades to hunt up until that fateful day he and the crew were attacked, he then subjected Chadgerwin to what little he knew about Gnomera and the reason they had come.

"I knew it," Rangus grunted quietly. "This *crew* is in search of the Source. That means there will be others too."

Chadgerwin nodded while massaging one of the scars on his face with his middle finger. Soothe eased from him. "Rixs, you said the crew believed Talents existed and believed that they were tied to the Source. What do you know about the Source?"

A wave of calm settled on Rixs. His shoulders sagged slightly. Muscles that had been tense since he had regained consciousness and realized he was in a prison cell had loosened up as an unseen force relieved him of his burden. Tranquility nudged his lips to answer. Instead, he tossed his head to clear oily hair away from his emerald eyes. Those eyes swept over the Counselor's face.

Never one to babble needlessly, he pressed his lips together to resist the urge to share what he knew, but he talked anyway.

"I was new to the crew, so what I know is … well, it is not much. I never thought much of Talents…" His gut tensed. It was not the truth. Rixs thought about Talents all the time – thought he might be a Talent but had never dared share that thought because of his father.

His father had been adamant, almost violent in insisting that he was no Talent. He insisted that Rixs simply had an uncommon ability and admonished that no one could know about his second sight lest his ability be used against him. So, the gift had been tucked away in secrecy.

The urge to correct what he had said overwhelmed him. "I … I …"

"You were saying?" The Counselor probed, amused at the young man's resistance.

"I suppose if Talents exist then it is possible for the Source to exist," he said with an exhale. "But my father always told me …" He quieted.

Chadgerwin grinned. "Go on," he urged.

"When I was younger, I fancied myself …" Rixs bit his tongue to keep his words to himself.

Rangus fidgeted and snarled deep and low. "Stop playing with the boy! At this rate, we will be here for days! I can have those answers by the time he takes his next breath, or he won't breathe at all!"

"Quiet, Rangus, or leave," the Counselor replied with a calm that provoked a red flare in the Sanguinary's eyes.

Though he was sitting, Rixs startled backward against the wall, his eyes wide. The stories Bronan had shared about Sanguinary Talent suddenly came to life.

Chadgerwin saw the surprise and fear in Rixs's eyes then glanced over his shoulder at the intimidating Talent. "Compose your eyes, Absolute, you are frightening our guest." Then he turned his attention back to Rixs. "You have a strong will," he said. "I like that."

"I feel … strange. Are … are you doing something to me?" Tingly warmth inspired Rixs to share everything and anything but he clenched his teeth and leaned back against the wall.

The stranger had an extraordinarily strong will, but Chadgerwin was a very strong Soothe. "I have sensed that you have a *special* ability, Rixs."

The vest still hung from the Counselor's clutches, fine sleek blades gleaming from their sheaths. He plucked one and held it up, turning and angling it in the light. The shiny black metal reflected hues of blue and purple. His eyes blazed, soaking up the artisanship required to make such a weapon.

"Workmanship as fine as this is intended for someone with skills to match – let's say a *Talent*, perhaps?"

Rixs glanced at the dark-skinned man briefly then closed his eyes, continuing to clamp his teeth together tightly. He refused to respond though his tongue battled for the freedom to speak.

"We know much about Talent here, Rixs," the Counselor continued. He waved a hand toward Rangus. "As you can see, we appreciate Talent." More Soothe flowed from him to Rixs as he talked. "Tell me about yours."

Rixs knew something was happening to him. Either the frightening Sanguinary or the deceptively friendly Counselor was doing something to him. The only way he could defend himself from the compelling desire to speak was to ask questions of his own.

"And what about you? Are you a Talent, Counselor? Are you doing something to me?"

Eyebrows arched high on Chadgerwin's scarred forehead, and his eyes twinkled. Most people were clueless when Soothe was exercised on them, especially if they had never been exposed to it before.

"And why would you think I am doing something to you, Rixs? I only ask questions to become better acquainted."

"No," Rixs tossed an arm over his face and focused on the shapes that filled the space close to him. He no longer had to see the red, hungry eyes of the Absolute since color was not a part of this ability. "I think you are doing something – I just need to figure out what." He squirmed a little to relieve the itch of a piece of straw sticking him in his side.

The Counselor's face practically glowed with excitement and anticipation. Still holding the blade in his hand, he took a chance to expose the thing Chadgerwin suspected. With a snap of his wrist, the blade was flying toward the young man who had his eyes closed and an arm slung over his face.

A reflex as quick as lightning had no choice but to act. Rixs reached out and caught the blade before it could pierce the same shoulder that had been healed earlier that day. Eyes now open, he glared at Chadgerwin, whose wide smug smile lit up the cell. Rangus released a growl of approval at the discovery. There was no way to undo his stupid mistake, but his only other recourse would have been to let the blade stab him. He had been tricked.

The Counselor flashed a victorious smile at Rangus. "I believe we have a new Talent in our midst."

SIX

The Gneiss Curtain loomed silently over Syersi. Purple glittering rock sparkled like lavender snowflakes. Absorbing the strange and breathtaking kaleidoscope of colors found along the base of the mountain range, she slowed Juju to a trot to better appreciate the view.

Her lessons had taught her that something in the gneiss gave the solid rock mountain range its unique color. It also had an unusual effect on vegetation that sprouted along its base where gneiss met soil. More colorful than a rainbow, the normally green vegetation exploded in hues of bright red, blue, orange, even pink, then gradually changed back to its traditional colors the further away they grew from the range's base.

Red grass flattened beneath the weight of Juju's hooves while Syersi grabbed at the blue leaves rustling overhead in the branches of the trees she passed. The odd mixture of colors depended on the types of trees or plants and how they reacted to the purple gneiss, but the results were always breathtaking – vibrant and unpredictable.

Though she had never left the boundaries of Isslewood, marked by Tower Wall, except when she had found her souvenir, the stranger, she knew this colorful phenomenon was unique only to the Gnomeran side of the Gneiss Curtain – the western side. The eastern side, and the four land realms that bordered it, were greeted with nothing but desert, and no one knew why.

Syersi looked around her. She had escaped the gaggle of frilly skirts that made up her retinue. They chased after her company daily, but this day the Empress Heir jumped on her horse for a solitary ride. Only her two guards followed at a distance. Their company was preferable to the five lucky daughters of the affluent aristocrats who had been selected to keep her company.

The great house, built with light lavender gneiss by her great grandfather, glittered a near blinding white causing her to squint as she rode up and looked around for someone to help her dismount Juju.

"You there! Do you not see that I am waiting to get down?" she called to a servant.

Out of nowhere, a strong hand came from behind and slid around her waist. "Allow me, Lady," Orris crooned while gently easing her to the ground.

He held her longer than necessary, their bodies nearly touching. Leaning into her, he inhaled deeply to catch the fragrance of her hair.

"Ummm," he moaned quietly. "I have missed that sweet smell."

Her bright blue eyes flashed from a combination of flattery and annoyance. "Careful, Commandant, or I shall have your nose cut off." He laughed.

The rise and fall of her chest caught Orris's eyes, drawing them to the drooping neckline of her red shimmering dress. After lingering there momentarily, he raised his focus upward to find her scowling at him. He had been caught ogling.

Orris had been the son of a farmer who had wanted more out of his life than growing crops. He had joined the Lothorian Guard as a boy, barely older than fourteen seasons cycles, and had achieved his rank through hard work and undying loyalty to the Emperor Lothorius. His hard work had ascended him to the rank of Commandant, responsible for the performance of the Lothorian Guard and the safety of Isslewood. It had also made Orris a contender for Syersi's hand in marriage – and he was determined to have it.

Extending the crook of his arm, Orris gestured silently for her to walk with him. In the distance, she spied the five females of her retinue giggling around a tall figure. Instantly, Syersi accepted the Commandant's arm and guided their walk in the direction of her retinue.

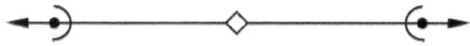

A dull ache throbbed in his leg. Rixs bent down and rubbed the still tender muscle. It had been a miraculous healing, his cloudy memory barely able to capture the image of the lean Imperial Physician working his Talent – for he had to have been a Talent to heal everything that was broken in Rixs.

Hunched over his leg, Rixs lifted his head and smiled at the gaggle of females that surrounded him. They had appeared out of nowhere to invade his privacy as he walked off the stiffness in his body. Thanks to the First Counselor's generosity, Rixs exchanged his prison cell for a comfortable small room at the training arena where the new recruits were housed. It had been the last place he expected to be ambushed by so many lovely faces. All were easy to look at, but one, with dark wavy hair and light blue eyes, was exceptionally lovely.

Perhaps this girl was the Princess of Gnomera, whose legendary beauty had traveled far and wide. Even as far as the coastal peninsula of the Bravura Strait where his home of Pax Valley sat isolated from the rest of the world.

Innocently Rixs asked, "Are you the Princess?"

Giggles burst around him.

The beauty beamed a sunny bright smile. "I think you mean *Empress Heir*," she replied, choosing not to correct his mistake. She knew who she was. She was part of Lady Syersi's retinue, a *lingering lady*. "You are a new face to me. Tell me, what is your name?"

Murmurs and gasps vibrated his ears and Rixs glanced from one girl to the next. They appeared to be surprised and offended.

"Have I said something wrong? Should I not have spoken to the Princess?"

One of the young ladies stepped into the beauty and whispered something Rixs could not hear. A look exchanged between them and the girl stepped back, seemingly chastised for whatever she had said. Then the beauty leveled her light blue eyes on him.

"You have done nothing wrong except for one thing."

His face fell and he tossed his head to shift rebellious hair from his eyes. He wanted to be able to see every small twitch of her expression. "What have I done?"

She laughed then told him in a low voice, "Your name. You have yet to tell me your name."

He blessed her and the other ladies with a crooked smile. "I am Rixsander of Pax Valley." There was a quick pause before he added, "But please, call me Rixs."

Chadgerwin had determined that Rixs was who he said he was and had no devious intentions behind his mischievous green eyes that sparkled like a polished emerald. Unbeknown to Rixs, Chadgerwin was not planning on letting him leave Isslewood any time soon. It was his unique ability, the Talent that was discovered, which had persuaded the Counselor and the Absolute to keep Rixs close by.

The clashing vest with its stash of blades was a treasure by itself, but Rixs had given away his closest held secret when he caught the blade Chadgerwin had suddenly thrown at him. Not only had he caught the blade, but his eyes had been closed when he caught it. After that, the Absolute had insisted on testing his abilities right in the prison cell, making Rixs catch blades repeatedly, sometimes two at a time with eyes open then eyes closed. Then the Sanguinary set up a target in the corridor so that Rixs could demonstrate his ability to throw his blades, only he had to make the throws through the cell bars – with eyes closed.

Both men grilled Rixs on the purpose of his blades – the two long blades that crisscrossed the back of his clashing vest and that he used as swords. The eight short blades arranged in two rows of two that hugged each side seam – four under each arm, they were his favorite. Easy to get to and quick to throw. Then there were his four medium blades which were hidden away on the inside of each front panel of his vest – two on each side.

Finally, Rangus had pointed to the finger-length ornaments that adorned the hem of the clashing vest. Rixs's throwing stixs. More like darts, they were inconspicuous and deadly, but no one knew other than Rixs – and Chadgerwin and Rangus. The heated red glow of Rangus's stare and the recurring smiles and head nods from Chadgerwin, was all the hint Rixs needed to assume he would be released from his cell. And he was.

Holding her hand up to block the sun, Syersi squinted at the crowd and the stranger in the center. "Who is that?" she questioned.

Orris followed her eyes. "That is the vagrant you found."

"Is he?" She arched a brow while smooth sapphire eyes glided over him. "Hobb did well."

From a distance, the stranger, who had nearly plunged through death's door, was transformed. He stood up straight to reveal a respectable height, and his skin appeared to be full of color. Hair that had been matted in clumps moved whimsically about his face. He was … *captivating*, she thought.

Silently, the Lady watched her retinue flirt with the property she had found. A tinge of resentment pinched her throat as she observed the smiles that he graced them in return. A frown arrested her face when she realized a certain member of her retinue had snagged and monopolized the stranger's attention.

Amused by the slow burn in Syersi's stare, Orris leaned close to her ear. "It appears that the vagrant has his hands full with all those girls. And I could swear he has an eye for Moniere."

She slanted him a look. "Not for long," her voice sang, her footsteps smooth as they walked toward her retinue and the stranger. "In the end, he will only have eyes for me."

Orris cocked his head to the side. "A bold statement," he snorted. "Even for you."

Her slender frame shrugged. "But true, nonetheless. All men eventually want me. Take you, for instance." She swatted his chest to make her point.

He sighed heavily understanding her meaning. "And you will tire of him just as you have tired of everyone else who seeks your affection."

Syersi's mouth curved. "Very likely. I became bored with you, after all."

Orris clenched his teeth. "You only think you are bored with me." He leaned in and gripped her attention with serious chestnut eyes. "We are not finished."

They had arrived at their destination, so he said no more as they came to a stop behind the crowd of recruits and retinue congregated around the stranger. Orris scratched his nose then cleared his throat as loud as he could causing the trill of feminine voices to cease. All eyes turned in his direction, but once realization dawned, the recruits hurriedly dropped to one knee while the ladies of Syersie's retinue dipped into a low courtesy.

Rixs tossed his hair away from his eyes and blinked at the sight around him. Even the girl he assumed to be the princess sank low to the ground. He glanced up to study the two bodies that stood before him. Of course, he had known they were approaching, the space around them filled and emptied as they walked, but he had paid them no mind, absorbed by the girls around him. Especially the one who still held herself low to the ground, her head bowed.

The man that stood straight as an arrow, Rixs recognized as the Commandant of the Lothorian Guard. He had ordered the move into his new quarters. As was explained to him, the Lothorian Guard was the Emperor's personal army and was responsible for the protection of Isslewood, the grand fortress and the lands around it that hugged the Gneiss Curtain to the east and was surrounded by what was called the Great Wall everywhere else. It was a formidable kingdom within an empire, and the Commandant exercised authority over its protection and the training of all the soldiers, not only of the Lothorian Guard, but of the many Gnomeran armies, as well.

Rixs recalled that he was not a particularly nice man. His actions indicated arrogance and enough self-pride to drown a fish. The man was full of himself and Rixs narrowed his eyes in wariness.

The young woman released the Commandant's arm and met Rixs with eyes so blue, he was certain the sky had lost its color – for she had stolen it. The woman ripped apart the true meaning of beauty, for there was no way to explain her. If his eyes could breathe, his emerald orbs would have inhaled her until there was no more breath to be drawn. The hunger he had never known he had until he laid eyes on her would have been satisfied with a mere glimpse and filled his belly until it overflowed into his chest. Rixs frowned at such sappy thoughts.

Exquisiteness aside, something was familiar about her – like he had seen her in a dream. An image of a yellow cloak came to his mind, but no more.

A swirling red tide of glimmering skirts played at the lady's ankles as she walked forward, but it was the tight bodice of her gown with a neckline drooping scandalously low that captured Rixs's eyes. Aware that he lingered too long on her chest, his attention traveled to her hair and the stunning jewels that were woven into an elegant braid of shiny black hair. Those jewels could keep a man living in great comfort for the rest of his life.

A gaping grin transformed Rixs's face. He tossed his head to one side, clearing his eyes of the rebellious hair that threatened to obstruct his color-filled view. Dark lashes framed her brilliant blue eyes – eyes that roamed slowly from his feet to his head. It was a good thing that he had bathed that morning.

Syersi tilted her head ever so slightly as she studied the man who gawked at her. Sandy brown hair hung provocatively in a pair of devastatingly gorgeous green eyes, and for an instant her fingers twitched to brush his hair away from his forehead. He had morphed from caterpillar to butterfly. At her scrutiny, she noticed a deep flush color his cheeks.

Even with his mouth gaping wide enough to catch a fish, his sharp cheekbones and strong jawline demanded she take notice. She sucked in a breath to seize the moment and snapped back to herself. With pink lips pursed, she arched a single dark brow at him and said, "You should close your mouth, stranger. You look like a fool."

Rixs stared at her, not comprehending her words. "Huh?" he mumbled while slowly closing his mouth.

Orris coughed to camouflage a smirk then observed, "Obviously, he wreaks of intelligence."

Quiet snickers sounded around him as the retinue continued their curtsies and the recruits lingered on their knees. The understanding that he might have been played a fool warmed his cheeks. The girl who had led him to believe she was the princess was poised so low she might have kissed the dirt.

"Do you know what to do when in the presence of royalty?" the beauty asked. Her voice was a melody.

Again, there were muffled chuckles and giggles, but no one dared look up.

A quick burst of nervousness leached onto him. "No. I come from the Bravura Strait. We have no royalty. Who is the royalty here?" He turned questioning emerald eyes to the girl who should have been royalty. She only stared at the ground.

The stifled giggles soured into gasps while the Commandant shook his head and dragged a large hand over his face.

Syersi's melodic voice cut to a hiss. "Are you mocking me, stranger?"

Looking to Orris for help, Rixs received a mocking smirk and everyone else seemed content to keep their heads in the ground. "Umm, no?" he murmured, again glancing at the girl who had deceived him.

"Stop looking at Moniere," Syersi spat. "She will not help you." Nodding at Orris, giving him a silent order.

Orris cleared his throat. "Woodsman, the First Daughter is already known to you, but clearly, your memory is as sharp as a dog's tail." He paused, then spoke with authority. "Allow me to introduce, Lady Syersi, the Empress Heir of the land realm, Gnomera, the daughter of Emperor Lothorius and his beloved Lady Saudria."

The little confidence Rixs possessed abandoned him like a coward. This young woman was important. Stumbling over his tongue, he managed to stammer, "Uh ... hi. I mean ... your heiress ... um... it is a pleasure!" With an unsteady smile he waved a hand. "I am Rixsander of Pax Valley, but please, call me Rixs."

Syersi held back a laugh and cut his confidence further. "Did I ask for your name?"

Crimson swelled up his neck and into his cheeks as a lump of humiliation formed in his throat. Rixs allowed his smile to drop.

Standing straight, and elegant, Syersi waited, her piercing blue eyes fixed to his humiliated expression. Then she blew a puff of air from her lips and gave a single nod to the Commandant. He stepped up and quickly swung his fist at Rixs's face, but the hit was intercepted.

Quicker than a snake's strike, Rixs caught Orris's wrist with a strong grip, but the trained Lothorian Guard countered with expedient precision.

Oomph! The force of the blow from the Commandant's opposite fist nearly knocked Rixs off his feet. He gripped and moved his jaw from one side to the other while swiping his tongue at the corner of his mouth to the drop of blood that had pooled there.

Rixs nodded, his green eyes glowing with appreciation. Back home, no one would have been able to land that blow against him. The hometown brawls of Pax Valley did nothing to prepare him for the honed skill of a Lothorian Guard. Rixs had never fought against a seasoned soldier, and clearly, he would need to do better.

"Heed my advice, Drifter," Orris quietly spoke in Rixs's ear. "Always bow in the Lady's presence, and never avoid a punishment dealt to you." He backed away slightly, letting his eyes touch on Rixs's cut lip. "And never, never underestimate me," he finished, flashing a smile that showed off his teeth.

Syersi, poised and calm, watched on, her blue eyes glimmering with expectation and Rixs finally understood. Slowly, he dropped to one knee.

"Stranger," said the deceptively sweet voice. "Maybe some sense has been knocked into you?"

He nodded and started to rise but a firm hand slapped his shoulder and held him down. "Never get up until she allows it," Orris said.

Rixs stayed on his knee. Time passed slowly. The wamps and retinue had it far worse. They had been frozen in place since the Lady had arrived. It was a bad idea, but Rixs opened his mouth regardless.

"Are we to kneel forever?"

Syersi blinked at him, then her gaze swept over the others. All their heads hung low. She turned back to Rixs. He should not have been looking at her. "Yes. If I wish it," she replied bluntly, her blue eyes challenging his emerald ones. "But I am merciful. You may all rise."

There was an audible sigh of relief as the retinue straightened from their curtsies, and the wamps rose from their knees. Rixs stretched to full height, and no sooner had he done so than a fist filled the space toward his head.

The Commandant's swing was fast but Rixs was already aware of the angle, the speed, the exact spot Orris's fist would land. He could have easily prevented it. Instead, Rixs stood still and prepared for the hit.

The sound of knuckles hitting bone preceded pain that erupted along his cheek. "Strikes!" Rixs yelled. "What did I do this time?"

Orris snarled back, "Never question the Empress Heir."

Rixs lost his temper. "By The Powers!" he growled through clenched teeth. "Have some patience! I come from the Bravura Strait! We have no royalty we must grovel to. There are no self-absorbed princesses to slap us or …"

Syersi's eyes flashed, but it was Orris who slapped the back of his head. "Watch your words, Straggler! People have died for the insult you speak!"

It was well known Syersi had a temper, her self-control fragile, at best. She had a reputation for being quick to act and slow to think. In an instant her hand found the first sword within reach and yanked it from its scabbard. The poor wamp cried out in confusion, and horror.

His inexperience and ignorance made him a green recruit. His stupidity and rash actions made him a *wamp*. Wamps were lower than dirt until their training made something more of them.

When the boy realized his sword was being yanked from his possession, he reacted without thought. He grabbed it.

New recruits were taught to maintain control of their swords — always. It was drilled into their heads over, and over again. This recruit had reacted too late. By the time his fingers closed around the sword, the double-edged blade pulled through the meaty flesh of his hand. That made him a *wamp*.

"Ahh!" he screamed as blood poured from two slices in his hand, one along the muscle of his thumb, and the other along the base of his fingers. He screamed again and dropped to the ground, huddling around his injury.

Syersi froze momentarily, horrified, and remorseful at what she had caused. Then her anger grew. It was the stranger, Rixsander, who was to blame. If he had not insulted her, she would not have lost her temper and the wamp would not have cut his hand.

The weight of the sword forced the tip of the blade to hit the ground causing Syersi to grunt as she used both hands to heave it back into the air. On wobbly legs, she pointed the sword at Rixs's chest, the blade swaying as she struggled to keep it steady.

Again, Rixs yelled without censuring himself. "Is she out of her mind?" After cringing at the sight of the wamp's bloody hand, he added, "She's mad!"

It was his words that drove Syersi to her rage. His disrespect could not, and would not, be tolerated. Without thought of consequences she grunted loudly and heaved the sword high in the air. She would sever his head from his neck then see if he had anything else to say.

Knowing the movement to come Rixs saw the look in her eyes. The girl meant to kill him, but he meant to live. "You are truly nuts if you think I will stand by so you can run me through!" he announced.

Reaching for his long blade, his grip caught air over his back. He was not wearing his clashing vest, so he had no protection. The well-defined shape of Orris stood next to him doing absolutely nothing to intercede, so Rixs found his own solution to the problem at hand.

One instant, the Commandant's sword hung at his side. In the next, Rixs had torn it free from its scabbard. It happened so fast Orris had no time to react.

Syersi swung the sword through the air toward Rixs's head. Her lack of speed and control guaranteed it moved with agonizing slowness. Rixs was already positioned long before the *clank*, of Syersi's weapon met the sword he held in his hand.

There were screams and shouts, but a deep and powerful voice cut through them all in a loud bellow. "That is quite enough!" A strong dark hand wrapped around the handle of the sword Syersi held.

"Chadgerwin!" she cried. "Let me go! He will be punished!"

Orris also yelled while lunging at Rixs. "How dare you steal my sword!"

Not to be left out, Rixs bellowed, "She's a nut!" and at the same time, easily jumped away from the Commandant's clutches. "And you are too! You did nothing while she tried to kill me!"

"Silence! All of you," Chadgerwin growled. The emotions that surrounded him made his ears ache. He drew in a deep breath then exhaled slowly and within moments there was a shift around them. The rage and panic that had rocked the air dulled to a mild tremble.

Even with the deep breath of calm, Syersi squinted her eyes at the Counselor and bit her tongue to keep silent. No one around them knew what had happened. Not the recruits, not the retinue, and certainly not the stranger she had just tried to kill. Not even Orris fully understood, but Syersi did. She knew the power of Chadgerwin's Soothe. He had calmed the entire crowd that surrounded her. Only a powerful Talent could affect so many at the same time.

Chadgerwin stared down at the girl who caused him so many headaches. His large hands still gripped her wrists tightly and he shook his bald head. If he strangled her, there would be too many witnesses.

SEVEN

Face after grimy face filed through the receiving hall. They came to seek pardons, ask for help, or settle disputes. Syersi, inexperienced in these matters and bored out of her mind, pretended to listen with a smile frozen to her ethereal face. Sneaking away was out of the question. Rangus would sniff her out in no time and drag her back.

Chadgerwin had been a tyrant after Syersi's display at the training arena. Her punishment consisted of the longest lecture she had ever had to endure in her seventeen seasons cycles of life, after which he forced her to receive her subjects. So, she sat. And sat. The ache on her bottom caused her to fidget on the polished stone of her father's throne.

Orris stood rigid and erect behind her. The scowl on his face gave away his discontent of Chadgerwin's order to endure Syersi's responsibility in the receiving hall as a reminder that his failure to maintain peace between Syersi and Rixs was unacceptable.

Not one to be humbled, the Empress Heir had wanted to shrug off the incident with the young wamp, but when left to herself felt genuine remorse for what she had done. It was because of this that she submitted to the Counselor's orders without loud complaint, but as the morning dragged into high sun and the line of people continued to extend past the exterior doors, her cooperation and patience began to fade.

The throne swallowed her up like a little girl barely out of swaddling rags. With an elbow propped on the arm, she plopped her chin in the palm of her hand and huffed. An older man dressed in dirty worn trousers and a stained smock continued to rattle on before her.

What did he say? His horse trampled his neighbor's garden, and he cannot make restitution? Or was it that his neighbor's horse trampled his garden, and he will not make restitution? And why do I care? I say they should fight it out.

Suddenly, she was aware that the man had stopped babbling and was looking at her eagerly. It was her turn to say something – give her judgment. Syersi looked at him with an uneasy smile then allowed her blue gaze to drift over the bodies waiting their turn. She was done.

Lifting a finger, Syersi said ever so sweetly, "Excuse me for one moment." Then she stood and walked out the private door behind the throne and kept walking, leaving a curious Orris behind.

"Where are you going?" a stern voice reached her ears. The mighty footsteps sounded angry as they pursued her.

"What does it look like? I am leaving," she said. "I have had enough for one day."

"You cannot just leave!" Chadgerwin stormed. "You have just barely started!" He caught up to her and grabbed her arm. Two of Syersi's shadow guards stepped forward, but the Counselor threw them a warning glare, his threat obvious if they interfered.

Swinging her around, Chadgerwin grasped both of her shoulders with his massive hands, forcing her to face him. Swept up in a fury of her own, Syersi yanked back but was no match for his powerful grip.

Only reaching Chadgerwin's chest, she tilted her chin up, sparks of blue heated her glare. "Let me go! Those people are complaining about trivial things that I find boring! I have had enough!"

Chadgerwin's exasperated laugh echoed through the corridor. He would have pinched her lips off her face but instead ordered the guards to empty the corridor of unwanted company. Once all extra ears had been shooed away, the Counselor gave her a stern shake.

"You think that *they* complain about trivial, unimportant things?

By The Powers! You should listen to your own complaints, Syersi!"
He let her go to avoid the temptation to bend her over his knee and
spank her.

"*You*, my dear child, complain when your bath is not ready at the
precise instant you demand it. Or when your attendant only braids
five jewels in your hair instead of six! Ah, now there is a tragedy! Oh,
let us not forget when your cushions are not fluffed to perfection!"
His nostrils flared. "*Those*, my dear, are trivial complaints!
Meaningless demands from a spoiled First Daughter!" He had a
fleeting thought to use his own Soothe on himself.

He swung a bare, muscular arm toward the receiving hall she had
just left. "Those people toil each day just to survive! Do they
complain their soup is too cold? No! They are happy to have soup at
all! And if you listened at all, you would realize they are not
complaining. They come here seeking help from their ruler who cares
about them. Lothorius cared about his people!"

"Then where is he!" Syersi screeched so loud, the walls
shuddered. "If he cared so much, why did he leave his people?
Obviously, he had no love for his daughter – at least not enough to
stay!"

Rendered speechless, the Counselor let her go and took a step
back. His thunderous eyes, now tame, searched her face. Syersi's
anger was no longer about boring lines of people. It was about
something she had buried on the day her father left.

"Do not speak to me about how that man cared for his people!
He should have cared about me! But he left me!"

Syersi had been the only child of a doting mother and a
protective father. Lady Saudria's murder four seasons cycles earlier
had left Syersi devastated, but it was when her father left Isslewood
that she felt abandoned and betrayed. Anger and bitterness festered
within her over the seasons since.

The Intimus had watched her morph from a sweetly spoiled little
girl to a spiteful, self-absorbed and reckless young woman. And the
burden to help her find herself and take her place as ruler of
Gnomera fell to the man who stood before her.

"Syersi," he said gently. "Your father did care about you. He loved you. You have no idea how much he loved you ... what he did to protect you."

"He had no love for me!" she shrilled. "I will not hear it!" Her scream caused the great warrior to flinch. She shook as the emotions that she had long held were finally released. "My mother was murdered! Tell me, Chadgerwin, what did he do? Did he come to me? Did he hold me? Did he comfort me for the loss of my mother?"

Desperation bled through her eyes. "No! He left me to cry ... alone!"

"You had Mazzlin, and me, and..."

"Mazzlin was not my father! You are not my father!" she screamed, the echoes wavering endlessly within the corridor.

The servants that had been shooed away earlier were drawn back, hiding in the shadows. Chadgerwin thought to Soothe Syersi but quickly discarded the idea. She needed to work through her feelings.

"My father locked himself in his chambers. I had to beg to see him. Even then he would never let me approach his bed." She furiously wiped at her face and nose. "He had abandoned me even while he was still here, and I grew to hate him. But I wanted to love him. I wanted to wrap my arms around him for the loss of my mother and for the loss of his lady." She looked desperately into Chadgerwin's eyes. They stood in silence staring at each other.

"And then he left. The gallant Supreme left Isslewood without a good-bye for his daughter. I knew then how I would honor him ... I would despise him with every breath of my soul. My joy would mean insult and shame to his name." Blinking tears from her eyes, she stared off into an unseen distance. "So, you see, Counselor, I do not want to be like Lothorius. I do not seek to fill his shoes. I hate him."

As though a great burden had been lifted off her shoulders, Syersi fell into the Counselor's arms in quiet sobs. She had never allowed herself to show the effect of her father's disappearance. Like Syersi was his own flesh and blood, Chadgerwin held her tight and stroked her hair while he offered a sad smile to Mazzlin, who had crept up quietly and was wiping her own eyes and nose.

He spoke softly to the broken daughter in his arms. "You do not yet understand, but you will very soon." He gripped her shoulders, pushing her back from him just far enough so he could peer directly into her red and swollen eyes.

"Believe me when I say, he loved you more than you know. Everything he did, *everything*," he tapped her nose with a finger, "was for your protection."

Wearily she pulled away from him. "What kind of emperor leaves his throne and disappears?" Syersi wrapped her arms around herself. "I don't care about his love or why he did what he did," she croaked, her throat swollen from her screams. "I do not want you to convince me of anything. I just want to hate him."

Taking a knee before her, he placed his right fist over his heart – the salute to a leader. Syersi's hand flew to her mouth. He had never shown her such honor.

"No! Get up!" she cried. "You bow to no one!"

He grabbed her hand with his free one. "Lady Syersi, First Daughter of Gnomera, and Empress Heir to the Empire, I, Chadgerwin of Birch, First Counselor of Gnomera, pledge you my life and my loyalty. Lothorius is no longer of consequence. You will rule this land as the Empress I know you were born to be. I have protected you since the day of your birth. You are much more than an Empress in waiting. You are more powerful than you can comprehend, and one day, soon, all will become clear, but until that day, you must trust me. You must become the woman who can lead Gnomera. That woman is strong, wise, and honorable. Be that woman."

Syersi sniffed, "I do not know how."

"The Intimus will help you," he whispered. "I will help you. Trust me?"

The heir to Gnomera had no words. With tear-stained cheeks and quivering lips she studied the Counselor, still on his knee. He seemed different – no longer an adversary. He spoke of her being much more than she knew – of having power she could not comprehend, and yet she did not feel powerful. She felt embarrassed, wishing to take back the pent-up emotions she had let slip. He must have thought her to be very weak, and yet, there was no accusation in his perpetually stormy grey eyes.

Chadgerwin waited anxiously on bended knee, fearing that she would throw his words back into his face. He stared into her doubt-filled eyes knowing she was unpredictable. He had never saluted her before. She had never deserved it, but he did it now. It was an offering of his faith in her. She was Gnomera's future.

Time lagged by and Chadgerwin fidgeted with his knee against the unforgiving stone, until the young lady heaved a sigh and hung her head low, nodding slowly and whispered, "Very well, Counselor. Help me become that woman."

A round of quiet applause and sighs fluttered out of hidden places as Chadgerwin stood with a satisfied smile on his lips. He placed his strong hands on Syersi's shoulders and squeezed.

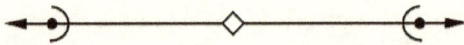

Vivid blue eyes and a smile as warm as a midsummer morning looked down upon her. "Be careful of the thorns, Syersi. They have a fierce sting."

The young girl mimicked her mother, picking up the roses from the table and arranging them in a vase all her own. A yellow rose, a white rose, a pink rose, began to fill her small vessel, while Saudria added her personal touch to a much larger arrangement. Syersi looked up into her mother's face and grinned from ear to ear.

A servant maiden sat nearby, assembling another arrangement which would grace the Emperor's table for the evening meal. The bouquet exploded with roses and marigolds in colors of red, white, and yellow. A particularly large velvety scarlet rose caught the young heir's blue eyes — eyes that mirrored her mother's. She snatched the flower out of the servant's vase.

"I want this one!" she cried, sticking the stem into her own concoction of flowers.

Calm and serene, Saudria arched her brow. "Syersi, we do not take from others. Please return the flower and apologize," her soft smooth voice aired with a gentle authority not to be underestimated.

"But I want this one! I am the First Daughter, and she must give it to me!" her little face scrunched with fierceness.

The servant bowed her head, talking humbly into her chest. "It be all right, Lady. She can have the flower."

A complexion as smooth as the rose petals in her hand, turned toward the servant. Dark, thick lashes fanned across almond-shaped eyes that were as blue as the sky, pinning the girl to her seat.

"No, Rayne," Saudria's full lips admonished. She arched a brow at her daughter. "Syersi?"

The miniature version of Empress Saudria crossed her arms and jutted out her chin. They stared at each other in a showdown, Saudria looking as though she were posing for a master painter and Syersi poised for a battle with furrowed brows and pursed lips. Rayne started to rise, but a soft hand pressed her arm, a tender command to remain where she was.

"Fine!" Syersi cried, putting the flower back into the servant's vase.

Saudria quipped firmly, "Syersi, you can do better."

The little girl frowned and blinked repeatedly. "I am sorry I took your flower."

Rayne smiled and curtsied to the girl then repeated the gesture to the Empress and excused herself. Once Saudria was alone with her daughter, she swiveled, taking Syersi's cheeks in her hands and pressed a soft kiss on each.

"Thank you, my adorable. You must always remember to treat others like you would want them to treat you. Would you have liked her to steal a flower from your vase?"

"She wouldn't dare," Syersi said with a frown. "She is just a servant ... Rangus says they are here to do whatever I tell them."

Saudria pressed her lips together. Leave it to the Sanguinary to encourage bad behavior from Lothorius's daughter. "Do not listen to Rangus."

"Yeah," Syersi agreed. "He eats people!"

"Oh, he does not eat people. He only wants you to think he does," Saudria smiled then turned serious. "You must remember, little Empress Heir. You should be kind and treat everyone with respect. It is much easier to be a flower than an onion."

"Huh?" Syersi's eyelashes fluttered in confusion. "Why would I want to be a flower or an onion?"

A hand stroked lovingly down warm black locks that absorbed the sun's rays. "It's an example. If you put out a bouquet of flowers and a basket of onions, the flowers will draw the butterflies, bees, and the hummingbirds. But the onions draw nothing. Not even flies."

The young princess, barely nine springs old, batted her lashes vigorously as though she were fanning herself. After a moment, enlightenment gleamed on her face. "That is because flowers smell sweet! Onions just make you cry."

A soft chuckle sounded in Syersi's ear as her mother bent down and kissed her temple. "Precisely, my adorable. And it is the same with us. When you are like a flower, sweet and lovely on the inside, you will draw everyone to you. If you are an onion on the inside, you will drive everyone away."

"But I am already pretty," the young girl stated thoughtfully. "Everyone says so."

"Outer beauty only draws outer loyalty, Syersi. It is the inner beauty that draws loyalty deep. Especially for you. Never forget, your inner beauty will shape you for two things, to become Empress one day, and to ..."

To what? The words repeated over and over in Syersi's mind. *Never forget...never forget...never forget...* But she did forget.

EIGHT

"Attack, wamp! Attack!" a snarl raked the air.

Rixs lowered his wood sword in frustration. "I have a name! It's Rixs, not *wamp*!"

The combat master bellowed back, "You have no name! Until you learn to attack, you are wamp!" A vein protruded from his forehead. "Stop holding back! You always defend! Instead, you must charge! Advance! Attack!"

Jerking his head to toss the sandy brown hair from his eyes, Rixs growled in return. "I win all my matches anyway! What does it matter if I win by attacking or win by defending, as long as I win?"

It was true. Rixs won all his hand-to-hand combat drills by waiting for his opponents to make their move. Once they did, he responded by blocking, evading, or hitting, if the situation called for it. He focused on every opponent in hues of grey and knew their movements – even those behind him. It was hard to explain, but he could see it. Almost feel it. He knew when space was closing in on him, and his body instinctively reacted by creating pockets of opportunity which allowed him to get the upper hand whenever he needed it.

"Don't be cocky, ya wamp! You fight other wamps. That's why ya win! If you fought against a seasoned soldier …"

"Bring 'em on!" Rixs challenged, dropping the sorry stick used for a sword. "What about you?"

The combat master gave up a tight grin. A second challenge was unnecessary. Showing off grey teeth, he muttered to himself while stripping off his weapons and rolling up his sleeves. "Boy, I'm gonna enjoy this!"

Waiting for the attack, as he always did, Rixs circled the combat master slowly while the other man jumped energetically on his toes, swinging his arms forward and back to show off his agility. The younger challenger watched with the eyes of a hawk, noting the pattern in which the space emptied and filled with every movement.

All the wamps formed a large perimeter around them and mercilessly taunted them on. For a while, it seemed Rixs and the combat master would only circle each other, Rixs observing while the combat master hopped about. Then the older man spat through his teeth, impatience getting the best of him, and lunged forward with such speed, Rixs barely had time to block the arm swinging toward his jaw. Immediately following, another arm swung toward the young challenger's gut. The combat master was clearly no wamp.

After having both of his strikes intercepted, the master growled through clenched teeth and faked to the left while charging to the right, but the Talent read his body's movements in dusky grey tones, easily avoiding the elbow meant for his face. And so it continued. Rixs sidestepped and dodged, never once trying to land a hit of his own. Meanwhile, the combat master was free to lunge, jab, and kick since Rixs remained in defensive posture. Even so, the master could not land a single hit.

Claps, hoots, and whistles soon became jeers, taunts, and rants. The wamps were impatient. They wanted to see a bloody brawl.

Frustration grew in the master's face. Rixs only grinned. He assessed the pockets of space that shifted with every movement, purposely staying within arm's reach to show he could openly hit the master, but he chose to evade the man's moves. Rixs was making his point.

"Hit me, you chicken!" the combat master yelled, his breaths deep and heavy.

His own breathing steady and unstrained, Rixs blocked a jab to his ribs then jumped out of the way when the man kicked out a leg, targeting his knee. "I don't want to take advantage of you!" Rixs teased, a cocky grin smudged across his face.

Growling and hissing, the trainer lunged in frustration. "Take advantage ... why, you arrogant ... What are you trying to prove?" He thrust a hand toward Rixs's windpipe, but it never made contact.

The wrist was caught with such speed, it surprised even Rixs. Then he twisted the master's arm behind him until the man grunted in discomfort.

With his mouth prickling the master's ear, he growled, "I want to prove that I can take you down whenever I want. But I do it my way. Not yours."

When the master countered this move with his opposite arm and planted his leg as leverage to flip his subordinate, Rixs used the trainer's momentum to his own advantage. Working in harmony with the space as it folded around him, Rixs successfully threw the man to the ground with a hard thud then dropped to his knee, swinging an elbow down and into his throat. A killing move. He stopped just before he crushed the master's windpipe.

"You're dead," Rixs announced.

Shouts and whistles heralded the wamps' approval that a student had triumphed over a master. Hands crowded in around Rixs, stretching and reaching to slap his back.

The combat master eyed the hand extended to him, then accepted it and was pulled to his feet to face a set of vibrant green eyes. He took hold of Rixs in a firm shake and said, "You could have won that match faster had you attacked."

"I do things my way," Rixs grinned at him. "Always."

A group had approached them during their match, but only Rixs noticed them, seeing their dull grey male and female forms long before he saw their bodies of color. A deep voice called out and everyone turned their heads.

"Let's you and I take a tumble, Woodsman!"

The Empress Heir jabbed Orris in the side with her elbow. "Take a tumble! That sounds terribly obscene," she cooed.

He murmured back, "I prefer to tumble with you." A wicked

smile stretched his cheeks.

Syersi rolled her eyes. "Only in your dreams, Orris."

Rixs turned stiff as he looked between Syersi and Orris. Since his last encounter with the Empress Heir when she had sliced the hand of some poor recruit, he had stayed as far from her as possible. The Commandant was bad enough with his veiled insults, but Syersi was a nightmare.

Moniere called out to him. "Hello, Rixs." She smiled demurely.

Hesitating, he returned her smile and waved. After letting him believe she was Gnomera's princess, he had kept his distance from her, as well. His eyes landed on a friendly and sincere face.

"Hello, Keedra," he called, a genuine smile making his dimples pop out for all to see. A few giggles drew his attention to the rest of the retinue. They were like a gaggle of geese following Syersi wherever she wandered. He grinned at the thought of Syersi waddling over the Isslewood grounds with a bunch of geese waddling behind her. No doubt the retinue all thought his wide smile indicated his level of pleasure at seeing them again.

Rixs acknowledged each of them as well, making sure to leave no one out, then eager to avoid another fist to his face, he bowed awkwardly to Syersi. "Empress Heir," he greeted. Once he stood straight, he grinned sharply at Orris. "Commandant, I would love to tumble with you."

Syersi's eyes brightened with delight and her ladies laughed.

With a savage smirk, all teeth on display, Orris began removing his cloak and weapons. "Let's not wait a moment longer."

A loud growl stole everyone's attention. "Commandant, I think I will get him next!"

The crowd turned to find the Absolute headed in their direction, consuming the ground in long powerful strides. Behind him, Chadgerwin's teeth were on display as he grinned in amusement while he showed off his well-defined arms and the myriad of scars they carried.

Disappointment shrouded Orris, but nobody dared challenge Rangus, so he exhaled his frustration before he announced, "You lucked out, Woodsman."

The crowd parted for the massive and muscular glory of the Absolute. Rixs was instantly nervous. When Rixs had first laid eyes on him in prison, the hair on the back of his neck stood straight on end. Seeing him again, nothing had changed. The hair on his scalp prickled to attention.

"I smell fear on you, boy," Rangus goaded.

Rixs nodded. "Well, I feel like prey. Why does everyone feel the need to challenge me?"

The Sanguinary laughed wickedly. "The others do not matter. Only I matter, and for me, you are fresh blood." He inhaled deeply and blew a satisfied, "Ahhh."

Rixs nearly wilted when the Sanguinary drew near enough that his big teeth clicked next to his ear. Rangus spoke low, "And I want to see your Talent in action."

My Talent! Rixs coughed in shock. "Are you sure I have Talent?"

The Absolute's expression fell flat. "Boy, do not ruin my opinion of you! Of course, you have Talent! Who else have you met with your ability?" Rangus rotated his scarlet gaze over the growing crowd.

Word had spread fast – Rangus had challenged Rixs. He never challenged seasoned soldiers, let alone the recruits. It seemed everyone wanted to watch.

It was hard for Rixs to believe he was Talented. His father had always insisted he was nothing special. Shifting his own perception of himself would be difficult and would take time to grasp that he was part of an elite group – like Rangus and Chadgerwin.

With pseudo confidence Rixs made his first mistake. "Get ready to have your hind parts kicked silly!" Rixs boasted. Then he made his second mistake. "But I confess, I fight defensively," he added, feeling a need to share.

Without warning Rangus swung a large fist while blurting out, "Never explain yourself, boy!"

Rixs hit the ground with a hard *thud* but was quickly on his feet again. He shook his head to clear his hair from his eyes.

Knowing Rixs was about to have the sense knocked out of him, Chadgerwin quickly defended, "Rangus, go easy on the lad. We prefer him alive!"

The crowd roared in laughter.

Rangus struck again, aggressive, and fast. Rixs twisted with lightning speed, just barely avoiding the extended fist and countered with a punch into the giant man's side. The hard contact paralyzed Rixs's hand. It was like punching a big rock.

The Sanguinary grinned at him. He had felt nothing. Rixs winced and hoped he was still alive when the fight was over.

NINE

Late into the night when the rest of Isslewood slumbered, the Intimus sat by candlelight around the big bulky chunk of wood that served as a table. They spoke in low voices.

"Tangrah continues to push their borders. I fear they will draw us into war, but my biggest concerns right now, are within our own borders," Rangus said. He gave Chadgerwin a pointed stare. "Two things." He held up his index finger. "First, the boy's crew is not the only pack searching for the Source. There seems to be several. What is unclear is whether these groups are all separate or if they are linked under a single ambitious effort." He added his middle finger to the raised index. "My second concern is the mysterious deaths being reported. Three to be exact. One happened outside of Gateway, and the other two, close to Sentur."

The Intimus quietly looked on, their gazes as piercing as thistles.

"I believe we have a Shade terrorizing the countryside. And I wonder if the Shade is somehow connected with these groups looking for the Source."

The docile Hobb jumped from his seat and exclaimed, "A Shade! How do we protect Isslewood from that? The Powers know what happened with Lady Saudria!"

Sitting back with his arms crossed over his chest, the relaxed Chadgerwin observed, "It poses a problem, we will need a way to keep the gates secure."

The Absolute popped a piece of sweet cake into his mouth, not bothering to chew before he swallowed it. "The searches risk Syersi's safety. The Shade risks Syersi's safety. Combine them ... she is in danger."

Mazzlin's eyes went wide. "Do not say that, Rangus!"

He threw her an exasperated look. "Fine! I take it back! Feel better?"

Her mouth drew tight. "Oh bother! How would they know about the Source?"

"Don't be daft, woman," Rangus snarled. "The legends have always sparked curiosity. There are always zealots ready to put half-baked theories to the test."

Hobb piped up. "Come to think of it, a few days ago I went to Ormolu to find herbs for my potions." He glanced around the table. "I heard of a stranger paying for information about Lothorius." The air paused as everyone looked at each other. He added, "Maybe someone has found out about Lothorius."

"Since you neglected to kill Moganar," the Guardian brooded, pointedly glaring at Rangus. "Someone should have run into him by now but there is nothing. Not even a rumor!" Mazzlin's eyes popped as big as twin moons. "It serves us right if Lothorius returned!"

An audible huff came from the Absolute. "You hate killing, Seer! What's your point?"

Chadgerwin shook his head. There was no telling where the Guardian was going.

Mazzlin dramatically clutched her chest. "I nearly choked when her feelings poured out to you, Chadgerwin!" She turned to Hobb and Rangus. "I wished you could have been there! She has stumbled in the dark for so long. And we have let her! Perhaps it is time we led our little Syersi out of the dark, Chadgerwin!"

The Counselor began, "Well, I think there is some ..."

"We can't keep her in the dark forever!" Mazzlin chirped sharply, interrupting the Counselor. The men startled a little when she slammed her round hand on the table. "We must tell her! She has a right to know! What happens if she falls in love with the wrong man?

Let me tell you what will happen! Chaos is what will happen! We will be cast aside like unwanted table scraps! She needs someone who is good, and kind, and will be faithful to her ..."

"Mazzlin!" Rangus stood from his seat to tower over everyone. "My ears have had enough! Do you have anything important to say?"

The Guardian blinked at him several times and puffed her cheeks in a scowl. "You are rude, Rangus!"

"I know! Tell me something new! Here is something for you! Your babbling gives me a headache!"

Shocked into silence for a moment, the plump Guardian stood to her full height. Undaunted, she stretched on her toes until she barely reached the Absolute's navel and tilted her head backward until her icy glare pinned his fire-filled sockets. "Dowse those eyes, sir, or I will dowse them for you! They do not scare me!" she declared with a pudgy frown.

"It is not my eyes you should fear, Guardian!" he rumbled, before snapping his large white teeth at her.

Unimpressed, she firmly held her ground with pooched lips and hands on hips. A growl vibrated deep in his throat. The standoff held, neither budging.

Suddenly, Rangus laughed. "Haha! You are a fierce one, little Miss Stubby!"

"Stubby, indeed!" she exclaimed, her chin raised high. "You can meet my stubby fist!"

"Take care, Mazzlin. You know how Rangus loves a challenge," Chadgerwin said. Then he threw out a thought. "I think we should make Rixs our Imperial Shield."

The verbal dual between Mazzlin and Rangus abruptly stopped, and three pairs of eyes turned their shocked focus to Chadgerwin.

"That is one of the most prestigious posts in Gnomera," Rangus said. "Why would we choose an outsider to fill it?"

"You know exactly why, Rangus. Look how long he lasted with you!" Chadgerwin leaned forward, clasping his hands in front of him.

Rangus snorted. "It was a short match!"

Shaking his head, Chadgerwin responded, "Give the man credit, Commander. It was impressive. He held his own with you, a

Sanguinary! He lasted longer than anyone ever has, including your seasoned soldiers!" He leaned back and stretched in his chair, the wood creaking with his weight. "Admit it. Rixs's Talent gives him the ability to protect Syersi better than anyone – even you, Rangus. And better than that, the young Talent will see people coming as no one else can."

The fight had been short, but Rixs had still lasted longer than anyone else ever had. After, Chadgerwin and Rangus had walked him to find Hobb, who patched up a sprained arm, a few cracked knuckles, two black eyes, and a grossly split lip. The Physician had eagerly engaged in his work to a fully conscious Rixs, who marveled at the Physician's Talent.

The Counselor smiled as he remembered Rixs's ability in action. He stood from his seat to walk over to one of the walls laden with bindings and tomes, and gazing at the thousands of records lining the shelves from floor to ceiling, he plucked one from the shelf and leafed through it.

"We need a Talent like him." He paused to stroke his goatee and said, "I think he is Sagacious."

"Who?" Rangus questioned.

Chadgerwin threw him an eye roll. "Who do you think? Our friend from the Bravura Strait, of course. I wish I knew for sure, but regardless, we need to convince the lad to stay."

"Well, he wants to leave," Rangus reminded him.

"Yes," Hobb agreed. "He seems to dislike Syersi."

"Everybody dislikes Syersi!" Rangus quipped.

Though engrossed in bindings, Chadgerwin still managed a dry, "Stop, Rangus."

The Physician continued. "He has that girl he is betrothed to …" He paused. "Did he tell you, Chadgerwin?"

Pulling a binding from one of the crowded shelves, the Counselor answered, "Hmm? Oh, yes. Cliessa was the girl's name. If he had really loved her, he would have never left her. What he feels is guilt for leaving, so he thinks he must do the honorable thing. Return and marry her."

Rangus, Mazzlin, and Hobb watched as Chadgerwin pulled

binding after binding, thumbing through each then replacing it.

"What are you doing?" Rangus asked impatiently.

"Trying to find that binding Lothorius always carried with him."

Mazzlin frowned and recalled, "Oh, yes. I remember it but never saw what was in it. He kept it to himself."

Chadgerwin turned and looked at her, his scars gleaming in the candlelight. "He never showed it to anyone, including me, but I saw it once when he was distracted. The encryption was very odd."

Thousands of bindings, tomes, and scrolls lined each wall of the records chamber from floor to ceiling. The daunting task of finding a single binding hidden amid the thousands would take seasons cycles. Even with the four of them.

Running an oversized finger along the bindings, Rangus stated the obvious. "Get the servants to help find it."

"No," Chadgerwin's answer was quick and final. "No one else can see it. We must look."

The three were confused. "Why must it be only us?" Rangus creased his forehead.

"Because," Chadgerwin said as he turned to face them, a binding held open in his hands. "I believe it contains the secrets of the Source."

TEN

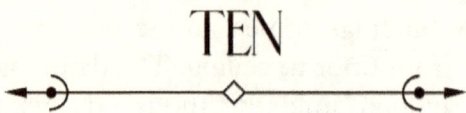

Long confident strides made their way to the tree where he grasped the sleek blade and yanked it free. His clashing vest had been returned to him, and Rixs gave up a crooked grin as he engaged in his favorite pastime – targeting. He jerked his head to the side, tossing a wave of renegade hair away from his eyes as he walked back to his place to throw again while Syersi's retinue admired him with lovesick stares.

The Empress Heir watched silently from a distance. He seemed to enjoy her retinue, talking and laughing with them as though they were old friends. Occasionally, his glance wandered in her direction where she had hidden herself behind some bushes. His focused gaze gave her the impression he could see her though she had taken great care to keep out of sight.

Moniere stepped forward and after a brief interlude of talking, Rixs handed her the black blade, showing her how to hold it. He demonstrated his stance and slowly went through the motions of throwing, then used his hands to guide Moniere. Syersi narrowed her eyes.

As Empress Heir to Gnomera, activities such as knife-throwing, sword-fighting, or even archery were withheld from her. These activities were viewed as unbecoming a lady of her stature, even though the desire to learn burned in her chest. She had given up convincing anyone to teach her.

"You are to be soft and delicate," Rangus had told her. "Leave the dangerous skills to those charged to protect you."

Chadgerwin had told her she had better things to do with her time, even though she was always bored and searched for ways to keep entertained. Even the guards had refused to teach her. It seemed no amount of threats, bribes, or seduction could convince them to disobey the Intimus, especially Rangus. They were eager to bend rules when it involved kisses and touches but drew the line when it came to sword play or daggers. Hypocrites.

Syersi watched for a time. The young man was incredibly accurate – more than any of the Lothorian Guard she had seen. When he threw, it was as if he became one with his blade. Goosebumps broke out over her skin.

Moniere repeatedly interfered with Rixs's practice, and Syersi studied Rixs as he endured it graciously, noticing how he subtly tried to brush her off and include the other girls. Tired of being a bystander, Syersi stepped out of her hiding place.

Rixs's attention shifted to her and he smiled, no hint of surprise on his face, as though he knew she was there all along. With erect posture, she elegantly cut her way through her retinue, drawing scowls from her ladies. She stopped at Rixs's side and not so delicately elbowed a frowning Moniere out of the way.

Sparkling green eyes peeked through sandy brown hair to study her. Their color danced in the rays of the bright spring sun, and Syersi stopped breathing.

He watched her sweep loose black hair from off her shoulders with a delicate hand. His eyes shifted to the jewels of yellow and blue woven into her long black locks then he let his gaze lazily travel down the blue dress she wore. It shimmered, reflecting bits of sunlight in his eyes that made him blink. Full pink lips dared to smile up at him, and Rixs curled his fists to make his fingers behave.

Moniere backed away until she stood at Keedra's side. The retinue fell quiet, their excited chatter suspended now that the high Lady had imposed on their fun.

Syersi's unspoken demand was obvious. Rixs looked at the blade in his hand then back at her. She smiled. She wanted him to show her how to throw blades.

"May I?" Syersi asked, her voice soft and musical. When she lifted her slender fingers, Rixs flinched and she hesitated, knowing she was the cause of this. Then she gently brushed away some hair from his eyes.

"Oh," Rixs gave up a reluctant chuckle. "My hair hates to obey me."

She dazzled him with a genuine smile. "Well then, you may count on my fingers to tame your hair when needed."

Instantly charmed, Rixs forgot Syersi's previous trespasses, and the retinue faded into the background. His attention belonged to the Lady with eyes of blue.

She was all friendliness as he demonstrated the proper way to hold a blade and how to bend her arm when throwing. Her excitement was something he could tangibly feel, and her genuine joy melted the ice wall he had erected the first time he met her, but it was her first throw that delighted him.

The short blade, black and shining, wobbled straight into the air. Rixs caught the blade easily, before it could hurt anyone, but he laughed so much, his sides ached.

"We undeniably need to work on throwing," he proclaimed between chuckles.

Syersi feigned a pout. "You mock me, Rixsander."

"Never, Lady Syersi," he replied.

She ran a finger along the front panel of his vest. "I've never seen anything like your vest," she said, finger gently stroking the worn leather. "Tell me, Rixsander. Do you wear it all the time?"

"Rixs. Call me Rixs." Two dimples graced his cheeks as he smiled proudly, his eyes looking down at his vest. "And yes, I wear it all the time. I feel naked without it."

His last comment earned giggles from the retinue.

"It must be extraordinarily heavy!" she exclaimed. "There are so many knives. You must stick yourself frequently."

He shook his head. "Not knives. Blades. These are blades … and no, I never get stuck."

Moniere leaned into Keedra, the retinue had no choice but to drop back into obscurity. "It's unfair. *She* takes an interest, and we have to yield," she hissed. "She will bore of him and discard him within days. Men are nothing but playthings to her!"

"Shhh, she'll hear you," Keedra reprimanded in a whisper. Then she added, "Why are you complaining? You are no different."

Moniere curled her lip and glared at Keedra. "I am not like her!"

Rixs's voice drew everyone's attention. "Watch closely," he said to Syersi. She, her girls, and her guards all watched with interest. In slow exaggerated movements, he demonstrated how to throw then he gave a blade to Syersi. "Here. Try again."

Rixs observed her closely but did his best to avert his eyes, as did Syersi's guards, when her hips swayed then shimmied just before she planted her feet. She awkwardly duplicated his moves and forcefully slung the blade forward. Instead of straight up, the blade wobbly sailed forward, spinning end over end until it hit the dirt with a thud.

"Ah-ha! This is such fun!" Syersi cried. "Better than a first kiss!" She turned and winked at her ladies.

Shocked laughter came from the retinue, their resentment of her temporarily forgotten. Even her guards forgot to observe proprieties and let loose their chuckles, one wagging his eyebrows at the other.

Raising a fist to his mouth, Rixs bit his knuckle to stifle his own surprise at Syersi's forwardness. Once in control of his voice, he said, "That was better, Lady." He pulled another short blade from its sheath and handed it to her. "Try again."

Syersi swept her big blue eyes over his sleeveless vest with its trove of blades. The vest fell just below his hips, black glistening blades hung everywhere.

"Can you show me all your weapons?" she asked, looking up at him through her dark lashes.

He obliged her request pointing out his short blades, the size of his palm, which hung in two rows of two at each side seam of his vest, just under his arms for a total of four on each side. He explained these blades were small and just the right size for quick throws.

He then lifted his front vest panels. Concealed inside each were more blades, two on each side, and explained that these were his

medium blades. Longer than the short blades, these were used for
targets that were harder to penetrate.

When Syersi tried to touch one, Rixs pressed the front flap
closed against his skin and moved to the two sword-like weapons
that crisscrossed his back. They were twice the length of his medium
blades but not quite the length of a sword, and though they appeared
awkward, he handled them with ease.

Syersi had heard from some of the soldiers that he was a master
at throwing anything with a sharp edge. Hearsay had spread that his
targeting skills had been unmatched by anyone who had challenged
him, and she remembered the match between Rixs and Rangus. No
one had ever lasted past the count of ten against the Sanguinary. Not
even Orris, and Rixs had lasted ten times longer.

Syersi's eyes fell to the hem of his vest. "What are these?" She
plucked an ornamental object from its place. "Is this some secret
weapon?" she teased with a light musical laugh, not realizing she had
guessed correctly.

He nodded toward the object she held. "That is a *stix*. They look
harmless, but they are as deadly as they are deceiving," speaking with
friendliness even though she had snatched the ornate weapon
without permission.

A quick flick of his wrist had the finger length stix whirling
through the air like a hummingbird, hitting the center of the target
right next to his medium blade already stuck in place. The retinue
applauded and squealed their approval.

"Impressive!" Syersi exclaimed with eyebrows arched high. She
finally reached for the short blade Rixs had been holding. "Your skill
is just as enviable as your knives."

"Blades," he reminded her a little harshly. "And, yes, people do
envy them. They have tried to steal them, buy them, even fight me
for them."

Syersi held up the black smooth metal and angled it against the
sunlight. "You cannot blame them. Look at the workmanship! They
seem … special."

"They are special. They were a gift from my father. Made only
for me."

Standing a full head shorter than Rixs, Syersi looked up at him with blue eyes coaxing. "I would love to have one," she said, her voice purring.

He returned her gaze but had no response.

"Perhaps you might part with one? For me?" she made a more direct plea.

"No," was the short response.

The abrupt answer took Syersi by surprise. "Such a quick dismissal of my request. Will you think on it?"

Rixs's answer was firm. "I do not need to," he said, and walked to fetch the blades that had been thrown earlier.

Anxious for the answer she wanted to hear, she thought to bribe him. "You would be handsomely rewarded."

Rixs turned toward her. "Open your ears, Lady Syersi. I said *no*. That answer will not change when you ask differently. These blades were a gift to me from my father. I will never part with any of them."

The air shifted and the guards tensed. This had now become a battle the Empress Heir was compelled to win.

"Stranger," she said with a cold, flat tone. "I could take all of them, if I wanted." Still holding the short blade in her palm, she fingered the handle anxiously.

He stopped and let impassioned green eyes duel with her. "You could try," he replied, his flat tone matched hers.

All movement stilled as the retinue and guards shifted their gazes between the two. Time seemed to slow as if to stall what was about to happen. Even the clouds slowed their lazy travel across the sky to watch the battle of wills.

Rixs broke his gaze first and picked a blade off the ground, aware of the stark blue eyes' glacial stare chilling his back. The hair at the base of his neck prickled a warning. *Be mindful of the space behind you. Watch shifts in the space around the Princess!*

He walked to the tree he had been using as a target and pulled the blades stuck in its trunk, careful to be mindful of any movement behind him. No sooner had his fingers wrapped around the last blade than he perceived the movement behind him. A fling. Then the familiar shape of his own blade whirling toward him.

By The Powers! Syersi had thrown his own blade at him!

Against better judgement, he let his anger take control. The best response would have been to let the blade sail past him since it posed no real danger. Instead, Rixs whipped around, thrust out his hand, and caught it by the handle.

He stood as straight and rigid as the Gneiss Curtain, glaring at the young woman who was ordained to rule Gnomera. His rage pounded in his temples.

The retinue strangled their gasps, except Keedra, who cried out in shock. "Lady! What have you done?"

The glower Syersi flashed her retinue promised pain-filled retribution.

Green eyes bright with fire fastened to the high Lady with each slow step Rixs took. Even as Syersi's guards flanked her, their hands ready to pull their swords, Rixs's deliberate stride never wavered, nor did his icy stare shift. With his eyes fixed on hers, he stopped a few strides in front of Syersi and slid the blades he held into their rightful sheathes.

Unyielding, she stared back. After the blades had been placed easily into each designated sheathe without Rixs so much as peeking at his vest, Syersi narrowed her eyes and frowned. He was more than he let on. No one could have replaced three blades and a small dart-looking stix, into their rightful places without a single glance.

Rigid and tensed, Rixs's chiseled arms flexed at his sides as he stood in front of her. His body was eerily still, like he was getting ready to hit something.

Blinking rapidly, Syersi slowly blew out a tuft of air. There were too many people around to demand an explanation for his ability to seemingly see without looking, so instead she said, "I apologize." It was a subtle confession for doing something thoughtless, and had she stopped at that, it might have assuaged his anger, but her need to make excuses for herself pushed her to continue. "It was an accident. The … the knife slipped."

He tossed his hair out of his eyes and frowned. "You lie."

His accusation left no room for explanations. There was no need. The blade had sailed straight at him. Anyone who believed it had been an accident was a fool.

Syersi's contrite expression was suddenly gone. "You might want to retract your words," she hissed.

"Why would I retract them?" There was a hint of a cruel grin. "It's the truth," he declared firmly, then turned and walked away.

The space behind him filled with the shadowed forms of two guards and smothered in around him. Although they were at his back, Rixs could visualize their every move and anticipate their actions. They were nearly upon him, and he smiled to himself.

Good! I need to blow off some steam.

ELEVEN

The pile of straw was better than sleeping on the ground, but it itched. Shifting and jostling to find a comfortable position, Rixs cursed under his breath. The cell was different than his first stay when Chadgerwin and Rangus had visited him then released him. This hole was enclosed by stone walls with a solid iron door which had a small window barely big enough for his face to peek through.

He touched the cut above his right eyebrow, then tongued his fat lower lip, very aware that his left cheek was just as tender. Undoubtedly, his face looked hideous, but he was confident he made out rather well in comparison to the other two guards who had tried to seize him after he had insulted the Empress Heir.

It would have been easier had he let the guards take him to lockup without trouble, but the scuffle had been worth it if only to see Syersi's shock after he had disarmed her two guards, then proceeded to beat them soundly. After Rixs had taken his frustration out on the guards, he willingly walked himself to the prison.

The grey form of a female came to view on the opposite of the stone wall – he could see the curves. Syersi was the last person Rixs wanted to see. He had demanded to speak to Chadgerwin but was ignored. Stewing on top of his pile of straw, all he wanted was to go home.

Rixs had done what he set out to do. He had found his adventure and so far, it had only brought him misery. He had trudged through rain and mud for days, was practically starved when food had become scarce along the journey, then he was nearly killed by an unknown group of attackers, and to top it off, he had almost died from jumping off a cliff. Now he was stuck in a cell at the whim of a spoiled princess. This big adventure had not shaped up the way he had originally envisioned.

It was time to go home and be reunited with his mother and brother. Thoughts of his home made Rixs smile, but then another thought weaseled its way to the forefront of his mind, and he frowned. It was time to make good on his promise to Cliessa.

He had avoided thoughts of his betrothed and the guilt that gnawed at his gut for not marrying her. Promises were always to be kept for a man of his word, and he considered himself just that, so there was only one thing to do. The idea brought him no joy, rather, it soured his stomach and left a bad taste in his mouth – like swallowing vomit.

Rixs shook his head. There were better things to think on, so he tried to find something else to occupy his thoughts. Rhages came to mind. The towering crude beast of a man that had befriended him and took him under his wing. If not for Rhages, Bronan and the crew would have abandoned Rixs long ago. He wondered if Rhages had escaped.

Having been ambushed by men covered in cloaks of black, the crew had found themselves in the fight of their lives. It had been Rixs's second sight that had kept them alive, releasing arrow after arrow which found their mark in numerous attackers. He saw the entire space around him and knew where every shape and form stood. The biggest challenge had been discerning between the friendly and enemy forms.

When Rixs saw Rhages take an arrow to his leg, he knew he needed to help his friend escape. Rixs relived the moments that he drew away the attackers and evaded the clusters of arrows. His heart leapt up into his throat as he remembered throwing himself off the cliff.

The door groaned open, pulling Rixs from his thoughts to face the female who had come to visit. A pang of disappointment pulsed in his chest when Moniere, not Syersi, stood in the doorway.

Taking in the small cell, Moniere's rich brown eyes watched Rixs hop to his feet and bow. She smiled, then her gaze wandered to the pile of hay before finally migrating to the bucket in the corner. When she realized its purpose, hot pink flushed her cheeks.

Not able to look at him in the eyes, she extended the basket. "I scrounged up some food for you. I hope you enjoy it. I have heard that prison food is horrible."

"Prison food is non-existent," he smirked. The aroma of cooked meet and freshly baked bread, among other things drifted out of the basket. Bright green eyes danced with excitement as he gave up a broad smile.

Stepping closer to him, Moniere lightly touched his bruised cheek. "Does your face pain you very much?" Her eyes landed on the cut over his eye then traveled to his fat lip.

Unprepared for her touch, Rixs sucked in a breath and avoided looking into her sultry eyes. He forced his fingers into the basket, grabbing the first thing he touched. His hand emerged with a piece of meat which was immediately shoved into his mouth.

Mumbling through his mouthful, he managed to say, "My face looks worse than it feels." He swallowed his half-chewed mouthful then added, "This was very thoughtful of you. No doubt the *Empress Heir*, would never do anything so kind."

The retinue pressed her lips together and wrung her hands. Her eyes dropped to the floor.

Tearing a piece of bread with his teeth, he chewed with his mouth open. "How can someone so beautiful be so rotten?"

"Oh, I do not think she is so very beautiful." Moniere scowled. "But she is rotten!"

Rixs laughed. "How do you and the other girls tolerate her?" His gaze suddenly shifted to the door.

"Well, she is the First Daughter," Moniere replied. "We must tolerate her."

His attention was still fixed on the door as he reminded her through the side of his mouth, "A very beautiful First Daughter."

Frowning at his words and his obvious enchantment with the Empress Heir, Moniere opened her mouth to refute. Words had formed but before she could say anything, Chadgerwin's voice belted through the door.

"What do you mean he already has a visitor?"

The cell door flew open and Chadgerwin's tall menacing frame froze in the doorway. His stormy grey eyes surveyed the cell and fixed on the retinue lady.

"What are you doing here?" he demanded.

The young lady curtsied low. "Counselor," she greeted nervously. "I was just leaving."

"She brought me food!" Rixs held up the basket.

Chadgerwin narrowed his eyes at the girl. "Why would she bring you food?"

"Because she is kind!" Rixs replied just as Moniere curtsied then ducked past the Counselor and hurried out the door.

Chadgerwin stared after her as she ran down the corridor. "What is she up to?" he mumbled. After extended contemplation, he finally turned to Rixs. "So, my good man," his tone was light and friendly. "It seems I am destined to always find you in lockup."

"And that is my fault?" Rixs huffed through a mouthful of bogroot he had pulled from the basket.

"Yes … it is!" came the response. "You have to get it through that skull of yours that Lady Syersi is the Empress Heir of Gnomera. You cannot argue with her, or show disrespect, even if she provokes it. You will lose every time. Learn *that* and your stay with us will be better."

"Why would you think I want to stay?" Rixs questioned. "Your Empress Heir is a mad woman! She threatened to take my blades. Then she threw one at me!" He paused. "Tell me. How is all this my fault?" He thrust his hand back into the basket. "Have you forgotten how she sliced a guard's hand with his own sword, then tried to attack me with it?" He shook his head and snorted, "I want no part of this place. If you release me, I promise to leave and never return."

Chadgerwin studied him. The young man clearly wanted to leave but Chadgerwin needed him to stay. A Talent like Rixs could not be allowed to slip through his fingers.

"I know she can be difficult." Rixs snorted at this but the Counselor ignored it and as he spoke, released a palpable wave of calm to the agitated prisoner. "Come now, Rixs. It is not for her to make the effort at amiability. It is yours." Chadgerwin pulsed more Soothe toward Rixs. "And besides, you know I cannot let you leave. I have only just discovered you."

Determined to hang onto his anger, Rixs shook his head to throw off the calm effect settling on him. It was a feeble attempt. Tranquility clung to him like honey.

Emerald eyes pierced the Counselor "I am not a possession! You cannot make me stay!". Rixs rubbed his face vigorously with both hands, his anger eroding away.

"Stop playing with my head!" he growled. Long fingers pushed through the rebellious hair that pestered his eyes. With a last attempt to resist the Soothe's effects, the young man petitioned, "Would you play with my head to make me want to stay? Are you a man who would cheat me of my choices?"

White teeth flashed against ebony skin. The Counselor's grin stretched wide. Rixs's attempt to block him was admirable. Chadgerwin could have pushed harder to break him, but that was not his intention. He would not obligate Rixs to a promise made under false pretenses.

"No. I would never rob you of your choices," Chadgerwin replied. "But make no mistake, Rixs. I want you to stay and will go to extraordinary lengths to keep you." He bored into Rixs with stormy grey eyes. "Your ability makes you valuable. I have never seen it and we need to explore your potential. Your Talent would be invaluable to Syersi's protection. And you would be richly rewarded." The Counselor wagged his eyebrows with his last statement.

Rixs smiled at the thought of riches. Then he smiled at the thought of being close enough to the Empress Heir to throw her off a cliff.

"How do you know I would protect her? I would sooner strangle her than protect her. Or maybe I'd let her would-be attackers strangle her. It would be worth it if I had to listen to her every day." He leaned into the Counselor's gusty stare.

Chadgerwin chuckled. "You forget, Rixs, the first time we met, I pulled deep from you to know the kind of person you are. If nothing else – I know your goodness."

He went on to recount how Syersi had found his body, broken and near death. She could have left him to die, but she saved him. It was Syersi that commanded Hobb to heal him and there was great significance in that act. As Chadgerwin spoke, Rixs noticed his sleeveless arms and the webbed scars that adorned the Counselor's skin like stitching on a fine-spun cloak.

"Using his Sanicle devours strength from his body." Chadgerwin's voice was barely above a whisper. "If Hobb exhausts his strength healing others, he risks not having enough for Lady Syersi should she need it. That would be tragic. She is the only born to Lothorius. Her survival is of the utmost importance for several reasons." Chadgerwin paused, eyeing Rixs.

"Protecting Lady Syersi eclipses everything. I know it. The Intimus knows it. Even Syersi knows it, and yet … knowing that you, a total stranger, would die without her help, she chose to risk her own safety by ordering the Physician to save *you*! That is not the action of someone who thinks only of herself." He shook his head, the large scars on his face were illuminated by the dim light.

"Had I been there, I would have forbidden it," he asserted. "The infection in your body was so severe, Hobb could not make you whole. He could not heal you completely. In fact, saving your life made him so weak, he could not get out of bed the next day as his body tried to heal itself."

Speechless, Rixs stared at Chadgerwin.

The Counselor's eyes wrinkled in a smile and he sighed. "Thank The Powers that nothing happened to the Lady that would have required Hobb's Talent. Remember, Rixs, this spoiled, demanding girl put your life ahead of hers. You should thank The Powers that she is hard-headed, and insistent on getting her own way. Without those qualities, she might have given in to expectations. She might have listened to Hobb and let you die, but she went against his wishes, and you are here because of it."

Mouth gaping, Rixs scarcely believed him and wondered if he would have to take back every unflattering thought he had about the Empress Heir. Worse, he knew he was obligated to repay her in some way. The only thing he could offer was to become her protector.

"Sharing that was a dirty thing to do, Counselor," Rixs huffed with shoulders drooped. "Now, I must repay her." He studied the floor then met Chadgerwin's eyes. "I am no warrior."

The dark-skinned man shrugged. "I have plenty of fighters. That is not what Syersi needs."

Rixs exhaled shakily. "Very well." He hesitated, as if to delay his agreement. "Grant me a trial period, but at the end of this period, if I wish to leave, promise you will release me."

Lines of tension relaxed in Chadgerwin's face. "You have it!"

The Counselor slapped Rixs on his back and he winced. His body was covered in bruises from the fight he had with Syersi's detail.

"Now, come," Chadgerwin said as he walked to the door. "Let us leave."

TWELVE

An arrow cut the air and thudded into the second ring of the target narrowly missing the red center. Cheers rocked the trees.

"There you are!" Syersi cried to no one in particular. The scene before her was of frenzied rivalry and it seemed no one cared that she had arrived.

Chadgerwin puffed out his chest. "Ah-ha!"

She cleared her throat loudly, then spoke again. "Excuse me!"

"Hush!" Rangus admonished as he stepped up with bow in hand. "It's my turn!"

Chadgerwin put a finger to his lips, signaling for her silence.

A scrawny wamp scampered to the target and pulled Chadgerwin's arrow. Rangus stood ready, his bow raised and an arrow in place. "Quiet!" he ordered the clamoring throng of observers. He aimed then released.

With a whir, the arrow sliced the air like lightning. It pierced the target just barely at the edge of the small red center.

"Ha!" he laughed and smacked his chest. "Look and weep, Counselor!" Then he spun around and screeched a war cry. The wamps and soldiers shouted their approval.

Orris stepped up. "Move aside, Absolute! Let me show you a real archer!" His eyes landed on the wamp ready to pull Rangus's arrow. "No, boy! Leave it! I want evidence of my arrow besting our fearless leader!" He laughed from deep within his belly.

Right-eye dominant, he held the bow securely in his left hand while his right three fingers wrapped around the bow string and smoothly pulled it all the way back until it nearly touched his chin. Then the arrow sped through the air.

Sitting atop Juju, Syersi gripped a handful of the white mane and pulled as she watched the arrow pierce the wood right next to the Absolute's. Two arrows stuck out within the small red circle that was barely big enough to accommodate them both. Orris pumped his fist twice, his arrow barely nearer to the center. The wamps and soldiers eagerly cheered for the leader of the Lothorian Guard.

Caught up in the excitement, it slipped Syersi's notice that not a single person had bowed or paid her any attention. The buzz of commotion tingled the light delicate hairs on her arms. Twisting her hands further into Juju's mane, the horse signaled discomfort by tossing her head and snorting.

"Sorry, girl." Syersi patted her neck and eagerly waited for the next competitor.

Rixs had stepped up, but Chadgerwin cut in. "I want another try!"

"It's the boy's turn!" Rangus growled. "You already had yours, and you missed! Ha!" the Absolute mocked. Bright red eyes danced like fire, celebrating the Counselor's failure.

"Rixs?" Chadgerwin appealed, already nudging him out of the way. "Do you mind?" The Counselor quickly nocked his arrow then raised it.

Syersi wondered at the Counselor. He never had fun with the soldiers. "Chadgerwin!" she cried out. "Since when do you play at targets?"

The Counselor furrowed his course brows and turned to her. "Quiet, Lady Syersi! You will cause me to miss!"

She grinned at him. Excitement thrummed the air. There was always an unmistakable spirit when the soldiers played together, and it caused Syersi's skin to pebble.

The Counselor's arrow sliced the air, postured to land solidly between the two arrows already in place. Instead, it skipped off one arrow's shaft and landed in a clump of grass.

"Ohhh!" a united and dispirited moan hummed throughout the sizeable group which kept growing in number. Syersi groaned too, disappointed for Chadgerwin's sake.

Another horse stopped alongside Juju. Syersi glanced sideways to see the rosy face of Mazzlin. She giggled at the Guardian.

"Rixs should be next," Syersi announced, and thought it was unlikely that he would find the target if Chadgerwin, an exceptionally skilled archer, was unable to do so.

Rixs had gone out of his way to avoid Syersi, even though she had apologized for losing her temper and throwing his own blade at him, then forcing him into lockup. It was obvious he held a grudge, so when she was told he was to be added to her detail, she questioned Chadgerwin's decision. Rixs neither liked her, nor was he an experienced soldier. The idea that he could or would protect her was laughable. Chadgerwin had merely told her to trust his judgment.

Botty, the old cook, had met Syersi's request and saw to it that Rixs was fed well while in lockup. The woman had a generous heart for the kind boy incarcerated. She had insisted that Lady Syersi had made some mistake. Rixs was too helpful and kind to be sitting in a prison cell.

Syersi had considered the cook's words and watched Rixs more closely. Botty was right. Rixs was like no other. He helped everyone, even going out of his way to assist the servants in their duties when he could. She needed to check back with the old cook to see how Rixs had accepted the basket of food she had ordered to be taken to him. It was to be a peace offering, but he had never given her a word of thanks.

Rixs stepped up to take his turn.

The Guardian inhaled the scene around her with a huge smile. "Well, well! What is happening here?"

"Silence your tongue, Mazzy!" Syersi hissed. "You will ruin his concentration!"

Mazzlin pressed chubby fingers to her lips and looked around. The quiet was palpable. Even the air stopped moving.

Rixs nocked his arrow with an ease unparalleled by Orris,

Chadgerwin, or even Rangus. Syersi watched with restrained breath. He stood with perfect form. At least, it looked perfect to her.

In one fluid motion, the bow and arrow lifted into position while simultaneously, Rixs pulled back the string. Syersi's eyes swept over every part of him and she noticed how the muscles flexed under his shirtless vest. A blush heated her cheeks. She also noticed something else.

"He uses his thumb!" she whispered to Mazzlin. She was no archery master, but she knew she had never seen anyone draw a bow string with their thumb.

Mazzlin's eyes went wide. "Oh, my! His thumb must be very strong!"

Rixs had pulled the string back to the corner of his mouth. The ladies watched with breathless anticipation. At any moment, both expected his thumb would snap in two.

The movement was subtle when Rixs straightened his thumb and released the arrow. In a blink, it hit the target, forcing its way to dead center. The thunder that erupted was ear-splitting, and immediately, the crowd squeezed around Rixs to slap his back and muss his hair.

Clap. Clap. Clap. There was a mouth-stretching grin on Chadgerwin's face as he clapped his hands slowly and deliberately. Even the hard-to-please Rangus nodded his approval. It was only Orris that remained unimpressed. He quietly watched the attention showered on Rixs.

"I congratulate you, Rixsander of Pax Valley!" Orris called out over the racket of voices. "It looks as if luck was your best friend today!" He flaunted a fake smile while running a thumb and index finger back and forth along the string of his bow.

Rixs responded with a crooked half-grin.

Chadgerwin turned to Orris. "Come now, Commandant!" he exclaimed. "It takes more than luck to stick a crowded target! You must admit, the man has incredible skill!"

Orris looked down at his boots and scratched his chin. "I will acknowledge his *incredible* skill if ..." he paused and looked Rixs in the eye. "If he can do it again."

Then the real games began. The rules were set forth.

Rule one. Each competitor had to place the arrow within the small red circle to advance to the next round.

Rule two. Each competitor had only one chance to hit the mark. Everyone pointedly looked at Chadgerwin.

"That goes especially for you, Counselor!" Rangus snorted, pointing an oversized finger at him. Chadgerwin merely shrugged.

Rule three. All could participate.

Those who chose not to compete were encouraged to wager on their favorites. So, the games began. Competitors eliminated during the early rounds tried to jump in on the betting. Praises and jabs thundered throughout Isslewood, the air throbbed with energy.

Round one began with twenty-seven men. Eighteen advanced to round two. In round three, seven more were eliminated, and by the fourth round, only seven remained. Then there were five left. And five again.

It was with great shock that Chadgerwin lasted until the seventh round as everyone had gambled that he would be knocked out earlier, but it was a greater shock when Rangus fell out in the ninth round. The Absolute had been expected to survive till the very end. He complained that a bug flew in his eye and argued for a second chance to which Chadgerwin promptly shut down. Only two competitors were left – Orris and Rixs.

There was a lively brouhaha to place final wagers. No one, except Chadgerwin and Rangus, could have known that the newcomer would do so well. The bets had started off in Orris's favor, but as the rounds progressed, there had been a shift in favor of Rixs.

Each time he hit the center of the target, Syersi stifled her squeals, but if she thought she was fooling anyone, she was mistaken. The expression she wore gave no doubt which competitor she hoped would win.

No longer competing, Chadgerwin found his way over and stood next to Juju. He patted the mare's soft muzzle while glancing at the young woman who would soon become Gnomera's ruler.

"I should observe," he chuckled. "This is probably not an appropriate event for an Empress Heir."

"Hmmm," she tapped her chin. "If a certain First Counselor had not abandoned me with hundreds of subjects, I would still be sitting in the receiving hall."

Chadgerwin noticed how her eyes never left Rixs.

"But I am glad you left, Chadgerwin," she continued. "Otherwise, I would have missed this great fun!"

Orris called for everyone's attention. "Since it is only Rixs and I, we should make this a little more interesting." He pulled a knife from its sheath that hung at his side, and the crowd silenced as he walked to the target. Using the knife's sharp point, he pierced his thumb. Then he pressed the bead of blood that had bubbled onto his skin into an unmarked area on the wood.

"Our new target!" he announced with a cocky smirk. Murmuring broke out and he hushed them with a wave of his hands. "The entire arrow's head must stick within the boundary of the blood." He paused, then proposed, "If I win, I take your clashing vest with its trove of blades."

Strands of wayward hair caused Rixs's eyes to itch. He blinked hard then flicked his head. "And what do I get if I win?" A deep frown menaced his face.

"I named my price. You name yours," Orris announced.

Cocking his head to see the color-filled frame of the Commandant. "There is nothing you have that equals the value of my vest."

Orris laughed then taunted, "You can think of nothing? You stand in the richest, most powerful land realm in the world, and you cannot think of anything you want to have?"

"Nothing matches the value of my vest and blades," the young Talent insisted. "Besides, you have no authority to offer me the riches of Gnomera."

Rixs reached over his shoulders with both hands and pulled the long blades from their sheaths on his back. He held them out in front of him and rotated them slightly so that the sunlight could dance along the black metal. Wherever the light touched, the long sleek blades turned several colors. He swung and sliced the weapons through the air to show off their unique and superior workmanship before easing them into their rightful places with fluid elegance.

"You are asking that I bet my very soul," Rixs said in a low and gentle tone. "I will not do it."

Syersi watched in fascination. Orris would find out, as she already knew, Rixs would never give up a single blade, but there was something else manifested in his demonstration. Replacing those blades so effortlessly without being able to see the sheathes – there was more to him than just skill.

The deep, authoritative voice of Orris cut into her distraction. "You refuse then, and forfeit."

"No, I do not forfeit. I will accept on one condition," Rixs said with a twitch of a smile. "If I win, I am free to leave Isslewood."

Orris bit out a laugh. "Of all the things the woodsman could ask for, this is his desire?" he cried in amusement. "To simply leave Isslewood?"

Rangus frowned and stiffened, the massive bulges in his arms flexing into hard rock. But it was Chadgerwin who voiced objection.

"Rixs, you and I have an agreement," the Counselor said, his hand planted firmly on his hips. "You cannot wager away your word to me. This is between you and Orris. Come up with something that affects him."

Rixs chewed the inside of his cheek. "Fine," he replied. Grinding his teeth as an alternative came to mind. "Then I require the title of Commandant of the Lothorian Guard."

The demand caught everyone by surprise and a dead quiet covered the ground then rolled into the hills before the murmurs began. Some agreed. Others opposed. Then a single voice shouted out to claim the crowd's attention.

"My title is not something to be wagered!" Orris bellowed. "You do not possess the skill to wipe my nose, let alone fill my shoes!"

"Take it or leave it," Rixs gritted out. The demand was bold – even arrogant. He had thrown it out, hoping to make the price high enough for Orris to back out.

The clashing vest was a constant reminder of a practical man who had taught Rixs to be modest about his abilities. The man who had taught him that no matter how skilled he was, there was always

someone better. The blades were more than weapons. They were a
reminder of his father's teachings. Orris could never offer anything
that equaled their value.

Musical laughter rang loud. "What will you do now, Orris?"
Syersi antagonized. "If you turn him down, you might as well
announce to the world that he is better than you!" She followed up
with another laugh.

With raised hands, Rangus stepped forward to draw all eyes on
him. "Silence!" he barked, deep and throaty, in a menace as only a
Sanguinary could. He turned full circle so that his blood eyes swept
over the crowd, daring anyone to make a single sound. Then he faced
Rixs.

"The Commandant is right. You cannot have the title of
Commandant of the Lothorian Guard."

Immediately Rixs rebuked, "Then there is no contest for that is
my price!"

"Let me finish!" Rangus snarled, flashing his large white teeth.
"I offer a suitable compromise." His blonde bushy brows were
creased together and nearly lost in the tangle of his equally blonde
and bushy hair.

"What if you had a title just as prestigious as Commandant? And
you answered to no one except to me and the First Counselor? You
would be free to make decisions as you choose with only us to answer
to. Would that be tempting enough for you?"

Big as apples, Syersi's eyes flashed to Rangus. She knew what he
was suggesting.

"What do you mean?" Rixs asked.

The Absolute invaded Rixs's personal space. He was close
enough their faces nearly touched. "Imperial Shield."

A shocked Orris quickly yelled, "With all due respect, Absolute,
the commission of *Shield* belongs to the Lothorian Guard, and must
be approved by the Governing Council!" Orris argued. "Like my
title, it cannot be won in a bet!"

Rixs seized his opportunity, "Then you renounce the
competition, Commandant?"

Boos and hisses mottled the air. Chants rumbled, "Wa-ger! Wager! Wa-ger!"

Orris glared at the faces crowding him then turned toward Chadgerwin, gripping his bow so tight that his knuckles turned white. "Counselor, you cannot allow this farce to continue. This woodsman has no training for such a prestigious title. It is too important to be won or lost in a wager."

Rangus had crafted the perfect solution to keeping Rixs around and Chadgerwin would not let it slip through his fingers. His only regret was that the idea had not come from him.

Only the Intimus knew the value of having Rixs as Imperial Shield. Even without formal training, Syersi could be in no better hands than those of the newly discovered Talent serving as her primary protector. It was a good strategy. There was no need to worry if the young man won because the prize would keep Rixs at Isslewood, and if he lost, he would still be around to serve on Syersi's detail. Whatever the political fallout, Chadgerwin and Rangus would handle it.

The Counselor turned to Orris. "This is your doing, Commandant. You changed the stakes of the game. Tables have turned. Rixs has the right to raise the stakes. You can always withdraw."

Rixs needed an offer too good to refuse. An idea took hold and he blurted, "Let the win or loss be decided by me!"

Orris narrowed his eyes at Rixs and snorted. "That sounds convenient."

"Hear me out," Rixs defended as he licked his lips. "You plant your arrow as planned. I will use a blade." Rixs looked at Orris and Chadgerwin eagerly, gauging their reaction. "My blade will unseat your arrow. It must fall from the target and my blade must stick in its place. If I succeed, I keep my clashing vest and become this Imperial thing. If I fail ... then ..." It was hard for him to say, and words failed him.

Orris finished. "If my arrow stands, you lose, and I take your clashing vest and blades."

Boisterous laughter drew everyone's attention. "That bargain is absurd! Do you honestly believe you can unseat his arrow?" Rangus snorted, then he laughed. He laughed so hard it became a spectacle and his outburst had Syersi laughing too.

"Rangus, I have never heard you laugh so unrestrained!" she cried in cheerful wonder. Mazzlin laughed along with her. "At the very least, Rixsander can be our tummler!"

They were making fun at Rixs's expense, doubting his ability to unseat an already embedded arrow from its place. Rixs glanced at Chadgerwin only to see doubt in his eyes as well. The increasing snickers from the crowd made him grind his teeth.

Undeterred, Rixs slipped a hand inside his vest and extracted a medium blade. "This is the blade I will use." He held it out to Orris. "Have we an agreement?"

Hesitant, Orris took and inspected the blade thoroughly. If he backed out, Rangus would never let him live it down, and his men would think him a coward.

He finally nodded. "How can I refuse? You practically hand me your clashing vest."

Cheers jolted the trees and vibrated the grounds. The excitement was not lost on Syersi and Mazzlin. They added their own hoots of approval to the crowd's roar.

"Let's do this!" Orris yelled, and the packed training field burst into thunderous cheers again.

Nocking his arrow, the Commandant waited for the noise to simmer. When nothing was heard except the buzzing of insects, he focused on the blood mark and released.

A *whiz* then *thunk* was heard. The arrow stuck cleanly within the blooded thumbprint. Ovations reached mountain tops and Orris grinned wide. Then all eyes turned toward Rixs.

Only the Pax Valley native would decide the victor in this bet. He alone would determine if he kept his blades or gave them up.

A hundred thoughts filled his head as he stepped up to the mark where he would throw. Doubts began to shake his confidence. His father's encouragement and his admonishment to be humble whispered to him. Perhaps he had let his confidence run away with him. He could have declined the competition and kept his blades safe from Orris's grubby fingers, but his pride would have suffered. Rixs wanted to win – to make a statement. He had been the best marksman in Pax Valley – the best in all the Bravura Strait. He could be the best in Gnomera too.

Clearing his mind of every thought, Rixs let the world around him narrow until all he saw was an arrow protruding from the round slab of wood. He stared long, his focus constricting further until only the arrow's shaft filled his vision. He fixed on the space the shaft filled, while his left hand held the blade loosely, his fingers rubbing the smooth metal.

The silence was overwhelming.

Syersi's hands twisted in Juju's mane. *By The Powers! Let him ...* What did Syersi want? Did she want him to hit or miss? If he hit, Chadgerwin would have him become Imperial Shield, and Rangus had been the one to suggest it.

Rixs as Imperial Shield would mean she would see him every day. Thoughts of him walking just behind her, watching her every move inspired mixed emotions – both good and bad, but if honesty prevailed, there were far worse fates than looking at a handsome face day after day.

Rixs closed his eyes tuning out the world around him. Summoning his strength, gathering it from his extremities, and concentrating it into his throwing arm. The world around him lost its color and the panorama of space became various shades of grey.

Within the sight of his Talent, there was no deceit. The eyes could be tricked. They could mislead what a person saw. When Rixs used Talent to see, the things that filled space could not be hidden, no matter how small. It was either there, or it was not. It was that simple.

A deep inhale calmed him. *By The Powers, let this be a good day!* Then, as only Rixs could, with eyes still closed and with all his strength, he threw the blade.

It was silent. He did not need open eyes to know whether he had succeeded or failed. Somewhere in the distance a mockingbird was calling. Then voices were erupting.

It was a good day.

THIRTEEN

Tower Wall was nothing like Rixs had imagined. Kissing the sky, it protectively loomed over Isslewood, spanning a distance around the Emperor's seat that required two days to travel. Within it was a labyrinth of stairwells and secret passages, including impressive stockpiles of weapons hidden at various intervals within the wall, and Rixs was now one of the few privy to their locations. Being the Imperial Shield had its advantages.

Swept from meeting to meeting, he tried to concentrate on the humdrum and exhaustive details of Gnomera's history. Everything from its geography to its governing structure and how it became a tremendous power was thrown at him. It was all very dry but had to be endured because of the position he now claimed.

Unprepared for the respect his new rank earned him, the biggest surprise came when he was moved from the soldiers' quarters to the great house and was given an expansive bed chamber on the same floor as the Empress Heir. While Chadgerwin, Rangus, and even Orris lived in the spacious palace in the wing opposite the imperial family, Rixs and Mazzlin each boasted a chamber just at the top of the stairs on the second level. Syersi claimed the rest of the floor.

It had been a shock when Rixs won the competition. After inspection of the arrow confirmed that the shaft had been split perfectly down the middle, Chadgerwin and Rangus announced him as Imperial Shield. Orris had still argued the legitimacy of Rixs being Shield because of his lack of training, Rangus contended that Rixs's deadly aim far outweighed any shortfall in training.

Slumped into a chair, Rixs stared out onto his own personal balcony. With only a small break in his activities, he had sought out the quiet of his chambers. The splendor in which he now lived was overwhelming. If only his mother and brother could see him. He even had personal servants.

Nothing was off limits anymore, and the fledgling Imperial Shield could go wherever he wanted in Isslewood. One of the best experiences of his life was his introduction to palace bathing. Living in the cramped soldiers' quarters with little more than a bucket of water to clean himself each day had been a hardship in more ways than one. Most of the soldiers chose not to bathe thinking it required too much effort. Their combined sweat from their arm pits to their feet nourished a putrid odor that seeped into everything, including Rixs's clothing. He could barely stand to smell himself even though he took advantage of his daily bucket of water.

That would no longer be a problem. The three fonts in the bathing chamber had given bathing a whole new meaning, but the two stunning females that arrived to help him bathe had been a dream come true!

Rixs stared blankly through the balcony doors. It had been a couple of days since he had seen the Empress Heir. He was kept occupied to the point of exhaustion. Indoctrination to his role as Imperial Shield was a priority. Part of it required tutoring in the art of patience and how to diffuse the First Daughter's temper.

A quiet knock on his door signaled that it was time for the evening meal.

Chadgerwin was attacking the enormous table burdened with food when Rixs arrived. "Ah, there you are!" the Counselor hailed. "Come get some food."

They loaded their platters then sat at the long table and ate. They ate and talked. Rixs asked the burning questions he had held back.

"May I ask a question?" Rixs asked. Chadgerwin stroked his goatee in contemplation. After a nod was given, Rixs continued,

"What happened to Lady Syersi's parents?"

There was a long, uncomfortable pause. "The Empress Saudria was killed by a Talent," Chadgerwin finally said. "Syersi was nearly fourteen springs when it happened." Chadgerwin stared off into the distance – somewhere far beyond the stone walls of the dining hall.

"She was beautiful, you know. Saudria." He placed his elbows on the table and clasped his hands in front of him. "She was the most beautiful woman I had ever laid eyes on."

Rixs remembered thinking the same about Syersi.

"Lothorius was very possessive and protective over Lady Saudria. He had been a mere twenty winters when he took Lady Saudria to wife. Six pregnancies were lost, and eighteen seasons cycles had passed before Syersi came along. When she did, Lothorius was the same with her … protective.

"When Saudria died, it literally broke his heart. He withdrew from life. Stayed in his bedchamber." Chadgerwin shrugged in resignation. "Then one day he left. Abandoned his throne. The Intimus took charge of Gnomera and raising Syersi.

"She has endured great heartache over her parents, but she will overcome," Chadgerwin said, his head nodding. "She must – for she is Gnomera's future. Rangus, Mazzlin, Hobb, and including me – we are the Intimus. We will see that Syersi fulfills her destiny."

Rixs chewed his mouthful mulling over what he had just heard. "After waiting so long for a child and with no others, it is no wonder that Syersi is spoiled rotten to the core." Realizing what he had said, he turned a deep scarlet. "Forgive me."

The Counselor suppressed a smile.

"What is her destiny?" Rixs's eyes were piercing.

Chadgerwin pressed his lips together. After some hesitation he spoke carefully. "To become Empress. And to find a companion to share her life with. Someone she can love and will love her back."

Leaning back in his chair, Rixs's emerald eyes danced. "Love," he made a mock cringe.

The twitch in Chadgerwin's cheek gave away his thoughts. "You have obviously never been in love."

A tuft of hair hung in Rixs's eye and he gave his head a jerk to see more clearly then changed the subject. "Why would you trust a stranger with such a responsibility?" he asked.

The change in subject had Chadgerwin blinking, but he answered. "I agree. It is strange that we have allowed a perceived stranger the honor of Shield, but you forget ..." He leaned over and tapped Rixs twice on his forehead with a long finger. "I know everything about you. Your secrets. Your weaknesses. I know I can trust you. And let us not overlook your Talent. It is quite ... unique."

Rixs shoved another handful of food into his mouth.

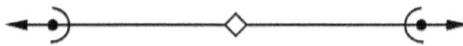

Syersi and Rixs walked in silence through the great house after the evening meal. It was an opportunity to talk about their new relationship – Empress Heir and Imperial Shield, but neither could find the words to start.

Syersi peered at him through her lashes and withheld the desire to touch his arms. He was not bulky like the Commandant, but he appeared feral and rugged, maybe even stronger than Orris.

Too distracted by taking peeks at Rixs and not watching where she was walking, Syersi bumped into a servant girl exchanging wilted flowers for fresh ones at the base of the stairs. The vase jerked then wobbled precariously on its pedestal. Trying to save it, the girl's fingers grasped for it but gave it the final push that toppled it over. The vase crashed to the floor breaking into a hundred pieces and scattering colorful blossoms everywhere.

"You, silly girl! Look at the mess you made!" Syersi snapped as her hands found her hips.

The girl stood rigid with head bowed and squeaked out, "I am sorry, Lady. I should not have stood in your way!"

"Next time you must be more careful!" she bit sharply. "Now, clean this up!"

The food in Rixs's stomach curdled as he watched the cold and unfair treatment of the servant. Dropping to his knees, he threw a glare at the Empress Heir and began helping the girl collect flowers and pieces of broken pottery off the floor.

Flower by flower, piece by broken piece, he helped the cowering servant while Syersi stood over them, her pink lips pressed flat, and her blue eyes scrutinizing.

Flowers gathered, and the broken vase collected, the Shield rose from the floor and extended his hand. The girl looked at it nervously then stole a glance at the Empress Heir, seeking permission. Rixs leaned forward to block the girl's view of Syersi. His expectation obvious. He wiggled his fingers.

Hesitantly, she lifted her trembling fingers which he took in a gentle grasp. After helping her off the floor, he picked up the basket and handed it to her. Her pink-rimmed eyes from tears held at bay, spoke a hundred thanks to him. She curtsied.

"Thank you, Master," she whispered before disappearing down the corridor.

Syersi stood in bewildered silence, perplexed by his actions, and sure that he had somehow insulted her. She blinked up at him. He had stooped low to help a servant. Botty's words rang in her ears. *He be a good soul – helpful and kind, that one.*

After brushing off his knees, Rixs straightened to his full height, towering over her. He responded to her dumbfounded stare with his own disappointed one.

"Why did you do that?" she asked.

Because it was your fault, not hers. Because I was disgusted that you blamed an innocent girl. He wanted to say those things but thought better of it.

"Because, Pixee, it was the kind thing to do."

"But it was her fault." Her eyelashes fluttered.

Annoyance stretched the lines of his mouth. "It didn't matter who bore the blame," he said. "Helping someone is never wrong."

She blinked. Then blinked again. Chadgerwin was kind, but he had never gotten on his knees to help someone. Nor had Mazzlin, who was the embodiment of kindness. Bored with the subject, Syersi shrugged then asked, "Did you ... call me something?" She wrinkled her nose at him.

The annoyance in his expression was replaced by a hint of guilt. "It's possible."

Her arms flew up in the air. "It is either yes, you did, or no, you did not. Now tell me!"

Clearing his throat, he said in a voice so low she barely heard it. "I might have called you, Pixee."

"Pixee?" she repeated. It was not a good sign if he had a name for her. "What an ugly name! Why would you call me that?"

Placing his hands behind his back Rixs nodded his head forward indicating they should continue their walk. "I have my reasons," he answered, sweeping a sideways glance at her, with a ghost of a smile.

"You refuse to tell me?"

"For now." He dared to grin.

She scrunched her face at him, mostly to hide her grin. "I could force you."

His emerald eyes shimmered. "You could try," he teased, repeating the same words he had when she threatened to take his blades. "And we both know where that would lead."

"With you in lockup," she squinted at him.

His response was quick. "And you apologizing for losing your temper ... again." Rixs held his breath, waiting for her reaction to his words.

Syersi abruptly stopped and turned to face him. After a pause she blew out a giggle, nudging him with her shoulder. She slipped her arm into his and pulled him along.

Rixs exhaled. For now, it seemed he was with whimsical Syersi.

FOURTEEN

Isslewood was a fantasy. Vibrant and peculiar combinations of color stretched along the base of the Gneiss Curtain. Grasses of lavender blanketed the ground. Trees covered in orange bark were heavily laden with blue leaves or pink leaves, or bright red leaves, depending on the tree. Green and black wildflowers grew along the ground in abundance.

It was the Gneiss Curtain wonder. No one knew why the flora grew in such shocking colors close to the mountain's base then gradually changed to normal hues the further away they grew. It was believed the poisonous substance found in the rock had something to do with it, but whatever the cause, it filled Rixs with awe. He had never seen anything like it.

He breathed in through his nose and let out a contented sigh. He was living his adventure.

When they had arrived at the stables, Syersi abruptly stopped and Rixs nearly ran into her. "Forgive me for throwing you in lockup," she blurted, eyelids fluttering. "I … I know I need to work on my temper."

He had heard that the First Daughter never gave out apologies. His cheek twitched a hint of a smile.

"An apology from Lady Syersi! I must be very special to receive something so rare!" he teased with a quick wink.

Syersi smiled. She would swallow her pride a thousand times to see that wink again. "Well, that was your one and only. I have satisfied my quota for this lifetime," she teased in return, then sashayed into the stable.

The smell of hay and horse slapped Rixs in the face as he followed behind Syersi and watched her with his mouth half open. She was skipping! He glanced around the stable thinking he might find the *real* Syersi.

Her body halted in front of a large stall where a head, as white as snow, accentuated in a long silver mane, hung over the edge. The white head with midnight eyes bobbed up and down in greeting. A light pink muzzle nudged at Syersi's shoulder, and thick lips nibbled at her hair.

"That is certainly a pretty white horse," Rixs breathed, recognizing the animal Syersi rode nearly every day.

"Shame on you!" Syersi scolded. "*That* is a, *she*, and *she* is not a white horse! She is Juju!" Syersi kissed Juju's muzzle. "Pay him no attention," she cooed to the horse. "He is only new at being an Imperial Shield! He still has a bumbling tongue!" She patted Juju's neck. "Did you miss me, girl?"

The horse nudged Syersi's side impatiently while Rixs silently looked on with curious eyes. The Lady reached into the folds of her elegant gown and pulled out a fat carrot which the mare eagerly plucked from her extended palm. After giving Juju a final pat on her head, Syersi strolled on, leaving Rixs to linger by the horse and ponder the side of Syersi he had never seen before.

Emerging from the stables to the fading light of day, the two wandered toward the low-hanging sun with silence between them. The ground crunched quietly under their feet until Rixs built his nerve to speak.

"I have a question to ask," he posed gently. Sandy hair slipped over his brows, barely hanging in his eyes.

Syersi curled her fingers to keep them to herself. "Will your question get you thrown into lockup?" When he shrugged, a laugh escaped her. "Very well, ask your question."

He straightened his shoulders as he kept a slow pace with her, and reflexively tossed his head to the side, clearing away the rogue strands of hair. "Are you nervous to become Empress?"

Her brows nearly jumped into her hairline. "I admit that was not the question I expected, but not at all. I have the Intimus, you know," she answered. "There is Chadgerwin, the mountain of wisdom who will always be there to guide me. Then, I have a *Rangus*," she laughed, exposing perfect white teeth. Her eyes danced as she looked at Rixs. "Try to ignore that one and see where it gets you! He is better than an entire army. Mazzlin keeps me safe with her ever-seeing eyes. In fact," she tapped her chin as if in thought. "It is very annoying! She is too good at keeping me out of trouble!" Her smile brightened her face. "And finally, Hobb is a lifesaver, in the very real sense. Without him …"

"I'd be dead!" Rixs suddenly interrupted. "Without him, I would not be here."

Syersi's face softened. He had been so close to death when she found him in the river near Trifalls. Her eyes swept him over appraisingly.

"And you," Rixs added. "I owe my life to you, as well." His eyes stuck to the ground. "I never thanked you. Had you not found me, Hobb could not have healed me. I would be dead at the river's edge, and no one would have known — my body would have been lost." He looked into her eyes. "So, thank you, Pixee. I owe you my life."

A large lump blocked her ability to swallow. *And I thank The Powers that guided me to you.* The words remained unsaid, tucked in her heart as they continued their walk.

"And now you torment me at every opportunity!" She nudged him softly with her shoulder, making him stumble slightly.

When the grass and trees had all returned to their normal color, and they arrived back at the courtyard maze, Syersi's curiosity got the best of her. "My turn to ask *you* a question." Her voice was cheerful though it quivered a little.

Movement compelled Rixs to use Talent to scan the area. He made a mental note of each male form positioned throughout the hedges and ivy walls.

Returning his attention to Syersi, he said, "First, I have one more question, my Lady!"

"No!" was the firm reply.

"Please, indulge a poor ignorant Shield," Rixs pleaded while waggling his brows.

She huffed, hiding her smirk. "Very well. Ask," she said with a twirl of her hand.

His gaze turned serious. "I was told you constantly scheme to escape Isslewood. Why is that?"

She reached for a jewel that had been braided into her long black hair and blinked into the distance as though she could see Tower Wall hidden behind the vines and groomed hedges that lined the courtyard's garden maze. The wall was a symbol – Syersi was nothing more than a prisoner.

"That is a personal question," she said.

Rixs tossed his head, hair flopping to the opposite side of his face. "Perhaps, but I am now responsible for your safety," he replied. "So, it is important to me."

In the waning light, her complexion glowed. "I doubt you would understand."

His fingers twitched. "Try me," he said as he curled his fingers to keep from touching her.

A heavy sigh left her lips. "You come from beyond the wall," Syersi lifted her head and nodded in the direction of Tower Wall and the lands beyond it. "Isslewood is a beautiful place," she confessed. "But I am not permitted outside of these walls ... have not experienced anything outside these walls ... until the day I found you. That was my first time to get by the gates and sentries. Do you know what it is like to feel trapped?"

Trapped. Rixs placed his hands behind his back. He understood *trapped*. Cliessa's innocent face and the betrothal she represented caused him guilt every day.

Pax Valley life was planned out for everyone by the township council. They had selected Cliessa for him. They were still children when they were betrothed, robbed of their choices. Though Cliessa liked the choice made for her, Rixs had fled when the time came to marry her.

The prolonged silence nudged Syersi to fill the void. "It is my turn to ask a question." Brilliant blue eyes rested on him. "What brought you to Gnomera?"

An itch on his chin suddenly needed a scratch while he contemplated his answer. "The very thing you scorn ... being trapped." As he spoke, a tentative grin poorly hid his true feelings. "My *prison* was a life in which my choices had been taken away. The township council in Pax Valley dictated everything for me, including which woman I would marry. I was only thirteen winters when the choice of my bride was made. So, before I took her as a wife, I thought I should first have a great adventure."

He cast a big grin her way and she blinked a few times to absorb his personal story. He continued.

"A poor excuse for abandoning a girl who expected to marry, but I kissed my mother good-bye, gave my brother one last wrestle, and set off without a single clue where I would go, or how long I would be gone. All I knew was I wanted a portion of my life to be on my own terms."

Syersi looked down at the ground while he spoke. It had never occurred to her that there was more than one way to be held captive. There were no walls in his story, yet he had not been free. Then something occurred to her. The Intimus had practically made him stay.

She murmured, "So they selected a wife for you? Do you love her?" When he shook his head, Syersi frowned and her eyes softened. "Even I am able to marry for love. It has been hammered into my skull for as long as I can remember. Mazzy always reminds me, *Syersi, you must find love and fall in love.* You would think that is my only calling in life." She shrugged her shoulders then let them drop like two heavy rocks. "What if they betrothed you to someone disgusting? What if the two of you despise each other? What if you want or love someone else?"

"Whoa, Pixee, that is ten questions!" Rixs laughed.

She gave him a playful shove. "It is not ten questions!"

"Almost ten," he insisted, leaning a shoulder against the ivy-covered stone lattice with arms crossed over his chest, which was always shirtless under his famous vest. His tone became serious. "You have no say. You must marry the council's selection."

"That is a crime!" she cried.

Both sets of eyes dropped to his arm where Syersi's fingers had gripped Rixs's arm. His muscles flexed beneath her touch and her gaze slowly drifted upward to meet his luminous green eyes.

Syersi exhaled and swallowed, her body easing forward. Heart racing, her chest rose and fell to the rhythm of her breaths. She held still, waiting for him to respond to her invitation.

Without warning, Rixs pulled back and shoved his hand through an opening in the stone lattice. Grabbing a handful of thick fabric, he gave a swift and forceful yank. There was a hard thud as a body slammed into the stone structure with a muffled cry. A face was smashed against the lattice, just visible through the vines next to them.

Rixs cursed under his breath. He had been too caught up in Syersi to notice the figure that had snuck up on the opposite side of the ivy wall.

Not good, Rixs! How will you protect the Empress Heir if you are too busy drooling over her?

"Doughty!" Syersi shrieked, at the member of her detail. "Why are you sneaking up on us?"

With nose flattened against the stone lattice and ivy poking into his mouth, the soldier mumbled through smashed lips, "Lady Syersi." Her name was barely recognizable. "The Commandant has …"

"Has no authority here," she hissed, cutting him off.

Keeping as still as possible, smeared blood tainted Doughty's face. His eyes shifted to Rixs then back to the Empress Heir. "He wants to prove the new Shield is incompetent."

At the words, Rixs clenched his teeth and pulled the guard harder against the lattice. Doughty moaned louder.

"Hmmm," an amused Syersi hummed. "This incompetent Shield was apparently perceptive enough to know you had snuck up on us, clever enough to take *you* by surprise, and skilled enough to incapacitate you." She tapped her lip with a slender nail. "On the other hand, you, a competent Lothorian Guard, wound up with your face smashed flat and bleeding." Syersi reached through the lattice and poked him on the forehead.

While Syersi enjoyed Doughty's discomfort, Rixs caught the movement of two shadowed forms displacing air as they weaved silently through the hedged walls of the garden maze, approaching them.

More guards to prove my incompetence.

"Sorry about this," Rixs apologized just before he shoved Doughty away from the lattice with the fistful of cloak clutched tightly in his grasp, then violently yanked him into the wall. The man's head bashed against the stone.

Syersi startled with eyes as big as melons when Doughty's head thudded against the lattice then disappeared on the opposite side of the ivy after Rixs released his grip. The sound of his body crumpling to the ground quickly followed.

Climbing the lattice wall like a squirrel, Rixs ordered, "Stay here!" right before propelling himself over the top and dropping to the other side.

He had abandoned her. Syersi looked around, blinking, wondering why he had scrambled away so quickly. Then she heard it – the sound of approaching footsteps. Two guards rounded the corner and stopped just short of running into her. They hastily scanned the area, their expressions revealing their shock to find her alone.

Using both hands to smooth her hair with chin raised high, Syersi addressed them as only she could. "I presume you have a good reason to ogle at me!"

They quickly dropped to one knee. As they rose, one spoke. "Lady, we thought the Shield was with you."

"He was." She sounded annoyed while she held out her hand to inspect her nails. "He ran off without telling me where he was going. I have a mind to throw him in lockup."

The guards looked at each other. Syersi's eyes flicked behind them and they slowly turned around.

"Hello. I take it you want to expose my incompetence." Rixs was leaning with one shoulder propped casually against the lattice wall, his arms crossed over his open vest, and a toothy grin was plastered to his face.

Neither guard could have known Rixs had already identified every shape on their bodies that resembled the form of a weapon hidden from view. Both wore swords, as all guards did, but in addition, one hid a karambit at his back, and the other concealed a dagger strapped to his ankle.

Suddenly, both charged, but before either could reach him, Rixs already knew what their movements would be by the way the open voids around their bodies shifted. It was easy to tuck and roll between them, giving ample opportunity to snatch the dagger at the ankle of the one guard, and as he rose behind them, he slid his hand up the back of the other and disarmed him of his karambit.

Syersi blinked as her eyes flitted with his movements and a smile grew too big for her face. He was fascinating to watch.

The guards found their own weapons pointed at them. Their stunned faces were enough to make the Empress Heir laugh. Rixs had skill – special skill. It was as though he had read their minds and knew how they would attack before they moved a single muscle.

The guards stood motionless and bewildered. The stranger had gained the upper hand against both of them.

Syersi squealed with joy and clapped her hands. "Oh, how I wish Orris were here to see this!"

FIFTEEN

Rixs had done the impossible. He had persuaded the Governing Council to let Syersi leave Isslewood.

Each spring season, Gnomera held its Spring Governing Forum. Leaders from the territories descended upon Isslewood to debate the issues facing the land realm. After the days of political debates were concluded, the viceroys and commanders stuck around Isslewood to enjoy the festivities of the Spring Celebration, a gala in honor of Lady Syersi's birth season. This seasons cycle, the celebration was to be particularly jubilant since Gnomera would coronate a new Empress.

Orris had gone out of his way to undermine Rixs in front of the Governing Council, reminding the Gnomeran leaders that the man the First Counselor proposed as Imperial Shield was little more than a woodsman with a new title he had won in a bet. It was Chadgerwin that helped the Council to see past Rixs's formal shortcomings and focus on the benefit of having someone like him protect the Empress Heir. Then the Counselor asked the new Shield for a demonstration of his skills.

All eyes followed the young Talent as he stood from his seat and grabbed an apple from the bowl in the center of the table. Rubbing the apple gently in his hands, he faced the large wood door. This demonstration would need to be extraordinary to win the confidence and approval of the Governing Council.

Rixs tossed the apple high into the air and, in a blur, threw a short blade, slicing it through the center. Reaching the apex of his toss, the apple halves slowed and reversed direction, descending toward the floor. Before they had fallen midway, the young Talent pulled two more short blades, one with each hand. A *zing* buzzed the air, followed by two, nearly simultaneous hard *thuds*. A collective gasp filled the chamber. The two sleek black blades had speared both apple halves into the wooden door.

The demonstration had sealed Rixs's confirmation as Imperial Shield.

A few days later, Chadgerwin exclaimed as he watched the group leave Isslewood, "It's a wonder Rixs hasn't fallen off his horse!"

Standing next to the Counselor, Orris muttered, "Behold your Imperial Shield! He is going to embarrass the empire!"

Keedra and Moniere sat on their horses behind Syersi, giggling at the spectacle of Rixs riding a horse. Violently, he bounced up and down while the horse trotted toward the Tower Wall gate. The quick riding lesson Rixs had been given prior to their excursion, had obviously not produced the results of a competent rider.

After clearing the gate, Rixs grinned sheepishly at Syersi and her two lady companions, knowing he was humiliating the magnificent horse he rode. "I guess I need more riding lessons. The poor horse will never forgive me."

Syersi held in a laugh but failed to resist the temptation of teasing him. "I don't know how I can stand to have a Shield who cannot sit a trot properly." She looked at him from the corner of her eyes and her lips curved into a half smile.

He grinned with apology. "I will try not to embarrass you too much, Lady."

Keedra and Moniere giggled as they watched his hair flap wildly with every bounce of his body. "His insides will be shaken to pieces by the time we reach the city!" Keedra snickered.

By the time they had reached Ormolu and the farmers' market, Rixs was thoroughly rattled. Walking to Ormolu would have been preferred to riding a horse had the distance not been so far.

The activity around Syersi had her head turning in every

direction and her eyes darting this way and that. Throngs of people walked from stand to stand, and cart to cart. Children ran the streets, dodging through and around adult legs, making a nuisance of themselves. The competing cries of vendors reverberated against the buildings as each peddler vied for fickle customers to purchase their goods. Merchandise of every kind dangled in front of her, all of it begging to be picked up, admired, and purchased.

Rixs, who had seemed to be the timid Shield while they traveled, had instantly become the master of manipulation. He skillfully managed and controlled everyone and everything that came within Syersi's proximity.

All activity came to a standstill when the Lady entered the market. The entourage of soldiers was proof enough that someone important was in town. Gasps and whispers sounded at every display. Glistening eyes stared at Syersi – hundreds of them. Something that had never been done before had finally happened – the First Daughter of Gnomera had left the boundaries of Isslewood.

Nervousness had Syersi staring back at the crowd. She stared at their tired and weary faces. At their worn clothes. At their weathered hands. Their appearance told the stories of their hard lives. Lives that she had been indifferent toward. Biting her lower lip, she blinked repeatedly.

Rixs leaned in. "Isn't it customary for you to say something? Address your people?"

"What should I say?"

"And how should I know? You are the First Daughter!" his annoyed voice clipped back.

Syersi returned, "In case you have forgotten, Shield, this is my first time any place other than Isslewood!"

He clicked his tongue and huffed, "Fine!" Then he turned to the crowd and improvised. "Kneel before your Empress Heir!"

A moment of hesitation passed. Rixs was nothing more than a stranger to them, but then one by one, the people fell to their knees.

Syersi's eyes were wide. "You sounded very harsh," she chastised.

"At least I did something," he growled.

The Guardian stepped into their bickering. "This is hardly the time to argue. Syersi, it is your turn," she urged quietly.

"My turn for what?"

"Acknowledge them then let them rise and carry on. Tell them to enjoy their day."

The people fidgeted on their knees. Syersi's throat felt dry. No words would come.

A distinct cough from Rixs had her scowling at him. "Stop pushing me!" she hissed. Clearing her throat, a musical voice projected her words for all to hear.

"I thank you for the warm welcome!" She paused, her lashes batting rapidly as she grasped at what to say. "Rise and enjoy your festivities. May The Powers bless you this day!"

Her smug glance at Rixs told him she was pleased with her words. A tick of his head replied, *it would do.*

The people rose to their feet, and all hesitation of her presence melted away. Bodies swarmed her without warning – hands reaching. Voices called her name. The space around her had quickly become too cramped and suffocating.

Rixs immediately signaled the guards who instantly became a human wall around the Empress Heir, protecting her from the throng of faces pressing in. While Rixs pulled Syersi close to his side, her detail forcefully pushed back the crowd of people.

After order had been reestablished, Rixs guided Syersi from display to display, unaware that he held her hand in his. It was only when a pair of sapphire eyes blinked up at him curiously, that he looked down and saw their joined hands. A rosy blush touched Syersi's cheeks and his own flamed hot when he realized his thumb had been circling over the skin on the back of her fingers. Her skin was soft.

"Forgive me," he apologized. Releasing his hold only to place it at the small of her back. That choice was not helpful either. The warmth from her body seeped into his hand and into his blood. Guilt, in the form of Cliessa's face, twisted his expression into a frown. His hand dropped.

Syersi frowned too. The warm sparks tingling in her chest fizzled away with the disappearance of his touch. The awkwardness between them drove her to say something.

"I am glad to be rescued from those dirty, disgusting hands reaching for me!" When she peered into Rixs's handsome face and saw his expression, she wished she could take back her words.

He shook his head. "Pixee, of all the things … you noticed their dirty, disgusting hands?" He stopped walking and leaned in so that his face was close to hers. "Did you notice how their hands bleed and crack in your service? Did you notice how they reach for you in excitement at having the Empress Heir in their midst?" His voice was calm, but his eyes sparked like hot coals.

"Did you bother to look into their faces, Pixee? If so, you might have noticed their sincere joy in seeing you! I saw it! They were genuinely happy and honored to have you at *their* farmers' market!"

There was no need for Rixs to look behind them. "Even now they follow you! If you told any one of them to drop to the ground … to give you the clothes off their back … I wager they would do it simply because you are their Empress Heir, and they want to please you. But no! No, *you*, Lady, only noticed their dirty, disgusting hands!"

All the air left her lungs, his words punching to the center of her gut. Then fury took her over. "You always judge me, Stranger! You always choose to see the worst in me!"

He quipped back without pause. "You are wrong, *again*! I look for the best in you, Pixee, and I feel disappointed when you show me anything less!" He stepped into her space, their noses nearly touching.

"I think, when you can get over yourself, and begin to show people the best you have to give, in here," he tapped her chest with a finger, "then, and only then, will you begin to see the best in others!"

Her bottom lip quivered. His words had cut deeply. Only her parents or the Intimus had ever dared to speak to her in such a manner. Scarlet flooded her vision, and her shaking hand found his cheek. *Whack!*

The act of hitting him had not given any relief, especially since she had the distinct impression that Rixs had allowed her to slap him. She stomped off, not bothering to look over her shoulder to see if he followed.

The eager crowd gave Syersi wide berth as she stormed through the central square, weaving around carts, wagons, and displays. After the initial shock at her presence, the city's pulse had quickened once again. Vendors shouted for attention, customers bartered, and onlookers hurried here and there. While gliding from one display to another, Syersi dragged one of her handsome blonde guards behind her.

Content to stay his distance, Rixs felt the lingering sting on his cheek. It was a good solid slap, but it would never be effective if she had to protect herself. He would need to teach her to ball her fists.

He stared at her openly from across the street and could see Syersi watching him from her periphery, pretending he was beyond her notice. She pulled the guard, Athan, close to her side, wrapping an arm around his. The guard stared at her through his blonde wavy locks and smiled.

There were penalties for touching the Empress Heir, but there would be no repercussions for Athan. She had sought his arm, and guards never refused Syersi – even if they wanted.

She spied on Rixs from across the square. His hair hung into his eyes, and as though he read her mind, he jerked his head to the side, effectively clearing away the renegade strands. He was blatantly watching her – an emerald gaze followed her every movement as he propped himself against one of the displays with his arms folded across his chest.

Never letting the First Daughter out of her sight, Mazzlin wandered from booth to booth, every now and again seeing the market through Syersi's eyes. Her Talent made it easy to surmise where Syersi's thoughts rested. Each time the Seer took a quick peek, the image of Rixs filled her view. It became obvious that her charge was preoccupied with the new Shield. Syersi might have been flouting the droolworthy Athan at her side, but her eyes were fixated elsewhere.

The Empress Heir slowly migrated through the displays. Voices called to her, bombarding her ears, coaxing her to try their goods. Under the Shield's explicit orders, Syersi's detail never allowed her to touch or eat anything until they had touched or tasted before her. So, it was the gorgeous Athan who chewed on a piece of mouth-watering sweetbread while Syersi had a mind to kiss him just to make Rixs angry. She would have done it had she thought Rixs would care.

"Hmmm. This is good! I think you will like this, Lady Syersi," Athan said, holding bread to Syersi's lips.

"You are not here to think, Athan. Just look good for me, and feed me," she said just before opening her mouth. Acknowledging her with a nod, he gently pushed the bite in. With closed eyes, she chewed slowly and licked her lips.

The spectacle was enough to dislodge Rixs from the wall, but before he could walk away, a voice stopped him. "Can I interest you in a lovely scarf, sire? Perhaps one for your sweetheart?" a bubbly female spoke.

Yanked from her own amusement, Syersi watched a young female with long blonde locks, flip her hair and smile shyly up at *her* Shield. And he had the audacity to smile back! Not to be out-done, Syersi smiled at Athan, though it was as fake as the jewels pawned in her direction.

They carried on as if they had known each other all their lives and she could do nothing except watch with clenched teeth. The girl was giggling! Syersi strained her ears and worked her way closer to the cart.

Always the gentleman, Rixs tried to look interested in the items the girl held up. When she asked if he was attached, he gifted her with a charming laugh, but did not answer. She lifted a yellow scarf from her display and draped it over his shoulder with a smile, teasing that it complimented his golden complexion.

Syersi snorted. *Strumpet!* The thought of her fingers curling around the girl's blonde locks flirted with her thoughts. Her hair was long enough to grab easily and could be completely bald in no time. As if in a trance, Syersi had shuffled her way close to the cart before she had realized it.

An arm discretely shoved the rack of scarves over. A waterfall of silky colors floated downward as the wooden rack toppled over and hit the dirt with a loud crash. Scarves blanketed the ground, and the girl frantically fell to her knees to gather the merchandise.

Syersi feigned surprise. "Oh! Did I do that?" she exclaimed. "Your display must not be stable if someone as slight as me can topple it with a little bump!"

Rixs hurled a dark glare at the Empress Heir while she batted her lashes at him innocently and bit her lip. He stooped over to pick up the rack and ordered *blonde boy* to help him reattach it to the cart.

Several displays away, a merchant handed Hobb a long, sleek dagger. Eyes slid along the sculptured bone handle and he paused to admire the intricate carved pattern. It inspired the Physician. The sound of his name caused him to wince and shudder.

"Hobb, there you are!" Syersi's voice sang into his ears. "Where have you been hiding?"

"If you had bothered to look, you would have seen that I have been in plain view, Lady Syersi," he replied. A glance behind her revealed Rixs reassembling one of the displays. "And I see *you* have been getting into mischief."

The merchant gasped when he realized the Empress Heir perched near his stand. His low bow went unnoticed as Syersi glanced over her shoulder, following Hobb's gaze.

"It was an accident," she shrugged, ignoring his skeptical expression. "And what might you be doing?" Her attention was riveted on the variety of knives on display.

Hobb rolled his eyes as he switched the dagger from hand to hand testing its weight. "An accident was it? Of course. What else could it have been?"

The merchant allowed Hobb to test the dagger on a large wood plank set up for prospective buyers. He was just winding up for a throw when a huffing Mazzlin came bounding up to them.

"Mazzlin! You made me miss!" Hobb cried.

"Hush, Physician!" was all she said to him before turning a stern scowl on Syersi. She growled as fiercely as a puppy's snarl. Only the Guardian could pull off such ferociousness. "Child, what have you done?"

A jeweled knife caught Syersi's notice, giving her an excuse to ignore the Guardian. It was a very sparkly jeweled knife.

"You must make things right!" Mazzlin huffed in a low voice.

Syersi extended the knife to the merchant. "I would like to throw this one."

"Of course, my Lady," came the reply.

Mazzlin creased her forehead. "Syersi! Do not ignore me!"

With a sweet smile, Syersi gently bumped Hobb out of the way with her hip. "May I throw, Hobb?"

It was posed as a question, but Hobb knew better. "Do you even know how to throw?" Hobb replied. There was a smile in his voice. "You might hurt someone … namely me!"

Before anyone could stop her, Syersi lobbed the blade at the target. The knife landed far wide of the wood plank, rolling in the dirt. The merchant cried out in horror and hurried to scoop up the knife, gently wiping away the dirt.

Syersi held out her hand and wiggled her fingers impatiently. Words were unnecessary. He shuddered as he reluctantly extended the work of art toward her outstretched fingers.

"Lady Syersi!" Mazzlin demanded.

Hobb piped up, "You need to throw with more force than that if you want to hit the target. Put your body into it!"

It had not been so long ago when Syersi had nearly stabbed Rixs in the leg, angry that he had refused to give up one of his blades to her. Before she had lost her temper and tried to stick him with his own blade, he had given her a lesson in throwing. Remembering what he had said, she mustered all the strength she had, swinging her arm back as far as it would go to gain as much momentum as possible.

It was at that precise point that the knife flew out of her hand, sailing behind her instead of forward. Mortified, Syersi whirled around with her hands clamped over her mouth.

Already in a foul mood from having to mend the damages from the Empress Heir's little stunt, Rixs was striding in her direction with a few chosen words hanging off the tip of his tongue when he felt it. The space shifted. His eyes could not see it, but he captured the shape looping clumsily in the air nonetheless, and there was no need to look up to know exactly what it was, but he did anyway.

There it was – a knife. Rixs instantly suspected that Syersi was somehow involved, and though the knife was headed in his direction, the worse part – there were innocent bystanders that could be hurt!

Strikes! She wants to kill me! How do I get out of this one without giving myself away or anyone getting hurt?

Determining where the knife would land was easy enough. Evading it would be simple – all it would take was one step to the side, but there were too many people. If he stepped away someone else could walk into the knife's path. Catching the knife was the obvious choice, but it could give away his ability.

Out of time, Rixs walked directly into the weapon's path. There was no appeal in getting stabbed, so only one choice remained. He jumped high, snatching the tumbling knife out of the air by its handle. He then landed lightly on his feet, and without missing a step, continued forward with the deadly weapon hanging loosely in his grip.

A self-assured swagger that reeked of rage, stopped just short of the Empress Heir. "Are you trying to kill me?" Rixs growled, his voice low so no one else could hear. He stood so close he could feel his own breath rebound off Syersi's cheeks.

Burning under the fire of his temper, Syersi had the good sense to look contrite as she stepped back to put some distance between them. "I … I am very sorry. It was an accident," her low tone matched his.

He moved forward, closing the distance again. "I've heard that before, Pixee. Your apologies fall on deaf ears."

Hurt welled in her eyes, but after a few blinks she was fine, and a curious face peered up at him. "How did you do that?" she asked. "You caught that knife while it was tumbling in the air! You could have been killed!"

"Well, thank The Powers! They must like me, since apparently, you have it in for me!" His voice was as rough as gravel. Then more gently he said, "You could have hurt someone … A child. The market is full of the little buggers!"

Mazzlin quietly nudged Hobb. "Did you see that?"

"I did," whispered Hobb. "I knew he was Talented, but this …"
He walked over to Rixs and patted him on the back. "You have my
vote, Shield."

A disturbance a short distance from where they stood caught
their attention. Two guards were throwing punches at two men while
more guards ran to the scene.

Repeated threats from a deep thunderous voice caused Rixs to
pause and stare. The tall, thick man stood out with his dark skin and
wild hair. Four guards tried to restrain the figure but struggled against
his powerful punches, and even though they snuck in a few of their
own, there was little effect on the giant.

Rixs froze, forgetting about the wayward knife that still hung in
his hand. Two blinks later, he was off and running.

"Keep the Lady here!" he ordered over his shoulder.

"My dagger!" the old peddler cried. Rixs dropped the weapon
and ran.

Curses were hurled recklessly for all to hear, coaxing the local
citizens to gawk at the escalating scene. Two soldiers were hurled
through the air, their cloaks flapping as they fell to the ground.
Energy riveted every vein under Rixs's skin.

I can barely trust my eyes!

Rixs thrust himself into the melee and a fist immediately
connected with his jaw, snapping his head to the side. It was as
though a large clay pot had been smashed into his face. He shook his
head, surprised that his Talent had failed to warn him.

He shoved a fist into a wide muscular jaw, then on the follow-
through, slung his elbow around and down onto a familiar fuzzy
head. Dark threatening eyes peered at him while a massive hand
fisted. Rixs prepared to avoid another punishing hit – and waited.
The fist had frozen in midair, and the man's eyes snapped wide.

"Kid! By The Powers, what ya be doing here?" Rhages cried.

SIXTEEN

Frizzy and rebellious black hair flopped from one side of Rhages's face to the other as he stood to his full height. He dwarfed the tallest guard by at least a full head. A wide grin covered Rixs's face as he took in the frame of the friend he had been separated from since the day he jumped off the cliff at Trifalls more than a moon ago and nearly died. Much had happened since then.

Rixs yelled for his men to stand down.

Shoving several guards off him, Rhages exclaimed, "Kid! We thought ya be dead!"

Rixs laughed. "Not yet!" He grasped his friend's hand in a hardy shake.

Rhages narrowed his eyes at their joined hands. "I be having none of that!" he growled, wrapping a big arm around his young friend's neck, and mussing his hair.

Remnant scuffling caught their attention toward a head of tangled red locks popping out from under the armpit of a large body. A soldier had the short man in a headlock. Rixs recognized the bright red hair that could only mean one thing – trouble.

"Let me go!" Fogle pushed his way out of the guard's hold. He stumbled back and straightened his shirt while glaring at the man who was twice his size. "Lucky for you I don't beat you to a pulp!" Fogle puffed out his chest.

None were fooled. Fogle was all talk.

"Ya hot-tempered fool!" Rhages huffed. "That guard will have ya for a midday meal!"

The short man squinted and frowned at Rhages, then his eyes grew big as platters. "Well, well," he said slowly, sweeping an assessing gaze over Rixs. "Is that Rixsander of Pax Valley?" His eyes caught on a ring circling Rixs's right index finger. "Donning jewels like a woman, I see! Where'd ya get *that*? It looks valuable!"

Rixs glanced down at his hand and curled his fingers. The thick gold band trumpeted its own worth. A swirl of engraved lines rolled in circular patterns converging to the center of the ring where a single blue stone sparkled – the *Seal of Syersi*. It was the pattern the Empress Heir wore in her crown. Chadgerwin had forced Rixs to take the ring as a symbol of his title and authority, but Fogle or Rhages did not need to know that.

"I found it, so it's now mine."

The guard placed a hand on Fogle's face and pushed him back then walked away. Fogle flexed his arms and punched the air at the guard's retreating back. Rixs shook his head and suppressed a smile while Rhages rolled his eyes.

"Stop it, ya twerp! Provoke that soldier and he be kickin yer tail! He ain't gonna be afraid of the likes of you!"

Fogle snorted. "Oh, yeah? He left in a hurry, so I'd say he didn't want to mess with me!"

Rixs had to speak up. "Make me a wager, Fogle. If you do that to his face, I'll give you the coins in my pocket. That guard is trained by a Sanguinary, the scariest man I have ever seen, and the leader of the Gnomeran armies. Facing him will scare the snot out of you! So, believe me, it takes more than a redhead jabbing a few punches in the air, to intimidate these soldiers."

Snorting, then spitting a large wad on the ground, Rhages eyed Rixs. "So, Bronan be right! Gnomera's army is led by a red eye!"

The high sun compelled Rixs to wipe an arm across his forehead. "Yep. And he's every bit as fearsome as the rumors say."

Rhages ran his tongue over his teeth. "Well … Bronan says, where there be one Talent, there surely be more! Have ya seen more?"

Not inclined to answer, Rixs shook his head. In Gnomera, it was common knowledge Talent existed – Rangus was evidence of that. Even so, the topic was always avoided in public conversations, almost like it was a secret, but an open secret that everyone already knew. Rixs was unsure who else knew that Chadgerwin, Mazzlin and Hobb were also Talents, so he kept his mouth shut.

"That the Princess?" Rhages nodded his head down the street where an impatient young woman fixed a curious stare on them both. He whistled. "Trotts! She be a beauty!"

Rixs flashed a glance toward the Empress Heir and muttered, "Follow me." Then he slipped into a side alley.

Eyeing the lovely vision, Fogle sputtered. "Whoa! Is my mind playing tricks? Sorry to disappoint you, Rhages, but she ain't looking at you! Her eyes yearn for me!"

"In yer dreams, Froghead!" the giant quipped.

Nothing had changed since Rixs was separated from the crew. Fogle was still annoying, and Rhages was still ... Rhages. Cantankerous on the outside, soft on the inside.

"Enough gawking, you two," Rixs chided. "Rhages, what are you doing in Ormolu? Where's the rest of the crew?"

The man squinted as if to search for words, but it was Fogle who blurted out, "Careful to give anything away, Rhages, especially *you know what!*" If there was a secret to be kept, it would burn a hole in Fogle's tongue.

The crew had traveled to Gnomera to look for the Source. All they knew was that it was an object of power, and that someone very wealthy would reward an incredible sum to those that found it. Word had spread far and the race to find the Source was on.

Rixs's green eyes shifted from Rhages to Fogle then back to Rhages. After spending time at Isslewood, Rixs wondered ... perhaps the Intimus protected more than Syersi. It did not matter. He was Imperial Shield. Only Syersi's safety mattered.

"What should you not give away, Rhages?" Rixs asked as he flipped his hair then stared at his friend.

"Trotts, Froghead! Ya twerp!" Rhages fumed. "Let's see if we can shove three pair o' feet in that big mouth of yers! Why be satisfied with one pair when there's mine and Rixs's feet standing here with nowhere to go!"

"What?" Fogle cried.

Rhages fisted his giant hand as if he intended to pound Fogle's head into the ground and his expression confirmed he would do just that, then stomp on it for good measure.

"Rhages," Rixs began warily. "What are you and Fogle up to? And where is the rest of the crew?"

The response was stern. "We be up ta nothin' so just stop acting like we be some kind o' scoundrels!"

Teasing and yet serious Rixs reminded through a clenched smile, "You forget, my friend, I traveled with you for a season! Who was it that said I'd have to learn to *curse, spit, and fight dirty* if I hoped to travel with the crew?" He slapped his forehead with the heel of his palm. "Oh! I remember! It was you, Rhages!"

"Fine! I be a scoundrel! What's it to ya, kid?" he growled.

Rixs narrowed his eyes at him. "Because the scoundrel watched my back when I needed it. Stop avoiding the question, my friend. Why is the crew in Ormolu? Is there a connection to what we were searching for?"

Suddenly, Rhages swung his fist hard. Rixs's eyes popped wide and he would have dodged out of the way had he not already known that the fist was not headed to the space where he stood. In an instant, Fogle was sprawled on the ground – out cold.

"That's for opening yer big mouth, ya good for nothin' Froghead!"

Fogle never heard a word. Breathing hard, Rhages looked at his young friend, the internal struggle showed in his dark stormy eyes. "At least now, I can deny I told ya anythin' important!" he grumbled. For a long while there was only choking silence as he studied the young man before letting out an exasperated groan. "Ya gotta promise not to tell a soul, kid! It be my neck if they find out!"

"This is starting off bad, Rhages," Rixs warned. "I hope you're not stealing from these people!"

The man held up his hands. "I ain't be a thief, kid! Well ... most of the time! You know what the crew be looking for … that rare treasure …" Rhages scanned the alley.

Rixs knew there was no one within hearing distance. He waited patiently for something more.

"After we be separated, I made the crew go back … see if we could find ya, but there was no sign of ya nowhere."

Rixs swallowed a lump in his throat. "Thanks for going back for me. It means a lot to know you would never leave me behind."

Rhages snorted, waving it off. "If we left ya, who be doin' all the huntin'?" He grinned. "Then we met up with … uh … that man who hired Bronan ta put together a crew. He thinks that the red-eye means somethin' … wants us ta dig up stuff!"

"So, who is this man?" Rixs asked. "Has he described what he wants you to find?"

Rhages scratched a scraggly, dirt-covered beard. "Remember all them talks about Talent?" Rixs nodded, and Rhages nodded too. "Yep, we talked up Talent a lot. Now, I still ain't never seen a Talent, but others have, and now you seen one too, so I think that be good enough for me to believe in 'em. Anyways, this man has lots of hunches. Talked about somethin' that were lost during the Long Wars…" He paused and poked the unconscious Fogle in the side with his boot then said. "Hey! Bet he'd hire you too! You 'n me be a good team!"

"You evaded my question." Rixs crossed his arms over his chest.

"Trotts, kid! You know what it is. You were part of the crew for a while! It be the *Source*, but no one seems to know what it looks like. The interesting part is … he thinks the Source be somehow connected with Talent. So, where we find Talent, we could find a giveaway."

Rixs scratched his head. The Intimus had been right – the search for the Source had brought treasure seekers close to Isslewood. Rhages rambled on while he had been thinking.

"Wait," he said, picking up on something that had slipped by. "Are you saying that there is a connection between Talent and the Source?"

When Rhages nodded, Rixs laughed. "What be funny, kid?"

Another laugh caused Rixs to turn his head away. "What makes you think they have a connection? Possessing Talent is much like having rare abilities. It pops up without warning or reason. As for the Source … well, it surprises me that you have fallen for that nonsense. It is nothing more than an exaggerated tale concocted during the Long Wars to give people some amusement while they killed each other." He ran both hands through his hair. "Think about it. How can touching an object make a normal man turn into a powerful being?"

Rhages kicked at the dirt while listening to his young friend. "Look, kid, I don't care if somebody be sending me on a tail chase as long as I get paid! He pays us good so, it don't matter if it be true or not! What matters is he believes it! Rhages don't mind working for a fool." He thoughtfully paused, pursing his lips. "But I don't think he be a fool."

The two looked at each other. Rhages frowned and tapped, rather forcefully, at Fogle's splayed out and unconscious body with the toes of his boot.

"The crew split up to find stuff and I got stuck with Froghead cuz none of the others can stand him!"

Rixs snorted and gently bumped Fogle's body with his own boot. "I knew you were a good man, Rhages."

"Yeah, well, don't be tellin' nobody!"

It occurred to Rixs that while Chadgerwin had asked him his thoughts about the Source, the Counselor had never divulged what he believed. He speculated but never stated if he believed the Source was real. Maybe answers could be found in Ormolu. Maybe there was a tie to Isslewood. Perhaps the crew's benefactor had tangible evidence to shed light and support the connection.

As if he read Rixs's thoughts, Rhages exposed more forbidden light on the subject. "I can tell ya that this man be thinking the Emperor is the key, but since he disappeared and no one's heard nothin' from him, we had to find another connection. Vic…um, … I mean … trotts!" Rhages bit his tongue.

"The man that hired us thinks that where there be one Talent there's bound to be more. He also says that if there be more, then there be somethin' to find cuz they be protectin' somethin'!" He scowled and scratched his beard. "Strikes! I don't know! Makes sense ta me!" he shrugged.

Rigid with unease, Rixs grimaced. There were more Talents at Isslewood, but they were protecting the Empress Heir. There was nothing mysterious about that. He reached out to fixate on Syersi's light grey form moving among the sea of shapes. Considering the information Rhages had shared, it was best to return the Empress Heir to Isslewood.

The crew would not be as identifiable in Rixs's world of grey as Rhages was. Rhages was abnormally large, so he took up a lot of space — his shape was easy to recognize. The rest of the men were average. They would not be so easy to pick out with his ability. They would blend with everybody else in Ormolu and could potentially get too close to the Empress Heir without him being aware. Rixs would need visual sight to identify them. They posed a threat.

"Your turn," Rhages said.

Feeling obligated to share, Rixs quickly gave an account of all that had happened to him, leaving out the part about three other Talents living at the palace. He also omitted the fact that he was a Talent too.

Rhages slapped him on the back and Rixs lurched forward. "Survived a fall! Found by a Princess! Now yer the Imperial Shield! Ya wanted an adventure, kid, and ya got one!"

Their time was up. "My friend, it has been a pleasure, but it's time to part ways." Rixs had picked out Syersi's petite and curvy form making her way down the street in their direction. Apparently, she had waited long enough for him to reappear.

He nodded at the mess of arms and legs sprawled on the ground in front of them. "What will you do with him?"

"Leave him!" Rhages exclaimed with a wink.

Shoving the guards aside, Syersi was no longer interested in cooperating with the request to *stay put*. After Rixs and his friends had disappeared in the alley, her curiosity was piqued. She had waited for them to emerge, but she had waited long enough.

Lead guard, Pravin, caught up to her. "Lady Syersi, the Shield desired that you remain in the square."

Sweeps of a sky-blue critical eye made Rixs's second in command flinch. "You can either take me to him or stay behind," was Syersi's ultimatum. Her steps were quick and deliberate. "Take your pick, Second, but do not bother to keep me where I prefer not to stay, or I assure you, it will be the last thing you do."

There it was. Nothing Pravin or anyone else could do would influence the Empress Heir once she had made up her mind. With no other choice, he walked beside her.

Only steps away from the alley, a lean figure hurriedly rounded the corner and nearly collided into Syersi. She found herself body to body with Rixs, his hands grabbing her arms to keep her from stumbling backward. Their eyes locked and their gazes danced around each other until Rixs found his tongue.

"I thought I made it clear you were to remain back there," he nodded his head in the direction she had come.

"I was certain you had abandoned me," she replied. "You left me unprotected. Lucky for you, your second kept me safe!"

The Lady had never been in danger the entire time Rixs spoke with Rhages. *He* had been *watching* her every move. "Pravin is a very competent guard," he replied.

Her response was a dissatisfied, *humph*, as he guided her back in the direction she had come. She pointed out, "*You* are my Shield, Rixsander. If anyone fails to protect me, it will be your head on the chopping block, not theirs."

"I concede your point." He placed a hand at her back to hurry her along.

She abruptly stopped and swirled toward him. "Why are you hurrying me? And why did you not introduce me to those men? Who were they?"

"No one of importance," he answered. "Come, it is time to leave and head back to Isslewood. The sun is nearly half past high noon. I want to make it back well ahead of dusk." Rixs held his breath. When she made no argument, he sighed with relief.

Both Syersi and Rixs gasped when they saw the wealth of treasures Moniere and Keedra carried when the guards had fetched them. It had been a busy day for them, but Syersi, too, had managed to purchase an entire cart's worth of scarves. The same scarves she had effectively knocked over. Syersi had Mazzlin to thank for scarves that would last her a lifetime.

Rixs effortlessly lifted Syersi onto Juju with strong hands that closed around her waist. She held her breath at the warmth of his touch. Once situated, Rixs walked along side Juju, holding the reins.

The faces of Ormolu surrounded them, waving their hands in farewell while the detail formed a protective ring around the Empress Heir and her Shield. Syersi waved back, all charm and grace.

It was then that the explosions began.

SEVENTEEN

A shattering boom sent tremors under the feet of hundreds of marketgoers, interrupting the activities of the city's square. Dark smoke plumed into the air on the far side of Ormolu. As the people began to yell, a second explosion shattered buildings and spewed rubble in all directions, this time, too close to Syersi and Rixs.

A baker's shop, not far from where Syersi sat atop Juju, erupted in a mixed cloud of dust and debris. Wood and stone flew in all directions, pieces raining down on Syersi's head. No sooner had the second explosion sounded than a third rocked the city.

A spooked Juju reared up on her hind legs then took off in a run, yanking the reins free of Rixs's grip. Nearly falling off her horse, Syersi desperately grabbed at Juju's mane to hold on.

Cursing out loud, Rixs ran after the horse. A naturally fast runner, he pushed his body to move like it never had, while keeping his eyes on a struggling Syersi. She was an incredible rider, evidenced by the skill she employed just to hang on. Rixs would have fallen off as soon as the horse reared up.

The frenzied commotion only served to scare the animal more. Syersi leaned low against Juju's neck, keeping her fingers tightly twisted in the horse's silver mane, and strained to cinch her legs as tightly as she could around Juju's midsection. Daring a glance behind her, she saw Rixs running after them, his face pulled tight in concentration.

A wagon stopped directly in the path of the frightened horse. Juju skidded into a side alley then reared up, pawing her two front legs in the air as three men stood in front of her waving their arms. Already exhausted from hanging on, the sudden movement threw Syersi to the ground with a hard thud. Breath knocked from her, she lay stunned beneath Juju's hooves and was nearly trampled before her horse ran off in the opposite direction.

Male voices spoke in low hurried tones as Syersi lay on the ground with the breath knocked out of her and too stunned to move her muscles. She realized she was being dragged by her feet. Dirt kicked up into her face making it difficult to breathe or open her eyes.

The tugging stopped and rough hands forced her to stand. Wobbly on her feet, she nearly fell but a nasty hand kept her up and stable while a scrawny man thrilled over the jewels in her hair. Rixs rounded the corner at high speed and skidded to an abrupt halt.

Syersi struggled against a thick arm that wrapped around her neck like a snake. She could not see this man. The scrawny man fumbled with the gems woven into her dark braid, and another stood by assessing Rixs.

"Let go of my throat!" she coughed, clawing at the arm that held her, not thinking about the danger of her situation. "Ouch! Stop that!" she snarled at the man with grimy fingers plunging after the jewels.

Her eyes finally landed on Rixs to find him panting and staring at all of them, his emerald gaze glancing between each man. "Shield! Do something!"

Too winded to respond, he launched a scowl that said, *Did you just see me run across town after you?*

The grip tightened around Syersi's neck, and the big man growled, "You can leave the same way you came, boy! There is nothing that concerns you here!"

Breathing with effort, Rixs lifted his hands in submission, but his tone was anything but submissive. "That girl is my concern." He sucked in a few gulps of air. "If I leave, she goes with me."

Syersi hissed, "Did you refer to me as, *that girl?* Do these men know who I am?" Another hard yank to her head had her screaming. "Ahhh! That hurts! I already told you to stop!" The bony male was determined to own every gem in her hair.

She swiped out to claw his face, but the big smelly one gave her a hard jerk. His growl stopped abruptly, and all eyes turned to a nearby doorway where a hooded figure emerged into the alley.

"Hate to break up the warm gathering," a smooth masculine voice said. "But, I will take the girl."

Two additional figures slid into place behind him, each with arrows raised and aimed. One arrow targeted the head of the man holding Syersi – the other arrow was fixed on Rixs.

The arrow trained on Rixs lowered. "Rixs?" The man shook the hood from his head. "Ha! I thought I recognized you!"

Rixs cringed. It was Bronan, leader of the crew and the man who would have abandoned Rixs a dozen times had Rhages let him.

"Someone you know?" the smooth voice asked.

Bronan's voice hinted of disgust. "Yeah. His name is Rixs. He traveled with my crew until we were attacked." He turned back to Rixs, "I'm surprised you're alive. Thought you to be dead!"

Nodding thoughtfully, Rixs responded, "Sorry to disappoint. You can stop pointing that arrow at my head."

While Rixs and the new intruders parlayed with one another, the big smelly man holding Syersi tight around the neck, thought to ease away with his catch. He edged backward little by little.

"Stop moving," the words floated from beneath the hood of the man with the smooth voice. "If you want to leave here alive, hand her over." He held out a pale slender hand.

"We take our chances! If I hand her over, our master will skin us alive!"

Rixs frowned. There were at least two groups wanting Syersi – the man who hired Big Smelly, and the man with Bronan. Since the crew searched for the Source, he wondered if the other group was doing the same, and how the Empress Heir was connected.

"Stop talking!" Syersi hissed at the man who held her. "Your breath stinks of rotten eggs!"

The man jerked Syersi's head producing a whimper, then

growled in her ear, "You shut up before I snap your pretty little neck!"

Rixs tensed. It would have been easy to eliminate Big Smelly. His entire head was exposed, and a single well-placed blade would have dropped the scum. He could have taken care of his friends, as well. The only thing that held him back was the second group of men. Bronan and his friends complicated matters.

The Governing Council had been hard to win over. Convincing the voting members that Syersi would be safe with him if they left Isslewood required that he minimize the dangers posed from the search for the Source. He also reminded the Council of the benefits that freedom from Isslewood could provide. The obvious benefit was that the Empress Heir would be less inclined to escape at every opportunity. However, with two separate groups trying to abduct her, it seemed Rixs had been wrong about her safety.

Chadgerwin had required him to bring fifty men on this first excursion. The chaos of the explosions, and Juju's runaway stunt had made it difficult for the detail to follow. His Talent, Sagacious, as Chadgerwin had guessed, gave him the ability to see that the guards were scouring the alleys. They would not arrive to this alley in time. Rixs needed to do something.

In the few fleeting moments that passed, Rixs assessed the space consumed against the six male bodies. There was a knife strapped to the back of the man who held Syersi. It was just under his shirt. The scrawny one with his fingers perpetually tangled in Syersi's hair had no weapons at all. It was the same with the third man. Those three would be easy to overtake. He would deal with them last.

The other three were a different matter. The one with the smooth voice was the obvious leader, and probably the one who hired the crew. A sword and dagger rested at his waist, under his cloak. If the man tried to pull them, they would be difficult to get to quickly. That would be an advantage for Rixs. The man also carried a knife strapped above his ankle. That would be the weapon the man would go for first. Rixs would go for it too.

Bronan and the third man each had a bow and quiver of arrows. At close range, flying arrows were always a challenge to evade. A long dagger hanging from Bronan's belt was hidden beneath his cloak. Rixs knew, firsthand, that the crew leader needed to be taken seriously when there was a weapon in his hands. The third man carried a sword strapped across his back.

A defensive strategist, Rixs liked avoiding danger, but in that moment, he had to attack first and wished he had paid more attention to the offensive fighting style the combat master had tried to drill into his head.

Smooth voice announced from under the drape of his hood, "Enough delay. No one here is ignorant of the Empress Heir's identity. Hand her over or prepare for an arrow in your chest."

The man winced, then adjusted Syersi in front of him while she struggled to hold her head high. "You are all dead men!" she hissed. "My Shield will kill you all!"

Bronan turned a sideways dawning glance at Rixs. "By The Powers! You are the new Shield!"

"You are obviously not too bright!" Syersi hissed. "Do you not see the ring on his finger?"

All eyes landed on Rixs's index finger. He exhaled heavily with an annoyed glare fixed on Syersi willing her to shut her mouth.

"A striking ring. Toss it over here," Bronan ordered.

"That is not why we are here, Bronan," the leader admonished. He turned to the one holding Syersi. "Why are you here?" he asked.

The man responded flatly, "We were offered gold to snatch the girl."

"Who offered?" Rixs interrogated. "Did you set the explosions?"

"No, but they were handy. She came right to us!"

Bronan flashed a cocky smirk. "You can thank us for the chaos, Rixs."

The callous confession made Rixs itch to grab his blades. People were suffering because of the explosions, and the Empress Heir was in danger. Rixs silently prayed to The Powers for guidance – he needed to wait for the right opportunity before he began tossing his metal.

The choking arm that, no doubt, would leave bruises on Syersi's neck, reminded Rixs to tread lightly but he could already see the impatience in her eyes. She expected action and was tired of waiting. He hoped she would resist taking actions into her own hands.

Abruptly, Syersi threw her head back – a resulting *crack* split the air. Two voices cried out in pain. Syersi rubbed the back of her head, while the anguished howl of the man that held her rang loud around them. While he grabbed at his bleeding nose, she stomped on his foot.

It was enough to motivate the big smelly man to release his hold. It was also the cue Rixs needed.

Neutralizing both arrows was top priority. In simultaneous motions, each of his hands plucked a short blade from the outer side seam of his clashing vest and released them before anyone could blink. His objective – slice the bow strings. He could not let those arrows fly, especially the one that could accidentally hit Syersi.

The Shield's aim was precise enough to stick a fly to a wall, if he had wanted. Bronan and the other archer cried out as each blade hit true, slicing through its intended bow string, and causing the poised arrows to fall limply to the ground. Unfortunately for them, in need of a final resting place, the blades sank deep in the shoulder of each man wielding the bows. Bronan staggered back but managed to stay on his feet while the other man fell to the ground.

Not bothering to take notice of his handiwork, Rixs dove into a roll toward the feet of their leader, sliding both hands underneath his pant leg and disarming him of the knife strapped above his ankle. It was a move that had been too easy and he was standing with the knife pointed at the leader.

Over before it began, the hooded man twisted around to find Rixs pointing his own knife into the hollow of his throat. Knife in one hand, Rixs used the other to roughly yank the man's hood off his head.

"Time to introduce yourself," Rixs demanded. "And forget about reaching for the dagger under your cloak."

A pale-skinned man with ebony eyes and matching hair met Rixs's gaze, his hand that had twisted into his cloak to clutch his dagger, suspended its movement. "Impressive," he said, careful not to move so the knife at his throat would not draw blood.

Gasping in pain, Bronan managed to growl as he pulled the blade from his shoulder, "I am going to shred you with your own blade!" he spat.

Before Bronan could make good on his threat, the Shield had already reached over his shoulder with his free hand and pulled a long blade from his back. Bronan met the tip of it with a scowl. A cocky wink from Rixs made Bronan's scowl twist further.

A low chuckle was heard. "You know, I could use your skill on my team," a dark smile accompanied the smooth voice of the pale-skinned man. "Bronan, who is this man again?"

With the grimace of pain leaching across his face from the blade wound in his shoulder, Bronan grunted his reply. "He is Rixs, a scab the crew picked up along the way to Gnomera." He blew out a measured breath and added, "I knew he was great with his blades, but apparently, I underestimated the level of his skill."

"And now, your turn – who are you?" Rixs demanded of the man.

The pale face crooked slightly, then after a prolonged moment he finally announced, "I am Viktus."

Rixs looked at him from under a blanket of hair that had found its way into his eyes. "Just, *Viktus*? You have no home of origin?"

Another smile, "Just, Viktus. I do not know where I come from."

"Very well, Viktus, from nowhere. Please tell your men to toss my blades gently by my feet, or I may need to give you a token of my affection in your throat," Rixs spoke with calm.

Viktus studied him for a long moment. "Do as he says," he relented.

Syersi's abduction might have gone unnoticed while Rixs dealt with Viktus and his men, but he knew the exact moment her light grey form had been dragged from the alley, leaving only empty space behind.

He groaned. Before any rescue could be attempted, Rixs needed to finish up with the current problem, and incapacitate Viktus and his men until the guards could find them.

"Sorry. I cannot chat longer," Rixs apologized, then he swung the blunt handle of the knife and hit Viktus on the side of his head. The man fell in a heap onto the ground.

Bronan roared and sprang into action. As if he had never been stabbed in his shoulder, he spun in the air, poised to stab Rixs with the dagger he had pulled from his belt. The third man instantly found his strength too, and abruptly jumped up, groping, with effort, for the sword hanging on his back.

A quick duck allowed Rixs to avoid Bronan's attack. He dropped the weapons he held and hooked an arm through Bronan's injured one, then swung around, twisting the bleeding arm behind him. *Pop.* Bronan's scream of agony as his shoulder dislocated caused Rixs to shudder.

"Sorry for that," he winced.

The form of the third man with sword raised high shadowed over him. Rixs whirled both he and Bronan around just in time. Lucky for Bronan, his thick cloak took the brunt of the vicious slash so that only a superficial, but sizable wound cut across his chest. Bronan screamed again.

Rixs said remorsefully, "Again, sorry, Bronan." Then he slammed an elbow into the side of his head knocking him out. *Two down, one to go!*

Breathing with little effort, Rixs narrowed his emerald stare at the third man who was already swinging down once again with his sword. There was barely enough time to jump back and pluck his long blade from the ground, but he did it, then swung around in time to block the man's swing. Rixs stayed in defensive form and successfully blocked several deep thrusts, one that would have impaled him in his groin. He sent a silent prayer of thanks then quickly countered the move by kicking the man in the gut, causing him to stumble to the side.

Dirt-smeared cheeks gave Rixs the appearance of a rambunctious boy. "Are you sure you want to fight with me?" he questioned, swinging the long blade comfortably at his side. But there was no more time for chitchat. He feigned left with his ebony blade drawing the man's block, then spun opposite, leaping high and smashing a foot into his head. Like an unwanted rag, the man hit the dirt.

Finally, able to toss his hair out of his eyes, Rixs heaved a sigh of relief. He looked up as though he could see through the buildings, which he could, and took off in a sprint.

EIGHTEEN

A thick calloused hand pressed so hard against Syersi's mouth, her teeth cut into her lips and blood tinged her tongue. Dragged from alley to alley, she kicked and scratched to break free, but there was too much meat on her captor's bones for him to feel any of it.

Ducking into a shop that appeared empty, they stumbled upon the shopkeeper picking up shattered glass from bottles that had rocked off their shelves during the explosions. She looked up and noticed the three men hurrying through her shop with a girl in tow. She yelped in alarm seeing a hand clamped over the young girl's mouth.

"What is this?" she cried. "Unhand that girl!"

"It's all fine," Syersi's captor hastily explained while hurrying past. "My daughter is throwing a bit of a tantrum. That's all! You know how young girls are!" he chuckled, pushing through the door at the opposite end of the shop. The four of them spilled out into the street, and quickly slipped down another alley.

Syersi had never had to endure being a victim. She had not been educated in the delicate art of behaving when one was a captive. So, she behaved as badly as she ever had and bit hard into the smelly man's palm.

A warm, wet sensation caused her to gag. The thought of big smelly's blood seeping into her mouth sent a cringe up her back, but she soldiered through and kept her jaws clenched tight.

The man yowled and pulled his hand away, leaving a bit of his flesh in her mouth. Syersi nearly vomited as she spat on the ground then poised herself to run. His other beefy hand grabbed her by the hair and yanked her back.

A shrill scream, the likes which shattered ear drums, erupted from her plum lips. The scrawny man covered his ears and hissed a *shut up*! For all her efforts, it did little good. Chaos from the explosions held dominion over the streets and no one paid her any mind.

The slap was unexpected, swift, and hard. Hard enough that her ears popped. Blinking back tears, wide blue eyes stared up at the abuser and for the first time, Syersi experienced true fear.

Never had anyone touched her in such a manner. The snatched Empress Heir of Gnomera rubbed her cheek and swallowed back a choked sob. Her captors had managed to slip away, and Rixs would never find her despite his skill at blades. She was alone.

"Every time you scream, that's what ya get! Understand, Princess?"

She bit her tongue and glared.

"Do you understand me?" he yelled. The ferocity of his voice shook her from the inside out. There was no doubt he would hit her again, and again. She nodded.

"Now, tell me about the Source," he growled.

Dark lashes fluttered in confusion and she shook her head. A thick calloused hand raised to strike her, and she flinched away from him.

The third man scampered back toward them. "Guards! They come this way!"

Syersi's abductor snatched a handful of hair and yanked her head back, her eyes forced to stare into his. "You gotta know something!" he snarled. Yanking her hair again, he threatened, "Start thinking or I'll grab your tongue and pull it outta your mouth!"

"Do that later!" the third man pleaded. "We gotta hide!"

Tugging her along with an arm wrapped around her head, and a big grubby hand clamped over her mouth again, he kicked in the first door available. They all stumbled inside and slammed the door shut.

The place they invaded was small and sparsely furnished. Syersi dared to hope that the occupants were somewhere inside, but it seemed The Powers had ignored her prayers yet again. The scrawny man went from room to room and confirmed that all was clear. Syersi's heart sank and despite her best efforts, tears spilled onto her cheeks.

Removing his hand from her mouth, Smelly pulled a soiled scarf from his pocket and cinched it tightly around Syersi's mouth then he pulled a rope for her hands. She struggled but he backhanded her into compliance. Once her hands were firmly tied behind her back, he pointed a big finger between her eyes. The warning was clear. Remain silent – or else.

Rangus would demand she be fearless and strong. Syersi hoped her returning glare camouflaged the tears trickling down her cheeks.

The third abductor kept vigilance at the window. "Ha!" he exclaimed in a loud whisper. "The soldiers walked past!"

The soldiers had been Syersi's best hope at rescue. Head down and shoulders drooping, despair took over. The young woman sobbed quietly.

The irony of the situation was not lost on her. Syersi had been consumed with breaking free of Isslewood's prison, and yet here she was, free of Tower Wall, yet nothing more than a blubbering prisoner. She had been dragged through the dirt, choked, and slapped. Grimy hands had pulled her hair to steal her jewels, and her tongue wrestled with the filthy rag while rope gnawed at the skin of her wrists tied behind her back.

Syersi hiccupped. At that moment, she would have given anything, and everything to be back within the smothering confines and ultimate safety of Isslewood. Her chest cramped. She had never known what it was like to be terrified. Certainly, no one had ever touched her in a threatening manner, although she did remember a few times when her father, Emperor Lothorius, had threatened to bend her over his knee. Only the dark had ever made her truly afraid, and even then, there was always her mother, a servant, or Mazzlin, to make her feel safe and secure.

"It's that boy again ... the fast one!" the watchman hissed a little too loudly. "He's walking this way!"

"Keep your voice down, ya fool!" smelly man warned in a hushed growl. "There ain't no reason for him to come in here, so calm down. But grab that chair and stand ready to hit him over the head just in case he opens the door."

Syersi's heart thudded loudly against her ribs. *Please find me! If you do, I promise never to insult you again!*

Her abductor leaned in. "Don't even think about screaming, or crying, or breathing! One sound, one move, and I'll slap you so hard, your eyes will pop out!" Again, he pulled her hair so that she had to look at him.

"No one said anything about the condition ya had to be in when I hand ya over!" Then he squeezed his hand around her throat to make his point.

"He's slowing down," the man reported. "And he's staring at the door." A few eternal moments passed then a barely audible whisper. "He stopped and he's standing ..." watchman pointed at the door, then lifted the chair over his head.

"What?" the leader mouthed.

With his head jutting toward the door, the man exaggerated the pronunciation of his words. "He's standing outside the door, and his eyes are closed!"

"Eyes closed?" the leader breathed.

A quiet knock sounded at the door. The chair, positioned high and ready to strike, shook slightly. Then without warning or time to react, the door burst open and the Shield grasped the chair, ripping it free from the man who held it.

Rixs already knew the position of each body. He had paused outside to make sure of it, so his next move had already been calculated before he burst through the door.

He flung the chair across the room where the scrawny man stood. The chair hit him in the chest, the impact throwing him on his back. His body slid across the floor until it slammed against the far wall.

Once the chair was out of his hands, Rixs threw an elbow into the face of the watchman standing next to the door. There was a crunch then his head slammed into the wall with a loud crack. Only the whites of the man's eyes were visible when his body slid down the wall into a crumpled heap on the floor.

Recovering, scrawny man grabbed the chair and charged. There was little effort expended when Rixs yanked the chair out of his grip and slammed him over the head with it. Scrawny was on the floor – out for good.

Emerald eyes took in Syersi. Rixs inhaled every detail of her, noting the wad of material in her mouth, the tangled mess of her hair, but mostly, he took heated notice of her swollen lip and cheek. His face darkened.

Had she been able, Syersi would have thrown herself into his arms and smothered him with kisses of gratitude. He had come for her, and against the odds, he had found her. His bright, beautiful eyes were a blessing from The Powers.

Tipping his forehead ever so slightly, Rixs acknowledged Syersi. His gaze bore into her soul, appealing to her silently with an arch of his brows. *Are you all right?* She blinked back, her bright blue pools glistening with tears.

Green eyes tore away from her and Rixs pronounced through clenched teeth and pulsing veins, "Time is up! Give her to me – now!"

"Don't come any closer!" the man growled and grabbed her head in both hands. "Or I'll break her neck!"

"No. No, I trust you won't … for two reasons," Rixs challenged with a tight smile. "One," he held up an index finger. "The man that hired you to take the Lady won't take kindly to you killing his prize and ruining whatever plan he had for her. And two," Rixs added his middle finger. "Because if you do, I will make sure you won't live to take another breath." They stared at each other.

The man's muscles tensed as he narrowed muddy eyes at the Shield. Rixs knew he was about to make a move – his body said as much.

Without warning, he pushed Syersi into Rixs and took off running toward the back exit. Rixs grasped her by the shoulders, sliding his warm hands over her arms and looking over every portion of skin. He pulled her into a tight hug.

She mumbled through the scarf and he cracked a quick smile. "I like that rag interfering with your lethal tongue." She snorted and he shrugged and grinned wider. She mumbled frantically through the filthy scarf and shoved him with her shoulder. Her message was clear – he pulled a short blade from his vest and cut the scarf from her face. Then he cut the twine binding her hands.

"You play while my abductor escapes!" she cried while rubbing her wrists. "The scum will never pay for what he has done!"

Guiding her into the alley, Rixs responded, "He shall pay, but first, I must get you to safety."

"He's already gone! You will never find him!"

The frantic tone of her voice stirred him to tenderness. "Pixee … I will find him. I promise."

Rixs left a flustered Syersi in the care of two guards and ordered them to find her detail. He instructed that once she was safe, they were to retrieve the string of bodies he had left behind. Then he took off in a run.

Tracking down the last man took no time at all. Had he found a hiding spot and stayed put, he might have blended into the environment around him. It was easier to spot a grey form on the move than it was to find a grey form that was statue still. Gray shapes tended to dissolve into the background when they were motionless, but as soon as a shape moved, it was like waving a white flag. *Come and get me!* So, Rixs did.

Shockingly, it was Rixs who took the first swing. His fist plowed into the man's jaw, but his head barely jerked to the side. Then the favor was returned. A hard punch was delivered, and Rixs was quick and ready to block it, but the sheer size and weight of his adversary powered through Rixs's arm and pushed all the way through into his face. Bright stars twinkled in swirling circles like a sparkling cyclone around his head.

Mentally kicking himself in his own hind parts, Rixs knew he should have dodged out of the way. The man was much stronger than he appeared, he would not underestimate him again.

After being stomped on, choked, and thrown ruthlessly into a shed, which collapsed on top of them, Gnomera's new Shield finally got the upper hand. Jumping onto the man's back, he wrapped his arms in a choke hold around his massive neck and squeezed, and squeezed some more, clinging like a leach while his nemesis tried to throw him off.

All the air was knocked out of Rixs when *Big and Smelly* threw his weight back into a stone wall. Another *whoosh* of air left him when *Smelly* did it again. Then again. He used Rixs's body like a battering ram.

Stars danced around Rixs's head and darkness dimmed his vision. The assault on his body continued. His back slammed into the wall over, and over again until his muscles felt like bread dough. It was a miracle he hung on, squeezing the man's neck, and cinching tighter and tighter like a snake coiling around its prey.

He willed himself not to black out first. The muscles in his arms trembled and the veins in his neck pulsed with effort.

The man's efforts slowly lost its force and Rixs caught his breath. Finally, torture gave way to triumph. Big and smelly staggered. Then he wobbled. Not a moment later the big body toppled to the ground, and an exhausted Rixs rolled off him onto the dirt.

NINETEEN

The ride back to Isslewood proved interesting for onlookers as Rixs bounced roughly, clinging to Syersi's waist. The gash on the back of his head throbbed with every trot the horse made.

Juju had fallen out of favor with the Empress Heir, and she refused to ride her horse, so she traded with Rixs. He carefully mounted the stunning white mare, but Juju promptly bucked him off. The horse had only ever carried Syersi, and so after several attempts to climb the fickle horse only to find himself sprawled on the ground, Rixs gave up.

"Everyone keeps looking at us," he said while trying to keep his voice steady. He shifted his hands for the hundredth time trying to find a way to hold Syersi's waist without looking gropy.

The Empress Heir turned her head to the side and spoke behind her. "To be clear, they are looking at *you*, not *us*. Can you blame them? Look at the way you bounce during a trot! I feel as though you will bounce yourself right of the horse and pull me with you!" She smiled, then winced when her split lip gave a sting.

"Well, if you rode your own horse, I could ride mine and only embarrass myself!"

Syersi's two retinue rode just behind them. "Shield," Keedra called. "If you continue jangling like that, you won't be able to walk for days!"

He turned to look back at her, but every rib screamed in protest. "Too late, Miss Keedra," he called over his shoulder. "I'm already beaten to a pulp. Walking would be a miracle!"

Leaning over so she could speak without anyone hearing, Moniere murmured, "I would be happy to rub his body so that he forgets all about his soreness."

"Shh!" Keedra snapped. "If the First Daughter hears you, she will have your head!"

"Oh, Keedra! You are no fun!"

A messenger had been sent ahead of Syersi's entourage to inform the First Counselor and Absolute of the explosions in Ormolu. Before long, Chadgerwin and Rangus came into view with a large contingent of the Lothorian Guard.

As the group approached, it was Rangus who growled to Chadgerwin, "What in holy sanguine is that boy doing?"

Sanguinary eyes were much keener than normal eyes, so Chadgerwin had to squint to study the bouncing figure behind the First Daughter. "I believe he is riding."

"Well, he looks ridiculous!" Rangus growled.

Chadgerwin scratched the scar that stretched across the right side of his face. "Yes, he does, but the bigger question is, why is he riding with Syersi? And why is Juju without a rider?"

When Chadgerwin reined his horse close to Syersi and Rixs, he reached out and gently touched Syersi's face, frowning at the marks and bruises he found. His mouth kept silent but grey stormy eyes revealed dark and dangerous thoughts. His expression did not bode well for the men who tried to abduct the Empress Heir. Their fate had been sealed the moment they laid hands on her.

"You look like a beaten pile of dung!" Rangus complimented Rixs.

Rixs gave a droll reply. "Thank you for noticing, Absolute. I hoped to impress you. Dung is a step up from wamp."

Rangus responded with a smirk, though his eyes were the color of blood. He then barked orders for the Lothorian Guard to proceed to Ormolu. They were charged with stabilizing the city, giving aid to the people, and reporting any supplies necessary to help rebuild.

Once satisfied the contingent was well on its way, the Absolute led the smaller group back to Isslewood, and insisted Rixs provide every detail of Syersi's abduction. Syersi listened with tear-filled blue eyes.

Once they had reached the safety of Isslewood, Chadgerwin and Rangus disappeared to enjoy quality time with Syersi's abductors. Rixs had wanted to go with them, mostly because the First Daughter yearned for a bath and he preferred to be as far away as possible while she soaked naked in her fonts.

Even standing behind a wall, every shadowed shape of her outline was available to him. Self-control was his forte, but he was also realistic. Unfortunately, Syersi had become clingy, fearful that someone could be lurking around every corner to snatch her up. When he asked to leave, she screamed so loud, he had to promise to stay to silence her.

During the evening meal, Rixs hoped to speak with Chadgerwin or Rangus, but his only company was Hobb, Mazzlin, and Syersi. Even Orris was eerily absent to torment him. And Syersi had eyed him like a platter of her favorite delicacy all through the meal. It motivated him to eat quickly and leave while she was diverted, talking to Hobb, but if he thought he could hide, he had been mistaken.

He tapped lightly on her chamber door while he shook his head, letting his hair fall into his eyes. Not waiting two heartbeats, Rixs turned to sneak away.

The door flew open. "Rixsander! You have come!"

"You summoned me?" he winced. *Not fast enough Rixs!*

Her bright blue eyes beamed. "I know you need to rest, but I could not let the night pass without telling you of my heart-felt gratitude for rescuing me."

Gratitude was not the look conveyed in her big pools of blue. Rhages would have called them *bedtime* eyes. Rixs's mother would have called them, *run away quickly*, eyes.

He swallowed hard and tried to think what he would call them. He would call them, *dangerous*. They certainly zapped his strength. He needed to escape – quickly. She slammed her door shut.

"I did nothing more than my duty," he choked out, his voice raspier than intended. "Any of your guards would have done the same thing."

Her face spoke of caresses and kisses. "No, my Shield. The other guards might have tried ..." She took a step closer. "Even Orris would have tried and not succeeded." Her foot moved another step forward. "You were brilliant. Fast ... and ... strong." She stood directly in front of him, only a breath away. An enchanting blue stare bore into his blood.

"The ... the Counselor ..." he stammered, then forgot what he wanted to say.

"Shhh. I want to thank you properly – with a kiss," she whispered through her plump pink lips.

Rixs blinked at her mouth then rubbed a hand down his face. His mind had gone blank. He grinned, then bowed to leave needing to escape.

"My apologies. I am too tired. I need sleep, as do you, Lady Syersi. We begin your training tomorrow."

Warm fingers had grasped his arm before he could open the door. Facing away from her, Rixs closed his eyes and froze. "Was there something else, Lady Syersi?" he had managed to mumble through a thick and paralyzed tongue. He willed the image of Cliessa into his head.

"Lady Syersi?" her soft musical voice questioned. "I thought you liked to call me, *Pixee*."

The muscles in his arms involuntarily flexed under her grip. "I call you that to tease you,"

Syersi turned him around to face her. They stared at each other for a long moment, then she lifted onto her toes and tilted her head toward his, a soft curve to her mouth. His gaze dropped from her eyes to her lips, appreciating their shape.

She closed her eyes, still perched on her toes.

It would have only required a slight dip of his head to taste her. A thousand fireflies had ignited the inside of his gut. He admired the soft velvet of her closed eyes, the shape of her nose, the color of her cheeks. He lifted a hand to touch her shining black hair but curled his fingers at the last moment.

The young woman waited patiently with eyes closed. When Rixs had finally resigned himself to giving in, it was Cliessa's face suddenly peering back at him. He stumbled backward into the wall, and Syersi's eyes popped open.

Legs nearly buckling beneath him, Rixs fumbled for the door handle and was through it before she could catch his vest. "We train in the morning, Princess. Sleep well," he called over his shoulder.

"But I'm afraid to be alone!" she cried.

"Your guards are right outside your door, Lady Syersi!" was his reply.

Rixs hurried down the hall, but it was not long before two smokey forms had quickly made their way behind him. He could have run, but he had already been beaten once that day. Instead, just as he reached his chambers, he let the two guards take hold of each arm and lead him away.

And so, the familiar smell of mildew and something else that Rixs could only attribute as rotting skin ambushed his nose. He was in lockup once again, in a cell that the prison guards had affectionately named *Rixs's Hole*. His reputation as Imperial Shield would suffer a terrible blow.

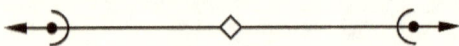

"Good morning, my dear," Mazzlin greeted with a cheery voice as she pushed open the shutters and terrace doors. Morning sun flooded the chamber.

Syersi responded with a grouchy, "Umm!" and pulled the bed covers over her head. She still burned after Rixs's rejection.

Men had always tripped over themselves to please the Empress Heir when she showed interest. It had been humiliating to stand with closed eyes, expecting a kiss, only to have Rixs turn tail and run like she was a nightmare. With her vanity and pride brutally wounded, his insult could not go unpunished.

The sound of another person entering her chamber coaxed Syersi out from under her bed covers. A servant girl had set her morning meal on the table.

"Bring it here, girl!" she demanded, her promise to herself just the day before, to be a kinder person was all forgotten.

The spindly female nodded and hastily placed the tray on the massive bed. She took quick glimpses of the Empress Heir and her silky black hair from under her own dull amber mess of tangles.

Gossip had spread like a lightning strike through the great house. Lady Syersi had thrown Rixs into lockup again, but the best part – rumor had it that the Shield was imprisoned because he had rebuffed her advances. Everyone wondered if it was true, including the servant girl, who lingered a little too long to study the Empress Heir.

There had never been a single account of anyone rejecting Lady Syersi when she chose to drizzle her special attentions on a single recipient. The idea that Rixs had refused the future Empress of Gnomera made him even more desirous to the women of Isslewood. He was a man worthy of their own hearts.

Mazzlin flashed a glance between Syersi and the servant. "Thank you, Lisserie," she said, and the girl took her hint and withdrew.

When the door closed, the Guardian poked around to satisfy her own curiosity. "I hear that our young Shield didn't spend the night in his chamber … again." She stepped back to appraise the flower arrangement she had just finished. "I wonder why."

A square jaw line, tempting lips, a straight nose peppered with light apricot freckles, and emerald eyes that competed with Syersi's most brilliant gems came to her mind. Even though his face had been beaten, bruised, and swollen, his lips had still called to her.

The recollection of standing on tiptoes so close to Rixs's body and her lips softly gathered into a pucker, flooded back to drown Syersi all over again. He merely walked away like it was normal to shun the desires of the most powerful woman in the world. He might as well have spit on her pride.

"How should I know why he didn't sleep in his chamber?" Syersi sassed. "I am not his keeper!" She drew a mug of soup to her lips.

Mazzlin was not deterred. "The great house is rumbling with gossip," she said, still fussing with the flowers. "He rejected your advances … at least, that is what the rumors say. Yesterday, the Shield could do no wrong, then suddenly he is in lockup. Do you have problems with your heart?"

"I am not having problems with my heart, Mazzy!" Syersi spat. Then her mouth dropped wide with realization. "Mazzy! Were you spying?"

The expression of guilt on the Guardian's round face told Syersi all she needed to know. The Seer had used her gift to watch the event from Syersi's own eyes.

"It was all in innocence," the Guardian defended. "I was checking on you, as I always do to make sure you are not embroiled in mischief ... the boy appeared in my face! I ..." Mazzlin stopped and chose her words carefully. "But I can hardly call him a boy! I thought the man might hurt you, so I watched! See? My snooping was very innocent. But let me tell you! If I were but twenty seasons cycles younger ... it made me reminisce of my own youth, and romance, and ... well!" Mazzlin giggled. "I was quite a lovely in my day! You would have had competition!" She closed her eyes and sighed. "His eyes made my knees wobble."

Syersi snorted and plopped her mug of soup on the tray. "Eew! That is not what I needed to hear, Mazzy! It places disturbing visions in my head!"

The Guardian clamped her lips together with her thumb and forefinger.

Blue eyes pitched forward and squinted at her. "You watched until I closed my eyes! Admit it!"

Mazzlin blinked and her round cheeks blushed a deep pink. Her reluctance to speak shouted her guilt.

"Oh, Mazzy!" Syersi plopped over on the bed, her face smashed into the blanket so that her words were nothing more than mumbling moans and groans.

"Syersi! I cannot understand what you are saying!"

The First Daughter snapped up from her covers and glared at the Seer.

Mazzlin continued with her assessment. "I could have sworn he was about to kiss you before he ran off ..."

"Oooh!" Syersi moaned, falling back into her covers once more. She was humiliated all over again. She pitched up straight and changed the subject. "What do you know about the Source? Those horrible men seemed to think that it was more than a myth and that I knew something about it."

The mood shifted. "Well, my dear," Mazzlin began hesitantly. "Some people believe the stories of the Source are true. Even I believe."

Syersi's lashes fanned her cheeks as she blinked in rapid succession. "You believe that a Source filled with power exists? Why is this the first time I am hearing it?"

Mazzlin tapped her mouth, thinking her words through. "Syersi, how do you think Talent originated?"

Somewhere in her memories, Syersi's mother had told her something, but the memory was too deep to grasp it. She blinked again. "But these are legends ..."

"And legends are long-ago truths exaggerated and embellished over time," the Guardian offered.

Syersi's eyes glazed over and a memory slowly spilled from her lips. "The Source created the supreme ones ... the Denier Cri." She surprised herself. "The Denier Cri were invincible. They could not die." Her eyes became wide. "Are you saying there is truth in those old stories?"

Light laughter filled the chamber. "My dear, of course they could die. They were killed off more than a thousand seasons cycles past, during the Long Wars. Denier Cri disappeared from the earth but then Talents started to emerge."

The young heir stared at her Guardian while she tried to remember what her mother had taught her. "The Denier Cri," Syersi whispered. "I have so much to learn."

TWENTY

Boredom drove Rixs to push the end of his nose up then down, over, and over, until the grey form caught his attention. It filled and emptied space as it rhythmically moved in his direction. Though his eyes were closed, he saw every movement. There was no mistaking the owner of this shape. Within moments the heavy door groaned open and the extraordinarily large form of Rangus entered the cell.

"Morning, you scoundrel!" the Absolute bellowed. Rixs winced at the ferocity and volume of his voice. "So, you think you can insult the Empress Heir, do you?"

Opening one lazy eye, the grey form of the Absolute was suddenly saturated in color. Rixs sighed relief when he noticed the Sanguinary's eyes were the hue of dull rust. A good sign that he was not to be the savage's morning meal.

Rixs opened both eyes. "Insult her? I did no such thing." Rixs defended. "I refrained from sullying her innocent reputation!"

"Who said anything about innocent?" Rangus lifted a big bushy brow while towering over Rixs. "The point is, Syersi gets what she wants. Apparently, she wants you."

Rixs sat up on his sleeping box, clenching his teeth with the movement. His body throbbed from the beating he had taken when rescuing Syersi. "If she wanted me, throwing me in lockup is a peculiar way of warming my feelings toward her!"

"And throwing her overtures in her face is a wampish way of maneuvering around her pride, boy!"

Rubbing both hands through his hair, Rixs replied flatly, "I am obligated to another."

Rangus placed his hands on his hips, his rusty eyes narrowed. "You make it sound like a prison sentence!" He cocked his head to the side. "She must be very ugly."

"To the contrary. She is very pretty."

"Boy, no female wants to be thought of as a chain to be dragged around. Do you think she waits for you when you willingly abandoned her?"

It was true. Rixs had willingly left Cliessa. Running away from Syersi's kiss was nothing compared to running away from a life with his betrothed. A lump formed in his throat.

The subject abruptly changed when something caught Rangus's eyes. "What is that?" He walked over and pressed a large, calloused hand onto the sleep box, his massive arm flexing with the movement.

Rixs answered with a snort, "Something you sleep on."

Flaring his eyes to red, the Absolute growled, "You dare to be snarky with me, boy?"

The cocky expression faded and Rixs shrugged. "Since it seems I am to spend many nights in lockup, I thought either you or the Counselor felt sorry for me and had it placed here."

"Don't be a fool, boy!" Rangus barked. "I could care less where you sleep, and Chadgerwin would think sleeping on the floor would build your character! The fact that you have something nice to sleep on makes you a boob!"

Rixs laughed, though he tried not to. "Well then, a boob I am because I'm not the slightest bit ashamed to have it!"

Rangus narrowed his eyes and shook his head slowly. "We have a boob for a Shield! Come on, *Boob*! Time to get you out of here."

Unconcerned with the lacerations and bruises covering Rixs's body, the Sanguinary grabbed him by the arm and yanked him to his feet. Rixs sucked in a deep breath. The Absolute curiously looked him over. A gleam in his eye hinted that he remembered the beating Rixs had taken the day prior. He gave Rixs a hard slap to the back anyway and the young man managed to hide his whimper and grunted instead.

Lacking any pity, Rangus said, "Suck it up, *boob*. You shall live."

Rixs gritted, "This coming from the man who most likely stabs himself daily just for fun and eats his morning meals raw." His curiosity got the better of him and he had to ask, "Tell me, do you consider yourself a man, or a beast?"

Rangus growled before responding. "What kind of a question is that? What do you think?"

Rixs paused to contemplate his answer. "I think …" he began, but Rangus cut him off.

"I care not what you think! And why should you care what I think! I am, what I am. You are, what you are. Live with it! Questions only make you doubt."

Rixs breathed, mulling it over. "I am, what I am."

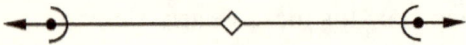

The sun's rays reflected off the six glittering palace spires and blinded Rixs forcing him to shut his eyes. It was lucky for him he could walk a straight line across the entirety of Gnomera with his eyes closed. He also noticed the smokey shape that approached and knew the figure's name even before the man called out to them.

"Ah, Rixs! There you are!" Chadgerwin greeted. "How was lockup … again? Did you sleep well?"

"He slept well, all right!" Rangus yelled loud enough that anyone within a respectable distance could hear. "There is a sleep box in Rixs's hole!"

The Counselor lifted his forehead and eyed Rixs. "Syersi must like you, Shield! Orris will be furious. He's consumed with jealousy already."

"Jealous of *me*? I sit in lockup!" Rixs scoffed. "Tell him I want to trade places!" There was a pause. "In fact, if I leave and return home, then there will be no need for Orris to be jealous. I am no Shield, and I don't belong here."

Rangus gave Rixs a sardonic grin. "What makes you think you

can leave?"

With a smirk to match, Rixs replied, "What makes *you* think you can force me to stay?"

Unless he was in a prison cell, Rixs knew he could leave whenever he wanted. Talent made it possible to avoid people who might see and stop him – especially guards.

Rangus, eager to please, gave the young man a demonstration and with an oversized hand grabbed Rixs by the neck, lifting him off the ground. Rixs grunted and his eyes popped wide as he clutched the Absolute's arm to relieve his neck of his body's hanging weight.

"Absolute!" Chadgerwin growled.

Rangus let go and Rixs fell to the ground. "That's why I think I can make you stay," he said with a sparkle in his eye. Rixs nearly planted his face in the dirt while he massaged his throat and coughed.

"What's more, I can run with the speed of a horse. Wait, I take that back. I can run faster than a horse, and just as far. My sense of touch is better, I hear better, see better ... well, maybe not see better, but I can certainly taste, and smell better than you." He sniffed the air. "I smell your blood."

Rixs grimaced. "Do ... you drink it? Blood, I mean. Do you like it?" He accepted Chadgerwin's hand to help him off the ground.

"My men know what it means when my eyes turn, and they fear it. I don't drink blood, but I crave its taste." Rixs turned pale and the Sanguinary laughed. "Relax, boy! I will not eat you today! We need your skills, but I might take a bite out of one of them." He nodded toward two guards who fidgeted under his scarlet gaze. Rangus laughed and grunted his contentment.

Flipping his hair out of his eyes, Rixs posed another question. "How many Sanguinary are there? How many other Talents?"

"Why am I answering all these questions?" Rangus snarled. "Chadgerwin, you are the one with the answers!"

Chadgerwin shrugged then clasped his hands behind his back as they walked. "Hard to know how many there are," he replied. "Talents are rare, and they like to remain anonymous. They like to blend in. Only Sanguinary stick out. They cannot hide what they are."

Rangus grinned wide at the comment, showing off large teeth.

"And what Talent am I?" Rixs had forgotten the supposed name for his own Talent.

"I cannot be certain until I find the binding, but I think you are Sagacious Talent." Chadgerwin beamed as he said it. "Lothorius had once mentioned a Talent of clarity – clarity of shapes, of space, or something to that affect."

Blood rushed to Rixs's head and it pulsed to the beat of an internal drum. Since his youth, his father had denied Talent existed and demanded, almost to the point of violence, that Rixs believe him. Deep down, Rixs believed his father knew the truth. *Sagacious*. The term rolled over his tongue.

Rangus whispered out the side of his mouth to Chadgerwin, but it was loud enough for Rixs to hear. "*Sagacious*. Kind of a sissy sounding Talent!"

Kicking dirt as he walked, Rixs said, "But a Talent, nonetheless. Tell me. What is the connection between the Source and Isslewood?"

Chadgerwin and Rangus simultaneously stopped in their tracks. Each glanced at Rixs, then looked around to see if anyone had heard.

Rixs eased their concern. "I made sure there was no one within hearing distance before I asked."

"Why would you ask such a question?" The Counselor failed to hide his surprise.

"Counselor," Rixs blew out between tight lips. "We know at least two groups look for the Source, and both have fingered Lady Syersi as someone they can use to get it. There are more likely other groups searching as well. I think you know more than you share. If I am to be Shield to the Empress Heir, I need the truth – time to come clean. Is the Source real?"

The purple glittering mountains of the Gneiss Curtain cast a bright hue of nearly white lavender over Isslewood. The light's reflection sparkled against the Counselor's dark skin as he thought his response through.

Few beyond the Intimus understood the Source. The power ignited. The Denier Cri born. The death it promised. Chadgerwin inhaled and brushed an imaginary hair from his nose.

"There are a few opinions," he began. "Some say the Source

must be real because Talents couldn't exist without it. Others say The Powers felt threatened by the Source, so they destroyed it and Talents are the residual of its power. Most say the Source was made up to amuse the people during the Long Wars and that Talent is a separate gift and has nothing to do with the Source." His dark, stormy eyes narrowed on Rixs. "I, personally, believe the Source exists, but I'll deny it in front of anyone."

Rixs stared at Chadgerwin. The Counselor was no fool and Rhages had mentioned that the crew's benefactor believed Emperor Lothorius was key to finding the Source.

"Tell me everything you know about the Source," Rixs almost sounded whiney.

"All in good time, Shield," the Counselor admonished. "Stay at Isslewood of your own free will and focus on Syersi's safety for now. Answers will come."

Rixs frowned and jerked his head to clear his hair out of his eyes. "Very well, but only if there is no interference in regard to Lady Syersi." He pointed a finger, wagging it between the two of them. "You will back me, no matter what I do!"

Narrowing his eyes, Rangus growled, "That depends on what you plan to do!"

The Soothe lifted a hand, gesturing calm. "You will have our support," he said. When Rixs creased his forehead, the Counselor added, "We swear it." Then he elbowed Rangus, who grunted with a nod.

And so, it began.

TWENTY-ONE

A plume of dirt puffed out around Syersi's head when her face hit the ground – again. She had lost count of the times she kissed the dirt. Luckily, her hands helped to break her fall – a little. Panting heavily, there was no way to avoid inhaling the thick cloud of sediment, and she coughed violently.

Stalling before having to get up and try again, Syersi dropped her forehead to the ground to catch her breath. A pair of thick-hide boots stepped in front of her nose. Face smudged with dirt and beads of sweat trickling down her temples, she pushed to her hands and knees, squinting into the sun as she looked up.

"Up with you!" Rixs ordered. "Try again."

"Orris will kill you," she hissed. "Even better, I will kill you myself!"

The two of them had left the great house alone. No guards. No escorts. No one except Syersi and Rixs. Observers were not allowed to watch.

Orris had objected, but he had no say in the matter. Chadgerwin and Rangus had sanctioned Rixs as Shield. They had promised their support and meant to follow through.

Rixs had explained why no one would be allowed to watch them. "I am training her, and I will be hard," he had said. "Those who watch will feel sorry for her and try to interfere."

"Bah! No one will feel sorry for Syersi," Rangus had quipped. "Have you noticed the way she treats people?"

It was Orris who had been outraged. "How do you plan to treat her? If you are forbidding people to watch, that means someone *should* watch!"

"She will be fine!" Rixs had bit back. "Maybe a little bruised." He smiled when the Commandant's face had turned red but dropped his grin and turned somber. "I require her to learn to protect herself and she will not like it. No doubt she will hate me by the end of the day, and all the days to follow."

"If you hurt her in any way," Orris snarled, "I'll rip out your teeth and use them to saw off your limbs!"

The Shield had grimaced.

There was a place north of the orchards and fields, nestled among the hills where a small stream danced its way around the landscape. It pooled into a shallow holding pond, before spilling over a cluster of rocks to continue its journey toward the river Giva. Rixs had discovered it shortly after arriving at Isslewood. The place made his chest hum with contentment, reminding him of his favorite river in Pax Valley.

It was at this place where Rixs brought the Empress Heir to train. And there was a happy thought that he could throw her in the spring to douse the flames of her temper when she threatened to kill him.

"I do not want to try again!" Syersi yelled at him, wiping sweat from her forehead with the back of her forearm.

Rixs stood firm without offering a hand to help her up. Syersi pushed herself into a sitting position. The training had just gotten started and already she was exhausted. *Stop being a princess,* he had said. *Walk this way, not that way. Tip your head forward. Put weight into your step. Do this. Do that.* She was tired of it! "There is nothing wrong with the way I walk!"

Placing hands casually on his hips, Rixs countered, "You walk like a princess."

"By The Powers! How dare I do such a thing!" she cried.

He wore nothing on his upper body, except the clashing vest

that had become synonymous with his name. It exposed the contours of muscle on his chest and abdomen which Syersi did her best to ignore. He never wore a smock or tunic underneath the vest and stood before her with a glistening sheen of moisture covering his gloriously well-blessed upper body. Syersi shook her head.

"Why are you sweating? You do nothing but shout at me and order me around!"

He cocked his head to the side, hair shifting around his face. "It takes effort to shout at you!" She slung a handful of dirt his way and he chuckled. "Come on, Pixee. Up."

"Make me!" she hissed, defiant blue eyes taking their stand against him.

"You bait me," he growled. "Very well." Without warning Rixs reached down and not-so-gently, grabbed her by the shoulders. With alarmingly little effort, he hauled her to her feet, shaking her before releasing his grasp. "Start walking," he demanded, his hair threatening to hang in his eyes. When she stood firm he added, "Please."

I will not cry! I will not cry! He will not get away with this! The thoughts whirled in her head, then she realized, he was getting away with it. Chadgerwin had let him bring her here without chaperones. Even Rangus had approved. Orris had been the only one to stand up for her, but he had been overruled by the two men who had the authority to do it.

A slight shove forced Syersi to move her feet. She jerked around and slung a quick slap to her tormentor.

Rixs clenched his teeth, bracing for the impact his Talent warned him was coming. Clamping his eyes shut did little to block her out as he tried to calm the rising heat of his temper. Before opening his eyes, he made sure he had reclaimed his patience.

Dangerously quiet, he said. "Start walking, Pixee. Practice what I've told you."

"Stop calling me that!" she cried. "I hate that name!" Then she stomped the ground with vengence while flinging and jerking her limbs.

Emerald eyes followed her. "Put your weight into each step.

Round your shoulders," he called as he walked behind her. "You are floating again. Stop floating. Stop walking like an Empress!"

Fire that matched the color of Sanguinary eyes in full bloodlust brightened her face as she swung around. "I am an Empress, you wamp! At least I will be! I do not know how else to walk!"

He pronounced each word with clarity. "Thus. We. Practice. How can you defend yourself when you worry over keeping your neck high and posture straight? How will you run for your life if your steps float gently across the ground!"

"It is who I am! You want me to forget all I've been taught!"

"You are wrong! I insist you remember what you have been taught! But you also need to learn to protect yourself ... to know enough to get away!"

"And why should I need to get away?" Syersi argued. "I will have *you* and my detail to protect me!"

"I told you!" he rumbled. "If, may The Powers forbid, you find your protectors have failed you, then it is *you* who must be your last line of defense!" She started to say something, but he shouted so loud the echoes of his words rang her ears. "Do it!" Veins throbbed in his neck. He could have boiled a pot of water for the rage that pulsed in his scarlet face. Steam could have whistled through his nostrils.

She jumped to his bidding, the threat of his voice prodding her forward, then backward, and in any other direction he ordered. Over, and over again, he exercised the Empress Heir, the fabric of her skirt tripping her up frequently. It was one more reason to see him skinned alive.

While Syersi and Rixs dueled each other, Mazzlin spied on them from her perch on the floating garden, suspended high above the palace courtyard. The battle of wills raged fiercely in the foothills of the Gneiss Curtain, much too far to see, but she was a Seer, so the great distance between them posed no obstacle.

The Guardian watched the unfolding events from Syersi's eyes. The first-hand view of Rixs's frustration and anger made goose bumps prickle her skin. His expressions told the story, and Mazzlin was thankful for the distance between them. If looks could murder, the First Daughter would have been buried a dozen times. A small fist whipped out of nowhere to strike Rixs's cheek and the Guardian gasped and slapped a hand over her mouth.

"What is it? What happened?" Chadgerwin asked, leaning forward with some concern. He, along with Rangus, sat at a table surrounded by colorful bursts of potted blooms and hanging vines.

Great care had been taken to make the floating garden an outdoor sanctuary – a hanging oasis that kissed the clouds. It was a place where the obnoxious noises of the world below chased the peace and stillness found higher than the treetops, but could never catch and dissipated unsatisfied into the air.

Mazzlin's stifled gasps cut the silence. She had an extraordinary gift and had been appointed as Guardian to Empress Saudria in the early days. The Talent could keep a watchful eye on the High Lady even though distance separated them. Lothorius had been ecstatic to recruit the Seer after discovering she could accompany him on his travels and report Saudria's activities to him. The only drawback was the pounding headaches Mazzlin suffered when she used her Talent for prolonged periods.

Hobb graciously stood beside her and cupped the base of her skull, absorbing the headaches into himself. Sanicle Talent was a blessing. The ability to spy on the two young adversaries, as Chadgerwin requested, the Seer needed the Physician to manage her pain.

"She hit his face! With her fist!" she exclaimed.

"Ha!" laughed Rangus, his big hand slapped the table with a loud crack. "Did he hit her back?"

Mazzlin sneered at him, "Really, Rangus! He would not dare hit the Empress Heir!"

Ignoring her, he declared, "I'll wager you, Chadgerwin. Before the day is out, he will lose his patience and hit her!"

Shaking his head, the Counselor leaned back in his chair, stretching his legs, and twirling the ornate metal goblet in his hand. "I say the Shield stays his hand. The man oozes with self-control."

"And Syersi oozes annoyance!" the Absolute retorted. "She can't help herself! A nudnik by nature. Mark my words, she will have him clawing out his freckles by the end of the day, and he will break down and hit her. It will be the boy's only defense!" Rangus took a big swig from the heavy goblet that had just been topped off by a voluptuous servant. He eyed her with craving before adding, "Unfortunately, I will have to kill him when he does. Too bad. I like him!"

Syersi's day dragged on. *Lead with your head! Put your weight into each step! You are floating again! Lift your leg higher! Swing your arms when you walk!* It went on and on. By the end of the day Syersi was sore, tired, and roiling mad. To further torment her, dark moist spots soiled her armpits. It was disgusting.

When the day was finally over, she walked toward her horse, itching to escape for the comforts of the palace, but Rixs had other ideas and snatched the reins from her. They would be walking back.

A shrill scream echoed through the Gneiss Curtain.

Rixs patiently waited for her to stop screaming, but when it became apparent that she was determined to scream until she got her way, Rixs began the long walk back to the palace, knowing that she had no choice but to follow.

TWENTY-TWO

Without command or compulsion, Rixs marched himself to lockup. He could have gone to his chambers to wait for two big burly guards to knock on his door and apologize for having to haul him off to *Rixs's hole*, but there was no point in waiting. He was exhausted. He had dealt with Syersi's bitter tongue all day.

The guards laughed as he marched himself into his open cell, flinging himself onto the narrow sleeping box. A meal arrived shortly after, and he gobbled it eagerly then settled in for the night.

Only a blink had past when the door to his hole opened the next morning. Rixs stretched out the kinks in his back then stiffly walked out the door ready to brave another day with the Empress Heir unless she chose to snub him for his cruel treatment of her.

The Counselor and Absolute had kept their word and Syersi waited by the horses, ready for another day of training. Despite her less than happy demeanor and crude rantings which spewed from her ethereal face, he was determined to ignore her fits and maintain patience throughout the day.

Patience was a virtue, and Rix's dwindled rapidly. Shadowed arms invaded the space around his head repeatedly. He could have blocked each swing with ease, but occasionally he allowed a strike to land to appease her temper. He dared not tell her he could see her swings coming, fearful that she would resort to screaming instead.

At least her swings were slow, and more importantly, silent.

While she brandished her tongue like the tip of a sword, Rixs merely looked amused, even pleased with the affect he had on her, and he did not let up. When she fell, he laughed which only fueled the flames.

"You need to pick up your feet like I showed you! Catch the material of your skirt with the tops of your feet as you walk so that it won't tangle around your ankles!"

"You try to walk in skirts!" Syersi howled, her bottom planted firmly on the ground. She grabbed the closest rock and slung it at him with all her strength. It was a good throw and would have hit him in the chest had he not caught it. "I should be wearing breeches!"

Shaking his head in a resounding *no*, he argued, "I told you, Pixee, gowns are your burden because of your status. You must learn to handle yourself while wearing them."

Syersi had pleaded with Chadgerwin to remove Rixs as Shield and begged for anyone else to be assigned to the post, even Orris. Her pleadings had fallen on deaf ears, and when she continued to whine, the Counselor had threatened to assign Rangus as Shield. Syersi had promptly shut her mouth.

"Come on. You are stalling! Get up!" Rixs said without offering any help.

Another strike against him. His strikes were accumulating rapidly. He never offered his hand when she found herself on the ground. He laughed when she fell. He mocked her by calling her *Pixee*. His list of strikes was a long one.

Again, he wore no shirt under his vest. Again, the delineation of his chest and abdomen distracted her concentration. He stood with feet apart, appraising her with emerald eyes, hands placed loosely on his hips, and head cocked to one side.

Syersi pushed off the ground and stood straight. "Where is your tunic?"

"Why would I wear a tunic? The heat is sweltering, and this vest absorbs it. I go without a smock or tunic when I can." Observing the direction of her eyes, a slice of a grin hinted at the corners of his mouth. He looked down at his exposed torso and flexed his muscles.

She huffed at him and said, "Well, I am hot too, but I am stuck in this dress! It is only fair that you should wear a shirt or something."

The gleam in his eyes and mischievous arch of a single brow spoke the words he held back. *You are welcome to remove your dress if you like.* The words he actually uttered were less intriguing.

"As I have said on numerous occasions, Pixee. Your position in Gnomera requires mounds and mounds of fabric. You must learn to …"

"Shut up!" she cried. "Once I am trained, you had better watch your back!"

"With pleasure, for then it means you have learned something," he replied with a grin that cared nothing for her threat. "But remember, I am no warrior. I teach you to defend yourself. If you want to learn to attack me properly, go to Orris."

He walked to the edge of the swollen stream and called out to her. "Now, if you can impress me, we can be done for the day. Remember, do not float! I do not want to see Syersi, the Empress Heir!"

Her steps began with heavy thuds as her shoulders swung in rhythm to each stride. *I may not impress you, but I promise, it will be memorable.* Picking up her tempo, her arms swung naturally, driven by the motion of her shoulders, and then it all clicked. Her body knew what to do and the gait became her own.

Leading with her head tipped forward slightly, Syersi let her feet stomp the ground while her hips swayed from side to side, synchronized with the movement of her shoulders. The motion was not a regal, fluid walk – it was a gutsy, self-assured swagger.

She felt powerful. Rixs was her prey. She knew what she would do when she reached him. Each time she had taken a tumble to the ground, her revenge had been rehearsed in her mind. Each time he laughed at her, the moves she would make became clearer.

One by one, the steps brought her closer to him, her stride long and purposeful, determined and strong. She could not hide the smile perched on her lips, even if she wanted to. For the first time in her life, she felt commanding, and it was all due to the simple technique of a walk. She was eager to see how her Shield would react to the surprise planned for him.

Rixs had to blink a couple of times. The woman approaching him with the bold, assertive gait of a warrior could not be the same female he had quibbled with over the last two days. Syersi, the Empress Heir floated over eggshells with her head held high wanting all to admire and adore her. This woman claimed the very earth she stomped on, her piercing gaze demanding all to respect her. His skin pebbled as he watched her gait eat the distance between them.

Dark spots on her bodice, moist with sweat, dampened Syersi's tight-fitting gown, accentuating her figure. Her shoulders moved in harmony with the tempo of an extended stride. She was walking fast, furious even, which exaggerated the swing in her hips, and he found himself distracted by her movements.

More disarming was the smile that radiated her face. It was more a tantalizing sneer than it was a smile, and it stretched wider the closer she came. He stared. This woman resembled nothing of the Empress Heir he had come to know. Rixs tossed the hair out of his eyes and crossed his arms over an exposed chest as though he was unaffected.

Syersi smirked to herself, a thrill hammered every fiber within her body. By the look in his smoldering green eyes, he was clay in her hands. He was steps away. Her mind worked through the plan one last time.

Control, Syersi. She inhaled through her nose and blew out gently through puckered lips to bridle her accelerated breathing. Rixs's eyes focused on her mouth. Swaggering straight up to him, she threw her fist into his stomach, stomping down on his foot at the same time.

Having admired her performance, Rixs hadn't paid attention to the changes in the space her body consumed. Suddenly, he recognized the signs of impending impact to his stomach and foot. At the last moment, he caught her fist in one hand and pushed her leg with his other before she could finish her intended attack.

Syersi knew he had fast reflexes and had anticipated his blocks. A quick knee was thrust up into his groin. Again, Rixs intercepted the move and pushed her leg down before cherished parts could be racked with pain. Adjusting to his countermove, Syersi hooked her foot behind his then pulled her leg backward. His balance wavered, and anticipating victory, she grabbed his shoulders while twisting her own body, and pulled with all her strength, grunting loudly with the effort.

Her goal had been to dunk Rixs in the stream, and at first it looked promising. He stumbled backward, kicking up water but didn't fall in. He grabbed hold of her and twisted his body to regain his balance, pushing off her in the process. Syersi tumbled into the stream belly-first, hitting the water with a large splash.

"Oh! Oh!" she yelled, the shock of frigid water instantly soaking her made her forget that just a step before she had been sticky with sweat.

A hysterical laugh echoed around her ears. Rixs had his head thrown back, hands clapping, and laughing so hard Syersi could scarcely believe it was him with the high shrill spilling from his throat. He grabbed hold of his stomach.

The Empress Heir had caught him by surprise, and amazingly, almost got the better of him. It was a good lesson to learn. Never underestimate an over-indulged Syersi. Though Rixs laughed, his chest swelled with pride at what she had almost accomplished.

The stream was little more than knee deep where Syersi sat, soaked and shivering. Each time she tried to stand, her gown, with its many layers now drenched in the frigid spring runoff, weighed her down like iron chains clamped around her waist. In the periphery, someone still laughed.

With legs spread out wide in front of her while her skirt surrendered to the water's current, Syersi hung her head. And the noise of a hysterical cackle pierced on. It grated at her spine and heated her blood though her muscles convulsed with cold. Narrowed blue eyes and chattering teeth faced Rixs's green gaze and echoing laughter. She had taken enough and dropped her head in her hands, then her slouched shoulders began to shake.

"I'm sorry for laughing, Pixee! I can't help it!" Rixs apologized between snorts and chortles.

The drenched young woman stayed silent with her face buried in her hands. Rixs stopped laughing. Only the bubbling stream made noise around them.

"Pixee?" he said gently as he stepped toward her. "Lady Syersi?" When she didn't respond, he crouched in front of her, fearful he had laughed too hard at her expense. "Pixee," he said with a gentle voice. "Please, no tears."

There was no reply.

"Come. Take my hand. Rangus will tear me apart if you freeze to death." He touched her fingers gingerly to ask permission.

Moving her hands from her face, she blinked up at him with blue eyes that matched the color of her frozen lips. He smiled and stretched out his hand.

Syersi inhaled and gripped his wrist securely with both hands, and as he began to pull her up, she tugged – hard. Using her weight to throw herself backward, the Empress Heir pulled with everything she had until her head and body were submerged beneath the water's surface. Rixs toppled over with a huge splash.

It was her turn to celebrate. Wave after wave of whoops and hollers rang into the hills. Syersi threw both hands up and cried, "I-I did it!" She jumped and splashed, suddenly no longer cold. A finger pointed in his face. "I f-f-finally b-bes-ted y-you! A-a-admit it!" She plopped into the water next to him.

Chuckling, Rixs rolled into a sitting position, the water cutting and swirling around him. Water dripped from his hair into his face. "I admit it!" he laughed. "You outsmarted me! Savor the feeling, Pixee. It will not be repeated." He shook a finger at her while his eyes crinkled at the edges. She grinned back.

Though it was a victorious moment, the water did not warm for the celebration. Syersi shivered violently. Rixs stood, hefted her into his arms and carried her to a large rock where he set her down.

"Ummm," Syersi hummed. Heated by the sun, the stone warmed her bottom and legs as she hugged herself. "Th-th-thank y-you," she managed to say, through chattering teeth. She stared at him as he removed his soaked clashing vest, nearly biting her tongue in two. The Powers had created an exquisite specimen the day they shaped the young man's torso. She was ogling a little too much. When his eyes flitted to hers, she blushed and hurriedly smoothed her dripping skirt.

"Tell me something," she said as Rixs adjusted himself on the ground. He looked at her and waited. She continued, "Why do you insist on calling me *Pixee*?"

He leaned back on his arms and thoughtfully sucked his bottom lip. "Hmm ... why do I call you Pixee ...?"

Syersi nodded enthusiastically, still shivering.

There was a long pause before he finally deliberated. "It is the name of a flower. You remind me of it."

"I remind you of a flower?" she replied with a lift to her forehead, eyes blinking as her mind turned. "Pixee ... I have never heard of it."

Again, Rixs considered her before he answered. "The flower is called *Pixee's Solitude*." Suddenly finding himself blushing, his fingers nervously began plucking the blades of grass in front of him. "It grows in my homeland. I have never seen it anywhere else."

Watching him slaughter innocent blades of grass, Syersi frowned as she asked, "Why does it remind you of me?"

He shrugged. "The flower is blue and looks much like a tiny rose bud. It is surrounded by spindly, long thorns that form a cage around it. It is unique ... very beautiful, but it draws blood when you try to touch it."

She pursed her lips. He had not answered her question. "Try again, Rixsander. You described the flower. Now, why does it remind you of me?"

A small pebble in hand, he threw it, then spoke with hesitation. "The blue reminds me of your eyes," he said.

His own eyes pierced her with a gaze so intense, Syersi had to look away. She found herself staring at the grass.

The remainder of the answer might very well land Rixs in lockup, again, but he pushed on anyway. "Remember, you asked for it, so have mercy on me." He paused then continued.

"I see a beautiful woman who lives inside a thorny cage ... she hides behind it. I think she has much to offer the world, but no one knows it. Like Pixee's Solitude, thorns and barbs get in the way when you try to touch it. In the same way, Lady Syersi wields thorns and barbs, while her blue velvety petals and sweet fragrance are tucked within." He dared to look up.

She blinked at him repeatedly. She was thinking.

He had called her beautiful and in the next breath compared her to thorns and barbs. To be complimented or to be insulted was the dilemma she faced. Cooly, she said, "Perhaps that is all she is – thorns and spindly barbs."

"Maybe," he agreed. "She is the only one who has the power to decide." Their eyes locked and they sat in silence for a long while, each refusing to look away.

Finally, Syersi nodded, her voice was soft. "Thank you. Now I know why you call me, *Pixee*."

TWENTY-THREE

Thumbing through the records that had accumulated dust over seasons cycles and seasons cycles, Rixs sneezed again. Each time he fingered a binder, dust tickled his nose.

"Ahh-chew!" He wiped his mouth and nose with his forearm.

Somewhere within the records chamber, a tome or binding captured the secrets of the Source and he was determined to find it. Chadgerwin and Rangus, too cryptic in their answers to his questions, had been no help to him so he dared to help himself.

The records chamber was a wondrous place. Shelves lined every wall from floor to ceiling, and on every shelf sat hundreds of tomes, bindings, and scrolls. There were thousands in total and it would take seasons cycles upon seasons cycles to search their contents. Of the truths or tall tales that breathed within their covers, there was only one Rixs desired. The single binding that gave up the secrets of the Source.

Rixs was poised high on a climbing frame perusing one of the highest shelves when the door opened and Chadgerwin walked in. "Oh! I didn't expect to find anyone in here!" he exclaimed. "You gave me a start, young man!"

Rixs had opened a thick, heavy record bound in nearly black leather and was searching its contents. "Sorry, Counselor." He inhaled as if to say something else, then stopped.

"Go ahead. Out with it," Chadgerwin urged.

Rixs hesitated before saying, "I need answers."

There was silence while Chadgerwin scratched his bald and scarred head. He studied the Imperial Shield with stormy grey eyes.

Perceiving an internal struggle, Rixs tried to help the Counselor along. "Viktus knew something, and he was willing to abduct the First Daughter because of it. I think he believes the Source is real and is connected to either Isslewood, Emperor Lothorius, or Lady Syersi."

He replaced the binding on the shelf deciding it held nothing useful. "If people believe the legend of the Source is true, it places the Lady in danger. I need truth and honesty, not secrets."

Rixs turned away, grinding his teeth when Chadgerwin said nothing. He pulled a sorely faded red binding from the shelf and opened it. Suddenly, he jerked around and released his anger on the Counselor.

"My ability to protect Syersi is not based on strength, or swordsmanship! I am not a strategist nor am I refined in tactics. I depend on avoiding danger – not fighting through it. I need to know what is out there … to see what comes, otherwise, I am no good to her!"

Chadgerwin exhaled. "To share the secrets you ask, I require your undying loyalty to Syersi."

"You already have it. I am Shield."

Brows creased deep in the Counselor's forehead. "No. I demand absolute fealty to Gnomera for as long as you live." He watched Rixs tense. "Swear to stay forever, and I will tell you what I know."

Forever. Rixs was unprepared for such a demand in exchange for a bit of information. The image of Cliessa's radiant face and golden curly locks spilled into his thoughts.

The township council had matched them at a young age with the expectation Rixs would marry her when he was old enough. It was the Pax Valley way. But he had left, not ready to be a husband, but with the intention to, one day, return and fulfill his obligation. He wondered if she had asked the council to annul their match, or if she waited patiently for him to keep his promise. Which was the greater betrayal? Never returning to marry her, or marrying her because he was forced?

Rixs had changed. When he had left Pax Valley, he was a hunter with an exceptional ability to mark targets, forced to marry a girl he had not chosen. Now, he was a Talent and the Imperial Shield charged with the responsibility of protecting the Empress Heir of Gnomera. That difference had changed his world.

His eyes slid past the Counselor to the hidden passageway on the opposite wall from where they stood. He had discovered it while exploring shortly after he had moved into the great house but had not been able to figure out how to open the entrance. The Intimus had shown him several secret passages. This one had not been among them. It might have been omitted on purpose, or maybe they were unaware of its existence.

The open space, hidden behind a wall of shelves, called to him. It tunneled downward past his ability to identify where it ended.

"Rixs!" the Counselor snapped. "I need a sign of your complete allegiance and life to Lady Syersi and Gnomera!"

"You ask much of me, Counselor. I need time to think on it." Rixs swiveled back toward the shelves and slipped the dull binding back into its proper place without looking at it.

Chadgerwin's features hardened. "Well, until you decide, we have the matter of Prince Tangorio. He comes for the Spring Celebration and we must not underestimate his motives for coming."

"Tell me about him." Rixs said. He jumped off the climbing frame, landing easily on the floor, like a cat. Standing to full height, he adjusted his vest.

Chadgerwin's eyes widened with a sparkle. "Tangorio is like his father, hungry for power, and very sly. He is no fool, and I imagine he has marriage on his mind."

Muscles twitched in Rixs's jaw. "The Tangerine plans to marry Lady Syersi?"

A grin simmered over the Counselor's features. "*Tangorio*," he corrected Rixs's slight, "is heir to the powerful land realm of Tangrah. Seasons cycles past, King Tangrin proposed a betrothal between Tangorio and Syersi. Lothorius gave no answer."

Void of expression, Rixs nodded and turned to thumb through more bindings. Chadgerwin shrugged and engaged in the same, while glancing at Rixs's tense face. They searched in silence, each consumed in their own thoughts, while throwing out the occasional question. Rixs cast intermittent glances toward the hidden passageway while Chadgerwin stewed over Rixs's hesitancy to pledge his life to Gnomera.

After the prolonged quiet had climaxed to a deafening ring in their ears, the Counselor could hold his tongue no longer. "I demand your loyalty, Rixs," he said while rubbing the scar on the back of his head. "So, I will tempt you with this." He leaned forward and lowered his voice. "But if you tell one soul, I will cut out your tongue," Chadgerwin rumbled. "Rangus is not the only dangerous Talent in Gnomera." He held Rixs's green eyes hostage, then he whispered, "Lothorius possessed a Source."

Rixs froze, all thoughts and words wedged tight between shock and disbelief.

Amid the silence, while the two stared at each other, a dull and faded red binding sat obscurely on the fourth shelf down from the ceiling, hidden among the thousands of tomes and bindings. Had the young Talent taken the time to scan its leaves, he and Chadgerwin would have had a much different conversation – equally mind shattering.

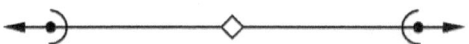

Rixs tossed in his bed, the hot and muggy night making it difficult to find sleep. Somewhere in the distance the night-watch was laughing. Rixs could have used a good laugh. His own thoughts would not leave him alone and he flipped from one side to the other.

Lothorius had owned a Source – had possessed it. The implications of that single piece of knowledge made his head spin. It changed everything Rixs thought he knew. Then there was the issue of his allegiance. If he wanted to know more, he would have to decide between two women, Cliessa and Syersi.

They were as similar as night and day, hot and cold, calm and

turbulent. Betrothed to one and protector to the other, they both
needed him. One needed him to marry her as he had promised, and
the other needed him to protect her from – what? What would Syersi
need because of her father's secrets? What did she know?

Too many thoughts bombarded his now throbbing head, and
the heat of the night made it unbearable to sleep. Sliding out of bed,
Rixs pulled on his breeches. Not bothering with a shirt, he grabbed
a single blade from his vest, slipping it into the back of his waistband,
then ducked out the door of his chambers.

He knew where he was going, and before long, the mysterious
passageway hidden behind the wall of shelves, stood before him. He
studied it. Talent had let him find it. He hoped Talent would help
him discover how to open it.

No obvious lever or knob flattered the wood. He felt around the
shelves. He pushed and pulled on the bindings and tomes. His foot
tapped along the floor panels. He eyeballed every small detail closely
then closed his eyes to critique the details again. Nothing revealed
itself.

A defeated sigh escaped into the shelves as Rixs leaned in and
pressed his head and hands onto the wood molding, his body's full
weight leveled against the frame. There was a creak and slight shift.

Rixs startled backward. Nothing seemed to indicate that
there was an opening. He placed a hand on each side of the panel
and pushed. There was only a slight shift in the shelves. Then he
bit his lip, grasped the shelving frame, and pulled. The panel of
shelves shifted and creaked open.

TWENTY-FOUR

A scream bubbled up through Syersi's throat and she shot up in her bed, clutching her chest. Hair matted to her sweat-soaked forehead. Trembling, she used her covers to wipe her face while images of her mother's dead body made her muscles shake.

"Lady Syersi! Are you all right?" a guard barked, barging into her chambers with another close on his heels. They both fanned out through her three large rooms, checking every corner and cranny.

She answered in a breathy voice, "Yes, I ... I just had a bad dream is all."

"Dear child!" Mazzlin's short body materialized at her bedside. "I heard you scream! Did you have a nightmare? Oh, tell me about it! I had a bad dream myself! I was being chased by Rangus. He was threatening to stitch my mouth shut!" She shuttered. "Then I could not get back to sleep, so I was tossing and turning thinking to myself that I would never sleep!" She drew in a breath. "I just knew that I would be all grouchy and groggy in the morning, all because of Rangus!"

Syersi rolled her eyes and cradled her head in her hands, scolding herself for crying out. Mazzlin would never leave her side now. She was stuck with her Guardian for the rest of the night.

"Come, come, don't be stubborn! If you talk about it, you will feel much better!" There was a pause. "I always feel better when I've aired my bad dreams. Well, I am waiting Syersi! You must …"

"Mazzy!" the Empress Heir cried. "How can I tell you anything when your mouth is moving?"

Snapping her lips tightly together and clasping her hands in front of her, the Guardian blinked thoughtfully.

"It was the same dream." Syersi pulled the covers up over her chest and shivered, even though just moments ago she was hot and perspiring.

After a quick thorough search, the guards informed her the rooms were clear. She thanked them, and they left to take their place outside her door once again. Syersi shifted to find Mazzlin's jaw hanging wide open.

"What?" Syersi asked.

Mazzlin shook her head in awe. "You thanked the guards!"

Syersi rolled her eyes. "Go away, Mazzy!" She flopped back into her pillows and pulled the covers over her head.

"Find love, my dear, and you will rest easier at night," Mazzlin said.

"What?"

"You were born to love. If you find love, your mind will be at ease and the nightmares should go away."

Syersi squinted her eyes and scrunched her nose at the Seer's flare for outrageously whimsical comments. It required great patience and interpretation to understand her Guardian.

"I am tired, and you speak gibberish, Mazzy. Go!"

The demand fell on deaf ears. "Everyone is born to love … to *find* love." Mazzlin made herself comfortable. "But you, my sweet child, you were born to *give* love. Wonderful things will happen when you do!" She placed her hand to her heart.

"I hear buzzing, Mazzy. The annoying kind."

"That boy is just the one for you!" Mazzlin cried as she clapped her hands.

Syersi stared at her eccentric Guardian. "Are there eggs in your basket?" she asked with narrowed eyes.

Mazzlin blinked. "What eggs? Well, anyway. Rixs obviously has influence over you. How often have we encouraged you to say a kind word to others? But *he* comes along and you are saying *thank you* to the guards!"

Springing to her hands and knees, the bed covers tangling around her ankles, Syersi cried, "You think that courtesy to the guards, translates to falling in love with Rixsander?" The Empress Heir covered her eyes. "You have lost all your eggs! I should keep my own mouth shut and not encourage you to ramble on." She flopped back into her covers. "I need sleep, Mazzy."

The hint went unnoticed. "Fall in love, Syersi. It is your calling. When you give your heart away, you will understand. Trust me." She winked. "If I were you, I would take a hard look at Rixs!"

As though she had solved Gnomera's greatest crisis, Mazzlin gave a single triumphant nod. Eyes shining, she patted Syersi's cheek, and left.

Syersi watched her Guardian glide from the room. Not the least bit tired, she pulled the covers over her head as an image of a young man with sandy hair took up a big portion of her mind. A tingle in her chest began to itch.

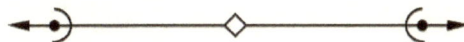

The little time Rixs slept, he slept like the dead. Up before the first bird's song, the enthusiastic Talent was eager to get a jump on the day.

He scrambled to be a nuisance in the baking house where the cooks all loved and adored him. He pandered for a quick bite to eat, and because he was the darling of their infatuation, he could raid food whenever he wanted, unlike everyone else, and he always got away with the very best of whatever they made.

After giving a quick peck on the cheek to each female cook, he hurried out the door to face the sun just winking over the Gneiss Curtain. The morning air was fresh and moist, the dew not yet evaporated from the flower petals and grasses adorning the walkway. He breathed in spring as if he could capture it. It was aging fast and would soon give way to the hot and heavy days of summer that would have Isslewood sweltering.

Ormolu felt sluggish and muted after the panic of the farmers' market only days prior. No vendors peddled their goods. Absent were the voices competing to be heard. Though there were plenty of people out and about, when compared to the throngs that had jammed into the city's square during market, Ormolu seemed desolate.

Debris from the explosions had been mostly cleared, and reconstruction was well under way. The distant pounding of mallets was testament that soon the city would be put back together. Soldiers walking the streets signaled that the First Counselor, on behalf of the absent Emperor Lothorius, was committed to seeing Ormolu mended.

Rixs walked the streets hoping to find Rhages again. Now that he had confirmation of the Source, there were questions he needed to ask his friend, and not knowing how to contact him, coming into the city was as good a start as any.

The main square had a few vendors set up, a young man sitting on the ground being one of them. With his back propped against a stone wall, it was clear that the man was unable to walk or stand on his own. A short table next to him displayed an assortment of pendants, rings, and trinkets.

As he walked by, Rixs nodded his head and vocalized a friendly *hello* while eyeing the fine work neatly organized on the table. Dark brown hair nodded in his direction.

"When you have more time," the peddler said, "perhaps you could come back and let me show you some beautiful pieces for your sweetheart."

Rixs thought on it. He had no sweetheart, but he stopped anyway, thinking he might be able to ask questions about the crew. "I have time now," he replied as he eyed the man whose body and legs sat unnaturally still.

A wide grin brightened the space above the table. The man waved his hand over his merchandise and boasted, "Take a look. I have some very fine pieces!"

The work was first rate. Rixs squatted next to the table and scanned over all that had been artistically displayed. Pins, chains, and bracelets of fine design caught his eye. With an approving nod, he extended a hand, "I am Rixs," he said. "Did you make these yourself?"

The man grasped his hand in a firm shake. "Annon, and, yes, this is my work."

Rixs's eyes widened at what he saw. "You are very talented."

Annon beamed, clearly pleased. "Perhaps you have a sweetheart that deserves one?"

Expecting golden curls to flow through his thoughts, Rixs was surprised to find no such image. There was no desire to select a keepsake for Cliessa even though he had plenty of coins. Chadgerwin rewarded him well as the Imperial Shield, and he could have obtained anything he wanted, but he wanted nothing.

The Shield confessed, "I do not have a lady, but if I did, I would deal with you."

There might have been a hint of disappointment, but it was quickly replaced with conviction. "Perhaps a piece for your mother then?" Annon's voice held hope.

Green eyes exhaustively assessed the jeweler. Rixs knew his story must have been an interesting one. He had been staring and realized it too late.

Annon looked at his legs. "I cannot walk ... or stand," he said as a matter of fact. "That is why I took up this trade."

"I ... I ..." he stammered, horrified that he might have been gawking. "Forgive me, I was not trying to be rude ..."

"Do not make yourself uncomfortable, friend," the disadvantaged man's voice was calm, his expression pleasant, and he gestured casually with a shrug of his shoulders. "It is one of those things. A nasty horse accident and ... here I am."

An awkward silence stalled their conversation before Rixs spoke up and expressed remorse for the stranger's terrible misfortune. Annon smiled and, upon Rixs's encouragement, launched into a short narrative of his love of horses, an accident while riding, and the result that left him without the use of his legs. Yet the man had grasped onto life with fervor and recreated himself into a master jeweler.

After listening to Annon, Rixs knew he must purchase something and fingered the pieces on the table. Finally, he picked up a simple, elegant pendant that reminded him of his mother. She had never worn a necklace before, but he was sure she would like the one he held.

"This is the one. My mother will love it."

Annon frowned in dissatisfaction. "Do not purchase from me out of pity."

Blushing with self-condemnation, the Shield defended his actions. "You have shown strength that surpasses even the Talents, but make no mistake, I do not pay for things I do not want. Will you sell to me or not?"

Their eyes dueled for a few moments. Payment was payment, and earning a living was hard. The corners of Annon's mouth lifted. "Very well. I only hope you can afford to pay my price."

Rixs grinned and pulled out his pouch then added, "I hope you would not take advantage of a lowly Shield."

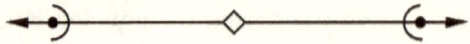

Gritt lazily walked toward the outer skirts of Ormolu with Rixs perched on his back. After asking around town about a giant, dark-skinned man with a big frizzy head, and no luck in finding him, he set off for Isslewood. Gritt meandered at a caterpillar's crawl and Rixs found he enjoyed the easy pace.

He might have missed the form if there had been no movement. With so many grey shapes taking up space in his colorless world, it was always the shifting of grey that caught his attention. His eyes moved in search of the figure's owner.

Against a large, neatly stacked pile of wood next to a nearby shack that someone undoubtedly used as a dwelling, a male form stood. The figure soundlessly ran a hand over what would have been his face. His Talent, Sagacious, never gave any detail in the contours of the physical form, so Rixs had to depend on his normal vision to provide the specifics. While he could not know where the man was looking, he could feel the prickle of eyes studying him.

Something niggled at him. Something about the silhouette was not right. Then it smacked him in the eyes. The man was not there, and yet, he was.

Had it not been for Sagacious, Rixs would have never uncovered the contours of a man's silhouette standing very still against the stacked chunks of wood. Using normal sight, only a vacant spot met his hungry stare. That was the trouble with eyes – they could be deceived.

TWENTY-FIVE

A Shade had been confirmed to him. It was all Rixs could think about as he raced back to Isslewood. There was no doubt in the truthfulness of a Talent that had been postulated to exist but had never been proven.

Shaken by what he had seen, or rather, what he had not seen, Rixs tracked down the First Counselor as soon as Gritt's hooves crossed the grounds of Isslewood. Using his gift, he found Chadgerwin and Rangus in the records chamber.

"A what?" Chadgerwin asked again, to make sure he had heard correctly the first time.

"A Shade," Rixs repeated, nervously pacing back and forth, excitement surging through his veins.

A growl vibrated the air. Rangus contorted his face into a deep frown and sat forward in his seat, his eyes brightening from rust to red.

Chadgerwin's voice resonated with hope. "You are certain?" he asked.

Rixs nodded, almost violently.

"Your Talent detected the Shade?" the Counselor questioned. "You could *see* him with ... Sagacious?"

"Yes!" Rixs replied, impatient with the continued questioning.

Eyes of bright scarlet, the Sanguinary looked Rixs over. "A

Talent that can detect a Shade! It's too good to believe!"

With a slight shake of his head, the Counselor exclaimed, "The implications are astounding!" He rubbed the deep scar running along the back of his head. "Do you know what this means?"

Rangus cut in with his thunderous voice, "It means we now have the upper hand! Boy, would you recognize him if you saw him again?"

"No." Rixs shook his head. "I see only the shapes that fill space. They are more like grey shadows that are precise in size and shape. If I need details, my normal sight provides that." Rixs suddenly slammed a fist on the table. "Start sharing what you know! I have given you honesty about my ability. I will answer nothing else until you give me something in return!"

The Absolute shared a look with Chadgerwin. "Found your fearlessness, did you, boy?" Rangus scowled.

The Counselor gave a nod to Rixs. "You know what I need," he reminded.

Rixs pushed back. "Why tell me the Emperor possessed a Source if I am not trustworthy?"

Rangus turned his blood-stained glare on the Counselor.

"Stop it Rangus! I had my reasons for telling him!" Chadgerwin defended. He turned to Rixs. "This is not about trust. I want to secure your loyalty to Gnomera, and to the Empress who will rule it."

Rixs jerked his head to toss the tufts of hair from his eyes that sparkled with excitement and resentment. "Forcing loyalty seems contrary to common sense," he said. "How can loyalty be trusted if it is forced?"

He did not mention that his loyalty had been settled the night before when he wrestled with the shelves in the records chamber and had effectively opened the hidden doorway. It had been tricky, but once opened, Rixs was rewarded with a stairwell that swirled down, down, down until the last remaining glow of light surrendered to the abyss of darkness, and yet the stairs descended deeper still. It had been a lengthy journey to the end.

No eyes could have penetrated the darkness so thick that it

plugged his nostrils making every breath a struggle. Had it not been for his ability he would have been utterly lost. Each step he took was as clear as if it were midday. And with each step, a thousand of them, Rixs mulled over his loyalty.

It was one thousand steps of thinking until he reached the bottom where a single door had waited to be discovered – waited for daring hands to push it open.

A throat cleared, pulling Rixs back from the cavern hidden far below them. Blinking a few times, he blew out through his mouth, then slowly pulled a short blade from under his left arm.

Chadgerwin inhaled with anticipation. Rangus stared on.

"Very well, Counselor. You win." Rixs flexed his chest and held out his arms with the blade in his left hand. "I stand before you and swear my loyalty to Lady Syersi, Empress Heir of Gnomera, until the day I die."

With two sets of eyes frozen to his movements, Rixs slid the blade across his right palm. As the blood oozed and pooled, he fisted his hand then slapped it against his chest, over his heart.

The other Talents stared at him. They had threatened and begged Rixs for something more than a promise. His blood declaration had come as a surprise. It was done. Rixs, the figurative Shield, had become the sworn Imperial Shield of Gnomera by blood.

Rangus slapped Rixs on the back, hard enough that the young man lurched forward. Chadgerwin clasped his wrist in a strong grip of approval.

"I am well pleased, Shield. Sit down." The Counselor waved a hand toward a chair. "Now we talk." His eyes bored into Rixs then delved into history.

"Long before the Talents were born – ages before the Long Wars began, there existed a source of power that could bestow sensational abilities to those lucky enough to possess it. No one knows how the source of power came to be created, but it held the Talents – Sanguinary, Sanicle, Soothe, and so on."

Ears red hot with eagerness tuned into the Counselor, not wanting to miss a word. Rixs cut in, "How many Talents exist?"

Rangus barked with a gritty voice, "Shut-up, boy, and listen!

Who knows how many exist? You were a forgotten surprise!"

"If Chadgerwin knew I was Sagacious, how could I be forgotten?"

"I said I thought you were," the Counselor replied. "Until we find Lothorius's binding, we will not know for certain."

"What else could I be?" Rixs continued to question.

"Just shut up and listen!" Rangus slapped the arm of his chair and the wood snapped under his strength, followed by a loud c*lank* as the arm fell to the floor. "Now look what you made me do!" he growled.

"My fault?" Rixs exclaimed in protest.

Chadgerwin loudly cleared his throat. "If I may continue," he grumbled and waited for them to be silent. "Whoever was lucky enough to possess the source of power, claimed all Talents." He looked intently at Rixs. "Can you imagine all of our single abilities in one individual?"

The idea was incredible and horrifying. One person with the abilities of Mazzlin, Hobb, Rangus, Chadgerwin, the Shade, and even his own ability would be scary enough, but to have all the Talents – Rixs shuddered at the thought.

"They would be unstoppable," he whispered.

The prospect of wealth and prosperity played through his head. With such power, much good could be done with it. But with power came the temptation of greed and the need for more power.

Chadgerwin watched as Rixs worked through the implications. "Yes, Rixs, they would be unstoppable. Before the Long Wars, I understand there were many who possessed sources of power. In fact, that is how the Long Wars began. Such power tested the very essence of an individual," the Counselor said as he placed his hands behind his back and began to pace slowly.

"These men were known as Denier Cri. They had the opportunity to make the world a better place. And they did ... for a while ... if the stories are to be believed. Yet greed seeped into their hearts until power and wealth became all they cared about. Skirmishes between the Denier Cri began. It was not enough to have wealth and power, they needed to know which among them was the strongest, the most superior. The skirmishes blended into war, then one war spilled into another, until …"

"The Long Wars," Rixs mumbled. He tossed his head to clear the hair from his eyes.

Chadgerwin nodded. "The Long Wars."

A question tumbled from Rixs's mouth. "Why didn't people stop the, De … Den …"

"The Denier Cri," Rangus finished. "There was only one way to kill a Denier Cri," he said. "The source of power had to be destroyed."

"So, destroy the source of the power and be done with it," Rixs pronounced.

Rangus shrugged and leaned back in his ruined chair. He swung his large legs on the stone chunk of table in front of him as he spoke, "No one knew the secret, but it is obvious they figured it out, because eventually, the Denier Cri were all killed off during the Long Wars."

"And so was most of humankind!" the Counselor exclaimed. "Humanity had to start all over again."

Rixs soaked in his words. It was too fantastic to believe yet too believable to disregard.

"Back in the day, thousands of seasons cycles in the past, the name of the source of power was common knowledge. That knowledge was how they killed off the Denier Cri, but over time, its identity has been forgotten. Anyway, the Denier Cri took whomever they wanted to bed, leaving an unknowing posterity in their wake. We believe the Talents are a residual of powers the Denier Cri possessed. The power of the Denier Cri became known simply as the Source. And there is your connection between Talents and the Source, Rixs."

After a moment of stunned silence, the young man hopped out of his chair, placing both hands on the top of his head. He paced wildly back and forth as he spoke. "And Viktus thinks that the Source is here at Isslewood," he exclaimed. "He's trying to find it so that he can turn it over to whoever has hired him and the crew." He mumbled something to himself then looked up at Chadgerwin and Rangus with the light of realization brightening his features.

"If Viktus finds the Source and knows what it is, why would he bother to give it away? He would be a fool to give away such power!"

A look passed between the Absolute and Counselor. The young Talent was bright as well as gifted.

Enlightened further, Rixs cried out, "Wait!" His veins pulsed with energy as his eyes flashed to the Soothe. "You told me the Emperor possessed a Source! Did he have all the Talents? If he did, why did he leave? I mean, is that why Lady Syersi's mother died? Because someone was looking for the Source and she got in the way? Is that why the Emperor left? To protect his daughter?" Rixs rubbed a hand over his face. The accelerated pulse of his heart told him he was on to something.

Half of the Counselor's mouth crooked up in amusement. "Something like that."

The young man was sharp and dangerously close to the truth. Even though Rixs had sworn his loyalty and allegiance to Syersi and Gnomera, Chadgerwin was not entirely certain Rixs was ready for the entire revelation.

"Lady Saudria was murdered by a Shade. And as you have seen for yourself, Shade Talent has the capability to create the illusion of invisibility. That is what makes them so dangerous. You never know who has Shade ability unless they decide to tell you, and no one has actually seen one ..." Chadgerwin's eyes lit up and a grin pulled his scar tight across his cheek. "Until you."

"How do you keep them from sneaking into Isslewood?" asked the Shield.

"You don't!" answered the Sanguinary. "It is very difficult."

Rixs's features turned smug. "You need me."

Chadgerwin came to stand in front of the Talent and placed a strong, firm hand on his shoulder. "Yes, we need you to protect the Empress Heir. Your Sagacious ... your second sight, makes you the perfect Imperial Shield. Do you honestly think I would be foolish enough to allow some stranger to win that bet and become Syersi's protector without an extraordinarily strong motive? And now that you have seen a Shade ... well, to put it mildly, Rixs, we will not let you go."

TWENTY-SIX

Orris pulled his black horse next to the Empress Heir then raised his hand, signaling his men to stay back. Casting a sideways glance at the Commandant, Syersi patted Juju's neck and shifted her eyes anywhere but toward him. She had been ignoring him since Rixs had become Shield.

"Commandant," her voice was syrup. "Whatever have you been doing with yourself these days?"

He grinned, surprised that she had spoken to him, even if she would not look his way. Orris had made no secret of disliking Rixs or holding back his disapproval of an outsider being elevated to the rank of Imperial Shield. It also rankled the Commandant to have the outsider so close to the woman he considered to belong to him.

His brown eyes scanned over every curve of her figure before he replied with a low voice, "I have been cleaning house, my Lady" He waited for it, knowing his comment would trigger some sort of response from her. She did not disappoint.

Gracefully, Syersi turned to him with wide blue eyes. "Cleaning house?" she asked. "I am happy you have finally found a chore worthy of your skills, Orris."

He inhaled a deep breath of patience. "I see you are in a teasing mood, Lady Syersi. Well, you will be happy to know that yes, I did find a chore worthy of my skills, and am happy to say, you no longer need fear your abductors will ever see the light of day … or inhale another breath."

Her dark brows drew together. "Orris," she said slowly. "What have you done?"

With impeccable posture the Commandant sat upright on his horse, his well-defined frame pulling his uniform tight across his chest, arms, and thighs. Striking in his own right, it was his presence that made the man. His bearing drew people to him. Syersi was no different though she resisted better than most.

Catching the sweep of her eyes, he smirked and replied, "If Rixs was even a pebble's weight of the Shield he should be, he would have taken care of the problem before returning to Isslewood."

Syersi gasped, catching his meaning. "You executed them!"

Drawn by squeals of delight, Orris turned away from Syersi's hateful glare to find the retinue cheerfully engaged with Mazzlin and Rixs. His features darkened as he watched the females practically pouncing on the young man.

Not inclined to let their conversation drop, Syersi prodded, "Ignoring me only tries my patience, and your avoidance convicts you. Why would you kill them?"

Orris deflected her accusation. "Since when do you care about what happens to people?"

Syersi flinched at his words.

"Come now," he contended. "You know better than anyone. They sealed their fate the moment they abducted you. When the leader hit you, he determined the level of his suffering."

Her color blanched. Orris was Commandant of her father's Lothorian Guard. Delivering punishment without conscience or hesitation would have been easy for him. He had always been swift and exact when it came to matters of justice, especially when it involved her safety.

"Did you even try to be merciful?"

"Humph! Do you really want to know?"

She frowned. "Orris! You swine!"

Stern dark eyes challenged her. "Swine? I can live with that, Lady, as long as you are safe."

The chatter surrounding Mazzlin and the Shield gave Syersi and Orris a place to turn their glares. Rixs courteously fended off question after question from the girls surrounding him, only to be greeted with a barrage of giggles after every answer he gave. It was as if he told the funniest story they had ever heard each time he opened his mouth. Though he tolerated the attention with graciousness, the squint of his eyes exposed his true feelings.

The verbal fondling was too much for Orris. "I need to throw up," he sneered. "What do they see in him anyway?" he asked. "He's a nobody from nowhere important who happened to get lucky and was rescued by Gnomera's Empress Heir."

Syersi pulled back on Juju's reins, the horse prancing in her place. "Why, Orris. I think you sound jealous. Not very flattering on you."

A dangerous chuckle rumbled around her. "He is just a fleeting fancy. You will tire of him, just like all the others, and I will still be here – waiting. You shall see."

She waved him off. "Keep telling yourself that, Commandant."

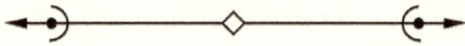

Not only was her temper at its finest, but Syersi could see Rixs had reached the end of his rope, as well. The day, like so many of the others, had been contentious. He wanted to start their day with a lesson in archery. She wanted to throw blades. Rixs won.

The complicated task of nocking an arrow tested the dubious cooperation between them. She refused to try, and he would not give in. If anger could be measured in smoke, there would have been plumes of it billowing from Syersi's ears.

"I don't like archery!" She threw the bow then stomped on it before storming off.

"*Piixeeee*," he warned. "Get back here!"

Not bothering to listen, she marched to the swollen stream's edge and plopped to the ground.

Rixs rolled his eyes at the blue sky. Warned by Chadgerwin that she would push him to the edge of his sanity, the Counselor had not exaggerated. She was combative more than she was cooperative, and he was ready to dunk her in the stream and hold her under.

Rubbing a hand over his face, a groan vibrated in his throat. A Shade jaunted the countryside past the protection of Tower Wall, his identity a mystery, yet it was Rixs's responsibility to make sure the stubborn girl pouting at the stream's bank was protected from him. Complicating matters, Rixs had never done anything like this before and had no idea what he was doing. All he knew was Chadgerwin trusted him, and failure meant Syersi's life would be in danger.

Syersi sat with her feet in the water, staring at nothing and grumbling loudly. The stream seemed to grumble back, roiling and sloshing as it charged over everything in its path. Footsteps crunched behind her then Rixs's firm body dropped down next to her. He said nothing but gazed over the bubbling stream. The corners of his mouth hooked upward.

Peering with a slanted gaze, Syersi absorbed the serenity of his face as he looked out over the water. The hard lines of his anger had faded, and a hint of happiness glowed in his expression. Running his hand over the ground, he picked up a rock and threw it into the stream.

He turned to face her, and she nearly laughed. Wayward hair hung in his eyes. It was a constant battle for him, and she gave his misbehaving locks a quick flick with her finger.

"Well?" Her blue eyes blinked at him expectantly.

"Well, what?" he mumbled, raising his forehead in confusion. Then he tossed his head to clear his eyes.

"Were you planning to apologize?"

"Why would I do that? I came over to listen to the stream. It calms me when a certain Empress Heir grates on my nerves." He crooked a grin then picked up another rock and threw it. It hit the water with a *plunk*. "Can you hear it speaking?"

Syersi rolled her eyes. "Water does not speak."

"Oh, yes it does. Just listen."

She turned an ear toward the stream. "Why, yes," she indulged. "I hear it! It is angry. It complains."

"Complains!" he exclaimed. "What makes you think the water is angry?"

Waving her hand over the water, Syersi enlightened him. "Look how the water boils and churns! It gurgles angrily and attacks everything in its path. Look how it assaults the rocks, breaks off branches, and carries away anything it can! That is anger."

Rixs considered her explanation a moment then shook his head and chuckled while the Lady frowned at him. He found a round, smooth rock, studied it for a moment, then tossed it into the churning water.

"Do you know what I see and hear, Pixee?" No reply was expected. "I see a bubbly, jubilant stream. The water is not attacking the rocks. It is happy and plays with them. It teases and dances with everything it surrounds. Look ..." Rixs leaned in close, pointing to the water's surface where brilliant flashes of sunlight reflected in their eyes. His cheek barely touched hers and a tingle stretched between them.

"It is all about your attitude – how you look at the things around you. See how the sun sparkles on the surface?" his voice was soft and low, almost a whisper, then he paused. She could feel his breath on her skin. "The water smiles at you. Can you see it?"

Syersi was afraid to move – afraid to breathe – fearful of interrupting the closeness they shared at that moment. His cheek grazed hers and she could feel the tingly fizzle of his touch. He waited silently for her answer, but she dared not speak for fear he would pull away, and the special moment would be broken. Something deep within her chest cramped.

Suddenly, Rixs jumped up and extended his hand toward her. "Come on, Pixee. Let us shoot some arrows."

The connection between them was broken. She blinked at him then took his hand and let him pull her to her feet. The Shield had coaxed her into cooperating. She ignored the cramp in her chest and stared at the hated bow and arrow he held out to her. Then to Syersi's own surprise, she took it.

TWENTY-SEVEN

The unabashed Rixs dug into the feast set to satisfy the eager rumblings of a hungry belly. He piled his heavy golden plate with several helpings of everything – roast pig, baked onions, hawknuts, yams, bread, and more.

Rangus eyed the boy's appetite then noticed Syersi, who eagerly scarfed down her food like a homeless urchin. It kept her mouth too busy to insult anyone, and the Absolute raised his mug to her silence. She blinked at him curiously.

Orris was enthralled watching her put food in her mouth. Then his eyes shifted to the Guardian and he shuddered. Mazzlin had stuffed her cheeks full. His eyes locked with the Counselor's as if to say, *that is disturbing!* Chadgerwin raised his eyebrows in muted agreement.

Oblivious to their stares, the Guardian chewed and chewed, while her own eyes never wavered from her charge.

"Why are you staring at me, Mazzy?" Syersi mewled. "Stop it! It gives me chills!"

"Oh," Mazzlin smacked her lips, voice wavering. "I was thinking. Forgive me for gawking."

Chadgerwin leaned over, concern edged in his voice, "Are you all right, Mazzlin? You seem ... pre-occupied."

She whispered back, "Have you noticed?" Her voice was

guarded. The Counselor raised his greying brows in a silent, *noticed what?* She answered his eyes. "The child rubs her chest."

His eyes popped wide, and he flipped his gaze toward Syersi, whose hands tackled her food brutally. Chadgerwin cocked his head and lifted his shoulders. "The only unusual thing I see is that the girl is eating ... for once."

Mazzlin hissed, "You men never notice anything beyond your own nose! I have been watching her the last few days, and I am telling you, her chest bothers her! It is beginning! I know it!"

Chadgerwin straightened in earnest. "If you are correct then we have a problem." His eyes squinted toward Syersi.

A soldier hurried into the dining hall. "Sire, we must speak!" All eyes snapped to the soldier, but he stood in silence, his eyes beseeching the Counselor for a private conversation.

"You may speak here," Chadgerwin encouraged.

The soldier glanced around the table, then he announced, "There has been a sighting of the Emperor!"

"My father?" Syersi gasped and looked to her Intimus for confirmation.

Suddenly, Rangus was on his feet. "Impossible!" he yelled. "Is this some type of prank?"

The guard's voice quivered as he spoke. "N-no, A-Absolute. The scouts reported it and were certain. It was Emperor Lothorius. He was sighted riding in the direction of Sentur."

The Absolute's eye sockets looked as though they were filled with blood and his skin glowed crimson. "It is not possible!" he snarled in a voice so low it could barely be heard. Everyone stood in tense wariness. Even Chadgerwin looked uneasy.

A decanter shattered into hundreds of pieces against the wall. Amber liquid raced in rivulets toward the floor. Everyone jumped to their feet and backed away from Rangus. He plunged his hands into the platter of meat, his hands fisting until pieces of pork oozed through his clenched fingers.

"Rangus!" Chadgerwin barked.

Rixs pulled a blade just to be prepared for whatever came next. The move did not go unnoticed by the savage Talent who shook violently. Narrowed eyes targeted Rixs like a snake focused on its next meal after weeks of famine, and he slowly stalked toward the young Shield.

Wrong thing to do, idiot! Rixs berated himself.

A wave of calm pushed through the dining hall. "Everyone out." Chadgerwin ordered with smooth composure. He looked Rangus's way and forced another wave of calm directly toward him, remembering too well, the one time he had Soothed the powerful Sanguinary, he nearly died. "Rixs, please take Syersi away."

A second request was not necessary. Everyone cleared the dining hall, leaving only Rangus and Chadgerwin behind.

"Steady, old friend," Chadgerwin Soothed. "You don't want to take your lust out on me. I'm a nasty-tasting bit of flesh."

Rangus clamped his eyes tight and he pushed his hands into the wiry curls blanketing his head. Pieces of pork from his fingers were left clinging to his hair. "Stop Soothing, or you will know how ineffective your Talent is on me!" he snarled.

Throwing up two hands, each lanced with scars, Chadgerwin capitulated. "Done!"

Several moments of guttural breathing vibrated the silence around them, then the Absolute spoke, his voice thick and fragmented as though sifted through gravel. "What could he possibly want?"

Eyes staring at nothing, Chadgerwin shook his head slowly. "His return can only mean one thing." He looked at Rangus. "He has most likely found out the truth about the Source."

Scarlet veins bulged along the Absolute's skin, making him look like a demon from the land of everlasting fire. Bloodlust triggered the insatiable urge to slay something. Anyone with eyes only had to glance at Rangus to know what he craved.

The Counselor cringed as he watched the Sanguinary sink his teeth into his own arm. Blood pooled and Rangus watched it curiously, drooling as he talked. "I should have killed him four seasons cycles ago!"

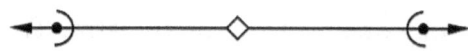

The layers of Syersi's skirt purled about her feet in graceful waves as she hurried through the corridor. Rixs led her with a hand at her back, while Mazzlin and Hobb pulled up the rear. The Guardian's legs moved in double step to keep up. Orris had peeled away with his guards to retrieve full details about Emperor Lothorius and his exact whereabouts.

The wide ornate staircase that circled upward along the glittering stone walls came into view just ahead of Syersi and Rixs. Upon seeing it, the Empress Heir stopped and spun around to face Mazzlin and Hobb.

"I want answers!" she demanded. "What was that all about in there!" She pointed toward the dining hall.

"We must get you to your chambers, child," the Guardian coaxed. "We can talk in the morning after a good night's sleep."

Hobb added, "It is for the best, Lady Syersi. Mazzlin and I need to make sure Chadgerwin is still alive, but first we must see you to your chambers. The answers will come in due time."

Slanting her eyes at Hobb, Syersi sneered, "Oh! The silent Physician has an opinion, after all?"

He inhaled deeply, then fell back into a silent observer.

Mazzlin's frown sounded vividly in her rebuke. "Your rudeness offends me. Start acting like the ruler you will be in just a short time. Now, we will take you to your chambers. Rangus in one of his moods is a threat to anybody!"

An idea sparked in Rixs's eyes. "I will get her to her chambers," he said eagerly. Syersi whirled on him, dirty look in place, but he quickly whispered to her, "Trust me."

Eyeing the two of them suspiciously, Mazzlin relented and nodded to the young Shield. She grabbed Hobb's arm and they hurried back in the direction they came. Back to Chadgerwin and Rangus.

Once they were out of sight, Rixs leaned in close enough that his lips brushed against Syersi's ear. "Come!" he whispered with a wide toothy grin. "Time for mischief!"

Suddenly, he was dragging her by the arm. They sped through

the halls, Syersi's face stretched in a smile and her small feet moving quickly to keep pace with his long strides. Heads gaped at them as they passed in a blur. He pulled her one way then backtracked to another. Some halls he took twice. And he mumbled as he hurried.

"I should have thought of it sooner! It will be perfect! Give her the edge. I know it!"

"Are you talking to me? Or have you lost your mind?" Syersi bit out as she nearly ran into a column. "Slow down! You almost made me run into that ..."

"Shh!" He threw back. "Let me think!"

"Stop dragging me!" she hissed and pulled her arm out of his strong fingers. "Where are you taking me?"

"Keep your voice down," he hushed, though he knew there were no ears close by.

In no time, they were pulling the heavy doors closed behind them. Rixs spun around, bouncing on the balls of his feet, his bright eyes meeting Syersi's confused gaze.

Curious eyes, the color of blue moons mused over her surroundings. "The records chamber," she announced. "It is an interesting place for a tryst, but I could have come up with better." She blushed just enough to set her cheeks glowing.

"What? A tryst?" He looked at her in bewilderment then strode to the far wall. Running his hand along a section of the crowded shelves, Rixs fumbled over the wood and molding until he found what he wanted.

Syersi frowned. "I thought you wanted to seek a place for a bit of romance."

"Romance!" He laughed and she glared at him. "No, Pixee. This is what I wanted to show you." Firmly grasping the edge of a shelf, he pulled hard. The entire panel, shelves, and all they held, swung out toward them to reveal a dark passageway.

TWENTY-EIGHT

The clicking of sandals reverberated in the dark winding stairwell that led down, down, down. The noise echoed loud enough that it seemed the stones trembled with each click of Syersi's footsteps.

"If you ever find yourself in a position of hiding to save your life," Rixs said, his voice bouncing off unseen walls in the inky darkness. "You might want to remember to remove your sandals."

The stairs took them deeper into a thick shroud of unending blackness. Goosebumps prickled Syersi's skin and the fine fibers of hair at her neck were stretched to attention. She clutched Rixs tightly.

"I want to go back!" she whimpered. "How can you possibly see?" Holding a hand in front of her face, all she saw was black. She even struggled to be sure her eyes were really opened and not closed.

His voice cut through the darkness. "I can see, Pixee."

"I do not believe you," Syersi insisted edging over to the other side of the stairwell.

Rixs yanked her back sharply, wrapping an arm around her waist. "Careful! There is no railing to the left! It drops off."

She stopped and patted at the thick blackness until her hand met with his cheek. "How do you know?"

He held her hand then eased her to the far side of the step. "Ease your foot to the edge of the step where the wall should be."

She did as he said, and her foot dropped off the edge. She

screamed and he pulled her close. "I have you," he reassured her. "Though you just shattered my ears."

"You can see! But if you can see in here, that would mean ..." She stopped short of saying it.

"Go on," Rixs coaxed. "You have hinted about it before."

"Talent?" she breathed. He chuckled. "I knew it!" she shrilled. It was the wrong thing to do. Her voice bounced back at them over, and over, pummeling both their ears.

Rixs sucked in air. "Please watch your voice," he said.

"I knew there was a reason Chadgerwin and Rangus wanted you around!" She paused. "What is your Talent?"

"Chadgerwin told me he thinks I am Sagacious."

"Sagacious," she repeated. "I have never heard of it."

"Chadgerwin says it is rare."

"This is unbelievable! What can you see?"

"I can see the drop off," Rixs said. "It would be a shame if I had to gather up your mangled body at the bottom of the stairwell." He took her hand and placed it on the wall. "Keep your hand or fingers touching this wall," he cautioned. "It will guide you and keep your senses oriented."

Her fingers dragged against the rough stone. Touching the wall gave Syersi back her bearings, and the inability to see no longer made her dizzy. Her legs moved forward confidently with her hand sliding along the wall, though she still clung to Rixs until the very last step had given way to stone ground, and a single door.

"Open it," Rixs told her, his voice sounding muffled in the tight space.

"How? I can see nothing!" she whined.

"Pixee, open it. Work it out for yourself, or we can stand here all night."

Grumbling, Syersi groped along the door frame and fumbled to find a handle. She pushed. No movement followed – not even a tiny creak.

"It will not open," she announced with finality.

"That was a poor attempt."

She tried to back away. "You have the Talent to see! You open it!"

A strong arm held her in place. "What would Rangus say if he were here? Would you shame him with your pitiful attempt? Put your shoulder into it," Rixs ordered.

"Shame Rangus!" she hissed. Patting at the air until her palm found the contours of his warm chest, she groped upward until her fingers found his face. Promptly, her hand swung to deliver a slap.

"Strikes, Pixee!" Rixs growled, holding her wrist with a strong grip. He had intercepted her slap.

"How do you do that?" she shrieked through gritted teeth.

Instantly, Rixs's hand was over her mouth. "Do you want to wake the dead? Just open the door!"

A loud "grrrgh" rasped from her throat as Syersi did her best to shove at the door. She pressed and pushed as she grunted and groaned with each effort. When her attempts failed, she threw herself at the door.

Her form was as clear to Rixs in the inky darkness, same as when they were running through the corridors and he grinned as he watched her efforts to budge the door. He stood back with folded arms, thankful to The Powers for the Talent that allowed him to see her struggles. He stifled a laugh repeatedly but eventually took pity on the girl and reached out to give the door a push at the exact moment she gave it a hard shove. It opened with a loud groan.

In the blackness, she heard a *clap, clap, clap*. "See? I knew you could do it!" he praised.

Pride swelled in her chest, giving her newfound courage. With outstretched hands patting at the air in front of her, Syersi led the way through the door into the unknown. Rixs smiled and followed her in.

The hollow echo of voices answering voices in undulating waves, revealed the enormity of the cavernous chamber. Syersi's courage quickly faded, but Rixs was not about to let her give up. He led her around the cavern, having her trace the wall with her hands to feel the size and shape of its space.

The stone was abrasive against her palm and several times she tried to pull away. Each time, Rixs stepped next to her placing a hand at the small of her back to resuscitate her bravery. They continued to pace their steps.

"You might be able to see," she whispered, the darkness demanding quiet. "But how do you know there is nothing lurking down here? Like a demon or a monster?"

He chuckled. "I have been here before and explored every nook and cranny. It is completely safe."

Syersi sucked in a breath. "If I had Talent, I could be as brave as you." She paused and groped for Rixs. He answered by extending a hand where she could find it. Once in his grasp, she asked, "Tell me, are my eyes opened or closed?"

"I cannot see like that," he explained. "I see your form but not the details of your features. I need my eyes for that." He gripped her shoulders. "I can see the lines of your shoulders, arms, head." He tussled her hair. "But I cannot see the color of your eyes, the definition of your nose, or the shape of your mouth." He gave her chin a playful bump with his fist.

"It seems impossible. How can you make out forms in the blackness? Even if you do have Talent."

Her question caused him to hesitate. It had always been a secret. Even his own mother had no idea of her son's ability. "Well ... my eyes see darkness, but my *second sight* sees the forms that take up space. I see the space filled and empty. Everything has its place, even if it is moving – it has a place in a moment in time and takes up a portion of an area. It is manifested to me in the form of a shadow." He thought for a moment, then continued. "Every shadow has a different shade of grey, from the lightest to the blackest. I see them all."

Her ears perked up to hear every word Rixs spoke. Each time Syersi slowed, engrossed in his revelations, he would nudge her on.

"I have placed a great deal of trust in you, Pixee. I have never shared any of this with another soul."

"Your trust is not misplaced, Rixsander," she whispered. "Thank you."

They walked along the entire chamber with Syersi's hands pressed against the jagged uneven surface, following the wall until she had paced every turn, every cubby, every bulge, and indentation of the massive space. The stones were like splintered bones of the dead beneath her hands and they reached out to prick her skin. She squealed.

"There is nothing that can hurt you," Rixs reminded her repeatedly, never venturing more than an arm's length away.

The night rolled on with Rixs requiring Syersi to perform various drills to familiarize her with the vast chamber. He was determined to have her know her way from wall to wall, and corner to corner. With no way to get her bearings within the shroud of darkness, her feet frequently veered from their intended course, but he was there to steer her in the right direction.

Rixs positioned the Empress Heir in the middle of the room and told her to listen to the sounds around them, then he had stepped away and left her vulnerable to the murky and penetrating chill that pressed upon her skin.

Syersi blinked frantically, not sure if her eyes were opened or closed. "Rixsander! Where are you?" she cried. The fine hair on her arms flared to life.

"Shhh, I am here," he comforted, reaching out to touch her arm. She grabbed him and held on tightly. "Listen," he said as he pulled away again. "What do you hear?"

"Nothing! I hear nothing!" she cried. "Take me back! I want to go back."

Rixs almost pulled her into his arms but held firm. "Pixee," he responded gently. "We will leave soon. Now listen." Then he lowered his voice and chided. "If you say you hear nothing, then you are not opening your ears. Calm you heart and be still."

Wrapping her arms around herself with teeth chattering, she drew in a deep breath then blew it out through pursed lips. Moment after moment crept by and she listened to the silence.

Then there was a faint noise.

Rixs watched as she tilted her shadowed head toward the sound. "What do you hear?"

"I hear … I hear … your breath! I can hear you breathe," she whispered in triumph, blinking through the dark void.

"Good," he praised. "What else?"

The silence screamed in her ears. Then, there was the faintest *tap, tap, tap*. It was familiar. Syersi searched through her mind.

"A drip!" she laughed nervously, vaguely remembering the damp stone along the far wall. "I hear a drip!" If she could have seen his smile, her heart would have melted.

"See, Pixee. I knew you could do this."

When her courage was emboldened, Rixs walked away from the young woman, then toward her without making a sound. He circled her. Each time he walked by, Syersi was able to feel the air as it stirred with his movements. He forced her to challenge her fear of the suffocating blanket of darkness by allowing the air around her to help her know her surroundings when her eyes could not.

The night's training had been long and tiring. Syersi said, "Can we go? We have done enough for one night." Emphasizing her point, she swung to face him and planted her hands on her hips.

A booming laugh came from behind her and instantly she knew her mistake. She pivoted in the opposite direction.

"You should beware of laughing at me," she teased as her own voice cracked with a smile. "I might throw you into lockup."

"Oh, no! I beg for one last indulgence," he propositioned. "Guess the number of steps I am from you."

Syersi moaned into the darkness. "Why?"

"Please, Pixee. We stay here until I get my answer."

A sigh heaved into the dark. "I can hardly know … perhaps four steps?"

He challenged her. "See if you are right."

His voice indicated the mark she should follow. Within the darkness, the long pleats of her dress swished like waves around her ankles with each step she took. One. Two. Three. Four.

Syersi extended her hand in front of her. There was nothing. She moved her hand to the right and felt nothing. Biting her lip, she slowly extended an arm to the left and nearly cried out in fear when she felt the firm lines of a chest. Then she squealed.

"I did it!" Her high voice echoed around them.

There was a roar of triumph. Rixs plucked up Syersi and swung her in a circle. Caught up in the moment, he pressed a hard kiss to her cheek, only realizing what he had done by the intake of Syersi's breath. Her giggles stopped.

There was a moment of awkward silence as Rixs planted her firmly on the ground and cleared his throat before summarizing the lesson. "Remember, even when you cannot see you are not helpless. Let your other senses speak to you."

Her hands had never left his shoulders. "I am still ignorant of the purpose for bringing me here."

The Counselor and Absolute had not wanted to tell Syersi about the Shade. They believed it was unnecessary to upset her. Rixs had disagreed. Knowledge was power and he was Imperial Shield, the one appointed to determine how best to protect the Empress Heir. If he expected Syersi to be her own last line of defense, then she needed to know.

"Rangus will rip my heart from my chest for this, but ..." He hesitated.

Syersi waited patiently, still holding onto his shoulders.

"A Shade was spotted in Ormolu," he blurted.

She sucked in a breath and blinked into the black void. "What do you mean? How? No one can see a Shade."

Rixs announced flatly, "I can."

Syersi's grip tightened on the young Shield. She remembered his words explaining his Talent. He saw space when it was filled and space when it was empty. His ability took on new meaning. She whispered her realization. "The Shade takes up space. You see his form!"

"Yes," Rixs confirmed with a tight smile that went unnoticed in the heavy blackness. "Though my eyes saw nothing, my Talent saw his form. You may not be able to see the Shade, but in this place, he cannot see you either. This cavern makes you equal."

"But what if we run into each other ... you know ... because we cannot see?"

"No," Rixs was shaking his head. "By the time we are done with this place, you will know every crack and crevice. You will run and know when to stop. You will know where to turn —

when to turn. This place will be as comfortable to you as the palace corridors, and you will be at home in its darkness." He took her hand and squeezed it. "May The Powers forbid it, but if there is no one to protect you, Pixee, then you come here and make your stand on equal ground."

TWENTY-NINE

Early dawn was winking over the Gneiss Curtain by the time Rixs and Syersi dragged their tired bodies toward her bed chamber. Already knowing that someone waited within, Rixs held up a finger, signaling her to wait in the hall. He had a good hunch who he would find but took precaution just in case. Of course, Syersi could not be bothered to listen and followed him in. He shot her a daggered glare.

"Thanks for waiting," he snarled quietly. She smiled and shrugged.

Both pairs of eyes traveled to a pudgy limp body slumped and sleeping in the chair next to Syersi's bed. Mazzlin snored lightly.

"Looks like you are safe!" Rixs whispered with a grin. "Goodnight, Pixee!"

"You cannot leave me to face Mazzy alone," she frowned.

"But I can. You are the one who ignored my order to wait outside. Be strong!" Rixs chucked her shoulder with his fist, bowed, then walked away.

"Coward!" Syersi hissed at his retreating frame. He turned around, nodding his agreement. Some things were too terrifying to face, and Mazzlin's lecture was one of them.

Before Rixs could make his full escape, the Guardian snapped awake. "Oh! By The Powers! Where have you two been!" she exclaimed, a hint of anger resonated in her normally sweet voice.

"Rangus will have your hide, Shield! There are soldiers all over the grounds looking for the two of you!"

"Why?" Syersi was confused. "I was with my Shield."

"They wait for you in your chambers," Mazzlin told Rixs, but he had already seen the two grey forms approaching the chamber.

The door burst open. Just as he had expected, Rangus had crashed through and in a flash breached the space toward Rixs, grabbing for his neck.

The young Talent pivoted and dove to the side, countering the direction of Rangus's groping hands. Blood-colored eyes followed the Sagacious around the room. The Sanguinary spun on his feet, showing an impressive amount of agility for one so large.

"Hey!" Rixs cried, dodging another swipe from Rangus, this time coming from the opposite direction. Syersi and Mazzlin screamed as a chair tipped over. A beastly growl filled the chamber.

Mazzlin pulled the Empress Heir close to her. "Stop it, Rangus!" Syersi screamed. "Chadgerwin! Do something!" But the Counselor stood at the door watching the tussle with a combination of muted anger and amusement.

Had Rangus chose to pull his dagger, the outcome would have been swift with Rixs gutted and scattered across the floor. But Rangus preferred his hands when tearing apart his victims. That gave Rixs a miniscule chance of surviving.

A fleeting thought to draw his own blade came and went. A blade would only provoke the Sanguinary further, and Rixs dared not do it.

The Sanguinary sidestepped several times, but Rixs had eyes in the back of his head – of a sort. His Talent was just as good as several pairs of eyes. He was being maneuvered into a corner where a table and chair waited to block him in.

"What have I done? At least tell me why you are ..." Rixs didn't have time to finish. The enraged giant reached out to grab him and the young man pitched his body into a backward roll over the table, landing in a crouch on the floor behind it. Without pause, Rixs thrust himself into a forward roll under the table toward his attacker. This was accomplished so quickly that as Rangus lunged forward, leaning over the table to grab the evasive Rixs, the young Talent was standing up behind him.

"Stand still so I can tear you apart!" the Absolute's shout caused veins to pop out of his neck and forehead. Then Rangus graced Rixs with the full dose of his Talent.

The blur of a body leapt at Rixs with such speed, it caught the young man off his guard. A meaty palm thrust into Rixs's chest with Sanguinary force, the blow sent Rixs flying across the room. He slammed against the back wall with a loud crack, and his body slumped to the floor in a heap.

Oversized boots clomped on the floor, and a pair of large, calloused hands seized the collar of Rixs's clashing vest, roughly lifting him off the floor.

Rixs struggled to draw in a breath. He gritted his teeth as searing pain spread across his chest.

"Hold up, Rangus," Chadgerwin finally ordered. "Let us not kill the boy ... just yet. Give him a chance to explain."

Breaking free of Mazzlin's grip, Syersi stomped over to the Absolute of the Gnomeran armies and jumped to her toes to slap his chin, not quite tall enough to reach his cheek. He flicked an annoyed sneer her way then released Rixs, who wrapped an arm around his chest as he stumbled to a chair.

Each breath filled with fire, he struggled to say, "You might tell me what I did to deserve this!"

Chadgerwin had taken a chair nearby and leaned forward in it, looking nothing like the calm, appeasing man Rixs had come to know. The Counselor pierced him with cold eyes and a grim countenance.

"You disappear with the Empress Heir, have her out all night without telling anyone, and do not bring her back until dawn, and *you* wonder why you deserve this?" The Counselor laughed. "Come now, Rixs. I know you to be a clever man! By The Powers! I have Orris, at this very instant, scouring the palace and grounds looking for Syersi!"

"That, alone, merits a serious flogging!" Rangus snarled.

"I am the Shield!" Rixs burst out then winced in pain. "You

should trust me!"

Syersi stepped to the door and commanded a guard to fetch Hobb. Walking back to the Counselor, she stuck her finger in his face. The long nail which threatened to poke his eye startled him to lean back.

"Mazzy is a Seer! If you had used her Talent, you would have known that I was perfectly safe!" she hissed, her face flushed in anger with dark circles under her eyes from lack of sleep.

The sound of a chair scraping against the floor forced Syersi back two steps. Chadgerwin loomed over her, his voice authoritative and impatient. "I did utilize the Guardian's ability! She could see nothing but black. There was no light whatsoever. Not even the slightest hint of a shadow! I thought you might have been buried alive!"

A pucker hid the smile threatening to burst free on Syersi's face. She gave a giggle while sharing a conspiring glance with Rixs. He maintained an impassive expression but managed a wink without anyone noticing. The chamber was their secret.

An acute interrogation followed. *Where were you? Why will you not tell us where you were? What were you doing? What could possibly keep you occupied till morning? Did you violate the First Daughter?* The last question caused a hearty laugh from the young Talent, and he paid for it dearly as his chest wrenched in two. When Hobb's face finally poked through the door, Rixs could have kissed him.

"I will not have Syersi listen to this insulting line of questioning!" the Guardian chided. "Out with all of you! I must help her to bed!" Before they knew it, Mazzlin's hands were pushing them out the door.

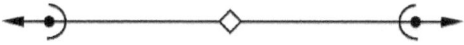

"Two broken ribs," Hobb declared, casting a wry look toward the Sanguinary. "If you want to kill Syersi's best hope for protection, Rangus, then you had better find our young Shield's replacement before you eliminate him!"

The only reaction from the Absolute was a loud grunt as he

scratched his neck.

The young man relaxed into the comfort of his bed and moaned while the Physician's Talent worked miracles on him. In the background, Chadgerwin's voice drummed on like an unwanted rain shower, probing Rixs for more answers. The questions brought no results, so the Counselor took matters into his own hands to *help* him along.

The warm mist that settled over Rixs's skin in a soothing velvety sheen could have easily been mistaken for Hobb's handiwork. Reluctance to answer Chadgerwin's questions rolled into cooperation.

"I was training her ... finding a place in the palace that can give protection if she ever needs it," he said almost groggily. The effect of Hobb's and Chadgerwin's artistry turned Rixs into a blob of putty, but his mind was still exceptionally sharp. Turning a distrustful eye on the muscular dark-skinned man, Rixs added, "Are you pulling your tricks on me, Counselor?"

"I beg your pardon?" Chadgerwin responded innocently, but he was impressed with the young man's ability to tell when Soothe was at work.

Talkative for a change, Rixs surprised himself by explaining why he and Syersi had disappeared for so long and swore that he had behaved with the utmost propriety, keeping his hands to himself. Both, Chadgerwin and Rangus, pushed to know the location of the secret chamber but even under the powerful influence of Soothe, Rixs somehow resisted.

"How many times did you kiss the Empress Heir?"

Chadgerwin arched a brow. "Obsessed with kisses, are we, Rangus?"

"You may trust Rixs, but he is still a man – with manly urges, and he had Syersi to himself all night!" the Absolute grumbled. "Throw some more Soothe his way, Chadgerwin."

"I can hear you, you know," Rixs mumbled.

A sensation, not much different to a moist warm breeze raced along Rixs's arms, legs and chest. His skin absorbed it, and it saturated his blood. Like flickering flames skittering over dry ground, the heat settled into muscles, warming him to his core and murmured peace to his mind.

Chadgerwin nodded to Rangus signaling to him with a knowing smirk, to ask his question. The warrior narrowed his brows and spoke. "Did you take advantage of the Lady Syersi ... especially while you were in the dark?"

Rixs flopped his head to the side and squinted at the Absolute. "She is beautiful when she wants to be," his unfocused eyes looked at the wall.

Rangus growled and thrust a finger at Chadgerwin. "See! I knew it! He wants her!"

With eyes closed Rixs finished his defense. "Let me finish. I did not take her there to kiss and ravage her. It was a lesson. I ignored her lips – though they called to me."

Chadgerwin raised his eyebrows. Rangus gave a single clap, snapping the air. "Her lips call to him!"

Like a scalpel slicing through skin and bone, a sharp and fierce sting ran from Rixs's outer ribs all the way to his breastbone. Pieces once cracked and separated abruptly snapped together. Eyes that had been closed popped open and a noisy slurp of air sounded just before the yelling began.

"Eeeowch!" Rixs cried, flexing every muscle in his body. "Strikes! What'd ya do that for?" He jerked away from Hobb, arms flexed, and hands fisted as though he would punch the Physician. Hobb raised his hands in calming apology.

The Absolute guffawed. "It always hurts when bones finally seal back together! The Physician should have warned you. Shame on you, Hobb!" he said with a grin.

A hard, impatient knock shook the door. Orris thrust his head through the opening, glaring around the room until he found the object of his search.

"I heard you suddenly turned up!" he spat, stepping into the chamber without waiting for an invitation. "Do you know how many squads I have searching for the Lady Syersi? Ten! Ten squads saturating Isslewood! I ought to slay you right where you lay just for wasting our time!" His hand reached for his sword.

The Absolute moved in front of the Commandant. "First slaying rights belong to me!" He jutted an oversized thumb into the hard flesh of his massive chest.

Orris scowled at the Absolute then returned his glare to Rixs. "Fine, but I get the leftovers!"

More footsteps echoed the approach of another person. The sound stopped just outside Rixs's door and a firm knock followed.

"Enter!" Orris commanded.

Sharp green eyes glared at him. "The last I looked, Commandant, this was *my* chamber!" Rixs snarled. Then he called toward the door, "Come in!"

Athan, a favorite of Syersi's, stepped through the doorway. Spying the Counselor and Absolute, he dropped to a knee. "Apologies for the interruption, Counselor, but I was sent to deliver a message." His eyes flicked toward Rixs. "There is a man at the main gate who insists that he must speak to *the kid from Pax Valley.*"

All eyes curiously turned to Rixs's hooked smile. There was only one person who called him, *kid.*

The long walk to the main gate of Tower Wall during the early dawn would have been quiet and peaceful had a certain red-eyed terror not accompanied him to the gate. Rixs shifted glances between the Absolute and the path they walked.

"Tell me about this *friend* of yours!" Rangus ordered.

By the time they arrived at Tower Wall, the Absolute had all he desired to know concerning Rhages of Lugger. A nod of his head gave the silent command for the sentries to open the gate.

They stepped back as the gate opened, their eyes alert and their hands ready to pull their swords at the slightest sign of trouble. A colossal, wild-looking man strode confidently through the opening. His sheer size almost matched that of Rangus, who was easily the tallest man in Gnomera, and who not only studied the newcomer, but sniffed at the air around him.

Bulging masses of muscle covered by a healthy layer of fat, gave away that Rhages was more weight than brawn. Nonetheless, even with his ominous pudgy physique, it was apparent he was still a formidable opponent. His menacing appearance included gobs of kinky black hair which stood on end as though he had been struck by lightning. A matching beard provided the final touch.

Rixs grinned. "Rhages! My friend! What brings you to Isslewood?" He extended a hand for a good hearty shake.

A gaping smile revealed big, white teeth. "Kid!" Rhages hooped out. He ignored Rixs's hand and pulled him in for a crushing hug and a solid slap to the back. "Glad ta see ya!"

Rixs clamped his eyes shut as he absorbed the pain that exploded through chest and ribs. It might have felt better if Rhages had stuck a knife between his newly healed ribs. Rixs's body was still tender and Rhages packed a heavy hand.

"Absolute, please meet my friend, Rhages," Rixs introduced. True to his nature, Rangus glared at Rhages with scarlet eyes tinged to intimidate while taking his hand and wrist in more of an arm wrestle than a greeting.

Rixs was relieved when Chadgerwin showed up on his horse, pulling Rangus's horse behind him. It was his arrival that kept the Sanguinary in check and forced him to let go of Rhages so that quick introductions could be made to the Counselor, who perused the visitor with grey, scrutinizing eyes. Seeming satisfied with his assessment, Chadgerwin and Rangus left to find Lothorius.

It was an unprecedented decision for the First Counselor and Absolute to be gone for an extended period at the same time. It had never been done before. Always one or the other had remained at Isslewood to ensure its safety.

As the last clouds of departing dust settled in the light breeze, Rhages gave up a long whistle. "Now, that Counselor be a grand-lookin' man! And be it my imagination, or was that red eye sniffin' me?"

Rixs could only laugh.

With an eagle's sharp eye, the guards watched Rhages with suspicion as he walked along the wall, dragging his hand against the stone while speaking with Rixs. The unique lavender gneiss from which the wall was made captivated him. As they made small talk, Rhages would pull his hand away from the stone to inspect it for any sparkly residue that might have stuck to his skin.

"Oh, this'll prick yer ears up," he said. "Viktus's been meetin' in secret with some fella. I never seen him, and Viktus don't tell us who, but he met him a couple times since the explosions in Ormolu."

"Do you think he lives there?"

"I be thinkin' not." Again, Rhages rubbed his palms over the rough stone wall. "Never could get over this gneiss." Giving the wall a final pat, he pulled away and folded his enormous arms across his chest. "Anyways, this outsider keeps hidden. Hides good too! None has ever seen him."

That bit of information pricked Rixs's ear. The elusive man working with Viktus could be the Shade. He might have followed Rhages to Isslewood. His heart thrummed in his chest as he immediately set his sights in search of a shadowed form that had no visual body.

"Rhages! What if this stranger followed you here?" Even as Rixs searched, his rapid pulse began to slow. Scanning the area with his Talent, he found nothing. For the moment, all was safe.

"Trotts, kid," Rhages hissed. "Stop being paranoid. I be knowin' when someone follows me!"

Not this person. You would need my Talent to see this stranger. It was a thought Rixs left unsaid.

A snort rumbled and a big wad of spit hit the ground. "Anyways," Rhages said as he wiped his mouth with his forearm. "This Source that Viktus be searchin' for, he thinks this Princess is key to gettin' what he wants. Just thought I be warnin' ya."

Eyeing his friend, Rixs said, "You know I won't let him, or anyone, take her."

"Figured as much. How did *you*, of all people, wind up being Imperial Shield?" Rhages questioned.

Leaving his question unanswered, Rixs countered, "Why do *you* work for Viktus? Do you even believe in the Source? What if it's all nothing but tall tales and you follow blindly? You put her life at risk."

"I ain't followin' blindly, kid!" Rhages muttered. "Viktus pays good and as long as he pays, why should I be carin' if he, or anyone else, be a fool? Near as I figure, gettin' paid to look for a myth is a sweet bargain." He leaned over and narrowed his eyes at Rixs. "But

I ain't thinkin' Viktus be a fool. He knows somethin' so beware. The idea of power makes men crazy and dangerous." Rhages rubbed a large dark hand over his face.

"And you beware," Rixs replied, his own eyes nothing more than slits. "Friend or no, I will crush anybody who tries to hurt the Empress Heir."

Rhages nodded as he swiped his tongue across his teeth and stared blankly at his young friend. Suddenly, he grinned. "Awe, this be talkin' nonsense. Tell me. Why they pick a hunter for Shield? You ain't no warrior! Do ya even know how ta fight?"

Rixs shot him a snarky look, his posture suddenly erect and arms flexed. "You are a funny man, Rhages! You know I hold my own."

A deep, hearty laugh rumbled from his friend. "Yeah, that ya do, kid! Ya saved my sorry rump cheeks that night! Seriously though, how did ya come to be such a high and mighty?"

Rixs shook his head in awe of his own story. "My friend, it is a story you would not believe."

Rhages leaned into him. "Try me."

THIRTY

Waking up to a pinching ache that bordered on pleasure, Syersi moaned and stretched in her bed. A smile ghosted her lips in remembrance of her dream and the handsome face that claimed it. Lively green eyes made her heart burn.

Always pushing her beyond her limits, Rixs had guided her through the cavernous chamber shrouded in endless darkness far below. His confidence in her boosted her own courage to do things she would have never imagined doing. She had pushed herself and she felt stronger.

Each time the stranger from Pax Valley popped into her thoughts, a mallet beat against her ribs threatening to crack her chest in half. The annoying burn that had started as a flicker of heat now plagued her with constant discomfort, getting worse with each passing day. Syersi inhaled and exhaled, pushing both hands into her breastbone.

"My dear!" Mazzlin fretted. "Are you hurting?" The fleshy matron leaned over her charge and gently ran her hand through Syersi's silky hair that slid evasively through her fingers like sunlight. "Is it your chest?"

After settling into a relaxed rhythm, her breaths deep and easy, Syersi replied. "I don't know," she breathed. "I swear my heart is on fire."

The Guardian sat on the side of the bed and rubbed her shoulder, studying her with somber eyes.

"It all started as a tickle ... something I could easily ignore," Syersi confessed. "But now, I can hardly breathe when it happens." She glanced at the Guardian. "I need Hobb. I think I am afflicted with a breathing ailment."

It was no secret to the woman who looked upon Syersi with eyes reflecting the love of a mother. Mazzlin fumbled with her own wavy curls before she spoke.

"Chadgerwin may never talk to me again for telling you this ... Well, he barely speaks to me now unless he is frustrated with you ... and that happens quite often – that he is frustrated with you, I mean," Mazzlin clarified.

Syersi rolled her eyes.

Then the epiphany gleamed in the Guardian's eyes and she snorted with a chuckle, "Come to think of it, Chadgerwin talks to me frequently!"

Syersi sighed and flipped her covers back then hopped out of bed. Padding to her wardrobe, she called over her shoulder, "Spit it out, Mazzy! What will Chadgerwin *never speak to you again* if you tell me?"

Like a shadow, Mazzlin followed her and pondered what to say. "You know," she tapped her chin as she spoke. "Love is a curious thing."

Wondering what love had to do with her chest pains Syersi silently groaned then appeased her Guardian. "Yes, Mazzy. I know you itch for me to find someone to love. Someone who can rule Gnomera at my side."

Mazzlin's head bobbed from side to side while her plump hands absentmindedly fingered every dress Syersi touched. "True, true. But that is not why your chest hurts ..." There was a quiver of nervousness in her voice. "That ache in your heart, my child, is tied to your love."

After passing by a few more dresses, Syersi stopped and cocked her head to one side. "What did you say? My pain is tied to my love?" Blue eyes assessed the Guardian from head to toe. "Mazzy, do you have a fever?"

Undeterred by Syersi's skepticism, the Seer chirped happily. "I'm quite well. Thank you." There was a delay, then, "The pain will grow until you give your heart away – completely. Once you do, the pain will stop."

Mazzlin had declared it with such certainty, Syersi had no words. Excessive blinking that resembled an atrocious eye tic was her only response.

"Guardian," she said and wetted her lips with her tongue. "I hope this is a teasing prank, otherwise, you would sound like a *crazy*."

"Yes, yes," Mazzlin agreed. "It does sound crazy – doesn't it? But love is a crazy thing. Few understand it, yet that doesn't mean what I have said is less true."

Faces, such as Athan, a blonde favorite and excellent kisser, and Orris, all muscle and a worthy distraction, came to mind as Syersi speculated on her Guardian's words. There had never been a single love interest. If she settled on one, she would miss out on so many others! And most of the fun was in chasing what wasn't hers – the anticipation of catching them. Tangorio, Prince of Tangrah and object of her infatuation, appeared in her head. Rumors boasted that he could melt the heart of an ice sculpture. She loved him from afar.

She laughed to herself. The notion of giving her heart to a single candidate was out of the question. Even if she believed Mazzlin, she could not, and would not ever do it.

Small fingers dug into Syersi's shoulders and swung her around with unexpected force. "Do not treat this lightly, child!" Her gaze was piercing. "This is serious business. Your heart is already burning, and it will not ask your permission when it settles its affection." Her fingers dug deeper. "You will be bound in a way you cannot imagine, and you will be helpless to stop it! You will be tied to that person for better, and for worse, and there will be no going back. So, beware that your choice is worthy of you!"

The urgency in Mazzlin's voice made Syersi pause in her musings. The old woman was serious! Even as she considered her Guardian's madness, an emerald gaze hidden behind sandy strands of rebellious hair, and the smell of leather washed over her senses.

Rixs. But did Syersi dream of him because of love, or because she wanted to conquer him?

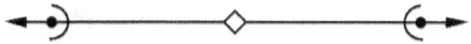

"I hate you!" Syersi hissed for the tenth time.

"*Humph*. You already said that!" Rixs snorted.

The large knobby tree, with leaves big and full, provided little relief, to the Empress Heir who strained under the weight of two palm-sized stones, one in each hand. For generations the tree had provided protection from the mid-day sun, but it offered Syersi little comfort.

Trembling arms extended to each side threatened to collapse under the weight of the stones. She cursed at her arms to stay strong while Rixs stood tall, feet spread wide, with arms folded across his chest. He counted.

"Sixteen, seventeen … keep your arms up, Pixee, or I shall start over!" Rixs threatened as he watched her struggle. "This will help build some muscle in those soft arms."

Again, he wore no shirt under his clashing vest, but in Syersi's agonized state, tired and sweating, she paid no attention. "A woman should be soft!" she snarled.

A quick moment passed as the thought of her soft arms brought a smile to Rixs's face. "Nineteen, TWENTY!" he cried out in victory, as though she had won a war. Groaning with gratitude, she threw the stones at him. He easily danced out of the way. "Such violence for a little thing!" he teased.

Each day Rixs forced her to work on strength. Each day Syersi threatened to have him beheaded, drowned, drawn and quartered, or whatever form of torture was equal to the soreness of her limbs. She rubbed her arms and forced the biggest frown she could muster.

"That is an ugly face!" he told her. She threw another rock at him.

Syersi recalled the Seer's explanation that her chest pain was a sign of pending love. "It certainly will not be you!" she grumbled under her breath.

"Hmm? Did you say something?" Rixs cocked his head to the side, his hair falling over his eyes.

Then they both heard it. The sound of drums. Rixs turned with interest, but Syersi jerked in surprise, understanding the meaning behind the drumbeat that echoed across the palace grounds.

She hurried toward the front of the palace not realizing she was running until she heard the annoying voice behind her. "If you are going to run, then run! Stop prancing! It is an insult to running!" She turned around and stuck out her tongue. Rixs laughed as he followed her toward the gates.

She attacked the narrow passageway that wound upward through the innards of Tower Wall. The dark stairwell circled up, up, up. When the dark gloom of the passage gave way to the light of the wall walk, the huffing and flushed Syersi nearly cried in both relief, and awe. Relieved that the claustrophobic, exhaustive climb was over, and in awe of the view that greeted her.

High atop Isslewood's Tower Wall, a set of fingers could tickle the clouds if stretched high enough. The view was endless. But it was the drumbeat that had summoned her, so the view needed to wait for another day.

Hobb stepped to Syersi's side while she and Rixs watched the evolving scene below. A strangled noise drew their attention to the dank stairwell just in time to see a panting, red-faced Mazzlin emerge from the doorway. Both hands covered her chest as she tried to catch her breath.

"That is a horrible climb!" she declared between gulps of air. Mazzlin hobbled to the parapet next to Syersi and followed her eyes to the mass of bodies approaching the gate. The Seer's eyes popped wide.

"What say you, Rixs? One hundred?" Hobb guessed.

"At least," Rixs replied with a frown. He could see the placement of each space filled with a body, even as it moved, and knew the number instantly. One hundred thirty and seven, but he kept that to himself.

There was a sharp hiss from Mazzlin. "What is he doing here?" she cried, pointing to a figure in the lead. "I thought he was headed for Sentur!"

"Who is he?" Rixs asked.

Syersi replied barely above a whisper. "My father, I think."

The drumbeat had been an announcement to all of Isslewood. *The Emperor is coming.* It should have been an occasion for celebration, but it seemed no one was eager to raise a merry goblet to his return. Rixs studied Mazzlin – especially the Guardian.

Orris was walking toward them with a handful of his men. Like the title he claimed, the Commandant assessed the situation as he spouted orders with confidence. After barking a final instruction, he stalked along the wall walk toward the Empress Heir.

"My Lady, you grace us on Tower Wall." He was tall and strong as he purposely edged his way past Rixs to stand next to Syersi. Taking note of her untidy appearance, he smirked. "You look ... interesting." She threw him a glare and he chuckled, then tossed a dismissive glance at Rixs.

All eyes transferred again to the scene unfolding far below them, but it was Syersi's eyes that stung with the flood of memories. Her mother's death. Her father's withdrawal. Her abandonment. Sorrow, anger, hope – they all competed for first place in her broken heart.

"So, my father has returned," the mumble was barely loud enough to hear.

"That is not your father!" Mazzlin snarled, her expression dark. "That is an imposter!"

The Commandant leaned over the parapet and squinted. "Open your eyes, Guardian." He nodded toward the man leading the company. "That is our Emperor. Of course, we are a long way up, but there is no mistake."

Hobb shook his head, eyes riveted on the man far below. "Do not believe everything you see, Commandant."

"You are absolutely right, Physician. Shall we confirm then? Let us go inspect the man then give our returning Emperor a proper welcome."

"You cannot open the gate!" the Guardian cried.

"Yes, I can," Orris responded. A muscle ticked in his jaw. "I am in charge."

Rixs remembered the Absolute's orders. "You swore to Rangus you would not open the gate under any circumstances …"

"Rangus did not know the Emperor would show up here!" Orris growled through clenched teeth. "Neither he nor the Counselor would want our Emperor locked out and begging like a fool to gain entrance to his own home!" He turned and walked toward the stairs then stopped and looked at Syersi. "I will understand if you choose not to greet your father, Lady Syersi," he said, then turned into the stairwell and was swallowed up.

Something unsettled Rixs as he scrutinized the view below. He swept his eyes over the riders and footmen for the tenth time. Something was not right. And then he saw it. Easy to miss with all the shapes and visual distractions, a grey form walked along the perimeter with the footmen. Each man marched with a corresponding body that laid over their grey form, and that Rixs could mark with his eyes. Except this one grey form that walked along the perimeter. His eyes could not mark its match.

It had to be the Shade and Orris planned to open the gate. Whether the Commandant was right or wrong in his decision did not matter. What mattered was that if he allowed them into Isslewood, the Shade would have access to Syersi. Rixs could not allow this threat.

Grabbing Syersi by the shoulders he pulled her close so that no one else could hear. "Get back to the great house and hide!" His stare was piercing, the brilliant emerald hues all jumping with urgency. "You know where to go. Stay there until I come for you!"

THIRTY-ONE

Orris controlled the security of Isslewood. Rixs controlled the safety of the Empress Heir. When the two conflicted, Syersi's protection had to take priority. It was the reason Rixs refused to back down.

The standoff between Commandant and Shield nearly degraded into a physical fight. Open the gate to admit the Emperor and his party. Keep the gate closed to ensure the Empress Heir's safety. Orris had insisted that the man waiting outside the gate was Lothorius, Syersi's father, and thus she was safe. Rixs argued that there were more than one hundred unknown and potentially dangerous men (one hundred thirty and seven to be exact) with the Emperor which threatened Syersi's safety. Orris observed it was a risk too small to worry over. Rixs was adamant that the smallest risk was a risk too big.

Unsure how much Orris knew about Talents, or what Chadgerwin may or may not have shared about his own ability, Rixs chose not to mention the potential danger involving the Shade stalking outside the gate. Trusting Orris did not come easy – even if he was Commandant.

"I will not yield on this, Commandant. You know I am justified in my position, but I will compromise," Rixs said. "The Emperor and three of his men can be admitted. The rest can set up camp outside the gate. No one else enters or leaves Isslewood until the Counselor and Absolute return."

It was not an easily won compromise, but Orris finally agreed. Then they tried to appease an angry Lothorius, who was not quickly appeased, but at long length, gave in for the sake of his daughter. Though he was Emperor, he acknowledged that it had been four seasons cycles since Syersi had seen him last. She had been a young and vulnerable thirteen Springs when he left, so he acquiesced his demands.

Rixs slouched against the wall eyeing Lothorius and each of the three bodies that walked through the gate. Each had a body his eyes could focus on, and a grey form that filled the measure of their space. He waited for a fourth unseen figure to sneak past, but none came. Having eliminated the Emperor as Shade, he only needed to keep an eye on three men.

"Where's Mazzlin and Hobb?" Lothorius demanded. "On second thought, where is my daughter?"

Eager to impress, Orris immediately spoke up, "Lady Syersi wanted to make herself presentable, and I am sure the Guardian and Physician will make their appearance shortly."

"And who are you?" Lothorius squinted at Orris.

He cleared his throat. "Supreme!" He knelt and saluted then rose to his feet. "I am the Commandant of the Lothorian Guard. We met twice when you were confined to your chambers."

No other explanation was necessary. The Absolute of the Gnomeran Armies, Rangus, had executed the preceding Commandant for failure to protect Lady Saudria. He then had appointed Orris as Commandant.

The Emperor nodded in bare acknowledgement then turned to Rixs. It was his story that captured the Emperor's attention.

"You must have skills beyond my comprehension if Chadgerwin and Rangus allowed an outsider to assume the post of Imperial Shield." He eyed the young man with faded blue eyes. Rixs did not reply.

Lothorius gave him one last look then turned to Orris. "Please reacquaint me with Isslewood, Commandant."

After Orris escorted Lothorius away, Rixs ran to his chambers to retrieve a bundle before setting out for the hidden chamber. He hurried to close his chamber door when he realized that Syersi's silhouette was not where it should have been. Tense knuckles rapped on her door.

"Open up!" he growled in a low tone. She had barely cracked the door when Rixs pushed through without asking. "I told you to hide in the cavern!" He looked around the expansive chamber. "I highly doubt this is it!"

Syersi produced a scowl. "Stop yelling at me!" she yelled. Then her face suddenly changed, and her hands dropped limply at each side. "I went to the records chamber and opened the panel, but I froze." She closed her eyes as she talked.

"I stared into the dark. I remembered the choking blackness. I was too terrified to step through the door, so I came back here." With hunched shoulders, Syersi hugged herself.

The stern lines of his forehead relaxed and Rixs quietly held out the bundle. "I need to remember that it is different for you than it is for me when you see nothing but dark." He smiled. "Here, put this on."

Curiosity made her fingers twitch. "What is it?" Eagerly taking the bundle, she found herself holding up a gown in one hand, and something that looked like a body shaper with a pocket in the other.

"This goes around your waist," he gripped the shaper. "It is to be worn under this dress. I need you to try them both on. Hurry." He nudged her to do as he asked.

A crease appeared between her brows. "What is this?" Syersi shook the shaper in her hand.

"Just do what I ask!" his whisper was impatient. "I will show you once you have it on. Make sure the sheath hangs over your right hip, then put on the gown. Now, hurry!"

"I need my servants to help me!"

"Strikes, Pixee! Can you not dress by yourself? Shall I help you?" She glared at him. "I thought as much. Figure it out! And hurry!"

She stomped into the wardrobe and slammed the door. He winced, hoping no one came to investigate. Thuds against the wall and floor told him she was angry, no doubt throwing whatever she found.

When Syersi stepped out, she was overcome with shyness and looked down at the floor, glancing up at him intermittently while his green eyes scoured over the gown, pausing to peruse the lines of her hip and thigh. Her cheeks reddened.

"How does the cincture feel?" he asked.

Before she could answer, Rixs yanked a short blade from under his left arm and held it tightly in front of him. The speed and abruptness of his movement caused her to jump. Twin orbs as blue as the sky regarded him warily. It was a reminder that he could slit her throat in an instant.

"Sorry to startle you. I would never hurt you, Pixee," he said, extending the blade to her. His eyes had softened. "Here. Right here." Rixs tapped her right hip. "There is an opening so that you can reach the sheath in the cincture you are wearing."

His fingers began fumbling through the gathers of the dress. A thrill ran up her spine, fanning wide across the back of her neck. With quick breaths she watched his hands tickle and explore the gathers at her hip. Syersi pressed her lips tight and dragged in deep breaths through her nose.

"There it is," he said, his hand sliding through a slit in her gown. "Put your hand in this opening and see if you can find the sheath."

She did as she was told. "I found it," her voice wavered, still recovering from his touch.

Nodding in satisfaction, he placed the short blade in her hand. "Until we can find you a suitable weapon, use my blade."

Wide blue eyes shot up to meet his gaze. "You … you are giving me your blade?" her voice held surprise under a stunned smile.

Rixs held up a finger. "I am lending it to you," he corrected. "Tell no one. Not even the Guardian." He lightly pinched her chin between his thumb and curled index finger. "This is your last line of defense. Your secret weapon. All of your dresses and skirts that have gathers or pleats at the waistline must be altered to accommodate the cincture and allow you access to your blade." His eyes bore into hers. "Do you understand?"

"Of course, but where did you get this?"

"I made it." Rixs shrugged.

Syersi's head jerked up. "You what?"

"Why the surprise?" he chided. "I mended my own trousers and tunics as a youngster. There were no servants for me!" He tossed her a teasing scowl. "Anyhow, I found some fine leather and made the cincture for you, then worked with your dressmaker to alter this dress to test it. I left instructions to alter all your gowns. Make sure she does this."

Syersi blinked at him, her mouth open.

Dramatically he grabbed his chest. "Are you impressed? How shall I bear it?"

"Do not gloat, you swine!" she ordered, pushing a finger repeatedly into his chest, his muscles remaining firm under the pressure of her pokes. She thanked The Powers he wore no tunic under his vest. His skin was warm under her fingertip.

She cleared her throat. "You know some of my dresses are without gathers and pleats. They are made to boast my curves."

Rixs scanned over Syersi quickly, nodding his head slowly with hooded eyes. Such a dress would indeed show off her exquisite figure. By the way she pursed her lips and abruptly planted her hands on her hips, he had no doubt Syersi knew where his thoughts had wandered.

Recovering himself, he said with a scratchy voice, "For the dresses that have no pleats or gathers, I will need to rig something for your ankle." His eyes dropped to his feet. "But anyone wanting to find a weapon will first look at your legs. It is the obvious place for a woman to conceal a weapon. If you have sleeves, your arms would be another obvious place, and ...," Rixs paused, and cleared his throat. "Your, um," he nodded at her chest.

"These?" she asked, dropping her eyes to her breasts. She grinned in delight because the swine had red splotches on his cheeks and neck. "I insist you to think of a weapon to conceal here." Syersi's smile grew wide as Rixs's face grew redder. "Perhaps one of your throwing stix would be perfect tucked with my cleavage?"

He coughed and changed the subject. "Try to place the blade in its sheath."

The cincture was genius. It snuggly hugged her waist like her own skin, the sheath pressed securely against her upper thigh. When wearing a gown, no one would suspect that under all the pleats, Syersi had a weapon easily accessible. And the Shield's blades were different than most knives. His were honed from a single piece of metal and they were very flat. Even the handles, though rounder and thicker than the sharp portion of the blade, were flat. This provided for a good grip. But the transition from blade to handle was smooth and seamless. If thrown hard enough, the entire blade from tip to handle could embed into its victim.

Syersi carefully tucked his short blade through the slit in her skirt and clumsily found the sheath. It was tricky and took time, but eventually she was successful. With practice she would become proficient.

A hard swallow filled her throat. He had let her borrow one of his blades, and she knew how much they meant to him. Rixs had already suffered in lockup for refusing Syersi's demand to give up one of his blades to her, and now he had offered one willingly. Without uttering her sentiment out loud, she mouthed, *thank you*.

He squeezed her hand gently. "Come on. The Emperor wants to see his daughter for the evening meal. But before we join him, we are going to conquer your fear of the hidden chamber."

Syersi shuddered visibly at the mention of the terrifying cavern but remained silent. As they were leaving, Rixs stopped abruptly, "And, Pixee," his voice was begging. "Please, please, please, try not to stab me with my own blade!" His eyes danced and a broad smile showed off his white teeth and irresistible face.

THIRTY-TWO

The evening meal summoned all high-ranking soldiers to dine with their Emperor. The dining hall vibrated with flirtatious female giggles as Syersi's retinue took quick advantage of their invitation to join. Blustering male laughter competed for the attention of the females.

Lothorius sat in the middle of the head table with Syersi to his right and Mazzlin to his left. The Guardian bristled at his nearness. Orris sat opposite the Emperor, and Rixs sat across from Syersi. Hobb faced Mazzlin and looked as if he would throw up. The remaining guests sat at tables set up in long rows.

Syersi and Rixs had just returned from the chamber of darkness sprawled far beneath the palace floor. It had frightened her just as much as it had the first time she walked its stone floor. It was hard to decide which was worse, the smothering darkness of the gaping cavern, or eating with Lothorius while a gawking crowd watched their reunion.

Stiff as a dead duck, Syersi endured the long hug her father bestowed on her. His fingers clamped into her skin to hold her in place, as if she would run away if they relaxed. She pushed away at the earliest opportunity, cringing at the affection he seemed too eager to give.

A quick study of her father's features gave away nothing unusual.

His eyes had dimmed from the vivid blue of her memories. Though weathered after roaming Gnomera's territories for seasons cycles, his features were still striking. The only thing that set her on edge was his embrace. It was too soft. Too tender. Something not reserved for a daughter. It was a stranger's embrace with the face of the Emperor.

"Eat up, everybody!" the man commanded then leaned over into Syersi's ear. "And pay no attention to my etiquette. I have picked up bad manners during my absence." The touch of a hand squeezed her thigh under the table.

The touch made her flinch with teeth clenched tight to keep her bottom jaw from unhinging. This was not the father she remembered.

He rubbed her tensed knee. "I should never have stayed away so long. It was selfish, but I was hurting. Please, forgive me, Syersi."

"I forgive you," she croaked, scooting her chair away so that his hand fell from her knee.

Orris lifted a goblet. "To our returned Emperor, Lothorius, the Supreme!"

Every hand lifted with a goblet, though Mazzlin barely raised hers and decided not to drink. Hobb was more civil and toasted with respect along with all the others. Then chatter filled the hall as everyone enjoyed their food.

Mazzlin took the opportunity to address the Emperor, her eyes flashing at Syersi while she spoke. "*Lothorius*, I wonder why you are here instead of Sentur. The Counselor and Absolute set out to meet you there."

Syersi was about to chastise her Guardian for the familiarity by which she called the Emperor's name, but then it struck her. Mazzlin had never addressed him by his name. Her father would have never allowed it.

He answered easily, no trace of annoyance in her breach of formality. "Can you blame me for wanting to come straight here? Look at my daughter!" He smiled as his gaze scoured over her. "She is the loveliest creature on the face of this earth!" He nodded toward Orris and Rixs. "Do you agree?"

Cheeks bulging, Rixs had just finished shoving a barrel-sized piece of meat wrapped in bread into his wide, engaging mouth. When he felt the attention of blue eyes upon him, he froze mid-chew.

Orris hurriedly filled the gap. "Supreme, Lady Syersi has no equal! She is the dream of dreams – the treasure hidden beneath the sea. The man that wins her hand will be most fortunate!" he proclaimed, confidence pouring from every word.

A spontaneous snicker unexpectedly slipped from Rixs's food-filled mouth after the Commandant's passion-dripping declaration. The man's nose was as brown as his boots. Attempting to cover the laugh with a cough, a chunk of soggy bread splatted onto the table. Rixs ducked his head apologetically and wiped an arm across his lips.

Syersi blushed on behalf of both men. One was ridiculously overblown, and the other was painfully unrefined. Orris sat like a tree trunk in his seat, meticulously rehearsed in his mannerisms and conduct. Her Shield hunched over his plate, chewing vigorously with his mouth embarrassingly over-stuffed and oblivious to everything but his appetite.

"And what do you say, Shield?" the Emperor asked.

Stopped short of filling his mouth again, Rixs vacillated his gaze between Syersi and Lothorius. Silence fell in the hall. Every hand and mouth ceased to move, and all eyes turned to the young man from Pax Valley as though his reply would be the most important thing ever said. Critical green eyes fixed on the Empress Heir and she fidgeted in her seat.

Syersi feared his words. The Shield was honest to a fault and her biggest critic. There would be no attempt to hide his opinion of her, and his opinion of her, on most days, was not flattering. A blush betrayed her attempt to look uninterested.

His stark gaze turned warm as the silence lingered on and he swallowed the last remaining pieces of food hiding in his mouth. Finally, Rixs began to speak, a twinkle illuminated his gaze.

"Supreme, the first time I laid eyes on the Lady Syersi, I knew I had never beheld a woman more beautiful. She is the dream of dreams as the Commandant so eloquently stated. I cannot do better." Rixs looked around the hall. All ears eagerly waited. "But I now know I only saw half of the Lady. There is much more to Lady Syersi than a flawless face. And sadly, I suspect there are many here who do not know that. She is stubborn to a fault, but it drives her courage, her determination, her strength. And she is clever. When I train her, she keeps me on my toes! Yes. There is more to our Lady than her beauty. I challenge you all to take a second look."

Applause filled the dining hall, and Syersi dropped her eyes to her lap, unable to look at anyone. Never had such a compliment been given to her – one that hinted she was more than just a pretty face. When she dared to steal a look at the Shield, she was greeted with a subtle wink. No one noticed as she pressed her fingers against the pain in her chest.

After the meal, when Lothorius found himself alone, he wandered into the receiving hall to reacquaint himself with Gnomera's throne. He approached it as he would a sleeping infant, quiet and cautious. His eyes hungrily followed every line chiseled into the bleached stone, sanded, and smoothed until it shined like a layer of ice covering a pond on a bright winter's morning. As if stroking a kitten, a calloused palm gently slid down the back of the chair, caressing it. Long fingers danced over each armrest, his fingertips following the whirling grooves that created an elaborate art-scape over the sparkling smooth gneiss.

The man sat on the throne and whispered to himself. "You kept much from me, Lothorius. Now that I have uncovered your secrets, I will take the possession you fiercely protected. The Source is mine."

THIRTY-THREE

The rumors spread like wildfire. The First Counselor had wasted no time in taking advantage of the devasted Lothorius after the tragic death of Lady Saudria. Chadgerwin had assumed power in the Emperor's behalf and after he and the Intimus had a firm grip on Gnomera, they forced Lothorius to leave Isslewood.

Gossip had it that he was forcefully taken to the northern-most region of Gnomera, where they executed all of the guards that had accompanied them. There could be no witnesses. They would have killed the Emperor as well, but he managed to escape, and had been wandering the land realm over the last four seasons cycles, hiding, and devising a plan to take back his empire.

The servants buzzed with the news, and though Rixs had his doubts, it was difficult to refute the rumors. His best sources for the truth had disappeared. Mazzlin and Hobb were nowhere to be found. Chadgerwin and Rangus had only been gone one day and since it was a three-day ride to Sentur, it would be another five days before they returned.

"I think something is not right," Rixs said when he met Orris in the corridor.

Orris glowered at him. "Who cares what you think? I think you should leave the thinking to me!" He spied the clashing vest and its missing blade. "What happened to your precious blade? Did you lose it?" he pointed to the empty space just under Rixs's arm.

"Yeah, I lost it."

"Hmm, too bad." The Commandant began to walk away but stopped abruptly and turned back. "Before I forget. You are no longer allowed to be alone and unsupervised with Lady Syersi." His voice was smug.

"What do you mean? I am the Shield," Rixs argued.

The Commandant rolled his thick neck then squared his shoulders. "Emperor's orders."

Flexing his arms and fisting his hand, Rixs flashed his teeth in a tight grin. "Jealous, are we? Had to cry to the Emperor?"

With eyes that could impale, Orris poked the Shield with his finger. "Careful. Chadgerwin is not here to protect you." Then without warning, Orris swung his fist.

The grey form of an arm devoured the empty space as it traveled toward Rixs. He coolly leaned out of the way then slammed an elbow into the Commandant's shoulder.

Orris growled and pivoted, grabbing Rixs around the neck. He used his free hand to snatch one of the sheathed short blades, but the Talent was already one step ahead.

Every curve and shadow of the Commandant's form was visible to Rixs. He could see the areas where Orris was most vulnerable, most off balance, and he effortlessly exploited the soldier's weakness.

He hooked a leg around Orris's unstable side, and simultaneously used his arm to block the hand that grabbed for his blade. Then Rixs twisted his body, thrusting his shoulder into Orris's gut, pushing the man back into his unstable leg. The air was knocked from the Commandant's chest as he hit the ground.

Orris snarled, "You worthless wamp! I'll teach you to …" His words were cut short by the sting of a blade's sharp point in the hollow of his throat. Though scarlet beads pooled where the tip pressed into his skin, he quietly swore, "You are a dead man."

Nostrils flared as Rixs warned with a hushed, yet savage growl, "No. You are the dead man if you ever try to take one of my blades again!" Sheathing the medium blade in the inner panel of his vest, he added, "Never attack me with my own weapon." Rixs walked away and left Orris to plot his revenge in solitude.

The evening breeze cooled the heat pulsing in Rixs's veins. Orris would never know how easily the young man could have broken his jaw. Anyone who fought Rixs was always at a disadvantage. His Talent made him a superior fighter, but it was his easy temper that made him an honorable adversary – someone willing to walk away. His brother, Rollin, had teased that mild mannered Rixs was a flower, not a fighter. And each time his brother called him out, Rixs would provide Rollin a sound pummeling to demonstrate his *flower*-like qualities.

The tree-lined path, with its aromatic scents did little to ease the edginess twitching under his skin. With the First Counselor and the Absolute days away, there was no one to refute the charges the Emperor was spreading about the Intimus. Mazzlin had claimed the man to be an imposter, yet she had disappeared along with Hobb.

He was suddenly aware of a shadowed curvy form approaching.

"Rixs," a soft voice called.

He frowned. "Hello, Moniere."

It was an inconvenient time for company. Rixs ignored her swaying hips, but his inherent kindness compelled him to give a stiff smile.

She brushed the hair away from his eyes. "There!" she said. "I can see your striking face."

He stepped back placing distance between them. She stepped forward. Warm sultry brown eyes met his annoyed emerald ones.

"I am poor company." He swallowed hard.

Moniere traced a finger down his arm. "These little bumps covering your skin suggest you want company. My company at least." Her lips were plump, her voice, heavy. She stepped into him so that only a finger could slide between them then leaned on her toes. "Would you like to kiss me, Rixs?"

Syersi stepped through the wide front doors of the great house and strolled along the stone walkway. She needed to speak with Mazzlin, but the Guardian had vanished. Thinking of Mazzlin's best hiding places, Syersi trotted toward the maze garden, hoping to find her, when she stumbled onto a pair of bodies nearly melded into one.

Her feet halted in their tracks and she stared. That same male body had been the central feature of her dreams. She squinted at the female. Moniere. The girl who chased men like dogs chased squirrels. Of course, Syersi conveniently ignored the fact that she chased men too.

The retinue's arms were wrapped around the man who had complimented Syersi so sweetly just the evening before. Even worse, she knew he was a Talent. He would be aware of her standing there gawking and speechless.

Throwing them both into lockup would serve them right, but instead, she spun on her heel and stormed away. Let them finish what they had started. There was a tall blonde who was always willing to make her smile.

Cursing under his breath, Rixs stepped back from Moniere, repulsed by her boldness and disgusted at his own moment of weakness as he had allowed his fingers to curl around her waist. No doubt, Syersi would have the wrong impression. He pushed Moniere away.

"Kiss me," she pleaded.

Rubbing his face, he said, "Moniere, you seek something I will never give. I am betrothed."

Using his betrothal to escape from one girl to go to another plagued Rixs with guilt. Cliessa's memory stared at him until a lump formed in his throat. She was faithfully waiting, and he was embracing a girl he did not want, while wanting another girl he could never have. Neither of them was Cliessa.

Things had changed between Rixs and Syersi. They had settled into a comfortable tug of war – he *tugged* while she *warred*. She commanded, and he ignored. He trained, and she rebelled. A smile crept upward. The girl who threw tantrums, spat insults, and thought herself above everyone, had somehow managed to dig her way into a portion of his heart.

Before he could take off after the Empress Heir, someone called out, "Shield!" A guard approached him. "The Supreme requests your presence."

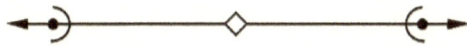

"Ah, there you are!" The Emperor sat at the table in the records chamber with his nose pressed into a binding. "Come. Sit down. Let us talk."

Rixs sat, green eyes studying the Emperor through strands of wayward hair. Though he did not know the man, there was something that felt wrong about him.

The Emperor eyed Rixs's vest. "A fine piece of work you have there," he said. "I am told you are an expert marksman. Better than Rangus, even." His gaze dropped to the hem of the vest. "And what are those? Knives?"

Following the Emperor's eyes, Rixs pulled one of the finger-sized weapons and handed it to him. "These innocent ornaments are my throwing stix. They look harmless but can be quite deadly."

"Fascinating!" Lothorius said. After a thorough inspection of the stix, the Emperor handed it back to Rixs. "If your marksmanship is better than the Absolute, there must be something more to you." His focus moved to the short blades sheathed under each arm.

"I hold my own," he shrugged.

Not mincing words, the Emperor's eyes dug into Rixs. "I know my First Counselor well, Rixsander of Pax Valley. He would have never allowed a foreigner to be Imperial Shield unless the foreigner had something extraordinary to offer ... like *Talent*, for example."

Rixs stared at the piles of bindings strewn along the desk and floor. *He searches for something.*

He replied to the Emperor without expression. "I know how to throw blades, and you heard the story of how I came to be the Empress Heir's Shield."

The Emperor nodded and waved an impatient hand in front of him. "Very well, shall we slash through the dung?" Suddenly, the Emperor stood from behind the desk and threw a dagger. It hurled straight at Rixs.

The narrow grey shape of the dagger's tip was poised to stab him in the throat. Rixs reacted and leaned left, out of harm's way, while he caught the dagger with his right hand. Afterward, when he looked at the Emperor, he realized what he had done.

Strikes!

Lothorius laughed in delight, his dull blue eyes sparkled. "What is this? I doubt even the Sanguinary could manage such a catch! No wonder Chadgerwin wanted you to watch over the First Daughter!"

Pointing an accusing finger at the Emperor, Rixs let his temper fly. "You almost killed me!"

Another bark of laughter filled the chamber. "Oh, no!" Lothorius howled, his eyes sweeping over every detail of Rixs's body like he was a prized horse. "Someone like you is far too valuable to kill … unless your loyalties are misplaced. Tell me, Shield, where are your loyalties?"

Not with you. Lustrous hair the color of raven feathers and eyes as blue as the costal harbor at Pax Valley, spilled into his thoughts. His answer was as certain as the blood oath he had sworn to Chadgerwin and Rangus.

"I am loyal to Lady Syersi. Only her."

The man swept yet another piercing eye over Rixs. "And where does that leave me?"

Rixs shook his head. "With respect, you chose to leave, but Chadgerwin …"

The interruption was instant. "Chadgerwin, Chadgerwin, Chadgerwin!" Lothorius hissed. "Leaving was not my choice! The deceiver forced me to leave, then stranded me in the middle of nowhere! To die! And he took over my empire!"

Hair obstructed Rixs's vision. He scratched his head then smoothed back his hair. "The Chadgerwin I know would never do such a thing. There must have been a reason for his actions."

"Wrong answer, Shield!" A large vein bulged and pulsed in the Emperor's neck. "After Lady Saudria died, I was devastated. I withdrew from my throne. From my people." He paused, then whispered, "From my daughter." He straightened his shoulders. "I thought Chadgerwin was taking care of the empire so I could heal, but it was a lie. When I was at my weakest, he tried to have me killed and took over Gnomera. He loves the power. If he controls Syersi, he controls Gnomera."

The likeness Lothorius painted of Chadgerwin did not resemble the man Rixs had come to know. He listened in silence.

"Rangus took me north and killed my detail." The Emperor tilted his forehead in Rixs's direction. "No witnesses, you see. But I managed to escape. The Powers blessed me that day! Chadgerwin and Rangus have had patrols searching for me ever since. I have been in hiding for the last four seasons cycles, finding men that would be loyal to me."

The words were hard to believe. The man had to be lying, but something about it rang true.

"I tricked them into going to Sentur so I could take back my throne. Anyone loyal to Chadgerwin must be an enemy to me." He leaned toward Rixs. "The Commandant is loyal to the Emperor. Now, you must choose."

Without a thought, Rixs responded, "I told you. I was given the responsibility to protect only Syersi. I am loyal to her – no other."

A disquieting shadow passed over the Emperor's face, then it transformed into a pleasant smile. "Do you absolutely believe you can protect my daughter better than anyone else? Do you have the cunning, strength, endurance to keep her safe from everything?"

Rixs tensed, and the hair on his scalp tingled. He tossed his head to clear the hair from his eyes, wanting a colorful view of the Emperor, but made no reply.

Lothorius grunted and narrowed his eyes. His expression wrinkled with thought. A sharp inhale hinted the resolve in his decision.

"I will let you in on a secret, Shield. I doubt the Intimus has told you. I am sure Orris has not been in their confidence." He and Rixs stared at each other. "Do you know of the Source?"

Rixs nodded and cocked his head to one side.

"If I told you I had the Source, and it needed protection from the wrong hands, would you agree?"

Rixs nodded again then remembered something. "Chadgerwin told me you had the Source."

The Emperor's eyes popped wide. "Did he now? He must trust you very much to share such a secret."

It then dawned on Rixs that the man before him had possessed a Source – he should have powers. He should be Denier Cri. Rixs saw nothing. The man was either an imposter, or there was no truth in the Source.

"Did he tell you the identity of the Source?" The Emperor searched Rixs's face. When he made no response, Lothorius had his answer.

"Well then, apparently, Chadgerwin trusts you only a little, but I will share this in good faith, Rixsander. Syersi needs your protection not because she is Empress Heir. My daughter needs your protection because *she* is the Source."

THIRTY-FOUR

His lips skimmed over the soft spot just under her ear. Her head tilted back so his mouth had full access to explore her neck.

The stabbing pain of seeing Rixs embrace another woman stung less while in the arms of Athan. Syersi's back was pressed against the intricately carved stone lattice, her eyes closed while the stunning guard caressed her neck. Tiny beads of pleasure prickled over her entire body.

Tucked away in an obscure corner of the palace garden, no eyes would find them – no eyes except Mazzlin's. The Seer could find her anywhere – if Syersi kept her eyes open. If Rangus were nearby, he could sniff them out with his Sanguinary nose. Then there was Rixs. He had the ability to see forms without the use of his eyes. Whether he had the ability to find them in the courtyard maze was yet to be seen.

Athan's kisses were hard, almost frantic as his lips roamed Syersi's neck until his mouth covered hers with a moan. The low rumble vibrating in her ear unexpectedly precipitated a moment of clarity, and in that instant, she wished that another pair of arms held her. The mood was quickly fading. Athan was not doing it for her.

Before she could push him away, a pair of hands grabbed the guard by the collar of his tunic and the band of his britches, slinging him off to the side like table scraps. Startled, Syersi released a yelp at the same time Athan's face hit the dirt.

"Get out of here, wamp!"

Planted over Athan, ready to pounce, Rixs stood with fists clenched. He turned a searing glare on the lady he was sworn to protect. She returned it with a threatening glare of her own.

"What are you doing?" she hissed. "How dare you interrupt me," she hissed again, even though only moments before Syersi had wanted an excuse to walk away from her guard.

Dusting himself off, Athan growled, "You will regret this, *Rixs*."

Rixs narrowed his eyes into dangerous slits. "You forget, wamp! I am Shield, and *you* are abusing your post. Your charge is to protect Lady Syersi from molesters, not become one of them! Now leave. I will deal with you later."

Syersi might have kept her mouth shut had she not remembered seeing Rixs in the arms of Moniere. "I sought out his company, Shield," she challenged.

Shaking his head, Rixs responded, "That makes no difference. He is leaving now. Good-night, Athan." He waggled his fingers in a dismissive gesture.

Her pride would not yield. "I say he stays!" she spat. Her hand swung through the air.

There were two choices — allow the slap or catch the hand. *Whack*! It was mostly for her hand's sake that he turned his head to soften the blow.

"Feel better?" he asked.

A whirlwind snuffed out the light behind her eyes. She slapped at him again, but Rixs was not in the mood to take another hit. He caught her wrist in a strong grip.

"Athan, leave," he demanded while holding Syersi's twisting wrist. "The Lady and I must talk."

Syersi had wanted Athan to go, but that was no longer important. Winning against Rixs had become important. She had to win this battle.

"Need I remind you who I am?" she spat. "Your position has gone to your head! I will dismiss Athan when I am finished with him."

"Then dismiss him!" Nostrils flared, Rixs edged closer, eliminating the distance between them.

"No!" she yelled.

A movement cut the air behind Rixs. Though quick enough, Athan's swing was too slow to catch the Shield unprepared and he dodged the blow effortlessly.

A well-trained warrior, Athan expected to land all his throws and followed up with two additional punches. Rixs sidestepped the first punch, then blocked the second. With mounting frustration, Athan overcompensated heavily to one side, hoping to attack from a different angle. Rixs imposed on his vulnerability with a hard jab to the hollow point where Athan's breastbone ended. It was a tender spot.

"Umph!" Athan doubled over. All the air had been forced from his chest. He hit the ground just as a wave of nausea twisted his insides, and his evening meal heaved up and out onto the ground.

"Sorry," Rixs cringed. "That always happens when I hit people in that spot."

An acrid odor wafted upward toward Syersi's scrunched nose. "Athan! Stop it this instant!" she ordered as if he could control throwing up all over himself. It was the excuse needed to get rid of him without appearing like she had given in. "By The Powers, Athan! Go clean up!"

After wiping his mouth with the back of his hand, the guard picked himself off the ground for a second time. Throwing a final vengeful glare toward the Shield, he stomped off, disappearing around the hedge wall.

Syersi began to talk, but Rixs pressed a finger against her lips, his head cocked to one side. He barked, "Stop listening, wamp! Go!"

Wide blue eyes flashed at Rixs. "You knew he was there?"

She was met with a dark forest glare. "Why would you lower your standards for someone like that?"

Fire lit her eyes. "Are we the hypocrite? I believe your lips had low standards as well!"

"My lips have not touched anyone!" Rixs had planned to explain to Syersi about what happened with Moniere, but anger claimed the better of him. "And even if I had kissed anyone, I am not the Empress Heir, Pixee," he retorted. "You are the one held to a higher moral accountability! Not me!"

Chin tilted up, Syersi scowled at him and fisted her hands, eager to take a swing. Even as she did so her heart burned with an itch too strong to repress. Without thinking she massaged the skin at her breastbone.

For an instant, there was concern in Rixs's eyes as they dropped to her neckline. His neck flushed when he realized how it must have appeared with his eyes locked on her chest. The night suddenly felt too warm.

Syersi followed his eyes to her cleavage then looked up. "Why, Rixsander! You naughty Shield," she taunted. "Are you tempted? Would you like to kiss an Empress Heir?"

The embarrassment Rixs might have felt for staring at her chest was instantly dowsed by the vision of Athan's fingers twisted in her hair and his tongue plunged into her mouth. He shook his head.

"No, thank you, Pixee. I prefer to kiss lips that do not roam as often as yours."

The insult was obvious. Rixs could have slapped Syersi's face with a barbed switch for the same effect. Certainly, the comment slapped the desire from her eyes. There was no need to think her reaction. Without hesitation, Syersi reached into the folds of her skirt and grabbed the black shining blade he had given her.

Even with his eyes latched solely to hers, the shifting of space because of her movement was obvious to him. Rixs intercepted her hand as it withdrew from the slit in her skirt and slammed it roughly over her head against the gneiss lattice wall. Her hand opened at impact against the stone and the blade fell to the ground.

"Ow!" she snarled, baring a set of white teeth.

Rixs leaned in so that his breath tickled the hair at her temples, showing off his own clenched teeth. "You promised not to stab me with the blade I willingly gave you!" he growled.

"How dare you insult me in such a manner!" she struggled beneath his strong grip. "Your grip is hurting me! Let me go!"

"Oh, I think not! I am safer with you pinned to the wall!" he exclaimed. Sandy hair hung in his eyes as he peered at her in amusement. His gaze dropped to her mouth. It would have taken little effort for Rixs to lower his head and discover the secrets of her pink lips. *Kiss her. No!* He battled with himself.

With eyelashes fluttering, Syersi looked up at the strong hand that pinned her smaller hand above her head. She lowered a scorching gaze and fixed on his emerald eyes, only to find him distracted. He was staring at the heaves of her chest as it expanded and contracted against the dangerously low neckline of her gown.

He gulped a mouthful of air and quickly shut his eyes. "You will only hit me again if I release you."

Her free hand slapped him, proving she was still Syersi.

He cursed. Annoyed that he had been too preoccupied with her deep, quick breaths to see the slap coming. He snatched her other hand and thrust it against the wall as well, and they stood there glowering at each other.

The form of a woman interrupted Rixs's glaring match and pulled his attention to the silhouette approaching from the other side of the hedge. He knew who it was and began to release Syersi, then stopped. He and Syersi stood in what must have looked like a compromising position. An intimate position. An idea came to mind. He only hoped Syersi's temperamental disposition would play along. Rixs held her uncooperative arms in place and stared into her raging blue eyes.

The figure rounded the hedge and stopped short. Syersi heard a faint gasp and leaned to the side, peeking around Rixs's neck. Mazzlin was most likely looking for her. Syersi almost gasped.

Moniere stood frozen, her face twisted in a frown.

With strong hands pinning her arms above her head, Syersi knew how it must have looked. The table had turned. This time, it was Moniere with the privilege of seeing Rixs in an intimate embrace, though she knew it was far from intimate. She was smashed against the wall with her arms suspended overhead and Rixs pressed close to prevent her from hitting him – or stabbing him. Still, Syersi took advantage of the situation.

Her mouth hooked into a mischievous curl in one corner. "Did you need something, Moniere?" she breathed, soaking in Moniere's crushed expression.

Feeling a cold stare on his back, Rixs turned his head to look at the young woman, while maintaining his hold on the Empress Heir. "Moniere," he acknowledged.

Guilt flooded over him. Using Syersi's temper to discourage Moniere from chasing him was wrong and cowardly. Not able to stomach the tears that pooled in her eyes, reflecting off the moonlight, Rixs turned away. The infamous Lady had behaved exactly as predicted, playing into their embrace as though they were lovers stealing kisses under a blanket of stars in their own private hideaway.

Moniere was rooted in place, frozen and immovable, so Syersi thought to help her along. "As you can see, girl, we prefer to be alone." It had the intended effect. The retinue smothered her face with her hands and hurried away.

Rixs backed away and released Syersi the moment the young woman disappeared around the corner, muffled sobs leaking from her hand. All traces of anger had vanished in Syersi's expression.

"That was fun!" she said with a pat to his face. "What shall we do next?"

"Come on, Pixee, we need to talk. But we need to go somewhere safe." he said while picking the short blade off the ground. He extended it to her, grip first, and narrowed his eyes, leaning in with a voice as rough as sand and quiet as a spider's bite. "Pull my blade on me again and I'll give you a scar to remember me by!"

She sniffed at his threat but swallowed hard.

Rixs hauled Syersi through the great house while she struggled to yank free. He wondered if she knew who she was — what she was. They slipped unseen into the records chamber.

"Lead the way," Rixs said. He swept an arm forward toward the open door leading into the abyss of darkness waiting to swallow them up.

Her eyes popped wide. "Me?"

"Yes. You. Now hurry!" He gave her a gentle push, then followed, closing the entrance behind them.

Syersi groped for Rixs's hand as she led the way, unseeing, down the long winding stairwell. He let her touch his arm occasionally, so she knew he was close, but forced her to face each step alone.

It was legend that the Source held every Talent and the only way to obtain the Talents was to possess the Source. It was assumed that the Source was an object, but the Emperor had told him that Syersi was the Source. And yet Syersi was not an object – she was a girl. A young woman. And she had no powers from what he had observed unless it was the power to drive him out of his mind.

Small fingertips followed the wall cautiously. "You are quiet," she whispered, the tendrils of silence too fragile for loud voices.

"Sorry, my thoughts plague me," his voice filtered through the darkness while he kept awareness over Syersi's safety. Then he blurted, "What do you know about the Source? Do you think it is an object or a person?"

She stopped abruptly, and he nearly bumped into her, which might have sent her tumbling down the stairs. "What an odd question," she observed without providing an answer.

They both fell into silence until they reached the cavernous chamber where Rixs immediately set Syersi to work. Over and over, she navigated the perimeter of the vast space. He applauded her efficiency and skill. Then came his final request.

"Your last trial, Pixee," he said to her. "I will stay at the door and you will go into the chamber alone. Find the far corner then walk back to me."

She pawed the air until she found his muscled arms then grabbed hold of his vest. "No! Please. I cannot!"

"You can," he encouraged. "Reach within. You always forget. You are more than you realize. The strength required to lead Gnomera is no different than the strength it takes to walk into this darkness."

Time passed with Syersi whimpering into Rixs's chest. After considerable convincing, she gathered herself and shakily shuffled forward in small steps. It was a snail's pace, her feet worming into the void ahead, her hands patting at the thick darkness threatening to suffocate her. It cinched around her breaths, strangled her movements, and smothered her ability to think.

Unseen images teased her eyes. The deep hush drummed loud enough to make her head throb. She perked up for every possible sound that provided clues of her progress only to hear chilling whispers that brushed against her ears. She called out to Rixs for reassurance but there was no reply.

"Shield!" she cried out again. "Shield, answer me!"

Silence answered her.

"Rixsander, please!" she shrilled, breaths were fast and shallow. The darkness spun around her, faster and faster. Her stomach roiled into her throat.

Stumbling into something hard, Syersi screamed. Immediately Rixs's sleek blade was free of its sheath and gripped tightly in her hand. The blade sliced viciously through the air while loud and convulsive sobs heaved from her chest as she fought the would-be demon that had come to claim her.

Strong hands grabbed her arms to hold her still and a shriek shattered against the cavern walls threatening to reduce them to nothing more than rubble. Rixs ducked, missing a violent strike by the blade's edge, then he tightened his grip on both her wrists rendering her swings harmless.

"It's me! Pixee! Shhh, I pushed you too far. I'm sorry. Shhh."

Violent sobs echoed around them, the waves bouncing off the walls only to hit them again. Syersi yanked away from Rixs. She did not trust what she felt and touched. The mind could play cruel tricks.

Rixs pulled her back against his chest and tightened his grip, restraining her from pushing away. He held her against him and kept her body still as he whispered into her hair. A torrent of tears fell against his arm. He praised her bravery.

When they started the long climb back to the records chamber, Rixs reflected on what had happened. He had pushed Syersi too far, but only because urgency demanded it. Things felt wrong at Isslewood, and somehow, he knew danger would find Syersi. She needed to be ready.

With an arm wrapped tightly around her, he smiled in the dark. Just days prior he would have never dared hold Syersi as he was.

Partly because she was annoying, but mostly because his betrothal hung heavy on his shoulders. It kept him distant, but the many faces of Syersi had worn him down. Her head rested on Rixs's shoulder as he pulled her even tighter against him.

Almost at the end of their journey, Rixs tensed. "Someone is in the records chamber," he whispered.

THIRTY-FIVE

The shadowed form hurriedly leafed through binding after binding and tome after tome, which were carelessly tossed to the floor afterward. Syersi and Rixs sat quietly, trapped behind the door while he studied the form and its movement.

"I think it is the Emperor." Rixs muttered in a low tone. "Or the man claiming to be Emperor. I imagine you would know better than anyone. Is that man your father?"

Puny threads of light snuck through the cracks. It was barely enough for Syersi to make out Rixs's silhouette. She breathed easily, relieved to be close to the door instead of the cavern an eternity below.

His question about her father caused her to recall the man's dull blue eyes, the unsettling way he looked at her, and the unease she experienced around him. "The man behaves strangely, and it has made me wonder, but then I remind myself that he has been gone a long time." Her reply barely carried to him.

"Mazzlin and Hobb are adamant he is an imposter," Rixs said.

The slightest sliver of light glimmered under the edge of the door. Syersi stared at it, drawn to it like a moth to a flame. "It would certainly explain his peculiar behavior."

When Rixs caught the underlying meaning of her words, he probed further. "What behavior?"

She was hesitant to say anything but recalled the way Lothorius had touched her leg with a tenderness that wreaked of desire. How he had looked at her – the hunger in his eyes. Perhaps she read too much into his behavior.

She shrugged. Then remembering they still waited in darkness, she asked, "Did you see me do that?"

Rixs narrowed his eyes though she would not have seen it. "Did I see you shrug? Yes. Now answer my question."

A giggle came from her shadowed person, and she mused, "I wish I had an incredible Talent! I can do nothing."

He studied her form through the dark. Syersi held power. She had to know that. "You," Rixs started then paused, not knowing what he should say.

"Did you say something?" Syersi whispered, but he gave no reply.

Time dripped slowly – one sagging drop followed by another. When Rixs and Syersi finally staggered out of the passageway, the sun's bright rays poured through the high windows. Rixs cursed under his breath as he rubbed his stiff and aching neck while Syersi stretched and smoothed her skirt with her hands.

Long before they reached the top of the stairs leading to Syersi's chambers, Rixs detected commotion outside her door. "Great!" he muttered. "They know your bed has been empty all night."

Orris approached them flanked by four guards. The scowl on his face hinted of the trouble that was to follow. "I trust you have a good explanation for having the Lady out of her chambers?" he barked.

Syersi immediately chimed in before Rixs could speak, "Stop yelling, Orris! You will remember I can leave my chambers at my pleasure! Sleep evaded me, so I decided to take a walk. Unfortunately for the Shield, I required him to accompany me." With a tilt of her head, her blue eyes challenged the Commandant.

Orris accepted the challenge. "We saw no one walking the grounds." His wide shoulders were pulled back, his posture straight.

"Because I did not want to be found!" The dismissive wave of her hand implied she was finished. "Now move! I need sleep!" The swish of her gown sounded as angry as she looked.

Nodding to her, Orris then turned to Rixs. "Shield, I would have a word with you, but first, I must have a private word with Lady Syersi." The four hulking guards immediately surrounded Rixs in a cozy ring. "Take him outside to wait for me," the Commandant ordered.

Syersi's stepped into her room and hurried to push the door closed, but a hand caught its edge to keep it from closing. She pushed harder.

"Not so fast, Lady."

She scowled. "Get out, Orris! I am tired." She watched as he ignored her and stepped through the door then closed it. "What do you want?"

His eyes slid over her body, wandering possessively over every curve. He stepped close forcing Syersi to tilt her head upward to meet his simmering gaze.

"Where have you been all night?" he asked through clenched teeth.

She smirked "I do not answer to you, Orris."

Muscles flexed in his jaw. "Why do you push me away when all I have ever wanted was to serve and adore you?"

"Everyone adores me, Orris." She rubbed her forehead and eyes, then ran two hands through her hair. "I push them away too. Stop thinking you are special. Now leave."

A tight smile stretched his cheeks. He ignored her demand and strolled across her chamber, inviting himself onto her balcony. His smile relaxed as his eyes roamed the courtyard. He glanced over his shoulder, as if to beckon her to join him.

"Your father wishes to speak to you, Syersi," he said.

As if pulled by an invisible string, she mindlessly made her way out onto the balcony. A wide yawn stretched her mouth, then she replied with a groggy voice, "I will see him after I rest."

The sun's rays reflected off the sparkling Gneiss Curtain, making everything brighter and difficult to see. She raised a hand to shield her eyes from the glittering light and scanned the grounds until her attention landed on Rixs.

He was standing in the courtyard, but he was not alone. Yet

again, Moniere, stood too close to her Shield. Orris had wanted him to wait outside but that did not include allowing Moniere to have another opportunity to twist her arms around Rixs's neck. Keedra stood with them, making light conversation, but it was the kiss Moniere planted on her Shield that made her hiss and walk away, threats to hang him off Tower Wall just under her breath.

The instant Syersi withdrew from her balcony, he felt the chill of barren space. Her form had become known to him, as distinctive as her name, or the color of her eyes. Rixs knew every curve of her form and the way her shape occupied the air around her like it was his own body.

Syersi's abrupt retreat was not a good sign and by the time he wrenched loose of Moniere's snaking grip, it was too late. The damage had been done. A quick glance at the balcony was met with the Commandant's smug grin just before he retreated into Syersi's chamber.

Rixs glared at the vacant balcony and growled as he pushed the retinue off him, wiping the remnants of her kiss off his mouth with the back of his hand. "You make yourself easy, girl!" his voice was a low roar.

Keedra frowned and cleared her throat before speaking. "Moniere! I had no idea you were so bold!"

"Keedra," the retinue replied. "You are jealous because I got to kiss him first!"

"He obviously does not want your kiss! He pushed you away!" she replied.

The guards laughed and teased. "Give us a try, Moniere. We'll not be pushing you off!"

Orris ghosted a smirk as he turned to face Syersi. The encounter had been a success. Syersi had seen that Rixs was nothing special. He was just another man, susceptible, like most men, to the temptations of a gloriously beautiful woman. And Moniere was beautiful. He had enjoyed her kisses himself, from time to time.

Orris walked to the middle of Syersi's chamber, smugness set deep in his face. "It appears that Moniere has sights on your Shield."

"So what, Orris?" Syersi bit. "The Shield can do as he pleases."

The Commandant chuckled. "And he *pleases* to have Moniere in his arms with her lips all over him. Even I blushed as I watched them, and as you well know," he gave Syersi a knowing wag of his brows, "I do not blush easily. However, I do recall that time when you and I ..."

"Again – why are you still here?" Syersi demanded, barely managing to keep her temper from spilling through her ears. She wanted to scream or throw something at Orris because Rixs was not within reach. Uncharacteristic of her nature, Syersi controlled the tantrum trembling beneath her skin. "As soon as you leave, I will lay down and rest."

The reaction was not typical Syersi. The Empress Heir that Orris knew was emotional, temperamental and had never backed away from the cliffs of her anger. She had always jumped. Orris had wanted her fury against Rixs. Instead, she unleashed calm.

Softening in the presence of her tranquility, he closed the distance between them and cautiously placed his hands on her shoulders. Her petite frame molded in his grasp, and he carefully pulled her into his chest, surprised when she let him. Syersi leaned into him.

There were times when Syersi had wished Rixs held her in such a manner. Held her because he wanted to and not because she was frightened. With eyes closed, she pretended the strong arms that wrapped her in warmth belonged to her Shield.

Orris kissed the top of her head and breathed in the scent of her hair. "You know I am devoted to you," he whispered.

Syersi pushed back, though his arms resisted. "Please. You are no more devoted to me than the fifteen other girls you have held in your arms this season alone," she countered.

"They mean nothing to me." He brushed the shining silky hair away from her forehead and stared into her eyes.

"You take me for a fool, Orris! And sound ridiculous while you do it!" Her ire was fully inflamed. Syersi had finished with him. "I go to speak to my father."

She turned and walked to the private garden – walked with a self-assured stride. Rixs's training had taught her to walk with purpose.

You are floating again! Stop floating, she could hear him say, her memory reliving the grueling days she spent walking back and forth in front of him. Determined to invade the airy garden like the fighter Rixs intended her to be, Syersi refused to *float* – she walked with swagger.

Keen interest sparked in the Commandant's eyes as he followed behind her. Amusement had his lips curling. Again, this was not the Empress Heir he knew. The woman in front of him swung her hips from side to side, and her shoulders pitched back and forth in a rousing rhythmic movement. Swiping a tongue over his teeth, Orris swallowed at the display.

There was an echo of voices when Syersi stormed through the high arches that gave way to the bursting colors of the garden suspended high above the ground, and her father sitting in the center. Kyerg, one of her father's confidants, leaned over the seated Emperor and listened with intent as Lothorius spoke. Upon seeing his daughter, Lothorius rose from his seat, then scowled when he noticed Orris nearly drooling behind her.

"You know what to do," Lothorius nodded to Kyerg in dismissal. After the man left, the Emperor turned to Orris, who had dropped to one knee. "Leave us, Orris," was all he said.

Expelled without consideration. Orris flexed his jaw, but he obediently lifted from the floor. After a final glance Syersi's way, he stormed out.

Left alone with her father, Syersi studied the man who was far from fatherly. In reciprocating stares, they eyed each other. While she critiqued him methodically, his eyes stroked over her in slow hungry sweeps. The overwhelming need to vomit smothered her.

Like a predator, the man stalked in her direction then stopped directly in front of her. He reached out and stroked the long black hair framing her shoulders, then pulled her into a hug.

"Alone at last," he breathed, and stroked her with a touch too urgent to be her father.

Syersi yanked away and briskly rubbed at her arms to rid herself of his grimy touch. As she squinted at him, she finally understood.

"You are not my father! You are an imposter!" She started to back away, but a strong rough grip clamped onto her hand.

Cold eyes pinned her in place. "Do you think you are leaving?"

Suddenly frightened, a silent scream raced through Syersi's blood, and she had a mind to pull her blade – Rixs's blade. *The blade is your last resort, Pixee. Once you have pulled it, you have lost the element of surprise. Do not show your hand too soon. Use it only as a last option.*

The blade remained tucked against her thigh. It brought comfort to know that a piece of her Shield was with her, even if she hated him for kissing her retinue. He gave her courage. He protected her. He would come for her, just as he had at the farmers' market.

Without the option of using her blade, there was only one choice to make. "Take your hands off me!" she cried, then made sure he made no mistake of her feelings for him. In typical Syersi fashion, the palm of her hand smashed into the side of his nose. A crack split the air, followed by two bellowing cries.

THIRTY-SIX

"You, gimcrack! This is a big mistake!" Rixs yelled. "I am not the enemy!"

After leaving Syersi with Lothorius, Orris had returned to the courtyard to retrieve Rixs, then promptly locked him up in the recesses of the prison. Rix had put up a noble effort to resist, but four guards were too many to fight at once. He was eventually overpowered.

Through the small window of the cell door, Rixs spat, "Worthless fool!"

"I dislike you, Woodsman! I especially dislike the way you have weaseled into Syersi's life. Even so, this was not my order. This was the Emperor's order."

"The Emperor asked me to join him!" Rixs snarled. "Why would he do this?"

Orris came close, spitting as he talked. "He does not trust you."

"When the Counselor and Absolute return..." Rixs began but was cut off.

"The Emperor will imprison them for treason!" Orris shouted. The flickering flames of the torch he held warped his face in twisted ribbons of shadow and light. "I know the truth, Rixs — what really happened behind the Emperor's disappearance. The Intimus betrayed him. They indulged and spoiled Syersi to keep her dependent on them so they could control Gnomera." Orris narrowed his eyes. "With a selfish child unfit to rule, the people turned to the Counselor as their leader!"

Rixs had heard the same thing from the man calling himself Lothorius, but it felt wrong. "It rings false," Rixs insisted. "Tell me your fat, swollen head can think! It must be good for something more than your mammoth ego! Do you think Rangus would have left him to die? He is Sanguinary! If the Intimus wanted him dead, he would be dead! Something is not right!"

Orris stood just out of reach on the other side of the door. His face was flat and Rixs knew his words fell on deaf ears. It would do little good to tell the Commandant the Emperor was an imposter, or that he was after one thing – the Source. Syersi was in danger.

Rixs grabbed the door and shook it. "Let me out!" he bellowed. "Syersi is in danger!"

"Syersi is safe! I protect her!" Orris yelled, jabbing a thumb at his own chest.

Growling, Rixs thrust an arm through the window. He needed to hit Orris, but the distance between his fist and the Commandant's face was too far. "You, gimcrack!"

Startled by the quick movement, the Commandant jumped back. "You already called me that," he spat. His hand smoothed an invisible wrinkle on his immaculately straight uniform.

Rixs kicked the door.

"Have fun rotting in your new home," Orris taunted. "Oh, I almost forgot …" he smiled wickedly. "Thanks for the clashing vest and blades." Then the echo of footsteps sounded in the fading torchlight.

Every vein in Rixs's body nearly exploded. Rage as he had never-before experienced choked the air from his throat and left him speechless and shaking. He turned from the door and punched wildly into the air but was left unsatisfied. He slammed his fist into the stone wall. Immediately he regretted it, blood dripped from his knuckles and his hand throbbed. He needed the pain to fuel his anger.

The cell was unfamiliar. Unlike his previous visits to lockup, this cell was several floors down in the far recesses of the lifeless prison.

He sat in the dark – in the silent deep reaches where people died without anyone giving them a second thought.

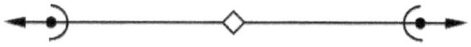

Syersi protectively cocooned her hand hoping to dull the excruciating pain. It was her reward for smashing the imposter's face. Short, quick gulps of air helped her bear the agony, but even better was the blood seeping from her so-called father's fingers as he held his broken nose.

Without warning, a hand struck her face, the force of it powerful enough to propel her into a nearby stone planter. Syersi threw her already injured hand in front of her to catch her fall and cried out as another sting burned through her hand and traveled up her arm.

"Imposter!" she managed to screech through numb lips that were swelling. A wipe of her hand drew away blood and confirmed what she already knew. She had a split lip.

"Guards!" she yelled while backing away, poised to run. "Guards!"

Without concern of Syersi's call for help, the imposter straightened his back and grabbed a linen from the table to soak the blood running from his nose. His face showed only calm.

"Who are you, and why are you impersonating my father?" Syersi's eyes wavered between him and the archway.

A tall, muscular body emerged into view. "You called, my Lady?" the guard asked.

Syersi visibly relaxed. With calm she ordered, "Take this man. He is not my father. Take him for questioning."

The guard looked at the other man but made no move.

"Well? I gave you an order!" she exclaimed, alarm rising in her voice. When he still made no move, she stormed toward the door. "Fine. I shall find the Commandant!"

The guard stepped in front of her.

Blinking at the guard's behavior, Syersi spun around and hurried to the opposite archway. She glanced behind her and noticed that the imposter had made himself comfortable in a chair, still holding a cloth to his nose. Faded blue eyes followed her across the floor.

An internal alarm drove Syersi's feet to go faster, but before she could disappear through the archway, another hulking body blocked her exit. Attempts to shove her way past were in vain. The human barrier shifted with her moves and effectively kept her pinned in. A scream pierced the air while small fists punched at the rock-hard body until the pain in Syersi's swollen hand forced her to stop.

"Bring her here," the calm, gravelly voice commanded.

While kicking and hitting, Syersi's body was lifted at the waist with a single arm. She thrashed at the guard, but he easily held onto her until he forcefully dropped her into a chair.

The quiver in her lower lip revealed that she was close to tears. She did not want to cry, but bravery seemed just out of reach. Rixs had tried to warn and prepare her for something like this.

Wintry eyes signaled the guards, and both men walked out, leaving the frightened girl alone with the man that she had stupidly mistaken as her father. She glared at him, hoping Mazzlin was watching through her eyes. She would get help.

"Wait until Rixsander finds me, or Mazzlin …"

Laughter cut her threat to shreds. He shook his head. "Your cries will summon no one, my dear." He glanced around them. "As far as anyone is concerned, I am Emperor, and your father. No one would dare interfere with me. And you are well-known for your screaming fits. Scream away. Though I would advise you not to." He leaned forward and stared down his swollen nose until his narrowed stare met hers. "It would grate on my nerves something fierce."

"Who are you? What do you want?" Syersi managed through a thick and heavy lip.

He tilted his head as if to study her from a different angle and leaned back in his chair. "You are ignorant," he exhaled with wonder. "Chadgerwin has not told you — has he?" He laughed and clapped his hands. "Oh, this is good! Very, very good!"

Tight lips drew her ivory skin taut, and she quipped, "Then out with it! What do you want?"

"I want you, of course."

Syersi's heart pummeled her ribs with fast beats. The man took her hand, which she instinctively tried to yank away, but his grip held firm.

"As for *who* I am. I am Moganar, your father's look-alike."

Her eyes batted frantically at his declaration, and her mouth had difficulty closing. "My father had no double." Though the moment she said it, Mazzlin's and Hobb's reactions came to her mind and Syersi realized they must have known.

They had tried to subtly voice their warning, but she had ignored them. She had ignored her Guardian. It was easy to do since the woman often rambled on about nothing. Generally, Mazzlin was too flighty to be taken seriously, but it occurred to Syersi that had she listened to her Guardian, she would not be stuck in this predicament. Another lesson learned too late.

Moganar placed a finger under her chin and pushed her loosely hanging jaw closed. "I was employed by your father to stand in whenever needed. I prepared for seasons upon seasons to walk, talk, and act like Lothorius. We already know I look quite like him. When he died, I slipped into his place."

It took a moment of dawning before Syersi cried out, "Died! What do you mean? My father is not dead!"

There was more laughter. "The Intimus has kept you in the dark, dear girl! Your father is dead." His laughter dissolved. "And now, you belong to me!"

"You are mad!" she snarled. Jumping out of her seat, she ran for the archway.

Moganar rose from his chair and shouted, "Are we starting this again? You know what happened the last time you tried to leave."

On cue, the same ominous figure appeared in front of her. She slid to a stop and ran in the opposite direction. *Run, not float! Run, not float!* The words rang repeatedly in her head.

The bands that held her courage paralyzed cracked enough to combat her terror. *Use your head. Think, Syersi, think!* When the guard lunged toward her, she pivoted around an enormous planter. Large fountain grasses, growing in dense clumps with fanning sharp blades poked at her. The guard was not so fortunate and fell into the welcome of those trenchant blades. He cursed loudly.

The second guard appeared and came at her from the opposite archway. Syersi was trapped. Moganar and the table blocked her from behind, and two guards closed in at either side. There was nowhere to run. The path directly in front of her was blocked by another stone planter overflowing with more sharp grasses. At its side stood an imposing statue carved in the likeness of one of her ancestors.

A narrow gap between the statue and planter offered the only hope of escape. She would need to suck in deeply to make herself as thin as possible if there was any chance of squeezing through, but there was no time for second guessing. Syersi inhaled and sucked herself in until it hurt – until she was sure she would turn inside-out, then she squished into the gap.

The three men converged on her. Her screams were not of fear, but of determination to push through the tight space, even while the skin on her cheek tore against the rough stone. Emerging on the other side, the Empress Heir dared not pause but instantly ran.

No prancing, Syersi! With purpose, Syersi!

Footfalls echoed behind her as she ran. Looking for a place to find help, she knew not to trust the servants to hide her. Moganar looked too much like her father, and they would hand her over in fear of him. Panic strangled her windpipe, and she fought to breathe.

Where are you, Mazzy? You always intruded on my fun, and now that I need you, you are nowhere!

Syersi's salvation was obvious. Rixs had tried to prepare her for it, but the mere thought of it still terrified her. The pit of despair – the black and horrible secret chamber. If she could master the abyss, Rixs would find her. Somehow, her heart knew he would come for her.

Racing through corridors and passageways, the clattering steps of her pursuers faded as distance separated her from Moganar's men. A sense of triumph gave her second wind. There was hope.

She burst through the last doorway that would take her to the records chamber and smacked into a hard body with an "umph!" Strong arms wrapped her up.

"Whoa! Where are you off to in such a hurry?"

The familiar voice caused a sob to bubble up from her throat.

Syersi sank into the Commandant's arms, tears spilling freely onto her cheeks. His entire body tightened around her and she shook with her cries.

"Syersi, what happened?" Orris asked as he held her back to run his eyes over her. His face fell at what he saw.

One of her beautiful cheeks was torn and bleeding. Dried blood clung to the corner of her swollen mouth where a cut on her lower lip could be seen. A bruise, dark and blue, colored her jaw.

"Who did this to you?" he growled.

The guards rounded the corner and slid to a stop, their chests rising and falling in deep quick breaths. Orris leveled a glare at them.

"Did you do this to her?" His voice rumbled.

"No, they did not," a voice announced. "I did," Moganar said as he appeared in front of them.

At the sight of the imposter, Syersi's cries escalated in volume and pitch. Moganar watched with an eye full of impatience. Orris tightened his grip on her and pummeled his Emperor with questioning eyes.

"My daughter is..." Moganar began.

Syersi screeched at him. "I'm not your daughter!"

The expression on Moganar's face, the sigh in his throat, the tilt of his head – all spoke for him. *See? Here is Syersi doing what Syersi does best ... throwing fits.* He closed his eyes briefly.

"Did you throw fits like this around your new Shield? No wonder he left so easily," Moganar said, staring pointedly at Orris. Rixs's imprisonment was to be kept a secret.

"You are a liar!" she screamed.

"Shhh," Orris murmured. Protectively he cradled her head to his chest. "It does no good to scream at him. And anyway, we all knew Rixs wanted to go home."

"No!" Syersi pushed out of his arms. "He would never abandon me!" After a few hiccups, she resolved to pull herself together and wiped her cheeks, only to be rewarded with a sting. She whimpered, having forgotten about her torn cheek and split lip.

A smile that dripped of concern graced Moganar's face. "My daughter, I am sorry about your cheek and lip." He shook his head and spoke to Orris. "She broke my nose, you know." He grinned wide. "I'm actually quite proud of her."

"Why would the Lady break your nose?" Orris frowned at the swollen nose and blood-smeared face of the man he thought was Lothorius. "Your face fared better than your daughter's. It seems only a vicious man would do such a thing to his own daughter." It was a bold thing for Orris to say.

Moganar spoke pointedly. "I do not explain myself to anyone, Commandant. But rest assured, my daughter's safety is my utmost priority." His stormy blue eyes dueled with Orris. The elder triumphed, and Orris nodded his head.

"Bring her to the records chamber. I must speak with my daughter in private."

"No!" Syersi cried. "That is not the Emperor, Orris! I should have seen it sooner!" She pointed at him. "He is an imposter! He admitted it!"

Grabbing Orris, her fingers clawed into his tunic as she pleaded, "He is lying, Orris! You must believe me!" She jerked away and ran, but Moganar's guards were prepared and had her under their control swiftly.

Wary servants had gathered on each end of the hall to witness the spectacle. Syersi had always been difficult and unkind, but she had never acted in such a manner to her father. Her desperate behavior unsettled those within hearing distance.

"Enough! Take her!" The imposter signaled to his men, and they hauled Syersi, kicking and screaming, down the hall and into the records chamber. Then he swung his head from side to side, observing the servants. "Is there a reason to be gawking?" All eyes lowered and heads ducked in nervous apology as they scrambled away.

Screams were heard down the hall. Orris listened with clenched teeth and started in pursuit of the cries.

Placing a hand on the Commandant's shoulder as he walked past, Moganar said firmly, "Be at ease, Commandant. She is my daughter, and I will deal with her as I see fit. Now, bring me status on Chadgerwin. I want to know his whereabouts."

Orris stood stiff and defiant. Moganar stared into the man's eyes until he dropped his head in submission. He smiled and patted Orris on the back then ambled past to enter the records chamber where Syersi's muffled sobs still carried through the closed doors.

THIRTY-SEVEN

Chadgerwin had thumbed through the bindings. Rixs had searched the bindings. Now, Syersi watched as Moganar threw binding after binding onto the floor. He barely looked at any of them.

Alone with the imposter, Syersi slumped back into a chair, rubbing her arms briskly to warm the chill of Moganar's presence. She turned her head, surveying her surroundings, pausing to look longingly at the hidden door that could have been her salvation.

"What are you doing?" she whispered, her throat as gritty as sand.

After a moment of intense study of her features, he answered. "I am looking for a binding that was very important to your father … almost as important to him as your mother."

A wicked grin slid across his face and he walked over, kneeling in front of Syersi. The hard wood dug into her spine as she retreated as far into the unforgiving chair as she could.

His tone was soft and eerie. "Do you know why he protected your mother so fiercely?" Narrowed eyes bore into her.

A whisper of something she should have known, begged to be remembered, but Syersi was helpless to recall it. She provided an obvious reply. "He protected her because he loved her."

"You would think, but no." He leaned close, so that his breath tickled her skin. "You really have no idea, do you? You have no idea what your mother was. What you are." His eyes brushed over her face. "*You*, my dear, are more precious than all the world's treasure. A blessing from The Powers! And you are mine."

A shiver slithered up from the base of Syersi's spine to the top of her head. Every hair on her slender neck stood on end. There was nowhere to run – nowhere to hide, so she waited for him to have his say.

"For six seasons cycles your father tutored me. Mentored me to be just like him. Sometimes, he had me stand for him in the receiving hall. His adoring subjects never knew it was me to whom they bowed and groveled. And as I worked to become him, they never told me the real reason I needed to be ready to take his place.

"How naïve I had been. How deceptive he had been. How betraying the Intimus had been." Moganar's voice had become a quiet snarl as he talked. "They thought they could keep me from the truth, but I found out." His pale blue eyes stared into hers.

On so many occasions the Lady Saudria had admonished Syersi to sit still for her lessons. But the young Empress Heir already knew who she was. She would be ruler. What else was there worth knowing? At that moment, she wished she had sat still for her lessons.

Dredging through the abyss of forgotten and colorless memories, vague, ghostly reflections that had long since faded into nothing sat just out of reach. She stretched to claim something – anything.

You are very special, my adorable. Your love will bestow the most powerful gift in the world.

It had all been shoved deep into the caverns of emptiness, where Syersi had buried the memories of her mother. It only brought heartache when thoughts of Lady Saudria surfaced. Her touch. Her smile. But it was the way in which she had died that had made the memories of her too hard to bear, and she dealt with it all by not thinking about it. Another memory stirred.

Mummy, why is Father not afraid of Rangus? Everyone else is afraid of him.

Well, my adorable, it is because your father is ... how shall I put it? He is very strong, and very powerful.

But no one is as strong as Rangus, Mummy! No one is as strong as Sanguinary!

Syersi envisioned the hazy, faint recollection of her mother's smile.

There is another that is stronger, but it is a secret, Syersi. It is something we do not speak of. There is another that dominates the Sanguinary, the Soothe, the Sanicle …

The memory evaporated into nothing. Syersi could remember no more, but deep within, there was a hunch. Something itched at her.

"I found out, Syersi," Moganar's voice broke the spell and pulled the Empress Heir back to the records chamber. He spoke in a shaky whisper; his eyes were almost frantic. "I know all about the Source. I only came back to confirm what I know, and to do that, I must find the binding. It holds all the mysteries."

Eyes glazed over, Moganar might have sat on the moon for the far-away look that stilled his face. It was an opportunity to get away, but too soon he shook his head, and too quickly, he had returned from where he had gone.

"Perhaps you know the binding I seek. It is red." He scanned the thousands of bindings.

A quick sweep over walls of endless shelves, Syersi's wide blue eyes inhaled the task of finding a single binding in the sea of records. Even if she knew where the binding hid, she would never admit it. With the thousands of tomes and bindings before them, it would take seasons to find it, and with all Syersi's scanning, there was not a red binding among them.

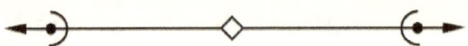

Low tones gradually coaxed Syersi from a restless nap. Every muscle screamed to stretch, but she forced herself to remain still and kept her eyes closed. A low gravelly voice she recognized as Kyerg spoke.

"Even if you never find the binding, you still have the girl," he had said. "Is there any way to tell for certain? Do you know if Talent resides in her and how to draw it out?"

Moganar shuffled to grab another tome. "No, and no. There are no markings on her skin that I can see." He paused then sneered. "But I have yet to see her without clothes ..." He stared at the endless records. "I need that binding! This is all speculation without it!"

Every moment brought a new revelation. Syersi contained her fear and through sheer determination placed a leash on her sobs. They spoke as if she was the Source. The giver of Talent. The legend linked to the Denier Cri. Moganar would be deeply disappointed to realize she had no Talent.

A shiver ran through her body. He planned to explore her body for some mark of the Source. *He believes the Source is a person.*

Rixs had asked a similar question. She remembered he had asked if she believed the Source was a person or an object.

What a notion! The idea that a person held all the Talents only to surrender them to someone else – it was preposterous. Why would they do that and not keep the Talents for themselves? And how would that work? How would the Talents be given away? Syersi's mind reeled.

Without permission, the Shield's face opened to her thoughts. Playful green eyes, full of mischief, taunted her. One had to look hard to find the light sprinkling of freckles that dappled his nose. A smile almost touched her lips at the vision of his soft, unruly hair that always found its way into his eyes. Her chest cramped so tight it nearly suffocated her.

Approaching footsteps pushed her daydream aside and caused Syersi's heart to drum hard and fast. It would thump straight through her ribcage if it pounded any harder.

The edge of a cloak brushed by. "She is a beauty. You cannot deny it," Kyerg's voice was low and quiet.

"Lucky me," Moganar's breath tickled her cheek.

At his voice, Syersi's eyes popped open, and she jerked away. Stiff muscles made it difficult to move but she was motivated. The hard and unforgiving chair only allowed her to retreat so far.

"Ah, the beauty wakes," the imposter cooed, stroking her cheek with a long finger. "Good. Now we can discuss our new arrangement."

Syersi winced away from his touch, which elicited a sinister grin from him. A quiet knock caught Moganar's attention just before the door pushed open.

Syersi held her breath and prayed to The Powers that emerald eyes belonging to a head of sandy tousled hair peeked through the doorway. Her expression fell when a square face and dark brown eyes framed by dark brown hair poked in the chamber.

"Supreme," Orris dropped to a knee and cast a quick stern glance at Kyerg. "We have word that the First Counselor and Absolute were spotted on the eastern side of the mole hills. They ride fast and should reach Isslewood by nightfall." His eyes scanned the room until they found Syersi.

There was no way Orris could miss Syersi's battered face. The swollen lip, bruised jaw, and scrapes along her cheek almost made her unrecognizable. A swollen hand was cradled in her lap. These injuries were easily fixed with Hobb's Talent, but he had disappeared along with the Guardian. Her absence was particularly puzzling since Mazzlin fussed over Syersi like a mother hen. Orris knew something was not right.

"I thank you, Commandant." There was not the slightest hint of unease in Moganar's features.

Orris addressed Moganar. "Might I take the Lady to her chambers to rest in her own covers?"

Moganar's reply was flat and cold. "You take an eager interest in my daughter, Commandant. Thank you, but no. I will see that she gets to her chambers."

"Commandant," Syersi quivered, her voice soft and hopeful. "Can you find my Shield?" Moisture coated her eyes.

He hated to be the one to snuff out her hope, but a quick look at the Emperor put him in his place. Syersi would hate Orris if she ever found out what he had done with Rixs. She would see it as a betrayal of her trust, but he had no choice. He was sworn to serve his Emperor.

Straightening the invisible yet persistent wrinkle in his tunic,

Orris said, "He has left Isslewood." Her scrunched nose made him faulter briefly, and for a moment, he thought she could smell his lie.

She replied, "He would never leave without ..."

Orris interrupted, his lie easily slipping from his mouth. "He left. I told you he would go back to his betrothed!" His voice was fierce in defense of his untruth, even though Rixs sat in the recesses of the prison.

"Be comforted, daughter," Moganar crooned. "Few men could resist the temptation of wealth in exchange of leaving Gnomera. I bribed him to leave."

Orris turned his stare on him.

Moganar continued, "He was an outsider. Chadgerwin had no right to appoint him Imperial Shield." He reached for Syersi with a sympathetic smile. "Anyway, he may have thought of you, *briefly*, before he walked out the gate with a heavy purse."

Syersi jumped away from Moganar's pending touch and shook her head. Dark lashes blinked away angry tears. "You lie! Everyone knows Rixsander has more honor in his little finger than most men have in their entire body! He would never leave without a word!"

Jealousy drove the Commandant to lose his temper. "Rixsander, Rixsander, Rixsander! I am sick of him! He hates to be called Rixsander!" he yelled. "And he could barely tolerate you! He would have had no problem taking his riches and leaving! And if he thought of you at all, it would have been *good riddance!*"

One step was all Syersi needed before she swung her fist. The hit had cracked him in the eye before a singe of fire exploded in her knuckles and burned through to her elbow. Orris roared at the hit while Syersi screamed at the pain in her hand.

With fists clenched tight enough to split his knuckles, Orris's entire body shook with the desire to hit the man with whom he was most angry. He moved toward the Emperor, but a blanket of calm came from nowhere to ease the tension in the chamber. His anger faded.

Syersi felt the air shift and knew immediately. She had felt it before. That feeling of tranquility that Chadgerwin had used so often to help dilute her outbursts and pacify her tantrums. No matter how subtle, she recognized Soothe – but Chadgerwin was not there. Syersi sat straight and looked around the room.

Typical for one under the Soothe influence, Orris apologized. "Forgive me, Lady Syersi. I am not myself."

"Leave, Commandant," Moganar ordered.

Docile and obedient, Orris bowed his head and silently left the chamber, his passion nothing more than a speck of dust.

It was the same for Syersi. The intensity of her fear and anger had deserted her – only remnants remained. Like Orris, Syersi felt calm, but unlike Orris, she knew why. Her eyes blinked at the only man who could have been responsible. Kyerg. He was a Soothe.

"We should be on our way," Kyerg said. "We have what you came for. The Counselor approaches."

"I hate to go," Moganar looked around him. "All this should be mine, but, yes, we should take our leave before it's too late." He nodded and reached for Syersi. "Come, my dear, it is time."

She jerked away. "I refuse to go anywhere with you!"

"My little ignorant one. You will leave with me. I cannot leave my intended bride behind."

Syersi froze, her mouth unhinged. Slowly, her head shook from side to side, then faster and faster. "Your bride!" she screeched.

Moganar replied pointedly. "You are the Source, Syersi. I *will* possess you. Your powers *will* be mine!"

Her slender fingers fondled at the pleats in her dress, the blade begged to be used. "What are you speaking about? I am no Source, and you are insane!"

"Maybe you are not and maybe I am, but you *will* come with me," he said coldly. "Of your own free will. There will be no screaming. No hysterics. No resistance. You will cooperate."

"You can drag my dead body behind your horse before I cooperate!" Syersi spat.

A dark shadow passed over his features and his lips flattened. "What if I drag the body of Mazzlin, or Hobb? Maybe both?"

Her face fell instantly.

"Your dead body would do me little good. I need you alive to have your Source's power." He lifted a brow and adjusted his cloak.

"The Source is a myth," her voice quivered. Moganar had obviously thought the Source was a person.

"No, my love. The Source is not a myth. It is you. Now come or I shall drag those who you care for until their skin falls from their bones." He leaned in close until she turned her head in disgust. "I have Mazzlin and Hobb tucked away. Their survival depends on you. The choice is yours."

Syersi groped for rational argument. "Why steal me away when you could stay here and continue to play Emperor and I would be your daughter. You would rule Gnomera." Her hands twisted in her skirt. "If you run off with me, people will come after you. Rangus will hunt you down." Visions of the Sanguinary tearing out Moganar's heart gave her a thrill.

"I will have Gnomera's throne," he said. "Once I have the powers of the Source, I can take any throne I please. I could rule the world." Moganar gathered up a few things from the table. "And Rangus will be no challenge at all."

A madman was always dangerous, Chadgerwin had taught the Empress Heir. There could be none more dangerous than the madman she stared down. Begrudgingly, Syersi stole a last glance at the door cleverly camouflaged among the ornate shelving. Its pathway to gloom would have been paradise when compared to the situation she faced. Would he follow through? Would she become a bedmate to the madman who had posed as her father? She shivered.

No one questioned them as they left. No one dared challenge Lothorius, the Supreme. Even the guards from Syersi's own entourage stood by as they passed, Orris not among them.

The soldiers who had camped outside Tower Wall flanked them as they rode. Syersi searched the grounds for anyone who might challenge the false emperor, but no one did.

Moganar set a brisk pace heading due west, avoiding Ormolu. The sun was directly overhead which meant there would be plenty of daylight to ride before suspicions were aroused.

Syersi watched as the majestic wall shrank into the distance. Quiet tears etched a moist path down her face. *Rixsander, where are you?*

THIRTY-EIGHT

Two lifeless forms sprawled across the floor above. Thanks to the Talent he held, Rixs knew he was the lone occupant on his floor, five levels down from the surface. The only company so deep beneath the prison were two limp and motionless bodies one floor above him.

No torches lit the halls. The young Talent sat in total darkness on the gritty stone floor, his back propped against the wall as he racked his brain for a way out. With legs drawn up so each elbow rested on a knee, he stared meticulously at everything and nothing.

Time dawdled. His chamber pot could have moved faster if it wanted, and that would have been amazing since there was no chamber pot in his cell. He would worry about where to relieve himself later.

He thought a lot about the Empress Heir — her forever blue eyes, her silky black hair always adorned with a gem or two, and the haughty attitude that made him want to turn her over his knee. She hid behind an angry mask to hide vulnerabilities. A subtle twinge just under his breastbone had him pressing his thumb into it.

The gnawing feeling that Syersi was in danger fed his burning need to escape. Far beneath the main prison floor, Rixs had no idea what was happening on the surface. He let his anger lead as he plunged into the task of exploring every stone for a weakness. Eventually, he slumped to the floor.

Drool seeped out the corner of his mouth and slid down his chin. It might have been the screeching silence that woke him, but his bones ached from the cruel stones that dug into his hip. He stood and jumped several times to shake off the haze of confusion before finally wiping the drool from his face. Then he saw the shadowed form, dark and full against the black.

A voice that half called, and half whispered rebounded off the walls. "Rixs! Are you down here?"

Rixs pressed his face to the opening in the door. "Pravin! Is that you?"

Torchlight bounced through the dark, the firm tap of footsteps picked up speed. Rixs closed his eyes in relief. If he had a friend at Isslewood, it was Pravin, his chosen Second Shield. They had not known each other long, but had struck up a rapport.

"Look for my hand sticking through the opening," he called.

A bright flame shoved toward the small window. Blinded, Rixs jumped back and cursed.

"Apologies," Pravin said and lowered the torch. "I did not think. Your eyes must be sensitive."

"Glad to see you, Second!" Rixs exclaimed.

"Glad I found you, Shield. Forgive me. I had not noticed you were missing until the Emperor left Isslewood with the Lady Syersi in tow. I wondered why you would let her leave."

"He left with the First Daughter?" Rixs yelled, hitting the door with both fists.

Pravin flinched. "That had to hurt."

Rixs grunted and punched the door again.

Pravin spoke again. "I knew something was wrong. Asked the Commandant but he said you left for Pax Valley." The Second looked at Rixs and shrugged. "I knew you would never leave without a word, so I set out to find you … been looking since yesterday at high sun."

Locked up for one day and a half! It meant the imperial imposter had a significant lead. Rixs paced in his cell as Pravin laboriously tried every key on the ring he had confiscated from a guard after knocking him unconscious. The man was only halfway through the keys when

Rixs cocked his head to the side.

"Someone else is coming," he warned Pravin.

The soldier froze. "How do you know?"

Rixs mentally kicked his own backside for the slip. "I ... I can hear footsteps."

Pravin paused to listen to the silence. He looked at the torch. There was no hiding with a torch in his hand.

It did not take long to spot another dancing flame down the long dark hall. Then footsteps tapped against the stone floor. The flame grew brighter, and brighter, until it stopped in front of Pravin.

An unseen voice sounded behind the second torch. "I wondered where those keys disappeared to." Orris stepped into view, like a bad dream. His expression was menacing, his posture, stiff as a board, and his clothing was tight enough against his muscular frame to tear at the seams. "I seriously hope you are not trying to free our dangerous prisoner," he mused.

"Commandant!" the startled Pravin cried while drawing his sword.

Orris regarded him with narrow eyes and bushy brows that furrowed into one. "I suggest you stand down, soldier." There was no hint of anxiousness to suggest he would draw his own sword. He was Commandant. It was common knowledge that he could take any Lothorian Guard easily. That included Pravin.

With a thick swallow, Pravin forced himself to re-sheath his weapon. Orris held out his hand and wagged his fingers, gesturing for the keys.

Rixs thrust his hand through the small window in the cell door. "Throw me the keys!"

It was a hesitation too long. Pravin tossed the keys toward Rixs's outstretched hand, but Orris easily intercepted.

"Enough!" Orris bellowed, the word ricocheted off the walls to assault their ears. "I came to let Rixs out, though I have a mind to leave him here." He glared at Rixs. "My dislike for you is obvious, but I may have made a mistake in placing you here." He hesitated, then sighed and slid a hand over his face. "Chadgerwin and Rangus should have arrived during the night but there has been no sign of them. The Emperor left with Syersi. He did it without telling me, which smells of something bad."

Had the Commandant been within arm's reach, Rixs would have punched him in the face, then punched him again. Orris held up a hand in defense of himself.

"I know, Rixs. You tried to tell me, but how was I to know he was an imposter?" he contended.

"By The Powers, man! Stop talking and get me out of here!" Rixs growled. "They already have a full day's head start!"

Knowing exactly which key to use, Orris slipped it into the heavy iron lock. After a loud *click*, he pushed, and the door grudgingly screeched open. As soon as there was enough space, Rixs squeezed through and without warning, threw a hard blow straight into the Commandant's gut.

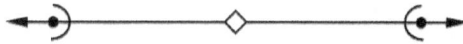

It had been a hard day of riding with barely time to stop and rest. The night had been no better, but though Syersi was miserable, she made sure Moganar and his men experienced a full dose of her. No opportunity to complain passed her by. The hard potatoes she ate. The hot sun. The cold evening. Her tiny tent. The flat bedroll. The journey was bearable knowing she could drive misery into the center of their spines with the whine of her voice. The best part – she was guilt free.

It had taken nearly all night to fall asleep, and just as she had winked off, Kyerg shook her awake. "We leave directly," he informed her.

Her pummeled bottom protested, and her aching legs rebelled against another day's ride, but she held her tears. A constant pain pulsed in her chest. It was like an invisible hand squeezed the air from her lungs and it was hard for her to breathe. At times, the pain in her chest felt as though a hatchet whacked at her ribcage. The pain was enough that tears fell, though she tried to contain them. Discretely, her dirty fingers wiped them away which left smudges on her face.

Do not be ashamed. This pain could bring any man to his knees! she told herself.

Grateful for her beloved Juju, the Empress Heir rubbed the horse's neck often. The feel of strong muscles under a coat of white comforted her and made her feel she was not alone.

As often as she dared, Syersi inconspicuously fingered the blade under her skirt. It was a piece of Rixsander, her biggest critic, yet fiercest champion. Only he could make her feel truly safe.

"We stop here!" Moganar called.

Grabbing some food for their mid-day meal, Moganar walked away from the rest of the group and ordered Syersi to follow. Once out of hearing range, he nodded toward the ground. She shook her head.

"Suit yourself," he said, tossing her food for her to catch.

Another potato landed in her hands. The Lady frowned at Moganar who sat on the ground and bit into his own potato without complaint. He shrugged his shoulders then let his eyes roll over her repeatedly, appreciation smoldering within his gaze. He smiled at her dirt-smudged cheeks.

If eyes could drool, his would have slobbered a bucket full. She quickly sat down. His eyes could not covet her curves if she sat.

He tossed her some dried meat. She caught it and looked around them, then let her gaze wander to the canopy of the trees.

A forced bite of meat helped take her mind off his stare. Her fingers itched to claw out his eyes. Pulling her blade and stabbing him was out of the question – there were too many soldiers.

"Sooo," Moganar began. "What do you know about the Source?"

"Nothing."

He chewed thoughtfully and watched her. "Did you know that Lady Saudria was a Source?"

Syersi bit her cheek to hide her surprise. "Is that so?" The imposter probably knew more about her parents than she did.

A deep flush crept up his neck. "I did not know it at the time, but your father wanted me to be his double, not for his own safety, but so he could create the biggest deception the world had ever known."

Dried meat found its way into Syersi's mouth and she bit off another piece.

"Your mother, Saudria, had been murdered. I was told that the Emperor had gone after the killer and was ordered to play the part of a sick, heartbroken husband." He took a bite, chewed then swallowed. "I stayed in that wretched bedchamber for a season! Day after miserable day I played the role. Then suddenly, I was told to leave and never come back. By The Powers! I had no idea what was happening.

"Rangus hauled me, and a small contingent of men, up to the northern most reaches of Gnomera, in Worstole. Then he started killing everybody. Mustn't have witnesses." Moganar's blue eyes shifted to his men that sat a little distance away, then looked back to Syersi. "Do you know how hard it is to survive a Sanguinary?" An answer was not expected.

"I hid for four seasons cycles, but I dug into the stories. Something was missing and I was determined to find out the truth."

Syersi growled through clenched teeth, "Get to the point!"

"Shut up!" he hissed. His teeth tore into a hard piece of bread and he chewed angrily while he relived the past. "The Intimus deceived me. They deceive you still. Your father died the same time your mother died."

Syersi stirred to get up. "You are full of lies. I will not listen to you! My father is not dead!"

A rough hand jerked her back to the ground. "Sit! I will tell you when you can go!" His mouth pressed in a thin line. "The Emperor's reputation was legendary. As a soldier, he was fearless. As a strategist, he was a genius. There was no greater politician. And he was an invincible ruler."

He took another bite of his food, chewed then swallowed before he continued. "I always thought he was too perfect. He controlled four Talents. That is no easy thing, especially to control Sanguinary. How did he do it? He seemed more than a man."

The beat of Syersi's heart fluttered rapidly, matched by the rhythm of her breaths. Moganar's eyes kept her prisoner while he talked.

"I'll tell you how he could control a Sanguinary! Because he had a Source … your mother. Because of Saudria, he owned the Talents … he was the Talents. He was Denier Cri, the supreme one." He snorted before adding, "No wonder he wanted to be called, *Supreme*. But there is a price for such power. Having the Source is to be tied to the Source. You know the tales, destroy the Source, destroy the Denier Cri. Lothorius protected Saudria so fiercely because his life literally depended on it! Then she was killed, and for all the good his protection offered, he died anyway."

A mallet beat against Syersi's ribcage. Her breathing huffed rapidly, and her lashes fluttered like butterfly wings, so fast that at any moment they would fly off her face. Her ears burned, listening but not believing. The madman spoke nonsense! His callous reference of her parents' death inspired the need to return his kindness with a blade through his eye. And still, he talked.

"Now we come to the important part. The deception," he announced. "Lothorius needed me. The Intimus needed me. They needed to keep up appearances and throw everyone off the trail of the truth. A precious little possession suddenly complicated Lothorius's life. A daughter born of a Source and a Denier Cri. Could it be she was a Source too?

"I have surmised that a Shade killed your mother to prove she was a Source. If she died, then Lothorius would die too. Long before that plot was hatched, however, Lothorius had thoughts of his precious daughter. He had trained a double to take his place. By having me step in when Lothorius died, the assassin would have concluded that Saudria was no Source, and therefore, you could not be a Source either. It drew attention away from you."

Moganar laughed heartily, eyes twinkling. "You are a Source, Syersi. Though I hate to say it, your father was a genius!"

Small hands tensed and twisted in Syersi's skirt. The imposter's words were unbelievable, and yet all of it was possible. The truth of it whispered to her soul. She forced her hands to be still and hoped to look stronger than she felt.

"You have nothing to say?" he cocked his head to one side.

Syersi had nothing to say. Moganar was right. Lothorius had devised the perfect deception. It was her father's ultimate gift to her. And Moganar had played an essential role to make the world believe Lothorius was still alive. The day of her visit to the farmer's market, her abductor had asked what she knew about the Source. Rixs had asked what she thought about the Source. It was becoming clear that there were those who believed the legends to be true.

Mazzlin had talked of love – had said Syersi was born to give love. Memories of her mother pointed to the same. Saudria had loved Lothorius fiercely. Had her love for him been the key? Syersi had never noticed any display of Talent from her father.

She reached deep within herself – there was nothing. No power. No Talent.

Syersi shook her head to clear her thoughts and leaned back on her hands. "And how does one retrieve power from this supposed Source?"

"I was hoping *you* could tell *me*," he replied flatly.

The corner of her lip lifted along with her eyebrow. If any of this was true, Syersi wagered to herself that she would have to fall in love to give up the Talents. That was what Mazzlin had hinted to her, and it would be a very hot day in Worstole, with an endless swamp of leaches bleeding her dry before she shared any of her guesses with Moganar.

"Sorry, I know nothing. I do not even believe in the Source."

He smirked at her. "It makes no matter what you believe or know. You are mine – *all* of you, and I have all the time in the world to find out your secrets. I am certain that you are a Source, but if I am wrong, you shall make a wonderful playmate."

THIRTY-NINE

Tower Wall had long since vanished from view and the irony of the hole it left in Syersi's heart was not lost on her. All her life, Tower Wall had embodied the captivity of an Emperor's daughter, but now that it was out of sight, all she could think about was the protection it had offered.

The remainder of the day had been consumed with thoughts about the Source. *Was she?* Anger swelled like a rising tide. The Intimus had kept her ignorant of her own identity – ignorant of the ultimate power her own hand could never wield. *You were born to give away your love.*

Then there was her Shield. The intense burning in her chest was no longer gentle and somehow, he was tied to it. As much as Syersi denied it, she had feelings for him. If Mazzlin told the truth, falling in love would make her pains go away. But if she was the Source, was her love the key to releasing her dormant powers?

The tales had always portrayed the Source as an object – a gem, a fallen star, a magic flame trapped in a carafe. It was not a person. A female. Her.

The burning, the cramping, the aching in her heart, it all seemed to lend credibility to Syersi's growing belief that she was the Source, and that her love was the key.

Falling in love as Syersi, the Empress Heir, offered the privilege to reign Gnomera by her side. Falling in love as Syersi, the Source, offered the Talents – all of them, and by doing so, she endowed the recipient with the mantle of Denier Cri. It was so much more than merely becoming a ruler.

Even so, along with all that glory and power, her love was also a sentence of enslavement. If Moganar spoke truth, whoever she fell in love with, their life would be tied to hers.

The night was muggy. Syersi tossed and turned in the privacy of her tiny tent. The crickets' song was especially loud, and an owl's continued hooting made a nuisance of itself. Syersi's attention was fixed on everything, but sleep. Rescue was also at the top of her thoughts but waiting for rescue seemed weak. Why wait?

"I am the future ruler of Gnomera!" she whispered to herself. "I wait for no one!"

A chorus of snores throughout the camp battled the night in discordant tones and rhythms. It was amazing that soldiers were able to sleep in each other's company. Unfortunately for the Empress Heir, her tent was secured in the very center of the sleeping men. There would only be one chance to get away. If she mucked it up, there would be no other.

She emerged from her tent in a crouched position and scanned the scene around her. The moon provided some light to help wind her way through camp. Fortunately for Syersi, the snores were loud enough to give her own movements the stealth needed to tiptoe around the soldiers sprawled on the ground in their sleeping rolls. It was a maze of bodies, her feet quietly stepped over one, then hopped over another. By the time she made it to camp's edge, the thrill of her success vibrated her spine so violently, she almost fell.

"And where ya think ta be goin'?" a low, raspy voice broke the silence.

Syersi jumped. "Oh!" she squealed but managed to maintain a whisper. "You scared me!"

A pair of thin arms folded over a flat chest. His face was unfamiliar.

Careful to keep her words hushed, Syersi said, "I have personal needs to attend to."

The guard glanced at the camp then back to Syersi. "They sleep. Do your needs here." A naughty grin crept across his face.

"I certainly will not!" Without asking she pushed by.

He followed. The ground crunched loudly with his every step.

She swung around. "You cannot watch me!"

"Course I can," the night watch smirked.

Her fist tightened into a ball. "Shall we wake the Emperor and see what he says?" The man's smile disappeared. "I thought as much. Sit here! I'll be just there behind that big rock."

With gritted teeth, the guard turned around and sat down. "Hurry up!" he huffed.

"You wamp! You never hurry a female! Especially me!" She almost forgot to keep her voice quiet.

Syersi walked away, the thought of using her blade to slit his throat came and went. She had no stomach for such violence. She could run and hide, but that would fail before it began. There were too many soldiers. They would find her in no time.

Her nervous steps caught against a rock and Syersi fell flat on her face. *By The Powers! I'll have the entire camp awake before I have a chance to get away!*

The man laughed at her. "Careful, your highness. The Supreme will never believe me if I tell him you broke your neck while trying to pee!" He started to push up from the ground.

She stopped him. "Don't move! And keep your voice down!" she hissed, picking herself up and brushing the dirt from her skirt. "You will wake the entire camp!"

His eyes danced in the moonlight as he lifted his hands in mock defense. "Hey! You are doing that all by yourself!"

"Shut up and turn around! And plug your ears! There is no need for you to listen!" she whisper-yelled. His head arced back in silent laughter as he turned around.

The large rock Syersi had tripped over caught her eye. It was big, and one edge had an impressive point. She stretched her neck to check that the guard was still turned around. Satisfied, she lifted the rock. It required the use of both hands.

On light toes, she silently snuck up behind the man. Guilt

washed over her when she noticed he had obliged her by plugging his ears. The nerve to go through with her plan nearly dissolved.

Whenever you hit someone, Pixee, never hold back. Use all your strength. Rixs was always in her head. Whether guiding her or taunting her, his unseen presence was a source of motivation.

The air that stirred caught the guard's attention and he pivoted just in time to see a large rock swinging toward his head. Before he could cry out, there was a hard thud, and his body fell over.

"Sorry," Syersi apologized before hastily sneaking off to retrieve Juju.

Rixs leaned over Mazzlin, her complexion too pale and her skin too clammy. He pressed a cup of water to her lips, coaxing her to drink. She was so weak.

After Orris had released him, it had only taken moments longer to find the Seer and the Physician. They had been locked up just above Rixs – it had been their bodies that he detected filling a portion of space. Without food or water for much longer than Rixs, it was uncertain if Mazzlin would pull through.

"We need your eyes for just a moment," Rixs pleaded, but she was in no condition to help. Even Hobb was helpless to heal her, as he needed to recover his own strength first and Rixs was out of time.

Resigned that Mazzlin was in no condition to help, he vowed to her quietly, "I will find her. I promise." He ran a hand over her clammy forehead then turned to leave. A weak grip clasped his wrist.

"Rixs," she breathed, her hollow cheeks and sunken eye sockets proclaimed she was at death's doorstep. He knelt at her side to hear her better. "She is very, very special."

He offered a tight smile. "I know … I know who and what she is," he whispered.

Clouds of confusion swirled in the Guardian's grey eyes while they searched his face. "You know? How?" Her eyes shifted about the chamber to check for unwanted ears.

He shook his head and touched her forehead with gentle strokes.

"Moganar. Now hush, Guardian. Rest. I must go."

"Listen." She fought for her voice. "Moganar may have pieced the truth together. He wants the Talent. He cares nothing for her. No doubt he will hurt her to get what he wants." She feebly squeezed his arm and licked her dry lips.

Mazzlin's confirmation of everything Rixs had found out sucked the wind out of him. He knew what Moganar had said, but there had still been an element of doubt … until Mazzlin gave it truth.

"So, she *is* the Source …" he whispered, but the Seer had closed her eyes and went still.

As he pulled away, her eyes flew open again, a flicker of life shown in them. "I see her, Shield! I see broken earth. She is riding."

"Broken earth? What is that? Where can I find it?" But the Seer had succumbed to unconsciousness.

"How can Moganar extract the Talent? Mazzlin! How do I stop Moganar from getting her power?"

There were no answers from the Guardian, and Rixs had no time. He barked to the servants as he hurried out the door, "Find the Commandant and tell him to meet me on the observation ring of Tower Wall!" Then he sprinted through the palace, past the courtyard, and down the manicured roadway until he was bounding upward through the winding stairwell that would take him to the wall walk, and the highest point where the view of the countryside was endless.

Rolling hills spread out before Rixs. His eyes could see Ormolu to the west. According to the watch, that was the direction Moganar had gone, so with closed eyes, to reduce the visual distractions, that was where he started.

Grey hues of rock, grass, trees – they were everywhere cluttering his sight. The city of Ormolu was portrayed in a disarray of chaos. Ashen forms of people, buildings, animals all competed for his attention. He summoned every bit of concentration, pushing the limits of his Talent farther than he had ever tried before. The shapes were difficult to identify so far away, but he could not give up, even when burning in his chest tried to break his concentration.

Orris finally joined Rixs on the observation ring. He listened intently while watching the Shield with a combination of distrust and disbelief. Rixs recounted Mazzlin's vision.

"You are a Talent." It was not a question. "No wonder you always had the upper hand when we fought." His tone hinted annoyance. "Now I know why Chadgerwin and Rangus dared to make you Shield."

"Does that really matter right now?" Rixs's annoyance resonated in his tone while he searched the landscape as far as his ability allowed.

"What kind of Talent?" the Commandant pressed.

"There are more important things to worry about than my abilities." His head rotated toward the open plains far to the west.

"Fine." Orris sighed then he smirked, "But it is good to know that it was never a fair fight."

Rixs paused long enough to smirk in return. "Whatever makes you feel better, Commandant."

They settled into a precarious and temporary truce. They would be allies for once, joined together for a single purpose – rescue the Empress Heir. To be successful, they would need to get along and make Syersi their priority.

"Broken earth. Broken earth, broken earth," Orris repeated to himself. He allowed the words to roll around his mouth, and on his tongue while he probed his recollection of Gnomera's geography.

"The Fractures!" he suddenly exclaimed, slamming his fist in triumph against the parapet which was the only thing that protected the two men from the long, deadly fall to the ground. "The Guardian saw The Fractures!"

He explained that it was more than a simple canyon. It consisted of broken ridges and mangled bluffs, wide and crumbling crags, and deep contorted fissures. It was terrain that a giant might have dug up and thrown around, leaving behind colossal piles of upturned and twisted earth. *The Fractures.*

Orris pointed to the southwest as he explained, and Rixs swept his senses in its direction. Its location was beyond his reach and he huffed in frustration. There was nothing to do but swing his view in another direction to see if he could spot Moganar's large company.

Nearly a hundred men would not be easy to hide or blend in with their surroundings.

Sweeping his Sagacious ability from side to side, Rixs stumbled on a single silhouette which appeared to be grossly malformed. The figure was too far for his human eyes to detect, but Talent helped the pieces take shape until recognition lit his face.

"Come!" he blurted.

Long before they reached the stoic figure trudging over the wild terrain, Rixs recognized Rangus. The fearless Sanguinary looked like the dead and walked with heavy footfalls as though boulders weighted each ankle. Dried blood colored every visible patch of skin in dull russet, and his clothes were smeared with the same. In his arms, the body of Chadgerwin bobbed and swayed with an arrow protruding from his chest.

After a three-day ride to intercept Moganar at Sentur, Chadgerwin had received word that the imposter changed his course and was headed for Isslewood. Wanting to return immediately, he and Rangus were stopped by the Second Counselor of Gnomera, Dodan, who was also the Viceroy of the territory Arvon. The entourage of Prince Tangorio, heir to King Tarrin, had set up a tent city on the outskirts of Sentur, the capitol seat of Gnomera. Dodan asked Chadgerwin to meet with the royal before he headed back to Isslewood.

The meeting was arranged, but the Prince had been detained with another matter. Chadgerwin and Rangus could not wait and departed without leaving their respects. They also left without waiting for their company, which needed to prepare for the journey back. They would catch up after they gathered the necessary supplies.

It was on the final leg of their journey, after they had entered the mole hills, that the scent of humans drenched the air. Rangus sniffed their blood, but by the time his own blood pulsed a warning, it was too late. Without the company of their men, the Counselor and Absolute were overtaken, ambushed in the lusciously green countryside of the mole hills.

It had been a full assault. Their attackers had known how to subdue a Sanguinary and Soothe. Had they not been taken down with the malignant force of a hundred arrows, all with lethal precision, the powerful Soothe would have had their assailants singing in the sunshine before they realized what they were doing.

A cloud of invading arrows sank into the Counselor's flesh. An even larger cloud struck Rangus – all in his stomach and chest.

Whoever the attackers were, they knew Rangus would be the hardest kill. Sanguinary were the ultimate warriors. They had speed, strength, and enhanced senses, but they also had the ability to heal. He might not heal as quickly as Hobb, but if left alive, Rangus would mend over time. To kill a Sanguinary, it was essential to strike the vital organs with deadly efficiency, and quickly overwhelm the ability to recover.

The arrows had flown in unison. All had found their mark in the Sanguinary's chest and knocked him off his horse. He landed on his back, sprawled across the ground, barely conscious and unable to move.

The paralyzed Absolute could do nothing but wait for the cowards to come out of their hiding places to finish him off, for it was extremely foolish to attack a Sanguinary and leave him still alive. Rangus waited … and waited.

The clamor of battle suddenly roused the Absolute. He had drifted into unconsciousness and woke to hear the clanking of swords and familiar cries of the Lothorian Guard. Not able to move, or open his eyes, Rangus listened. The Guard grunted and yelled as they hacked and sliced in fierce combat. Though he could not open his eyes to see, his keen senses provided a vivid depiction of the scene around him.

The echoes of exhaustion rang in his ears. The vibrations of the battle dance tickled his skin. The scent of blood seduced his tongue. It was as if his eyes were open. The fighting was severe and Rangus willed himself to heal faster so he could help his men.

He had counted fifty arrows in his torso. It meant that healing would be painstakingly slow. He could only hope his body would mend fast enough to give him strength to defend himself should someone decide to confirm his death.

Plop. One arrow hit the ground. His body had pushed out the foreign entity. One down, forty-nine left. When the fifteenth arrow had hit the ground, Rangus became aware of the silence blanketing him.

The worst had happened. The quiet indicated the battle had stopped. Dead bodies dotted the ground around him. Only two bodies approached. Friend or foe was the question. The stealth of their movements told Rangus *foe*.

"He looks dead," one said. "No way he survived all those arrows we stuck in him."

"Check his breathing," the other said.

Neither wanted to bend over – lean an ear close enough to a Sanguinary's mouth and listen for an exhale. After the challenge was tossed back and forth, one of the men found courage and leaned over.

"I don't hear nothin," he was saying when suddenly, blood red eyes popped open and a wide, gaping mouth launched upward. Iron jaws clamped around the man's throat and his shrill scream was silenced before it began.

While the Absolute bled the man dry, the second assailant backed away slowly. Rangus could smell his horror and locked a scarlet glare on him. Ignorant that Rangus was too weak to make chase, the man ran off, screaming. The fool would suffer the same fate, but it would have to wait for another day.

Rejuvenated after his kill, the Sanguinary pulled the remaining arrows from his chest and stomach. He stumbled over mangled bodies in search of Chadgerwin. When he finally found the Counselor, he cringed and immediately set to work. He treated as many wounds as he could but left an arrow that was stuck in his heart. It was too risky to pull out. With a grunt, he hefted the large man into his arms and set foot back to Isslewood.

FORTY

Hot jewels scorched Syersi's scalp. The gems woven into her messy and tangled hair had greedily absorbed the heat cast off by a spiteful sun. She was sure the rancid smell of burnt hair radiated off her head, and clumsily tugged at the glittering stones, trying but failing to get them out.

The uneven terrain had made it difficult to push Juju faster. The creviced ground was unforgiving and forced Syersi to dismount her horse several times to walk.

She swiped an arm across a wet forehead to clear the sweat dripping into swollen eyes. Her neck was wet too, and there were soggy dark stains under her arm pits. Syersi promised to throw herself into a mud puddle if she were lucky enough to find one. She squinted into the sun and sighed a begrudging thanks to no one for the large boulder that provided temporary shade for herself and Juju.

The drumming of hooves caught Syersi's ear, and she ducked behind the rock then dared to steal a peek over the top of it. Too short to see, she shifted higher on Juju's back, but the horse backed up a few steps, and Syersi slapped a hand over her gaping mouth as clumps of gravel tumbled down the embankment.

"What was that?" a voice shouted.

Another voice growled, "How should I know? Go check!"

Syersi hurled a harsh whisper into the sky. "I thank you for nothing!" The Powers had forgotten her – again. Blinking furiously, she willed her Shield to give her advice, but he was silent. "On our own, Juju. Up we go!"

Struggling against the loose dirt that gave way beneath her hooves, Juju fought for every step.

"Come on girl! You can do this!"

"There she be!" someone yelled.

When Syersi spun around, she saw the enormous dark-skinned man that Rixs had talked with in the farmers' market. Then Viktus came into view, the man who had tried to take her from the big smelly man who had abducted her at the market. These men were just as bad as Moganar. She had to get away.

Syersi loped up the hill, taking five riders on a wild chase through the jagged slot canyons. Then an idea hit her, and she hastily slid off her magnificent mare. With a quick kiss to Juju's muzzle, she choked a whisper, "Get, Juju! Take them away from me! Go back to Isslewood!"

Gulping back sobs, Syersi slapped her horse, and Juju took off in a sprint as though she understood what her lady needed her to do. Then the frightened Empress Heir hurried up another rocky crag. After she reached the top, she realized Rixs's daily torture had made her stronger and shuddered at what might have happened had he not forced her to train. She would have never made it past Moganar's camp.

Syersi dove into a small ditch and did her best to blend with the ground. Like the dead, she had lain motionless for some time while the sun beat down on her.

Then someone shouted, "We spotted her white horse!" Galloping hooves faded into the distance.

She sat up and sobbed through parched and cracked lips, thankful to be rid of them. A monstrous gurgle came from her tummy, and Syersi realized her last meal had been the day before. The ache was almost unbearable, but she was thirsty too. She wondered if it was worse to die of hunger or thirst.

A drip fell from her nose and Syersi wiped away the sniffle, then set her feet to march up the hill and toward the east. East, because the Gneiss Curtain and Isslewood lay in that direction. Up, because Rixs had told her during one of their many contentious training sessions, that being above your attacker was an advantage. It required more effort to pursue a victim uphill than to pursue them downhill or on level ground. She was just beginning to realize how much her Shield had taught her.

A snap of a twig caused her ears to perk up. The goose bumps along her skin told her to run, but before she could, a short man with curly red hair jumped in front of her. She recognized him from the farmer's market. He had been with Rixs and the large dark man.

"Hello there, Princess!"

He stretched to grab her, but she refused to give up so easily. Syersi flung her leg up and kicked outward with all her might, catching him square in the face with the heel of her shoe. His head snapped back violently and his hands immediately covered his mouth and nose.

"Hello!" she grunted in reply, then elbowed him in the head as she ran past.

The hulking dark-skinned man trained his eyes on her. He was almost the size of Rangus and had wild hair and a beard to match. He could have been a Sanguinary if his eyes had been red. He ran up the hill toward her, amazingly quick and agile for one so big.

The redhead recovered from the blow to his face and lunged for her.

Syersi grabbed for her weapon. With ease she pulled her coveted blade from the slit in the gathers of her skirt. It was ingenious. She would have to kiss her Shield for thinking of it.

Baring white teeth, she lashed out with the blade, immediately striking true. A thin red line instantly appeared across the redhead's cheek. Her Shield would have been proud.

"By The Powers!" he cried and slapped her arm. The blade flew out of her hands and tumbled in the dirt.

Freckled hands pulled her to his chest, but it was an unfortunate miscalculation on the redhead's part. Her Shield had taught her about close encounters.

Syersi's knee rammed upward – hard. She knew she had struck

treasure when his mouth stretched wide in a silent scream. Then she pressed her thigh between his legs and jammed her heel backward into his calf while shoving his shoulders away from her. When he fell to the ground, his hand still clutched his crotch protectively.

It was Syersi's chance to get away, and she turned to run but her face smacked into a big wall. Massive, calloused hands clamped onto her shoulders.

Syersi gritted her teeth, prepared for round two.

Already one step ahead of the Empress Heir, Rhages was prepared for her knee to target his precious parts. So, he screamed his surprise when a hard heel stomped on top of his foot.

"Arrgh!" he yelled and lifted his throbbing foot off the ground. Then her other foot provided the generous kick he had originally expected to the parts between his legs. Another cry had barely left his mouth before a heel crashed into his kneecap.

The big man hit the ground like a large falling tree. Plumes of dirt flew in all directions. Rhages roared like a wild beast caught in a trap. Syersi's trap. She might have gotten away but he was stubborn – and quick. He snatched a handful of skirts, making escape impossible, even while he twisted on the ground in agony.

Syersi fell beside him and tugged frantically to pull the gathers from Rhages's grip. The fight with both men had spent her energy. Her breaths were deep and labored.

With a fist still tangled in her skirt, Rhages lifted his head just in time to see the bottom of Syersi's shoe headed for his face. Ducking just in time, her heel stomped into the top of his head with a jolt. Then he felt her foot smash into his head a second time. Stars flashed before his eyes.

His regret manifested in a frown. Syersi had earned his admiration. Her spunk and savagery befitted the women from his own township, but he had to stop her from kicking him senseless. So, Rhages yanked her skirt with incredible force, pulled her close, and knocked her out cold.

"Sorry, yer high one, or whatever it be they call ya," he apologized to the unconscious young lady, while rubbing his head. "But I can't be havin' ya bash me senseless!"

Before long, Rhages had flagged the crew. Viktus, Bronan, and five other men took in the sight of battered Rhages and Fogle, then their gaze flitted to the unconscious female lying next to a big rock.

Bronan curled his lip in a sneer. "What happened here?" He twisted his head from side to side and looked around them. "You look thoroughly beaten."

Rhages ground his teeth and elbowed Fogle when he inhaled to speak.

Viktus's eyes studied the scene. The short pest, Fogle, championed a slash across his cheek, a bloodied nose, and puffy, bruised eyes. Rhages looked no better. Dried blood covered his swollen forehead in ruddy scarlet, and he moved with a noticeable limp.

Viktus scowled. "Please tell me you had to fight a band of twenty thugs just to get the girl."

Fogle shifted his eyes between Viktus and Rhages nervously, then blurted out, "We had to fight a band of twenty thugs! But in the end, we got the girl!"

FORTY-ONE

Viktus's men had caught up with Juju and subdued her. Once again, Syersi found herself atop her beloved white mare, only this time she had a throbbing headache, for which she had Rhages to thank.

She slanted a glance at Viktus. He might have been a handsome man if he were not so ugly.

She held her chin high and spoke. "You were looking for me in the market … why? What do you want with me? And how did you know to find me out here?"

Viktus's eyes stared straight ahead, and he blew a puff of air from his narrow lips. "Which question do you want me to answer?"

"Your choice."

"I have nothing to hide," he offered. "My … benefactor looks for the Source. I believe you are the key to helping me. I expect the Emperor will do anything in exchange for you."

Viktus had no idea that the very thing he searched for rode beside him and stared him in the face. Syersi looked down at her tied hands and bit her lip. Life had been simpler when the Source was nothing more than an old myth, short on truth, and tall on tales. When her only worry was how she could escape the walls of Isslewood.

They rode on in silence until Viktus stopped the group for a much-needed rest. Rhages sat with his back against a rock, his arms folded over his chest, while he guarded Syersi as she washed up in a stream the group had stumbled upon.

It had been a fortunate find. The swift current meant the water was moving along at a quick pace. Moving water meant safe water — safe enough to drink.

Syersi complained about the freezing temperature as she dipped her small toes into the stream and wiggled them. Then she splashed her face and neck, never once giving thanks for the cool, fresh water.

Rhages secretly stole quick glances at Syersi. He rolled his eyes when she complained, but mostly he frowned at her. Her beauty was obvious, but she was too young to be used as bait to find the Source. He glanced through the shrubs to check on the crew.

The shrubs and tall grasses that thrived along the stream's edge had mostly concealed Rhages and Syersi from view of the crew who relaxed and ate a short distance away.

"Listen," he whispered. "Rhages here, ain't wanted no part of snatchin' ya."

Syersi's eyes squinted into thin slits. "But the big dummy whacked me in the head anyway!"

"Well, you be kickin' my face!" His remorseful, gentle expression contradicted the harsh features of a broad and weathered face.

"Does Rixsander know he befriends a ... a ... criminal? Who hits girls? Then snatches them?"

There was a flash of hurt, then confusion clouded his face. "Who's Rixsander? Ya mean the kid?"

She gave him a curt nod.

"Listen! I be a thug, I's know it." Rhages thrust a thumb into his chest. "But be grateful that Rhages be the one ta catch ya. Who knows what the others would'a done! Ya be too pretty to have them find ya!"

Syersi scowled at him then pulled her feet from the water and propped them on the sandy bank. Rhages grinned at her.

"Yeah, I be seein' why the kid likes ya. Where's he anyways?" His forehead wrinkled and creased causing his brows to narrow while his big, calloused hands scooped up the cool water then splashed it on his face and neck. It provided instant relief against the heat of the high sun, and he moaned.

The question had been Syersi's too. Where was Rixs? He would have come for her if he could.

"Viktus got word the Emperor left Isslewood and took ya with him. So, we followed. Been trackin' him. Then you took off on yer own. That was stupid, ya know … leavin' the protection of yer father."

"He is not my father! He's an imposter who plans to …"

Riders echoed through the narrow passageway that led in their direction.

"Get her down and keep her out of sight!" Viktus called hastily.

It took little effort for Rhages to shove Syersi's head into the ground then practically lay on top of her. They were hidden behind the bushes while the crew ate their food rations a short distance away.

A sharp thump on her head prompted Syersi to look up. She found herself staring into enormous, hair-filled nostrils. "Ewww!" she cringed. "Get off me!"

"Shush it!" Rhages hissed and shoved shoes at her. "Git these on!"

Voices floated toward them. "Good day to you," a man said.

Syersi flinched and began to tremble. "I have to get out of here!" she exclaimed in a loud whisper. "He's a Soothe! He can make the men talk!" Nervous flicks of her tongue moistened her lips, and she scanned the area for a place to hide.

Rhages did not understand. "What's a Soothe?"

Syersi's words spilled off her tongue impatiently. "A Talent that can make you talk! I can explain later!" She started backing away upstream.

Rhages placed a firm grip on her arm. "A Talent, like a Sanguinary's a Talent?"

She hissed back. "Yes! Now we have to go!"

"We'll go," he nodded in the direction upstream. "But ya gotta listen to me."

Given her choices, she had no choice but to listen to Rhages.

"We never met proper," he said. "I be Rhages."

Syersi stared at him. "Is this honestly the best time for introductions?"

"It be as good a time as any." He held firm to her arm even though she tried to pull away.

"Fine!" She rolled her eyes. "I am Syersi."

"I know," he grinned.

She clenched her jaw and spoke through her teeth. "If you already knew my name, then what was the point of the introductions?"

"Well, ya ain't be knowin' my name!" Rhages almost looked offended.

Syersi froze with mouth wide open, disbelieving eyes pinned on him.

"Oh! Before I forget ..." he held something low to the ground between them. "I know the kid don't trust nobody with his blades, so there must be a good reason he gave ya this. I be giving it back to ya and trust ya not to stab me with it. Fair enough?"

A near-shrill escaped from her lips before Syersi clamped a hand over her mouth. The sleek shape of Rixs's blade brought tears to her eyes. She had dropped the blade when she tried to stab the short redhead with it.

She blinked up at the dark eyes that studied her closely and her fingers trembled as they slid around the handle. It was a meaningful gesture – Rhages trusted her with the blade.

A delicate hand pressed against his big one. "Fair enough," she said.

White teeth filled his open grin then his eyes popped wide. "Come on. We gotta git!"

Moganar's voice rang out and reminded Syersi and Rhages that danger lurked on the other side of the bushes. "The young lady we seek is the Empress Heir. I will only ask once. Do you have my daughter?" A cruel growl resonated in his tone.

"As I said before," Viktus's voice replied with a tinge of annoyance. "There is no woman here."

The whir of an arrow had resonated through the air before it found its victim. With an *umph*, one of the crew fell over.

"I told you I would only ask once!" Moganar yelled. "You have my daughter's white mare, tell me where she is, or you will all die."

They had made their way along the water's edge. Syersi and Rhages had shimmied and slithered along the ground placing precious distance between them and the others. It had been a gift from The Powers that the stream was as loud as it was swift. It easily drowned out any noise they might have made.

Kyerg would be exerting his Soothe, and while he was no Chadgerwin, who could influence fifty people at once, Kyerg was still capable of influencing a few people at one time. It would only take one person to get the information they needed.

Syersi left the stream and was careful to keep her body hunched low as she ran. The growth along the stream kept her hidden. She ran and ran, ordering her legs to move, repeatedly whispering gratitude for the strength Rixs had forced upon her. If she survived this mess, she would fling her arms around him and thank him, but in that moment, she ran — just like he had taught her.

Not knowing which direction to go, Syersi tripped over a small hole and fell flat on her face. Dirt plumed into her mouth as she inhaled sharply. Violent coughing and hacking followed while she hauled herself up and pushed forward.

A vague, distant voice yelled, "Keep going, Princess!" Syersi turned but Rhages was gone. She saw no one and wondered if what she heard had been real or in her mind. There was only one focus — get away and hide.

Up that hill. Her breaths came in ragged gulps. She struggled to get enough air in her chest. *Through those trees.* Her face scrunched at the deep burn in her legs. *Cut to the right at the boulder.* She looked behind her as she turned sharply to the right. No one there. *Jump that gully.*

Throwing all her energy into the jump, she propelled herself over the chasm. It was as wide as she was tall. She was sure she could make it, and for a quick moment believed she would, until her body hit the opposite side with a hard splat. With one side of her face smashed into the dirt, and legs hanging over the edge, she began to slide downward.

Clawing frantically at the ground to find hold of something, anything to keep her from sliding over the edge, Syersi cursed. "Rixsander, you wamp!"

He had never taught her to jump over things. Her failure to master the gully would be the Shield's fault!

Rescue came from a nearby tree perched precariously over the gully. One of its roots looped out of the ground and provided a convenient handle for Syersi. *Thank The Powers!*

The ground had given way beneath Syersi as she struggled to pull herself up. Her feet dangled in the air, but she swung a leg up onto the edge and rolled over onto level ground. Stumbling to her feet, she inhaled a ragged breath, then she forced her feet to move on.

"Here! I see tracks!" someone yelled in the distance. Another voice bellowed a response. Then there was still another voice that shouted from the opposite direction. "She can't have gone far! Split up! Find her!" And still, there were numerous additional shouts that rang out from other directions.

So many voices. It was impossible to know if they belonged to Moganar's men, or Viktus's. Both were equally bad. Hiding from everyone would be impossible.

A shallow hole in the ground caught Syersi's foot and she fell again. A cry nearly made it through her lips as her ankle twisted. She bit her tongue to keep it contained. Tears pooled along her lower lids while she whimpered on the ground.

It was time to give up. There was no strength left within her. Then she saw it. A narrow hole under a huge rock.

The opening skimmed narrowly along the ground, barely wide enough for her to fit through. She hesitated and imagined the crawly little vermin likely hidden in that crevice, but the voices that echoed against the broken terrain were motivation enough to throw herself, belly first, into the low fissure.

Her head hit the rock as she plunged into the narrow hole, and she cursed Rixs's name because of the sting that resulted. It was a tight fit, but Syersi managed to squeeze through, then pulled the layers of her skirt into the hole with her. Sweat rolled down her forehead and beaded between her breasts. She pushed back as far as the tight cave allowed.

Footfalls rushed by numerous times without discovery of Syersi. Then a powerful voice boomed. "I be tellin' ya, she ain't come this way. She ran that other way!"

Rhages. He was safe. The distant call came back to her, *Keep going, Princess!* It had been Rhages. He was helping her.

"How could you let that silly girl slip through your fingers?"

Syersi saw several pairs of boots from the craggy opening of her hiding place. A single pair of old raggedy boots dragged through the dirt, upsetting any footprints in the area and finally came to a stop in front of the crag's opening. She pressed back but there was nowhere to go.

"Shut it, Bronan!" Rhages snarled. "Would'a had her by now if ya didn't make me come this way."

Bronan. The way he had gawked at Syersi caused goosebumps to pock her skin.

More footsteps sounded and a new voice was heard. "Seen anything?"

"No!" Bronan bit out, "But we have to find her! That girl is too valuable to let slip through our fingers." There was a pause then, "Now, where can a little thing like her hide ..." His words stopped short and then he chuckled. Footsteps approached the opening of the tiny cave.

Syersi jumped as two sets of eyes appeared at the gap of her hiding hole. "Just leave her be!" Rhages grabbed Bronan by his arm and tried to pull him away.

"You knew she was here!" Bronan snarled. "I should slice you open! Get her out of there!"

There was a scuffle with several sets of feet and Rhages was pulled away. A face Syersi had not recognized filled the opening, and a large, dirty hand thrust in grabbing a fistful of her hair. She cried out and he yanked hard.

"Quiet!" he growled as he dragged her toward the opening. "Your father and his men are still lurking around! Viktus lost three men cuz of you!"

Syersi pushed against the rock with her hands. He yanked again, but she stayed in the hole and his hand came away with strings of her hair. With an angry grunt, he grabbed the front of her dress and curled his hand in the opening of her neckline. Fingers grazed the skin of her cleavage.

"How dare you! Get your hands off me!" she screamed.

He laughed and gave a final yank. Her head smacked into the lower edge of the opening before the man pulled her out and dropped her on the ground. Syersi laid unmoving.

"Ya hurt her!" bellowed Rhages. He struggled against the four men that held him.

Blurred faces came into view as Syersi regained awareness of her surroundings. She slowly lifted her hand to touch the sting on her forehead and drew back blood covered fingers.

It had only been a few days since Chadgerwin had left for Sentur, yet everything had changed during that time. None of it had been good.

Rough hands pulled her to her feet to stare into dark eyes.

"Leave her be, ya trott-head!" Rhages yanked free and flew at the man, landing a solid punch to his face.

Syersi was thrown back, and again, it was her head that suffered. It cracked against the large rock she had hid under, and her slender body slumped to the ground. Swirling stars interfered with her ability to see clearly. She stayed put, rubbed her head, and watched Rhages soundly pummel one of the crew – the one that pulled her out of her hiding hole.

A group brawl ensued. It was the way with men. A fight between two always became a free-for-all. The more, the merrier.

Firm arms lifted Syersi from the ground and pulled her away from the melee before an unyielding hand clamped over her mouth. With her back pressed against a hard chest, Syersi found herself helpless to fight or scream, nor could she turn to see the culprit that carried her away.

Walls of rocks and dirt slid past her periphery while she struggled in vain to break loose. Hands like iron clamps held her tight. Smothered cries found release only as far as the hand that bound her mouth and held her head immoveable.

The soft meaty portion of her assailant's hand pressed into her open mouth, so she bit down and locked her teeth like a diseased rat. The warm tang of blood trickled over her tongue and a male voice growled next to her ear.

Suddenly free, Syersi whipped around to face her abductor but stopped short and stared. There was nobody there.

Dark lashes fluttered wildly as she tried to make sense of the blank space in front of her. Turning around several times with a hand over her mouth, Syersi saw nothing, yet knew the hands that held her could not have disappeared in the blink of an eye.

Red drops plopped into the dirt. Syersi swiped a wary hand forward. Nothing. She pawed at the air again, and again, then switched directions. There was nothing.

With outstretched fingers, she twirled in a circle and yelped when they hit against something firm, but she saw only empty air.

Hair prickled at the back of her neck as if midwinter had iced her spine and burrowed deep into her bones. She eased backward, ready to break into a run when an invisible force grabbed her arm and pulled.

No! No! No! She was screaming in her mind, then she screamed out loud. She knew, and it was very bad.

Strong invisible hands had pulled her into a hard body and held her tight. A low and gravelly disguised laugh tickled her ear. "Shhh. You have nothing to fear from me," a raspy whisper told her. "I could never hurt someone so beautiful as you. Besides, you are my key to finding the Source."

Wide blue eyes blinked at what she saw. She saw nothing. "Who are you?" Syersi spoke to the air. "Why does every abductor think I am their key to the Source?"

He laughed, his breath warming her cheek. "I had no idea you would be so beautiful. I think I might keep you. Source or no Source."

The feel of a kiss brushed across her neck, and the young woman shoved away, but hands that were nowhere, yet everywhere, grabbed each side of her face. A mouth pressed onto hers.

It was an uninvited kiss. Syersi kicked hard and was rewarded with a grunt. The ghostly hands released her, and she ran.

Reflexively, her legs moved furiously. She had no idea where she was headed. All she knew was she had to keep moving. Too many people wanted her – Moganar, Viktus, and a Shade. Staying in one place made her vulnerable.

A sob bubbled up her throat. A Shade had murdered her mother. She might have had a chance to escape Moganar and Viktus, but she despaired any hope to elude an unseen adversary.

You are floating again, Pixee. Stop floating. This is no time to be Princess.

The crunch of dirt sounded behind her. Tears blurred the path forward. "No!" she screamed.

An iron grip pulled her to an abrupt halt and her shriek was choked into silence as ghostly fingers wrapped around her throat and squeezed. Invisible hands pushed her into a crevice just as Moganar's soldiers ran by, then once they moved on, the pressure around Syersi's neck eased. She bent over coughing so violently, snot spurted from her nose.

"If you want me to strangle you, then keep screaming," the scratchy voice threatened.

Still coughing, Syersi wiped her nose. "You coward! Browbeating a girl and hiding behind your Shade!"

Rixs had taught her how to see without seeing – how to detect her surroundings, the subtle movement of the air, the faint smell of sweat. She knew the man's face was close.

"So, you know of Talent? Good!" he continued to whisper. "Then you know why I want the Source. It is the means to own all the Talents!"

"You would be a fool to believe that!" the bedraggled Syersi mumbled. She turned her face toward the breaths that tickled her skin to let them whisper his location to her.

"I have spent seasons cycles searching for the Source," his mouth brushed her cheek lightly as he spoke.

Syersi flinched but stayed her place, an idea taking shape. Her words were a sigh, "What does that have to do with me?"

"Not sure, but I know you are somehow involved ... only ... I did not expect that ... you are temptation incarnate ..." His words fell away, and firm lips pressed against hers.

She stiffened, sickened by his kiss, but if her idea was to work, Syersi would need the man's hands fully engaged. She pulled back shyly.

He coaxed her. "Relax. Give in and enjoy."

Two hands that she could not see held her head in place as the man's mouth pressed against hers again. She struggled just a little, to make things interesting, and the kiss became harder, hungrier. His tongue parted her mouth.

The Shade delved into the kiss, and Syersi played along.

"Ugh!" the man gasped, as Syersi's hand pushed the blade deeper into his gut.

FORTY-TWO

Rangus led his group swiftly toward The Fractures, and with the efficiency of an eagle's eye, the Shield focused on every shape and form within the farthest distance he could reach. Syersi's form was a unique light grey, unlike all the other multitude of shapes that cluttered his range of awareness. He knew her every curve like the back of his own hand.

Walls of twisted rock jutted skyward from hard, packed earth and created passageways, both narrow and wide, that made it difficult to see more than a short distance. Orris had sent out three separate scouting parties to navigate around the narrow canyon walls and bring back word of the Empress Heir.

Unending thoughts of her had plagued Rixs. He saw her behind every tree and rock. Her scent tormented him when his eyes were closed. Her melodic voice hung in the breeze to tease him. His dirt-stained hand rubbed over his face.

It had been because of Orris that Rixs was thrown into lockup and unable to keep Syersi safe. He imagined the Commandant's face with his nose smashed into his chin. A growl rumbled deep in his throat.

"I found her!"

Through Rixs's Sagacious, he had found the horde of grey forms roaming through The Fractures and knew they hinted of Syersi's

location. After much concentration, he spotted the lightest of grey
forms he was looking for – Syersi's form. A long distance still
separated them, but every muscle twitched in excitement. *Keep your
head, Rixs. This is far from over.*

Rangus had carefully stowed his anger when they left Isslewood.
Once they had crossed into The Fractures, the Sanguinary's eyes
brightened from dull rust to hungry red. They nearly glowed, and
drool clung to the corners of his mouth. It foreshadowed the carnage
to befall the men who had dared to snatch his Empress Heir.

The Absolute solicited Rixs and his Talent to pinpoint the
positions of the scouting parties that Moganar had posted
throughout The Fractures. He could have used his heightened
Sanguinary nose and sniffed them out, but it would have taken more
time. Orris assigned his men to ambush the groups that were out of
the way, but for Moganar's men that were near Syersi's position, the
Absolute dealt with them personally.

The wet and gurgled screams of Moganar's men were felt all the
way to the bone, but it was what Rixs saw that would give him
nightmares forever. Unlike Orris and his Lothorian Guards, Rixs
could not close his eyes and turn away to avoid the mauling – the
torture. His Sagacious Talent cursed him to *see* through closed eyes.
To *see* behind his back as he walked away. And even to *see* when he
took cover behind a large boulder. The visions followed him. He
could only be grateful the scenes played out in hues of grey rather
than the full brilliant color his eyes provided.

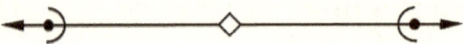

The air undulated in front of Syersi, like a ripple in a puddle of
water, and a body wavered into view. A man fell to his knees and his
hand quickly pulled a hood over an exposed head, but not before she
caught a fleeting glimpse of brown hair.

She covered her mouth as she remembered the blade puncturing
through cloak, and skin, and muscle. The sound as it penetrated the
man's body made her shudder, and she refused to check that he was
dead. Instead, Syersi ran.

Distance was her friend. Distance between herself and voices, so she wandered aimlessly, hiding with every suspicious noise. When she finally squinted at the sun and realized it hung low on the horizon, she nearly sobbed in relief. The tones of pink and dark orange cast into a purple sky meant that dusk was rapidly approaching. Concealed under a blanket of night, Syersi would be able to sneak away.

"Ah, there is my lovely girl!" Moganar chimed.

She had perched against a rock, needing a quick respite from running. Syersi nearly jumped out of her skin at the sound of his voice. She had hoped to evade everyone until the Absolute sniffed her out, or her Shield discovered her form outlined on the canvas of empty space, but it was not meant to be. Her hope shattered.

Her father's look-alike cocked his head to one side. "A lot of time has been wasted in finding you."

Exhausted to the point that she could sleep on her feet, it was no wonder she had not heard Moganar, or his men, sneak up on her. Her muscles ached. Blisters bubbled painfully on her feet. Bruises colored her swollen face, and there were gashes on her forehead. There were no more tears to shed, though she wanted to cry. Her tears had dried up like the dirt on which she sat. Syersi had no strength left to protest, to run – to hope. She had fought hard – had given it her all, and it was time to give up.

Her expression flamed Moganar's victory. "Are you ready to submit?"

Thick dark lashes blinked up at him and her mouth opened to give in, but her surrender stopped. A flower had frozen her tongue.

The flower was a tender blue bud surrounded in an oval cage of long spindly thorns. Pixee's Solitude. It swayed in a spring breeze until long slender fingers picked it and extended it to her. An emerald-eyed Pax Valley stranger turned Shield whispered to her heart. *You are strong, Pixee!*

Swiping a forearm across her nose, she hissed her words. "You will never get what you want from me. I promise you!"

Hot anger, manifested in shades of scarlet, seeped up Moganar's neck. Heavy steps warned of his intention, but the strike across her face still caught her by surprise. Syersi fell over on her side.

He yanked her up and shook her. "You are wrong!" he began as scouts hurried to him. "You will give me everything …"

"Emperor Lothorius!" one soldier cried. "The Absolute and Shield are coming!"

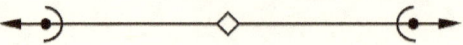

Unknown to Rixs, he stood at the same stream where Syersi had made her escape earlier that day. With subdued horror, he again watched the way a Sanguinary tortured and eliminated victims with merciless efficiency.

Rangus had attacked a group of unsuspecting guards taking watch near the stream. Single handedly, he took care of all of them with nothing more than two half swords, one in each hand.

It was a terribly unfair fight. The seven guards had no chance at all. Rangus stabbed two in the chest simultaneously then immediately pounced on two more, grabbing each by the throat and squeezing his fingers tightly.

Rixs would never forget the crunch of their windpipes under the Absolute's grip.

The three remaining guards stood frozen and watched as Rangus used his teeth to rip out the throat of one of his dead victims. Their fear became his pleasure.

"Run," he ordered them.

The poor fools obeyed, not knowing that by running, they only fueled his excitement. It was the chase the ferocious Talent hungered for. Rangus watched them with cat-like interest, his eyes glistening with savage enthusiasm. They were already dead men – they had no chance of outrunning a Sanguinary.

FORTY-THREE

The Absolute had disappeared. Conviction to get to Syersi made him impatient. His speed made him too fast for the rest of them to keep pace. Only Rixs held a glimmer of hope to keep up with Rangus, but even he fell behind. By the time Rixs, Orris and the rest of their party had caught up, Rangus was in a standoff with Moganar.

Rixs had stayed back, tucked out of sight, while Orris advanced and entered the fray. Moganar was no fool. He knew he would be at a severe disadvantage against the Sanguinary, so he used the only leverage he had — the Source. With a knife in each hand, one at Syersi's throat and the other poised at the side of her ribs, Moganar had kept Rangus at bay. Three archers with arrows pointed and at the ready to release them straight into Syersi's heart, gave him added protection and confidence that no one would make a move.

Orris called to him. "Let us talk. We all want to keep the First Daughter safe!"

Syersi looked a mess. Disregarding the knives pressed against the hollow of her throat and her ribcage, Rixs was more alarmed at what his eyes saw before the sun went down. Her flawless face was torn and swollen, bruised, and broken. Blood smeared her dress. The view of her had nearly caused him to lose all sense and jump from his hiding place too soon, but he managed to keep his head together and study the landscape around him as Orris tried to negotiate.

Fearful that nervous fingers could trigger the premature discharge of arrows pointed at Syersi, Rangus ordered the Lothorian Guard to stand down.

Moganar pulled Syersi tightly against his chest as he shifted against the rock embankment protecting his back and squinted through the waning light. Since the sun had set, it was difficult to see his adversaries as the fading sun cast shadows over and around everything. But this worked to Moganar's advantage. If he had difficulty seeing them, then it would stand to reason that they would have difficulty seeing him.

Moganar's shout reverberated off the canyon walls. "Rangus! The only way she comes out of this alive is to let us go!"

Orris put his hands up trying to calm the twitchy imposter. "We are prepared to trade riches for the First Daughter!"

"No! She is mine, or she is dead!"

"Over my dead body!" Rangus growled. "You already tried to kill me once! Do you think you can do it again?"

"What do you mean?" Moganar hissed.

"Do you deny it? You ambushed me and Chadgerwin in the mole hills! The Counselor still recovers!"

A hearty laugh rocked the terrain. "I do deny it! And I congratulate whoever was behind it! Too bad they failed, and you still live!"

"This is not about the Counselor or the Absolute!" Orris interjected. "This is about our Empress Heir! You know we cannot leave her behind. We will let you leave without harm, but Lady Syersi stays with us!"

While the Commandant tried to negotiate Syersi's freedom, Rixs absorbed the space around him taking great care to study the shapes of everyone and everything within proximity of the standoff. Motionless bodies laid scattered on the ground at odd angles and positions. Rangus had left his mark before the rest of them had arrived. The forms that remained standing, all matched up with a visible body. That meant either there was no Shade hiding among them, or the Shade chose not to shroud his identity and was standing in plain view. There was no way to be certain which it was.

Though Orris tried to step into Chadgerwin's shoes of statesman extraordinaire, no progress was made. He lacked the Counselor's diplomatic skills — and Soothe. They were at a stalemate.

It was time for Rixs to set his sights on Moganar. He studied every angle of his form. He determined the man's stance and the position at which he held his knives. Then he ran through numerous drills in his head, visualizing scenarios that could dispatch the evil man without harming the Empress Heir.

The stalemate dragged on and Rangus was out of patience. He stood rigid and still, the twitch in his cheek gave the only indication that every sinew in his enormous body trembled to attack. Even if he dared to make a move, his Sanguinary speed and strength would not be enough to save Syersi from the knives at her throat and side, and the three arrows aimed at her heart. The Absolute snarled in frustration.

Rixs finally stepped out into the open and edged his way toward the Commandant and Absolute. Syersi exhaled a breath at his appearance.

"Look who finally showed up!" Orris hissed. "We had hoped to rescue Syersi today! Not next spring!"

Rixs responded in a low mocking tone, "Then lucky for us all that I am here! If we relied on your negotiating skills, we would never leave this place! *You*, Orris, are no Chadgerwin!"

Orris scowled. "Save it, Woodsman! At least I tried!" It was more of shout than his intended whisper. "Do you think the Sanguinary could have come up with a diplomatic solution?" Both men flashed a glance at Rangus who narrowed his own red eyes at them.

"In case you were wondering, wamps! Yes, I can hear you!"

"Sorry, Absolute," the Commandant murmured.

Rixs purposely avoided the Absolute's eyes — they made him nervous. Instead, he levied a twisted face on Moganar. "Imposter!" he shouted. "You will pay for each mark made to the Lady's face and body! I promise you!"

"Great negotiating, Rixs!" Orris sneered. Rixs ignored him and kept his eyes fixed on the imposter.

Moganar squinted through the fading light. "Well, well, Rixs, the

Shield with the lightning reflexes, has finally come to join the stalemate!"

Rangus flinched.

"Try it, Rangus!" Moganar tightened his hold on the Empress Heir, adjusting his position so that his head was directly behind Syersi's. Only one eye was visible. "If you doubt my resolve to kill her, then make your move. I see the hunger in those evil eyes!" He nodded an unspoken message to Kyerg, and the man took his cue.

Quiet and subtle as a snowflake, the air kissed the Absolute's skin. He recognized it immediately.

"You have a Soothe!" he snarled. "A pathetically weak Soothe."

"It's Kyerg!" Syersi shouted, then cried out when Moganar yanked a fistful of her hair, tilting her head back and exposing her throat to the knife he held. Several drops of blood beaded on her skin.

Rangus sniffed the air. "I smell her blood," he murmured quietly. "He has cut her."

Rixs jerked forward but a grip, strong as gneiss, held him back.

"Be still, boy," Rangus urged quietly. Then with his face trained on Moganar, he bellowed, "Call off your ineffective Soothe! You insult me!"

Syersi's eyes locked on her Shield, and words she had heard yet not understood came to her. *You were born to love ... to give love. When you destroy the Source, you kill the person who possesses it. Their lives are tied together.* Her temples throbbed.

Moganar knew about the Source, but he did not know how to possess the Talents as his own. Syersi had finally understood. It was love – her love. Her love was a gift of power.

The myths and legends were right, yet wrong. The one with physical possession of the Source possessed nothing. No one could dictate the release of Talents from the Source. Only the Source could do that.

It was an epiphany! Syersi was the one in control. It was she who decided who she would love, and thereby, she controlled who would claim her power. Perhaps she could not use the Talents she owned, but only Syersi could select the next most powerful being in the world. Then it hit her like a club swung against her head – she would also seal their fate.

Her father died because her mother had been a Source and a Shade had killed her. Their lives had been tied together because her mother loved her father. It would be the same for Syersi. Whoever she chose to love, their life would be tied to hers. If she died ... Her eyes shifted to her Shield.

He watched her. While Orris tried to talk sense to the madman who had triggered blood and pain at her throat, her Shield never took his eyes off her. Had Syersi not just realized the ramification of losing affections to him, his burning stare would have melted her heart.

She knew he would get her out of this mess. More than Rangus, or Chadgerwin, or the entire Gnomeran army, Syersi trusted her Shield to take her home.

While everyone else struggled to see in the waning light, Rixs had decided on the two places he needed to hit Moganar simultaneously to ensure Syersi's survival. Both required an undeviating strike.

The first target was Moganar's right eye, peeking to the side of the Empress Heir's head. It was a killing shot, but a miniscule mistake meant Syersi would receive the fatal strike. The other target was Moganar's left hand where he held a dagger to her side. If Rixs was off by a little, he would hit her in the very place the imposter planned to stab her.

Those were the two places he had to stick with precision to secure Syersi's freedom. Both throws would have to be made at the same time – no easy task, but there was no other choice.

There was still the problem of the three archers who stood like stone, each with their arrows fixed on Syersi's chest. Timing was key. All three would have to be immobilized at the same time, yet they were spread apart from one another making the task a near impossibility. And if they were taken out too soon, the imposter would panic and kill the young woman who was to be the future of Gnomera.

Orris began speaking calmly to Rangus. "Absolute, let them go. We cannot be reckless with Syersi's life. We can plan and take the imposter another day."

Rangus curled his upper lip and grimaced at the leader of the Lothorian Guard. He scowled at what he saw in Orris's face.

"Get a grip on yourself, man!" Rangus barked. "That is a weak Soothe, and you are letting him affect you!"

"I feel it too," Rixs said quietly, as he swept his eyes around them. "He must be too weak to affect everyone. The soldiers seem fine. Kyerg must be focused only on us, but I can resist Chadgerwin fairly well, so this Soothe is less challenging for me."

Orris blinked at them. "I feel nothing."

"That's because you have already fallen to him," Rangus said with a sneer.

"I have a plan," Rixs whispered. "Ignore Kyerg for now. Absolute, when I take my third step, I need you to eliminate the archer on the left."

To reach the archer, it required a long jump, but a Sanguinary could manage it.

Rixs's voice was so low, only Sanguinary ears could hear. "Leave the other two, and Moganar, to me."

"You get three and I only get one?" Rangus complained, but there was no time to entertain his protests.

Rixs was already walking. He prayed to The Powers that it was dark enough that the archers would miss Syersi if they released their arrows. On his third step, Rangus made his move.

Like a winged predator, a single leap had closed the distance to the farthest positioned archer. Rangus snapped the arrow in half then twisted the archer's neck.

At the same time, Rixs snatched two short blades, one in each hand, and flung them at the remaining two archers. The pair of blades sliced through both archers' fingers pulling their bow strings taught. Amid the wails of pain, pieces of fingers fell to the ground, but most importantly, the blades had severed the bow strings.

Before the arrows could tumble to the ground, Rixs had already drawn his next two blades for Moganar. "Stop ..." was all the man got out before a medium blade sunk so deep into the socket of his right eye it nearly disappeared. In that same moment, a short blade struck his left hand. The knife Moganar had gripped fell into the dirt while the man who had convinced so many that he was Emperor of Gnomera, buckled over. He hit the hard earth.

Rixs's rhythmic strides did not falter or slow. Silence overwhelmed the early evening except for his steady footsteps crunching toward a dazed Syersi. Without hesitation he walked straight to the frozen and blinking Syersi, grabbed her shoulders in a tight squeeze, and pulled her into him.

No one spoke. Everyone stared as Rixs locked his lips with Gnomera's Empress Heir in a hard kiss.

With a heavy breath of relief, he finally pulled away but kept a firm hold on Syersi's arms to steady her. He searched deep into her eyes. She was safe and that was all that mattered.

Syersi's breaths were heavy and erratic as she looked into Rixs's green eyes then at the ground where Moganar's limp body sprawled. Her nightmare was finally over. Her Shield had saved her as she knew he would. In an unforeseen swift motion, Syersi swung her fist hard. Rixs's head jerked to the side and blood spurted from his nose.

FORTY-FOUR

Rangus laughed and laughed. The entire land realm shook under his thunderous guffaw while Orris had the look of murder on his face, and everyone else stared in stunned silence.

Rixs rubbed his face and squinted one eye. Blood dripped from his nose despite his efforts to pinch his nostrils shut. Syersi's reaction was not what he had anticipated, and though he had been aware her open palm approached, he had done nothing to stop it. It seemed that Syersi was the only person who could get away with slapping Rixs.

"What was that for?" he cracked with a nasally voice, suddenly remembering she constantly annoyed him.

Syersi slowly wiped her hand across the top of her right ear. Her fingers came away with blood. Rixs inhaled and realized some of her anger.

Rangus laughed harder. "You nicked her!" he laughed. "If she orders your throat slit, I shall be the first to offer my services."

Rixs tossed his hair from his eyes then tossed a glare at the Absolute. To Syersi he whispered, "Come now, Pixee. I had four targets to hit, all at the same time! Surely, you can endure a little blood in exchange for your miraculous rescue!"

"What a vain thing to say! Besides, you might have killed me!" Syersi declared. "But I forgive that!"

Indeed, Syersi was not angry that the Shield's blade had grazed her ear. A jumble of emotions left her elated that he had taken the liberty to kiss her, and yet indignant that he had assumed he could take the liberty to kiss her.

"Then why did you hit me?" Rixs questioned through gritted teeth.

The pain that seized Syersi's chest reminded her of Mazzlin's words. *Give your heart away and the pains will stop.* Then she thought of what she had pieced together. Love was knocking at her heart's door, and that was not a good thing.

Syersi's words were harsh. "Save your kisses for the girl waiting for you in Pax Valley!"

They were not the words she wanted to say. He had come for her. Again. Just like at the farmers' market, he had rescued her, and she wanted to fling herself into his strong arms and kiss him breathless. But she dared not. Her heart was already about to burst.

Blood continued to drip from Rixs's nose as he stared at Syersi. Perhaps kissing the Empress Heir in front of her Lothorian Guard had not been his brightest decision. He knew men had been beaten or strung up for touching the Empress Heir without her permission. Rixs quickly stole a glance at Rangus.

There was a sigh of relief when Rangus looked amused rather than angry. He bowed to Syersi. "My apologies, Lady Syersi. It shall not happen again." Rixs turned and walked away.

On the journey back to Isslewood, the soldiers had thronged around Rixs to talk about how he rescued the Empress Heir and how they might improve their own skills with blades and daggers. It was all anyone could talk about. The constant chatter ensured that Rixs and Syersi had no interaction on the three-day journey.

Isslewood had never looked so beautiful. Tower Wall had never brought such comfort. Something had changed in Syersi during the days of her abduction. She inhaled everything around her as appreciation for her home bloomed to its fullest. Yet she was not the same spoiled Empress Heir, and the twinkle that once consumed her brilliant blue eyes gave way to the realization – her Intimus had deceived her.

A newly healed First Counselor stood at the gate, the ambassador of majestic calm. Hobb's Talent had restored him perfectly, Mazzlin too. She stood next to Chadgerwin, as did Hobb.

A filthy Syersi pierced them with an impassioned glare and chin tip. "I will have a word with my Intimus after I have given a full day to bathing." Her voice was authoritative as she rode past without stopping for hugs or smiles. Secretly, she did whisper her thanks to The Powers for sparing the lives of her Guardian, Physician, and Counselor.

Mazzlin blinked as she watched Syersi ride past.

Chadgerwin arched a brow at the Empress Heir's command, his curiosity piqued. He found Rangus and said, "You saved my life, Absolute."

"If you thank me," Rangus grunted, "I'll finish what they started in the mole hills."

Chadgerwin laughed then nodded toward Syersi's back as she headed for the great house. "I take it that whatever happened out there has toughened up our First Daughter."

A guttural rumble came from the Sanguinary. "She thinks she's in charge!"

Chadgerwin and Mazzlin sat calmly while Syersi paced back and forth in her chambers. "How could you have kept this hidden from me all these seasons?" she cried while wringing her hands. "I trusted you and you deceived me! I thought Mazzy was out of her mind telling me that my chest pains would go away when I fell in love! How does that happen?" Syersi walked a few steps then turned and walked back.

Hobb had tried to heal her wounds but gave up and stood back to watch the anxious Empress Heir attack the floor with her quick footsteps. Rangus tracked her with his rusty red eyes as he leaned against the wall, his muscular arms folded across his chest.

"I should have heard about my father's death from you! It was bad enough to hear it from that bastard, Moganar, but it was the worst betrayal to learn that my father was dead because my mother was a Source … and you knew! All this time! And you knew I am a Source! I still struggle to believe it!"

Silvery scars gleamed white against Chadgerwin's dark, dark skin while stormy eyes tracked Syersi's movements back and forth. A thick eyebrow twitched.

"So, Moganar told you all that?" he asked.

The Guardian chimed in, "I had no idea he knew that much! What else did he tell you?" Having lost a little weight from her time in the dungeon without food or water for nearly three days, Mazzlin appeared gaunt and tired.

"What else is there?" Syersi questioned. "I could not stomach anything else!"

The Counselor quizzed her, "Did he know how to release the Talents?"

Syersi smirked and quizzed him back. "What do you know, Chadgerwin? Are the Talents released through intimacy?"

"Oh!" a plump hand flew to cover Mazzlin's mouth while red crept up her neck and into her cheeks. "Enough talk of such things!"

Syersi's return was immediate. "We must talk of such things, Mazzy! That is what Moganar believed. If he was right, I need to know."

The Absolute laughed while Mazzlin flushed a deeper red.

The Counselor made his way to the balcony doors and looked out past the orchards where the foliage shifted from rich green and brown to the outrageous grasses of bright red, and trees of vivid blue. The odd and interesting colors created a breathtaking landscape, and it was all due to the magic of the Gneiss Curtain.

Staring at the contrast in colors against the mountain's sparkling base, Chadgerwin chuckled while slowly shaking his head. "No, child. The Talents are locked away until you fall in love. And as for why we remained silent ... honestly? We did not know how to bring up the subject. It was your mother's responsibility, but obviously, she thought she would have more time to tell you. I think Saudria wanted you to enjoy life without the burden of knowing who you were." He turned and smiled. "I cannot blame her."

A crease formed between the young lady's brows as she joined Chadgerwin on the balcony. She quietly blew out a breath as her mother's blue eyes and bright smile came to her mind. Syersi's own blue eyes roamed into the distance and captured the glimmering yet jagged lavender spikes of the Gneiss Curtain.

"I need to know everything," she whispered.

Nodding in understanding, the Counselor asked, "You are ready then?"

She nodded and pulled back her shoulders, determined to hear it all.

Chadgerwin exhaled before beginning. "Your father was Denier Cri, or at least, to the best of our knowledge, that is what we think."

She interrupted. "You *think*?"

He held up his hand urging for patience. "The Denier Cri is the one in possession of the Source's Talents. Of course, your mother was his Source." He paused and studied Syersi, her blinking blue eyes riveted on him.

"When your father was a young man, he was found by your mother near the edge of a river in Janjene. Covered in war wounds, he was nearly dead."

Syersi mused at the similarity. She had found Rixs by the edge of the river, Giva, and like her father, he was nearly dead.

"Saudria nursed him back to health. She was young … about sixteen seasons cycles. It took a full season to restore his health, and along the way, he became infatuated with her which inspired him to stay longer. Then your mother fell in love with him. It is my understanding that she had no idea what she was, but there was a record in her possession that explained much. She could not read, nor could her parents who had found her and adopted her. Even Lothorius could only understand bits and pieces. It was after he was gifted with the Talents that the words came to life. That is the binding we search for in the records chamber." Chadgerwin rubbed a hand over his face.

"But that is its own story. One to revisit at another time. Anyway, according to your father, the moment her heart became his they knew it. It was excruciatingly painful for her, and her family worried she would die, as did he, but it was no walk in the meadow for him either."

Syersi winced, unconsciously lifting a hand to her chest, and pressing against the cramp that had plagued her for days.

All eyes focused on her hand, but none said a word.

Chadgerwin continued. "After that, Lothorius noticed changes in himself. Most occurred over time, but some were immediate. I knew him before the Talents and saw the difference … his strength, his sight, his mind … They surpassed anything normal. All the Talents we know of manifested over time."

The Counselor glanced at Mazzlin who nodded as he spoke. He absorbed the young Empress Heir before him. She was a Source – the very heart of the old legends, yet she knew very little of herself. Chadgerwin watched as Syersi blinked back glistening drops in deep pools of blue that threatened to spill from the corners of her eyes.

"Lothorius loved Saudria, or at least thought he did," Chadgerwin resumed. "He brought her back to Gnomera then wed her when she turned eighteen springs. By that time, Lothorius was incredibly powerful and hungry for answers. He studied the record, then traveled extensively, seeking all the information he could about the Source. When Garvier died, Lothorius ascended to the throne and his travels diminished, but by then, he was so powerful, his reputation had spread far and wide.

"Of course, no one knew anything about a Source, and your father hid the Talents well. But that kind of power affects a person!" Chadgerwin pierced her with his gaze. "Eventually, he realized everything was at his fingertips. No one could stop him and because he wanted Gnomera to be the greatest land realm in the world, he conquered territories. It came easily."

"That is the reason Gnomera is so great," Syersi whispered to herself.

He nodded and stroked his scarred face with his thumb. "Gnomera was already great, but he made it the ultimate land realm. Lothorius had become something born of legends. Some of the secrets he shared with me, but most he kept to himself. The more powerful Gnomera became, the more power he wanted … until you." He nudged her with an elbow, his eyes locked to the courtyard below.

"There was only one time that I saw tears grace your father's eyes. It was the first time he held you." The Counselor placed an arm around Syersi and gave her a gentle squeeze. "I was there, you know. And you had a shrilly voice then, too!" He smiled, the large scar on his cheek crinkling.

A lifetime of explanations cascaded from Chadgerwin's lips. Syersi had come along eighteen seasons cycles after Lothorius and Saudria exchanged their vows. It had been difficult for Saudria to conceive. She had lost many pregnancies. Once Syersi was born, Lothorius knew his daughter was a Source. He knew she would need protection, thus he devised a plan and searched high and low for a suitable double. The secret to his power compelled him – if anyone discovered the legend of the Source was true, and that his life was tied to it – to Saudria, her life would be in danger, if only to get at him. But worse, anyone with a taste for power and an understanding of the legend would clamor to possess the infant daughter, a Source herself.

Ice replaced the warm blood in Syersi's veins, and she shivered. A large warm hand covered her small petite one, and a subtle wave of tranquility caressed her entire body. Racing breaths eased. Tensed muscles relaxed. Syersi peered through her lashes at the man who had taken the place of her father and nodded her thanks for his help.

Unaccustomed to being thanked for using Talent to calm her, his thick eyebrows domed high on his forehead. She hated it when he Soothed her but this time, she welcomed it. Gnomera had fallen onto his shoulders while he patiently waited for Syersi to grow up. It seemed she was doing just that.

"Moganar was part of an elaborate scheme to throw people off the trail," Chadgerwin said. "But he didn't know it at the time. Lothorius had kept him ignorant." Chadgerwin leaned in and took Syersi's hand in both of his. "When that blasted Shade assassinated your mother," he paused to gage her reaction then continued when she showed no signs of distress. "Well … Syersi … your father died too."

She caught a breath and clung to Chadgerwin's hand. "Moganar said the same thing, but I had hoped he was lying," she murmured. "He also said the Intimus tried to have him killed."

The Counselor clenched his teeth. An eternity had come and gone before he spoke so he could choose his words carefully. "We are ruthless when it comes to protecting you, but do you really think Moganar could have escaped Rangus?"

The silent Absolute, still perched against the wall, snorted.

Mazzlin, who never held her tongue, could not remain quiet. "It was your father's plan, and it was perfect! Moganar thought your father left Isslewood to search for Saudria's assassin and did as was expected. He stepped into the role of an Emperor who was sick with grief over the death of his wife. It was necessary!" She clutched both hands to her chest. "Whoever killed my beloved Saudria needed to believe he had killed a mere woman, not a Source, and since Moganar played the role of an emperor who still lived ... No one suspected."

Hobb, who had startled everyone when he spoke, added, "Then after two seasons, we forced Moganar to leave Isslewood with a small band of guards and told the people he needed to get away from the memories of his lady. Moganar was never meant to return. And you were to ascend to the throne."

A low growl cut in, "It was a good plan, except Moganar decided to get greedy and come back." Rangus pushed off the wall and looked every bit like the wild beast he was.

Then all was quiet. In the silence there was an awakening.

"My father did not abandon me," Syersi's voice trembled, and tears spilled onto her cheeks.

Still holding her hand, Chadgerwin responded, "No. The sun rose and set in you. He loved you enough to orchestrate an elaborate rouse to hide the fact that you were ... *are* a Source. Somewhere within, you hold the greatest power any human could possess. His biggest fear was that someone would abduct you for your Talents."

Mazzlin added, "He wanted you to have the opportunity to find someone and fall in love, just like your mother found, and fell in love with him."

Syersi had hated Lothorius since his disappearance thinking he had abandoned her – left her alone and unloved. Her chest burned, and she closed her eyes.

"My child." Mazzlin's eyes were wide and glistening with

sympathy. "I notice how you hold your chest. Has your time come, Syersi?"

"No!" Her reaction was swift and abrupt. They gawked at her. In a calmer voice she amended her answer, "I have things under control."

Like a leaf fluttering in the wind, she floated about her chamber. "I will not subject anyone to a life enslaved to mine! That would not be love. Love expects nothing in return! How can I give my love knowing it demands his life!"

Rangus narrowed his gaze. "*His* life? You do have someone."

"I meant no one," she replied too quickly.

"It's that boy! That's why you hit him!" Rangus cried in triumph.

Chadgerwin found a chair and sat while his confusion shifted between Syersi and Rangus. "Hit who?"

"Rixs, of course," the Absolute responded.

"Why would she hit Rixs?"

Annoyance coated the Absolute's answer. "Because he kissed Syersi. Keep up, man!"

"Oh!" Mazzlin chimed.

Hobb chuckled. "I think we all saw that coming."

"Why would he kiss Syersi?" Chadgerwin questioned.

Rangus eyed his friend. "Why do you think? He obviously feels something for her. And she obviously feels something for him, otherwise she would not have punched him in the nose!"

Chadgerwin looked lost.

"Stop, all of you!" Syersi scolded. "I do not love Rixsander, or anyone else! Even if I thought I was falling for him or someone else, I would stop myself from loving him. He would be cursed to protect my life just to save his own!" She grabbed at her hair with a growl. "I cannot do that to him!"

"Love cannot be stopped," the Counselor said.

She knelt in front of the Counselor, her big blue eyes bulging out of their sockets. "There is still time. Strip Rixsander of his title and send him back to Pax Valley! Far away from me!" Her stinging gaze flashed between each of his eyes. "He wanted to leave, and we kept him here!"

The Counselor's scarred face was warm but firm. "I will not strip Rixs of a title he has earned. Rixs saved you, or have you forgotten? And he chose to stay of his own free will. We need his Talent. He is the best protector for you."

"I refuse him as Shield!" She jumped up and stepped away. "Make him leave, Chadgerwin, or I will!"

FORTY-FIVE

Precious stones and coins of gold thudded onto Rixs's bed. He stared at it, then at the First Counselor, who had casually dismissed him from his duty as Imperial Shield. It seemed Chadgerwin could not push Rixs out the gate fast enough.

Not fooled by the excuses, Rixs bit out, "You owe me an explanation! We both know I am the best choice to protect Lady Syersi. If it had not been for me, she would still be in Moganar's possession!"

He threw the large pouch of riches to the floor, his face twisted into a tight knot. "What has changed?" Not waiting for an answer, Rixs charged past Chadgerwin in the direction of Syersi's bedchamber and the Counselor let him go.

The Empress Heir had been avoiding him. She had kept to her chambers and assigned her imperial engagements to the Intimus. When she had emerged from her rooms, Rangus kept her company. Rixs was never summoned.

When he had first arrived in Isslewood, Rixs had gone out of his way to avoid Syersi. She was arrogant and temperamental and rude. A pain in his backside. Hard-headed and high-handed, Syersi blamed others for her mistakes, treated those who took care of her with contempt, and kissed nearly every guard she had. She was everything that offended him, and he had wanted no part of her but somewhere along the way something had changed.

He had discovered that while she was spoiled, she could also be considerably pleasant and little things about her made him smile. Like when her eyelashes fluttered wildly whenever she was curious or confused. Or when she had tried so hard to dunk him in the stream when they had been training. She never gave up until she finally succeeded.

They had settled into a comfortable banter between them that he had quite enjoyed. There were layers to the young lady, *Pixee*, and he had only scratched the surface.

Orris and two guards stood sentry outside Syersi's door. "Go away, Woodsman. She has nothing to say to you."

Every muscle in Rixs's body flexed. Anticipation of hitting Orris made him smile. Stopped in front of them, he cocked his head to study the men blocking his way.

"Try to stop me, Orris, please," he dared, itching for a fight. He further taunted, "I see Lady Syersi finally let you out of lock up for your blunder."

The guards tensed, and the Commandant showed his teeth but had nothing to say. It was true. Syersi had thrown Orris into lockup for a few days. It was his punishment for being part of the reason Moganar was able to steal her away, even though he thought the man was Lothorius.

Behind the door, Rixs was aware of a light grey figure. It was the space consumed by Syersi's body, and the form paced back and forth. In a voice smooth as cream, Rixs warned, "Out of my way. It seems I have nothing to lose, so if you try to stop me from seeing the Lady, I *will* hurt you." Emerald eyes squinted at each guard and Orris in turn.

When both guards foolishly reached for their swords, Rixs rolled his eyes. Two of his small throwing stix were already out of his hands and embedded deep into the sword hand of each guard. Their cries confirmed they were helpless to grip their weapons, and when they looked up, Rixs whirled two long blades in a graceful spin before each tip stopped to poise at their throats. Orris made no attempt to interfere.

Rixs held the long blades steady. "The Lady has nothing to fear from me. In fact, she is far safer with me than with any of you! Now, I suggest you stand down and move aside!"

"Stand down," growled Orris. "Let him dig his own grave!"

Once they stepped aside, the Commandant grabbed Rixs's arm. "Be warned. She is no longer the same starry-eyed girl who swooned every time you walked into a room."

He yanked his arm free and turned to the thick door. Nerves suddenly paralyzed his hand in midair as he attempted to knock. With a deep inhale he shoved his doubts to the side and tapped his knuckles against the wood.

It was Mazzlin's sweet round face who peered through the cracked opening in the door. Sharp eyes lighted over him before she swung the door just enough to let him through. When he turned to thank her, Mazzlin had already slipped out.

Syersi turned from the balcony and hitched a breath at the sight of Rixs standing in her chamber. Sandy hair hung in his eyes. She watched him toss his head of hair which resulted in revealing his brilliant green eyes. It threatened to break her resolve to banish him from her Empire.

"What are you doing here?" she managed to say.

A gentle curve hooked at the side of his mouth. Whether with his eyes or his Talent, Syersi's form was breathtaking, and especially when her mouth was shut.

Long and glossy black locks were woven into a single loose braid with her signature blue gems intertwined into her hair. He recognized the Seal of Syersi which hung at the center of her forehead. Layers upon layers of light sheer fabric in soft blue shifted in a subtle breeze which caught each layer in a slow dance and gave her the appearance of floating.

"Hello, Pixee," he said coolly. Then his lips hardened into a flat line, and he added, "You have been avoiding me, and now I hear I am no longer Shield."

Syersi swallowed at the nickname he had given her, and her chest squeezed tight. She needed to be rid of him immediately. If he lingered, she could not be held responsible for the demands of her heart.

Prompted by her silence, Rixs spoke. "I thought we were getting along. I thought we were becoming friends."

"Friends? Is that what we were becoming?" Syersi taunted and stared into his emerald eyes. They were full of life, brilliant and sparkling, yet they were angry. But these eyes were perfect for an Empress, even with their anger. "We both knew your stay was only temporary. You have a girl waiting for you in Pax Valley." She paused and took a step back — needed more distance between them. "And I have realized that we were wrong in making you stay. It is time for you to go home."

He stepped toward her to recover the distance she had placed between them. "What is the true reason you are sending me away? What have you found out over these last few days that has made you different?" Rixs asked as he took another step closer.

"I will not leave Isslewood just because you order it," he said as another easy step eroded their separation even more. With one more step, Rixs stood directly in front of Gnomera's Empress Heir.

They never had the opportunity to talk — for Rixs to tell her about Moganar's revelation that she was a Source. But they had the chance to talk now.

"You know, Pixee, Moganar told me you were the Source." Rixs tossed the statement into the air as casually as he would an apple.

Rosy cheeks drained of their color. That was the last thing Syersi expected to hear from his lips. Her tongue rolled in her mouth until her voice was steady.

"He told you I was a Source?" She forced a chuckle. "How amusing. And what did you think?" She batted her eyes up at him.

He was close. Too close. Syersi placed a hand on his chest to push him back but paused when her palm met warm flesh under his clashing vest. Naturally, he did not wear a tunic under his vest. She should have known better, but it was too late and the firm muscles of his chest and warmth of his skin inspired a shiver.

Rixs pressed a hand over hers and inhaled. "I was lost as to what to think," he replied in a low voice. "Enlighten me."

The hard lump in Syersi's throat made it difficult to swallow.

"Well … I want to know what you think."

The thoughts lingered on his tongue. He bit his lip and held her gaze as he said, "I think he spoke the truth. I believe you are the legend. Am I right?"

"Sorry to disappoint," she exhaled and finally swallowed. "I have no powers to use, and I believe the Source is full of power. All I know is that Moganar looked for a red binding. He said it was the key to everything …"

Serious emerald eyes studied her. A cramp squeezed the air from Syersi's chest, and she turned away. Rixs needed to leave Isslewood or he would break her resolve to keep her heart to herself.

"Look at me, Pixee." he hooked a finger under her chin and turned her gaze to his. "There is a Shade out there, and I am the only one that can protect you from him. You know this. So, why?" His eyes shifted their focus between each of hers. "Why do you want me to leave so badly?

Beg him to stay! Beg him to love you! The bite against her tongue kept the words caged deep in her throat. Relegating Rixs to a life of servitude was not a choice, and that was all he would be if he stayed – a slave to ensure no harm came to her so that he could continue to live.

It was settled in her head. She would make him hate her enough to leave.

Do not show your tears, Syersi! She was not fast enough.

When Rixs noticed glistening drops sliding down her cheeks, he instantly cupped her face with both hands and swiped them away with his thumbs. "Why the tears, Pixee? Talk to me." When she only responded with a quiver of her chin, he declared with a smirk, amusement resonating in his tone, "I am not leaving."

She did not move, and he slowly leaned in to make his intention known. He waited for her to react. She stayed in place and her blue eyes dropped to his lips. Soundlessly, Rixs made his move, aware as each tiny measure of space was saturated with their forms. The distance closed, until his lips pressed against hers.

It was soft and lingering, the kiss Syersi had waited for. The kiss of her dreams. A shiver flittered up her back, followed by the warmth of a silent sun.

The kiss spoke the truth. Rixs was resolved to stay, and it served to strengthen Syersi's own resolve to see him go. Fisted hands refused to reach for him, but Rixs wrapped her up and held her tight enough for them both. The kiss deepened.

He could not have known Syersi had already decided his fate and it would be their last keepsake. She put all she had into their kiss, ensuring it was worthy enough to cherish for a lifetime.

Both hands curved around the warm and hard plains of Rixs's chest and sides. She felt his muscles involuntarily flex – heard the small groan that vibrated in his throat. Every movement of his mouth inspired her craving for more.

Syersi's chest began to pulse, the reminder of her Source's curse pounded behind closed lids, and it gave her the strength needed to set in motion the events that would make Rixs hate her. Tearing her lips away from his, she released the scream that would seal her own misery.

FORTY-SIX

"You cannot do this!" Chadgerwin yelled.

Syersi's stone face defied the Counselor, her hands balled into fists on her lap. The Intimus sat around her in the governing chamber while Chadgerwin continued to unsuccessfully change her mind.

"You are mistaken, Counselor. I *can* do this, and I will!" She jutted out her chin.

Chadgerwin's scarred fist slammed on the table. He jumped out of his chair and ran both hands over his bald head to keep from using them to wring Syersi's neck. The inner circle shifted in their seats and watched warily between the two.

The day before, when Syersi had been gifted with the most meaningful and cherished kiss of her life, she forced a scream so shattering that Orris and her guards burst into her chambers. Rixs was wrapped passionately around her and Syersi pushed him off accusingly. The Commandant needed no further justification to have him beaten and thrown into lockup.

The look of bewilderment and confusion on Rixs's face had killed a portion of Syersi's heart, but she needed him gone from Isslewood. She steeled herself and accused him of placing his affections where they were not wanted.

At high sun, Rixs was to be brought to the receiving hall where he would be whipped for forcing himself upon the Empress Heir. A punishment of ten lashes in front of the ranking Lothorian Guard was his sentence.

Syersi knew it was a punishment he did not deserve, but it would provide the assurance that any affections he had for her would be whipped away and that hatred would take its place with every lash received.

"I agree with Chadgerwin," Rangus declared, his hard eyes fixed on Syersi. "Rixs is necessary to your protection. His Talent …"

"And that is another thing my Intimus chose to hide from me!" she interrupted with a shout that made the veins in her neck pulse. "You knew of his Talent but kept it secret!" She paused to control her breaths. "Regardless, you waste your time with me. I will not let him stay!"

Mazzlin sat straight in her chair. "Well, if you are set on forcing Rixs to leave, then have Rangus take him to Gateway. The Absolute can force him to leave, and no lashes are necessary. No cruelty is required, Syersi. Lashing him for kissing you is terribly unjust … especially when everyone knows you give your kisses away all the time." The Guardian blinked at her charge.

"Enough! Mazzy!" Syersi hissed as she stood from her chair. "The lashes will seal his hate and ensure he never returns!"

Clenching his fists, his powerful forearms cording, Chadgerwin walked to her, a plea in his eyes. "The sacrifice is not so horrible, Syersi. The young man will have the love of a beautiful woman. He will rule Gnomera at your side. He will have all the Talents entrusted to him. It is an honorable trade …"

"Honorable?" she cried.

Chadgerwin narrowed his eyes then raged at her. "It is an honor! Because of your love, he will benefit from the greatest gift he could imagine. Not only will he be certain you love him, but he will be the most powerful man in the world because of it. He will be thankful to protect you in return! By The Powers, Syersi, he will be Emperor! You act as if you are banishing him to live in the servants' quarters!"

Flat eyes and a face vacant of expression met Chadgerwin's argument. He could see it was no use. Syersi had already made up her mind.

She turned to Rangus. "Absolute, you will have Rixs brought to the receiving hall at high sun. I will let you decide which of your men will deliver the lashes." Without a second glance back at her Intimus, Syersi walked out.

"I told you," Rangus huffed. "She thinks she is in charge!"

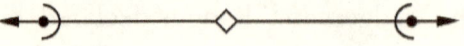

Stripped of his clashing vest, an angry Rixs leveled a deadly glare on the young woman seated on the throne. He was held in place by four guards, each holding a chain manacled to each wrist and ankle. Just behind him stood a large man with a whip hanging loosely in his grip.

Syersi sat straight as a board with Chadgerwin and Rangus standing at each side. She bit at her lip repeatedly and the taste of blood filled her mouth.

"I can smell that you know," Rangus whispered to her. "Stop it, unless you want me to drool over the dais."

She hurled a glare at him and he flashed red eyes and grinned back at her.

The Lothorian Guard's Commandant addressed the prisoner. "Rixsander of Pax Valley, you are here today to receive punishment for the violation of Gnomeran law which decrees that no one may touch the Empress Heir without her approval and consent, of which you are guilty. Such a crime is punishable by death, but the Empress Heir is merciful, therefore, your punishment is set forth as the following. Ten lashes to the back, after which, you will be banished from Gnomera for the remainder of your days! Do you have anything to say?"

Rixs glared at Chadgerwin and Rangus. *They* were letting *her* do this to him. He had nothing to say to anyone.

Orris nodded and the man with the whip stepped forward. *Crack!*

Syersi jumped at the sound of the first lash. Her tears were on the verge of spilling over as she watched Rixs flinch with the whip's bite on his back. The visible look of pain flashed in his eyes. *Crack!*

Crack!

Chadgerwin looked on with the strength he had always shown as First Counselor. The whites of his eyes against his black skin, gave away nothing but his teeth were clenched tight. Rixs would never forgive him for permitting the abuse inflicted on him. The Counselor only hoped he could forgive himself for allowing the injustice to continue.

The tang of fresh blood wafted up the Sanguinary's nostrils. Like the fearless giant he was, Rangus stood on Syersi's left, his hands hanging loosely at his sides. Displays such as this never bothered him. It was nothing more than the slap of a hand, but Rixs had not deserved this punishment, and that did bother him. Nonetheless, his Empress Heir had stuck to her decision, and she was not sniveling. He was proud of her.

Each echoed crack caused another stinging bite to the inside of her cheek. Syersi fought to hold her eyes steady on the man she would have dreamed to rule beside her. His eyes, turbulent with pain, betrayal and anger fixed on her in return.

Four. Five. Bile crept up her already constricted throat. It smothered her ability to inhale. She blinked repeatedly, willing her eyes to remain open and empty, free of emotion. Six.

Rixs's eyes never wavered. Each slice of skin made his entire body shake, but it was the nature of his punishment that cut and carved out his humiliation. He seared Syersi's image into his memory, her beauty marred by the cruelty of her false claim.

Again, the thin form of the whip split both air and space toward his already twitching and lacerated flesh. He clenched his teeth to prepare for the deep bite to come. *Crack!* Seven.

Body slumped in exhaustion and agony, the only thing holding Rixs up was the pull of the chains which had his arms stretched out wide and his legs straddled on the ground. Each time his legs faltered, the burly guards pulled his arms tight and high, making sure he stayed upright. Sweat-soaked hair clung against his cheeks and forehead, evidence enough of his agony, but if there was any doubt of his pain, every muscle visibly quivered to give testimony.

Syersi, held up a hand. "That will be enough." Surprisingly, her voice echoed calm. No one knew the strength it required to speak without falling apart into a sobbing spectacle.

"Feeling guilt, Syersi?" a tired, raspy voice cried out. Rixs breathed heavily, his hair, matted and dripping, hung in his eyes that had lost their vibrant color. "Ten lashes for my crime! Anything less stands as declaration that I was falsely accused and am innocent!"

Rixs had challenged the Empress Heir in front of her leaders. Her eyes swept over those watching, the same leaders that had been skeptical of Rixs in the beginning then came to embrace him as Shield. He had risen to Gnomera's heights but had fallen to its darkest depths – all because of her.

Knowing what it would mean if she walked away and left him without the full measure of his sentence, Syersi blinked into his acrid glare that could shrivel the dead. The hate reflected in Rixs's eyes was obvious. She had achieved what was needed. Without a word, Syersi gripped the gathers of her skirt, turned, and gracefully, like a queen, walked out.

Confused murmurs started low and grew to a feverish pitch as Rixs was taken away. The Empress Heir had made a statement when she exited the receiving hall, leaving his punishment unfulfilled and his declaration fresh in everyone's ears.

Mazzlin rushed to follow Syersi while Hobb went to Rixs.

"Get away from me!" Rixs snarled. "I neither want nor need your Talent!"

Covered in open gashes, Rixs's back looked like a slab of meat sliced repeatedly in preparation of an evening meal. The inflictor of the whipping had done his job well. Too proud, Rixs did not want the relief that only the Sanicle could give. He wanted nothing from any of them.

Loud hissing vibrated through Rixs's lips when he grabbed his clashing vest and stoically placed it over his shoulders. Every nerve burned when it settled on his skin. He spoke to no one, turned on his heel, and silently exited through the doorway. The sizeable pouch of riches remained behind.

"Be a good horse, Gritt, and kick these guys for me when you get a chance," Rixs managed a weak smile and patted the horse affectionately. Though the horse had been laden with supplies, Rixs refused to take him.

Almost to the gate, Moniere caught up with him, her own bundle gripped in her hands. She struggled to keep up with his long strides. "Rixs, take me with you!"

He only stared straight ahead and kept his quick pace, even though the heat of his wounds caused his muscles to fight back with every step.

"Rixs, slow down!" she pleaded.

He whirled on her. "Go back, girl," he snarled. "Take a hint. You are a nuisance!"

FORTY-SEVEN

Syersi had fled to her chambers, her stomach churned and tumbled while her heart cramped and threatened to squeeze the life out of her. She hurried to the balcony and leaned against the parapet, her false strength nowhere to be found. Her emotions shattered, like the vase she picked up and threw across the room.

Tears held back could no longer be contained, especially when Syersi noticed Rixs had emerged into the courtyard and refused to take the horse that belonged to him. Her heavy head thudded against the parapet and her body shook as the wails came.

She sobbed and sobbed as she watched the man whose dignity had just been whipped out of him. Too quickly, he had arrived at the opened gates. Even Moniere could not detain him, and in a blink, he walked beyond Tower Wall.

Rixs hated her. She had witnessed the transformation in his eyes. Her cries came in wave after wave, robbing her of the ability to breathe.

Mazzlin burst through the door to find Syersi crumpled on the balcony's stone floor. The Guardian dropped beside her and wrapped the girl in her arms.

And she cried. Her tears were one with Syersi. They cried together.

The sun made its way far past high noon and the broken

Empress Heir struggled to open thick and puffy eyes. The day was soldiering forward without any consideration of Syersi's broken heart. An aching throb stomped all over her head, and there was fire in her ribs.

Unseen flames licked at her bones. She moaned in suffering then shrieked when the heat became too much for her chest to bear.

Mazzlin had dozed off but blinked into sudden consciousness with Syersi's screams. She clumsily tried to guide her young charge to bed but could not budge her.

A phantom knife stabbed at Syersi's heart. She wailed and clawed at her chest. Orris burst through the doors, eyes searching for an intruder.

"Get out!" she screamed. "How dare you enter without permission!" The closest object, a vase, was hurled at his head. He ducked at the last moment and it shattered against the door. He flashed a questioning glance at the Guardian before hurrying out.

Syersi rolled back and forth on the balcony floor and clutched her chest. She panted and gulped for big breaths of air.

"Oh, my dear child!" Mazzlin cried, rubbing her hands over Syersi's restless body. "What can I do?"

Syersi pushed her hands away then shoved a portion of her skirt into her own mouth to stifle her screams. The veins in her neck bulged and pulsed with the heat of her blood.

Mazzlin hugged her tightly to keep her still. "By The Powers!" the Guardian cried. "Have mercy on her!" But she knew what was happening to the Empress Heir, and she knew there was nothing that could ease her agony.

Eternity passed. An exhausted Syersi shivered on the floor. Mazzlin tugged and pulled her toward the bed, but Syersi had fallen unresponsive. At her wits end, Mazzlin finally called for help.

"What is wrong with her?" the concern for Syersi obvious in his tone.

"She is ill. Place her in bed. She needs rest," Mazzlin replied. It was all he needed to know.

Strong arms effortlessly gathered the limp body off the floor then carried her through the spacious chamber and gently placed her on the bed. He hovered over her, his hand pushed away the sweat-soaked hair matted over Syersi's eyes.

"She's drenched!" Orris growled. "This dress needs to be removed!" His fingers fumbled just above her body without touching her.

Mazzlin slapped away his hands. "Well, you are not the one to remove it! Now out!" She shoved him toward the door. "And send for Hobb!"

He stopped before reaching the door, his eyes pleaded with the Guardian. "Please tell me this is not because of *him*," Orris mumbled. "Tell me those haunting screams are not because *he* left."

She sighed. "No, those screams were not because he left. Now, go get Hobb!"

A deep inhale conveyed his relief by the Guardian's answer. He nodded and closed the door.

"Those screams," Mazzlin whispered to no one, "means Syersi has given up her heart."

It was difficult to run, and Rixs quickly regretted not taking the horse with him. The blood-soaked clashing vest was removed to ease the searing heat it caused his skin. Riding Gritt would have made travel much easier. The horse did belong to him.

He jogged at a quick pace, needing to put distance between him and the object of his hate. The sun had made its way across the sky and Tower Wall and was no longer in view, giving Rixs some satisfaction. He had no sooner made the decision to slow down than he was hit with something that caused him to fall hard.

Sprawled across the ground, flat on his face and dazed, he gathered his wits and sat up, eyes and Talent scanning the space around him. Nothing. One moment he was running, lost in his anger, and the next, he was tumbling to the ground, hit by some phantom force.

He had just pushed off the ground when his chest tightened. The air was squeezed from his lungs, and he bent over to catch his breath.

Then the burning commenced.

There was a small flame that touched his breastbone. At first the discomfort was more a nuisance than anything else, so he rubbed his chest with both hands, but as its intensity roared to an inferno, he found himself roaring in return.

Muscles spasmed as fire lit his blood. It was as if an unseen dagger stabbed his breastbone. He clenched his jaw, while trying to control arms that flailed and legs that jerked him to the ground. He had no control over his muscles, and they convulsed violently. A snarl ripped through his nostrils. Then as suddenly as it had begun … it was gone.

Out of breath, with his face buried in the dirt, Rixs panted into the ground. His eyes were closed, but he scanned the area. There was no one around – nothing to explain his fall, not even a rock protruding out of the ground. There was nothing to explain the excruciating pain in his chest. He ran his hands over his skin. Everything felt and seemed as it should.

Rixs spat out a mouthful of dirt as he pushed up and sat on his haunches, preoccupied with trying to piece things together. There had been excruciating pain and then there was nothing. He sat and pondered it all for a time, and after some strength had returned to his limbs, he still had no answers. There was nothing else to be done except press on, so he did.

Lengthening shadows reminded Rixs that dusk was fast approaching. He had traveled the entire day without rest, and suddenly his bones and muscles were weary, worn out from his travels. There were few options to make camp, but he decided on a spot near a rocky ledge and settled atop his sleep roll.

There were endless twinkling lights in the night sky. The stars quietly danced for him, brilliant and sharp. Before he could rehash the events of the day, Rixs was snoring.

The bite of a whip's lash jolted him awake. He was still on the rocky ledge, alone, and the sun was long past its arc of high noon. Rixs rubbed the sleep from his eyes while he silently cursed himself. He had slept the day away.

Careful not to irritate his raw back, he stretched slowly only to find that the pain of the previous day's whipping was nothing more than a dull ache. He gathered up his sleep roll then slowly and hesitantly shrugged into his clashing vest. A grin stretched across his face as he twisted at the waist, swung his arms, and rolled his shoulders.

"You be a fast healer, Rixs," he said to himself. Then he turned to the south and walked.

Not much progress had been made before there were grey forms in the distance. Four of them. As the shapes became clearer, Rixs noticed that the normally dull smoky figures were no longer flat and featureless. He could make out the protrusion of their noses, the shapes of their eyes. His Talent had somehow matured to a new level.

The ashen figures sat around a fire, and two of the images were eerily similar in appearance to Rhages and Fogle. Rixs smirked, thrilled at the thought he might be able to discern identities of the forms that had always been nothing more than faceless shapes.

Still some distance away, he closed his eyes and concentrated. He smirked again. Their voices echoed on the breeze – voices that he should not have been able to hear. Something about him had changed. Not only had his Talent strengthened, but his vision was clearer, and his hearing sharper.

At long last, when Rixs finally emerged into view, all eyes landed on him. "Greetings!" he grinned.

"Who are you?" one man asked, eyes squinting.

The glimmer of recognition immediately lightened Rhages's face. "Kid! Be that you?"

Rixs walked to him, his wide grin exposed white teeth that glimmered in the firelight. "That be me, Rhages!"

Both Fogle and Rhages jumped up and slapped him on the back. He winced before he realized there was no explosion of pain. The sting expected from the lashes he had endured, did not come. He heaved a relieved sigh.

The two strangers nodded their introductions, but Rixs failed to catch their names. An odor had distracted him. The strange smell curdled in his nostrils and enticed him yet disgusted him at the same time.

Food was offered, but Rixs declined then realized he had not eaten in nearly two days. A thought crossed his mind that it was odd because normally as soon as he finished eating his stomach growled in demand for its next meal. Food was his joy.

The men clamored to congratulate the Shield on his rescue of the Empress Heir, and the four miraculous throws that had been pivotal in killing the imposter posing as Emperor Lothorius. Rescue had appeared impossible until Rixs arrived on the scene, then it was over before anyone realized it had begun, and not so much as a single hair on Lady Syersi's head had been harmed – except for the small nick in her ear.

"It seems you have not heard," he tossed his head to clear the hair away from his eyes. "I have fallen out of favor with the Empress Heir. I was stripped of my rank, whipped then banished from Gnomera. I return to the Bravura Strait."

"Dropped you like a piece of rotten meat, did she?" Fogle rubbed in.

Rixs wrinkled his already burning nose and placed his hands on his hips. "Seems you are right."

Rhages butted in, "Shut it, twerp! Or ya be findin' my boot in yer mouth!"

Lifting his palms, the redhead defended himself. "Calm down, brute! Rixs is the best marksman ever! She's an idiot for letting him go!"

The curious scent continued its assault to Rixs's nostrils and lingered on his tongue. After several swallows, he realized he was salivating and had a craving for raw flesh.

Through clenched teeth he said, "I may not be Shield, but you should not say such things of the Empress Heir." Then wondered why he defended Syersi at all. "I think I hear water nearby and am in need of a good washing," he huffed, and excused himself, following the sound of the stream he knew was nearby.

Emotions were on edge, and Rixs's senses played tricks on him. Anger coiled under his skin like a tightly wound snake, ready to strike, yet there was no reason for it. He had feared a single word might cause him to snap and needed to find distance between him and the smells that repulsed him but triggered a hunger he had never experienced.

Squatting by the stream's edge, Rixs splashed cold water onto his face and neck dousing the inferno within. Another splash of water extinguished any lingering heat.

Before the voice uttered a single sound, not only had Rixs seen the shadowed form of his friend approaching, but he heard his footsteps and caught the whiff of some odor that hinted of rust.

It hit him like a mallet cracking his skull. Blood. Rixs was smelling their blood.

"You okay, kid?" Rhages squatted next to Rix, studying his profile in the dim light. "Ya seem a bit restless and moody."

A rock the size of Rixs's fist, smooth and shiny, just under the gurgling water caught his eye. He plucked it up and turned it over, inspecting it. "Thanks for looking out for her, Rhages." Green eyes inspected him. "When she was trying to escape Moganar and Viktus," he added.

"It be nothin', kid." He reached for a rock. "But … I just don't get her whupping ya."

Rixs stared at him then mumbled, "I only wanted to give my thanks."

The muscles in his hand tingled and his temples throbbed. Thoughts of Syersi made his fingers tighten around the rock until his knuckles turned white. He squeezed without thought and squeezed until it cracked – then he tightened his grip still more. When Rixs opened his hand, the rock was in pieces.

Rhages's eyes were as big as moons, then he broke into a hearty laugh.

FORTY-EIGHT

Falling in love had left its mark. Pale skin and dark circles under dulled blue eyes gave evidence to anyone who looked at Syersi that something had leeched the life out of her.

Preparations for the Spring Celebration had begun, and servants scrambled among the gardens. Ripe cherries lined the orchards – baskets of them, harvested by the pickers who had been hired from Ormolu.

Mazzlin sauntered into the courtyard where Syersi sat. "How are you feeling, my dear?"

"Hi, Mazzy," Syersi greeted in a small voice.

Time hung in limbo since the day Rixs left Isslewood. Syersi had lain in bed for days and days. Recovery would have been even slower, had it not been for a Talent named Hobb, who had stayed by her side to restore her vitality. It was also the Sanicle who discovered the new mark burned into her skin.

Hobb had referred to it as the Mark of the Source. Apparently, her mother had one like it, in the same location, right between her breasts and a tad to the left, just over her heart. It was nothing remarkable, no illustrious color or shape identified it, but it was the mark that would forever remind Syersi of Rixs.

"I see a blush on your cheeks," Mazzlin chirped, sounding very much like the birds perched in the branches above them. "When the

Prince of Tangrah arrives, you will be as good as new!"

Syersi smiled half-heartedly and turned to look at the lake. Maybe a walk around the water's edge would ease her anguish. Had she known beforehand the misery and despair that would plague her after Rixs's departure, she might not have let him go.

Forcing Rixs to leave Isslewood should have contained her curse, for that was all her love was, a curse to the poor unsuspecting soul who received it. But despite placing distance between her heart and Rixs, she had fallen in love anyway. He was bound to her, and he had no knowledge of it.

"I hear that Prince Tangorio is the most handsome man in all the world," Mazzlin was yammering.

A lavish tent city had been erected just outside the gates of Isslewood to receive the heir of Tangrah. The tent city proclaimed his intent – he would linger for an extended visit.

"Yes, I know. I am also told he has an inflated ego. The biggest in all the world." Syersi stood from her bench. "My retinue have already forgotten about Rixsander of Pax Valley. They now focus their lustful attentions on Tangorio, hoping he will spare them a look."

Syersi turned to walk toward the lake, Mazzlin on her heels. A horn echoed and stopped them both. They squinted toward Tower Wall. There was commotion at the gates.

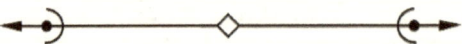

A hundred tents that bore Tangrah's banner cluttered the grounds outside Tower Wall. Rather than walk around it, Rixs tried to cut through the center but was stopped by four hulking sentries. He could have easily wrung their necks but that would have drawn unwanted attention. He walked around as ordered and noticed four tents, ornate and grand, in the center. He had never seen their equal. They were separated from all the remaining tents by a wide swath of ground. No doubt they belonged to the Prince he had heard so much about.

A muscle ticked in his jaw. It was no secret Tangorio had his sights set on the Lady Syersi. Rumors of her beauty, as well as her temper, had spread far and wide, even as far as Pax Valley. All the young men dreamed of meeting the dazzling heir to Gnomera's throne. But Tangorio's reputation had preceded him, as well. His romantic escapades and gifted abilities to seduce women had been the talk of the land realms from Janjene to Kelmar.

Syersi and the Prince of Tangrah will be perfect together! Rixs yearned to strangle them both. Whatever was happening to him, anger and aggression had become the first reaction. The need to tear something with his teeth constantly yanked on him, and fueling the madness was an ever-present bead of sweat that clung to his temples.

Isslewood should have been a memory, one to be forgotten. There was no desire to see the woman who had him whipped, or the Counselor who had failed him. Rixs flexed his back as he remembered each lash, but there was no other choice but to return. Too many questions needed answers. Rixs would demand explanations then leave and meet up with Rhages, who waited for him in the mole hills. Then they would return to the Bravura Strait together.

He had expected to fight his way through the gate, but they let him pass without question. Disappointment flared in his chest, as a fight would have worked off some of his anger, and because strangling Syersi was not feasible, Rixs chose to avoid her at all costs. He worked his Talent and searched for her light grey form, then purposely stayed as far from it as possible.

"What are you doing here?" the Commandant's voice was as cold as Rixs's rage was hot.

Rixs ignored him and walked on.

"Stop where you are!" Orris yelled. "Or I will have you whipped. Again!"

A dark grin that spoke Rixs's thoughts fixed to his face as he turned to face the Lothorian Guard leader. "Make me." His body trembled to throw a punch or bite off an ear. When Orris hesitated, he pressed him. "Please, hit me."

Hands that fisted and showed white knuckles stayed in their place. Orris scowled and stepped aside. Rixs wanted to hit him for being diplomatic – for being well behaved. For being a coward. Rixs walked on, his need for a fight remained unfulfilled.

Forewarned of his arrival, Chadgerwin, Rangus, Mazzlin and Hobb were already sitting in the governing chamber when Rixs stormed through the doors. Four guards nipped at his heels.

"Apologies, Counselor," one guard pleaded. "He barged in before ..."

Chadgerwin raised a hand. "We were expecting him. Leave us." He leveled an evaluating eye on the man he still considered Shield. "Hello, Rixs."

Standing in the doorway with arms flexed, his body tight and on edge, the changes in Rixs were subtle, yet obvious to Chadgerwin. Slightly taller. A little more bulk in his muscles. Had his eyes changed color?

Once the heavy door shut, Rixs spewed the words blistering his tongue. "You owe me answers!" He leaned on his knuckles against the table's surface and gave the Intimus a close view of his emerald eyes kissed with fire. Sanguinary eyes.

Stroking his groomed goatee and holding back a grin, the Soothe admired the eyes that danced with the sun's flames and were glaring at him. "What would you like to know?" Chadgerwin asked.

With bared teeth, the Talent growled, "You act innocent, Soothe! You know what I ask – what is happening to me? Stop the secrets and tell me everything!"

A snarl cut off Rixs's demands. Rangus jerked from his chair, scarlet eyes flared. "Watch yourself, wamp! You are in no position to demand ..."

A fist slammed the table interrupting the Absolute. The wood groaned then a crack split the table along the grain.

"Let us tumble, Rangus! Test my *position*!" Rixs taunted. His eyes flashed a brilliant apricot, a hint of emerald fought to remain in its place.

The Intimus stared at the crack, each speechless – except for Rangus. A deep guttural laugh sounded. "You need to learn to control that hot head, boy! Especially now! Or you will hurt someone!"

A wispy mist of calm settled in the room, flirting with Rixs's skin. His thunderous eyes shifted to Chadgerwin. "I do not need soothing, Counselor," he spat. "I need the truth!"

"The truth, my dear," said Mazzlin, "is that you are a victim of love."

Rixs stared at the Guardian. The creased forehead and opened mouth spoke his confusion. He glanced at Hobb, then Rangus, then Chadgerwin.

Mazzlin chuckled. "Please sit, Rixsander. We are here because we want to answer your questions."

Slowly, he took the seat next to her, then turned to Chadgerwin. "I am serious, Counselor. I am changing. I need to know why."

"We are serious, as well," the Counselor replied with a light smile, sitting back in his chair. "Sit tight. This will take some time." He then delved into the history of the Source.

"Thousands and thousands of seasons cycles past, superior men existed. These men had abilities like The Powers themselves. They could see things no one else could see, do things no one else could do, and they were clever. Because of their abilities they dominated quickly and became wealthy and powerful. They were known as the Denier Cri."

Rixs narrowed his eyes, watching every movement of Chadgerwin's mouth.

"They conquered and ruled with greed. Unless you were one of them, you could not fight back. Eventually, their greed for power turned them against each other. The wars began. Somewhere along the way it was discovered that these Denier Cri had a secret. They possessed a mysterious *source of power* which gave them their abilities. It was this *Source* that made them what they were."

Rixs thought back to Moganar's words. He nodded in cautious understanding as Chadgerwin spoke. Mazzlin's soft and cheery voice rang out next.

"It is a love story, Rixsander," she said. "Behind every Denier Cri is a Source who is in love. Their love is the key." She cautiously glanced at Chadgerwin since she had taken it upon herself to take over his story. He signaled encouragement to continue.

"Everyone assumed that the Source was an object, but that was false. The Source was a female ... always a female. Or, at least that is what we think. We have never heard of a male Source."

"Never?" Rixs questioned.

"That is what she said, wamp!" Rangus snarled. "Now shut up and listen!"

Ever patient, the Guardian reached over to pat the Absolute's hand. He growled at her, but she ignored him. "Anyway," she continued. "These powers are dormant and useless to the Source. The only way to unlock them is through the power of love."

Rixs sat with arms tightly crossed over his chest.

"Rixsander, Syersi is a Source," Mazzlin's voice was barely louder than a whisper. "Like her mother, and her mother's mother. She is special, she is the giver of Talent. And you are the recipient."

Confusion flickered across his face. "Are you saying Syersi loves me?"

She nodded. "Syersi is *in* love with you. It is the deepest love. The purest love. It has to be to release the Talents to you."

Wispy strands of sandy-colored hair tangled in his lashes as he blinked. He tossed his head to clear the hair from his eyes. It was hard to think of Syersi loving anyone – particularly him. He had been whipped at her hands, but he had healed – quickly. Not a single scar flawed his back.

The normally silent Hobb surprised everyone by adding, "You, my lad, are in a very envious position. If the people knew a Source existed, there would be a line of suitors as far as the eye could see, competing for Syersi's love. The Talents you are only beginning to receive make you the most powerful man in the world!"

"Only beginning to receive?" Rixs cried. "How many Talents will I have?"

Hobb shrugged. "No one knows."

Rixs sneered. "This is madness! But, if I ignore how ridiculous this sounds," he said, his leg bouncing under the table, "I believe you are telling me I am a Denier Cri."

"No!" Rangus cut in. "You are not a Denier Cri ... yet. You will be ... in time. You must hone the Talents. And, above all, you must remember, power can do strange things to a person. You must already see how Sanguinary traits make you act."

Lightning flashed in Rixs's eyes. "So how do I stop it?" Rixs remembered that the day prior, he had tried to wrestle a bear to burn off some pent-up rage. The scuffle had done him good, though he had some lacerations from the encounter. Those had healed, and the bear was released unharmed.

Chadgerwin shook his head, "You cannot stop it. Syersi has entrusted her heart to you. It is done. Now you must protect it."

Rixs rose from his chair. "Protect what? Her heart?" he spat. "That heart had me whipped then tossed me out on my hind parts. Do not tell me it is done!"

"No. You misunderstand," Mazzlin insisted. "Syersi tried *not* to fall in love with you. She had you whipped to make you hate her. She wanted you to leave Isslewood!"

It made no sense to him. He glared around the table. "And why did she not want to love me? Am I not good enough?"

Chadgerwin gestured calm with his hands. "Of course, you are good enough ... but ... she wanted you free from a life of ..." he was at loss for words. Telling Rixs that his life was now bound to Syersi's was a delicate matter. He fumbled for an easy way to tell Rixs that Syersi's survival meant *his* survival, and *her* death also meant *his* death.

"If she dies you die!" Rangus blurted out.

Chadgerwin sighed deeply. He no longer had to find a way to break the news to Rixs gently. Rangus plunged the dagger so deep, there would be no pulling it out.

The words had sailed over Rixs's head. "Come again?"

"You still misunderstand? Let me say it slower." Rangus leaned over the table. "If. Syersi. Dies. You. Die. Also! It is simple to grasp, wamp! Your lives are now tied together! It is in the myths about the Source. In addition to having all those powers, you have the obligation to protect the Source. Your life literally depends on it!"

A chair flew by the Guardian, and she jumped.

"What?" Rixs roared.

"Thank you, for your tact, Sanguinary!" the Counselor snorted. "Rixs, calm yourself."

"No!"

"I should have explained better," Chadgerwin apologized. "It will be easier if ..."

"Nothing you say will make this easy!" Rixs stood tense, muscles swollen with anger. "I knew Syersi was a Source, but ... I was not aware it would affect me!"

The Soothe inhaled with closed eyes. "Well, you would be unaffected if she had fallen in love with someone else. A Source's love literally creates a Denier Cri. One Source is needed for each Denier Cri. It was they who started the Long Wars so there must have been many like Syersi long ago. Anyway, the Denier Cri were impossible to kill. Normal humans stood no chance against them. Even the Denier Cri thought they were invincible. They were arrogant, bored, and greedy which led them to fight over land and riches. These were feuds and skirmishes mostly."

A heavy sigh interrupted Chadgerwin's explanation. "What does this have to do with my life?" Rixs asked.

"I am getting there, Rixs," Chadgerwin placated. He looked at the scars on his arm and cleared his throat. "Somehow, it was discovered that if the Source died, the Denier Cri died too. That sparked the beginning of the Long Wars. For seven hundred seasons cycles, the land was in war. Denier Cri fought Denier Cri, greedy for more power and wealth. The people fought to kill the Source and rid themselves of Denier Cri. The chaos went on forever. Eventually, the Denier Cri were killed off, but by then the people had forgotten what they were fighting for, and the wars raged on. Rixs, humankind was nearly killed off. It was assumed the Source were killed off too ..."

Silence filled the chamber. Rixs's mind worked through the tall tales he had heard as a child and the account of what Chadgerwin had shared. The Intimus watched him. The Counselor patiently waited for him to put the pieces together.

Rhages had been right. He told Rixs that day in the farmers' market that Syersi was the key to the Source. But Syersi was more than the key – Syersi *was* the Source.

Realization hit him in the head. "I am nothing more than a slave.

She deceived me," he mumbled, comprehending. "You all deceived me."

Mazzlin reached across the table and touched his arm. "Oh, no," her gentle voice chirped. "The First Daughter never deceived you. We, the Intimus, kept the truth from Syersi to protect her." She bit her lip. "She had no idea. Her feelings for you were already strong when she found out the truth. She was furious with us! She fought her feelings, Rixsander. Syersi did not want you sentenced to a life bound to hers. She thought if you hated her, you would leave. She succeeded in making you hate her, but love listens to no one ... she could not keep her heart from loving you."

The Guardian's gaze bore into Rixs, her voice determined. "Syersi, she needs you, Rixsander of Pax Valley. She loves you, and she is vulnerable without your protection. She has given all her powers to you. They are not hers to use. They are yours. Her love makes you powerful."

The Seer's words gave Rixs no solace. He clung to his rage. "Where is my choice in all this?" Heated eyes flashed to the Counselor as a fist slammed the table again. Another loud *crack* announced that the wood had split further. It was evidence that Rixs was growing stronger.

He placed his palms on the table. "I was nothing more than a prisoner in Pax Valley, captive to a marriage I never wanted. That is why I left. Now, I face the same, but this is worse. This time, my life is held prisoner. You say Syersi loves me. Well, I did not ask for her love and I do not want it!"

FORTY-NINE

Four magnificent guards carried Syersi's selle atop their shoulders, their drool-worthy features normally added pleasure to her day. But not this day.

The instant she had received word of Rixs's arrival, images of him consumed her thoughts. There were only two reasons for his return. Either he had chosen Syersi over his betrothed, or he wanted to kill her for whipping him. She bit her lip as she contemplated his motives.

The air thrummed with his energy. Syersi wondered if he had endured changes because of her Source's gift. The thought of seeing him made her body quiver and she knew sending him away again would not be something she could do. There was one irrevocable truth – she loved him with all her Source's heart.

The moment Rixs stepped out from the great house, Syersi's breaths stopped. Had he always been so large? Cords of muscle rippled in his arms and torso. It was a good thing he wore nothing under his clashing vest. Even his britches appeared to fit too snug. He seemed a little taller. And his eyes … they were the color of a green sun.

Syersi leaned out of her selle and greeted him. "I am glad you are back."

"I am not!" he replied sharply, his glower hard to miss.

Betrayed by his own conviction to ignore her, Rixs slid an appraising gaze over the Empress Heir. Dark circles around her eyes and hollowed cheeks told him she had neither slept nor eaten as she should. Her smooth ivory skin now pasty, conveyed she was battling an illness, and yet Syersi still was the most breathtaking woman he had ever encountered.

With a reckless swipe of his hand, he cleared the hair from his eyes then swallowed an oversized lump in his throat. "I am leaving."

The smile fell. Nodding in resignation, Syersi blinked repeatedly and quietly asked, "Walk with me for a moment, Rixsander? Please?"

So, he walked with her.

Along the path servants mysteriously disappeared wherever they roamed. Freshly picked cherries filled baskets along the orchard rows, their aroma calmed jittery nerves. The young Empress Heir was first to speak.

"I want you to know I did not try to deceive you. I did not know who I was ... what I was, until ..."

Rixs interrupted. "I know, Lady Syersi, the Intimus already explained it all to me." His gaze remained fixed on the treetops ahead of them.

Lady Syersi. That he had called her by her formal name did not pass her notice. She pursed her lips.

"I think when you purposely tripped me during our first training session, my feelings began to change," she hurried to say. She wore a smile so fragile, an unkind word from him would have made it crumble. Glancing from under her lashes she watched for a reaction. Before he left, she resolved to share her true feelings, and there was much to say.

Her steps touched the ground quietly compared to his which crunched the earth as he walked. Each of her steps were as thoughtful as the words she dared to share.

"There was this ache in my chest that became stronger, and stronger. The pain was linked with my feelings for you. As my feelings grew, the pains in my chest became harder to endure. Then I realized I was falling in love."

Rixs's continued silence made each of Syersi's words faulter at her lips. She had to drag each one out. Nervously wringing her hands, she forced herself to continue.

"Once I found out about myself, I tried to stop my feelings." She sucked in a throatful of air. "I would never wish for anyone's life to be tied to mine ... most of all, yours. So, I had to make you go ..." At a loss for words, she faltered.

The man's face was stoic as stone as was his gait. He walked stiffly beside her. They wandered slowly through the cherry orchard. Rixs dipped his hand in a basket filled to the brim with cherries and popped a handful into his mouth. As they walked, only the occasional *splat* of a cherry pit hitting the ground broke the silence.

Rixs brooded on. Syersi could stand it no longer. "I am sorry! So sorry for everything. I regret the way I handled all of this ... for your humiliation ... for the whipping ... it ripped my heart out!" She stopped and grabbed his arm forcing him to face her, but his eyes avoided hers. "I love you, Rixsander! Please forgive me. I beg you to forgive me ... and ... please stay. I will not be able to bear it if you go."

Green eyes finally met Syersi's blue eyes straight on. He pierced her with his gaze as though he could see her soul. "It is too late to apologize, Lady Syersi. It is simply too late."

His stomach churned. Heightened senses overwhelmed him. The scent of dirt, cherries, her skin, her breath, her blood. He craved the odors, yet they disgusted him.

"Your apologies do not set me free," he said, hand on his stomach. "It was not my choice to be bound to you. This is worse than my betrothal to Cliessa."

The bitterness of his tone, the truth of his words, sparked tears that trailed down Syersi's face. With his Talent stronger than it had ever been, Rixs saw her tears with exactness, every detail vivid, even though she turned her head to hide them.

Rixs clenched his teeth against the compassion threatening to soften his rage. He needed to hang onto his anger, not ready to let it go. His chest softened anyway without his permission, and he gently wiped her cheeks, rubbing the moisture between his thumb and forefinger.

There was a sigh of resignation. "I cannot forgive you now, Pixee. Do not ask it of me. Maybe one day I can put this behind me."

Syersi sniffled at his words – not what she had hoped to hear, but he had called her *Pixee*. It was a small strand of hope that they would find a way to each other.

She loved Rixs. While others could profess it with their lips and not mean it, or pretend with their hearts and not feel it, she could not. Others could hide their love. She had tried, but it had proclaimed itself without apology. Each manifestation of Talent Rixs claimed would be a testimonial of her love, and no one could doubt it.

The disappointment Rixs saw in her face reminded him of Chadgerwin's admonition. *The Source has always been defenseless, and more so when she gives up her Talent. Who knows why The Powers created it that way? There is only one means of protection – the life bond. The Source yields her power to love, and in return, the life bond ensures the Source has a means of protection. Syersi gave up the Talents to you, Rixs, and as a result, you are both left vulnerable because of the life bond. Yet you are both stronger also. Her life determines yours. You have the power to protect her. While she lives, you cannot die. But if she dies, you cannot live.*

It was hard to conceive, and yet Rixs knew it was true. Strength coursed through his veins. *While she lives, you cannot die. But if she dies, you cannot live.* He repeated Chadgerwin's words in his mind. His life would never again be his own. If he wanted to live a long life, he would have to keep Syersi safe.

With Rixs's shadowed face adrift in some foreign place, the Empress Heir drew breath to fill the gap. "The Source cannot access their own Talents. They are only a vessel ..."

"Yep," he bit out, not wanting to hear it all over again. "The Intimus already spilled the details."

"I did not intend to trap you, Rixsander, but I know it must feel like the worst betrayal on my part."

"You already said all of that."

Rixs had left Pax Valley because the township council had taken away choices that should have been his to make. They thrust a blonde, curly-haired girl with light blue eyes, at him when he was only thirteen winters. At the time, he was unsure girls were human. They had shrilly high-pitched giggles that clawed at his ears and spine. The funny thing was, had the township council left Rixs alone to choose his own bride, he guessed he might have picked Cliessa anyway. She was the loveliest, sweetest girl in Pax Valley. Instead, he grew up resenting the choice made for him, and he ran away rather than marry the prettiest girl he had ever seen — until his eyes beheld an obnoxious girl with an exaggerated opinion of herself, and a face The Powers had kissed to perfection, framed with black hair as slick as cream running through his fingers.

He let out an explosive breath of air. "You may not have meant to trap me, but I am trapped all the same."

There was nothing she could say in return, so they meandered on, with only the song of the crickets to keep them company while stars winked into the sky as night claimed the land.

The Intimus was sure Rixs would decide to stay. After all, keeping Syersi safe to protect his own life was a strong motivation. But he had never been one to adhere to expectations. Other than the Intimus, no one knew Syersi was the Source, except Moganar, and Kyerg, and they were both dead.

After Syersi's rescue, Kyerg ran to save his skin, as did many of Moganar's men. It was the game that Rangus loved to play. Chase. And chase he did. Kyerg never stood a chance.

Syersi was an Empress Heir, which was reason enough to guard her with every means possible. That was the pretense that needed to be maintained, but Rixs wanted his newfound status to remain secret. Convinced his plan was the best way to keep the Empress Heir safe, he discussed it with no one, including Syersi.

He would leave. Or at least he would make everyone believe he had left. Syersi would be heartbroken, but that was not his problem.

Even the Intimus would need to think he had left. It would be difficult considering Mazzlin's ability to see through the eyes of others, and Rangus's keen sense of smell. Both would be problematic, but until he felt compelled to openly return to Isslewood, Rixs would be as good as gone.

FIFTY

The line that extended all the way around the receiving hall and out the looming double doors was a great cause of panic. It was *The Welcoming*, and it kicked off the Spring Celebration. People traveled, both near and far, to greet the woman who would become their Empress.

Viceroy after viceroy, each from the Gnomeran territories bowed before Syersi. Beyond them, a sea of bodies waited their turn and signified a torturous day for the young lady. She glanced over the long line and eyed any male with brown hair scrupulously, her memory of the encounter with the brief tuft of brown hair still fresh in her mind. The Shade was still out there and Rixs was gone.

Her bottom had lost all feeling, as did her cheeks due to the stiff smile plastered on her face. The people lined up with no end in sight. Some were alone, some came in groups. They bowed, spat out compliments, then went on their way.

Pleasured by the panic he inspired, Rangus stood on Syersi's left, and watched the terror on every face that approached the throne. They eyed him cautiously, and he responded by throwing a blood-tinged glare their way.

"Blame yourself for the long line," Rangus's whisper was a rumble in his throat. "They come to see the *changed* Empress Heir. If you threw more fits and tantrums, this line would be half as long!"

A sneer befitting the *old* Syersi flashed at the Sanguinary. "You tempt me, Rangus." But an instant later, a wide smile fitting an Empress welcomed the next subjects waiting to greet her.

Filling the role of Shield, Orris stood behind the First Daughter. His flat eyes, tight mouth, and clenched fists easily professed that he was bored out of his mind. The role of Shield was supposed to have assured Orris alone time with the Empress Heir, instead, she ordered him around like a chamber maid, and he was forced to follow her wherever she went like one of her retinue.

The Intimus had high hopes Rixs would stay when he agreed to walk with Syersi, but then he had left, forcing them to deal with the Spring Celebration on their own. Rangus had even threatened to rip him apart if he left, but Rixs merely laughed at him.

In the end, the Intimus, and Syersi, watched Rixs walk away.

"I am trusting you to protect *my* life," was the only thing Rixs said to the Intimus before he disappeared.

The hollow thud of drums and a sudden halt to the progression of bodies drew everyone's attention to the double doors. Orris, Rangus, and Chadgerwin stood rigid as the crowds cleared a swath of ground wide enough for a distinguished party of eight to make their way, unimpeded, to the throne. Three prominent figures stepped forward, one man and two women.

Immediately, Syersi's keen blue eyes landed on a sight she had never seen before but had recognized instantly. The Talent was distinct from any other and always easy to identify, but this Talent was unique.

A *female* Sanguinary stood before the dais. Unable to resist, Syersi stole a glance at her Absolute.

Other than a single deep inhale, Rangus gave up nothing to indicate he had noticed the beautiful phenomenon standing before him. His nostrils flared with her scent. It was apparent that the curvy Sanguinary smelled as luscious as she was striking.

It was the stunning male with rich waves of dark amber framing a face worthy of a second and third glance that stole every pair of female eyes in the hall. He stood between the red-eyed temptress and another female, giving the impression that the two women were protectors rather than ornaments.

The man's dark brown eyes dared Syersi to blink first as he held her attention with an unwavering gaze that curled her toes. He could have easily contended for Syersi's heart had it not already been claimed.

It was the female Sanguinary who spoke. "Lady of Gnomera," she said with a surprisingly forceful voice that hinted of the power and strength surging within her seductive warrior's body. "I present, Tangorio, the Warrior Prince and Pride of the Land Realm, Tangrah, son of King Tarrin the Fierce."

The walking sculpture of lust stepped forward to within a deadly proximity of the Empress Heir. Orris sprung from behind the throne, and Rangus stepped forward with a snarl. The female Sanguinary responded with eyes that flashed bright red and a dagger ready in her hand. Tangorio waved an arm through the air in her direction – a signal to stand down.

The man dropped to one knee in a show of respect. "May I?" he asked, extending his hand with an upturned palm.

Syersi glided her cerulean eyes over the regal man on his knee and paused on the color of his hair. It was brown. Before she let paranoia rule her behavior, she waived it off. Many men had brown hair. Orris had brown hair. Many of her guards had brown hair, before she had Orris assigned them to other duties. It was a wonder why she kept Orris around.

Her dark lashes fluttered as she studied Tangorio who waited patiently for her next move. It was a bold gesture on his part and Syersi knew all eyes were keen on her reaction. A passing glance at Chadgerwin caught a barely perceivable shake of his head. He discouraged her from taking his hand.

Tangorio's face gleamed like the sun's reflection off the Gneiss Curtain, and before she knew it, Syersi had extended her hand, letting the Prince grasp her delicate fingers.

"It is an honor to finally meet the Jewel of Gnomera." The man exuded confidence. It dripped off him like liquid from a cracked goblet. Then he pressed warm lips lightly against the tops of her fingers.

Syersi let out a breath that she had been holding.

Hidden among the crowds packed into the receiving hall, Rixs watched with a silent snarl. It had been easy to slip by the door guards undetected since the Prince of Tangrah had claimed all attention. No one had given thought to the man with a patch over one eye, hunched over a cane as he walked.

Rixs scrutinized every particle of claimed space surrounding Tangorio. On his body a sword was strapped to his side, and concealed under his sleeves, knives were sheathed to each forearm. There was also a dagger tucked into the back of his trousers. The claim of *Warrior Prince* seemed to suit him.

Aside from identifying every threat within Syersi's vicinity, and thanks to his newly developing Sanguinary senses, Rixs was also keenly aware that her heart was thrumming wildly in her chest. She was taken with Tangorio.

A growl escaped his throat without warning. It caught the attention of nearby observers who looked at him like he was touched in the head. Unfortunately, both Sanguinary Talents, Rangus and the female with Tangorio, plucked the sound of his growl from among the many noises in the hall.

Rangus snapped his eyes over the crowd, stretching his neck to allow his scarlet orbs the best advantage possible to search the sea of faces, while he sniffed the air at the same time. Following the Absolute's lead, the female rotated her head from side to side, nose scrunched, dissecting each scent that cluttered the receiving hall. Tipped off by both Sanguinarys, Syersi, Chadgerwin, and Orris turned their attention to the crowds as well.

"Strikes!" Rixs whispered to himself, then cringed, realizing he had said it out loud. Another mistake for Sanguinary ears to hear.

It had been easy for Rixs to lose himself in the ocean of bodies packed in the receiving hall. He made himself small while eyeing the dais through matted and oily hair, hoping his voice hadn't singled him out. He held his breath.

Sweat and dried urine that had been left to simmer over days, not only affronted Rixs's nose, but everyone else unlucky enough to stand next to him. He knew he would need some way to conceal himself to avoid detection by Rangus, but since he slipped up with the sound of his voice, Rixs slumped further over his cane and slunk backward until he was outside.

It was Syersi's coronation day – a good day to sell goods. The air was fresh, the sun was bright, and people had come from everywhere to witness the young Empress Heir become Empress of Gnomera.

Forming long lines outside Isslewood's gates, peddlers took advantage of the crowds and lined Tower Wall to hawk their cheap wares. A cacophony of voices competed for attention making it difficult to hear anything. It reminded Rixs of the day he had taken Syersi to the farmers' market in Ormolu and he passed the time walking among the carts and displays. In his disguise, he walked among the peddlers, and it came without warning.

Images blurred before him. They rippled like water and crowded an already cluttered head. Rixs squinted to keep his balance and stave off the wave of nausea threatening to undo him.

It was the Source – *she* had caused this. The Talents that were useless to her now plagued him with fever, chills, nausea, and most of all, confusion.

His own Talent was strongest, the forms in endless hues of grey were no longer flat but defined in detail. Then came the added burden of Sanguinary sight. Sharper than eagle eyes, his vision was so clear, the colors so brilliant, his eyes watered constantly. Both *sights* combined required him to interpret their detail so as not to misunderstand what was around him.

The new images came in waves and looked nothing like the visions he already tried to navigate. Something entirely different was manifesting. Mentally exhausted from the many changes he already endured, Rixs found an unoccupied space against the sparkling stone of Tower Wall and leaned against it.

He shut his eyes tight to block out the world, but the undulating figures still plagued him like ghosts. He realized that these were different than what he saw in his world of grey. The scenes were not the same as what was immediately around him – these images came from a different place.

Syersi's face peered at him through a fog of undulating air. He jumped off the wall, his heart nearly stopped thinking she had found him, but she was beyond his touch. Like a dream, the Empress Heir was in his head. Only the boisterous throngs of people buying and selling goods stood around him.

Rixs relaxed back into the wall and heaved a groan as he watched Syersi's mouth move as if she spoke to someone, though he could not hear her voice. Behind her, wide double doors stood open to a balcony. He laughed. She was in her bed chamber, but more important, he realized he was a Seer. He could boast having Mazzlin's Talent!

At that moment, Rixs boasted nothing. His mind and body were overwhelmed with the changes taking place. Bile rose unbidden in his throat. It overpowered his control and he doubled over – vomit spewed from his mouth.

"Hey! Don't be smelling up the place! It will drive away the customers!" A vendor to his side complained.

Humped over and bracing himself with his hands against his knees, Rixs wiped his mouth with an already filthy sleeve, and looked up into the gaze of an old woman with wrinkles on her face as plentiful as thorns on a rose bush. Her nose crinkled at him.

"Must have got a bit of spoiled food. Nothing catchy," he flashed a humble smile, but was rewarded with a scowl.

"Not worried about the *catchy*. Worried about the *smelly*! Ya already stink of pee! I be selling nothing with you here!"

Rixs stood to his full height and towered over the woman. Her eyes traveled up his body and widened. Worry replaced her contempt.

Rixs pushed off the wall. "Forgive me for the inconvenience," he said before he walked away.

He trudged toward the trees and away from the commotion and noise surrounding Tower Wall. A secluded patch of grass caught his eye and he dropped to the ground on his hands and knees. The curdled contents of his stomach roiled, and he vomited. Then he vomited again, and again. All through his misery, the watery images continued to plague him.

When all contents had been emptied, Rixs lifted his head, and focused on the dream-like visions before him. A pudgy finger tapped on Syersi's chest and Rixs's eyes snapped wide and fully open when he realized what was on display.

Syersi's cleavage swelled into view. It was a lovely sight, and he might have wrestled with guilt for admiring it if it were not for the knowledge that these images came unbidden. He was not acquainted enough with the Talent to know how to make the visions stop. Mazzlin needed to close her eyes to prevent Rixs from seeing too much. So, he looked on with admiration.

The Guardian's finger pushed aside the fabric at Syersi's already plunging neckline and Rixs instantly closed his eyes, hoping to preserve Syersi's reputation. It did not help. The images continued anyway.

Then he saw it. The dark patch of skin just on the inside swell of the Empress Heir's left breast which looked like a birth mark. Determined not to ogle, Rixs tried to discretely study the mark. Then it suddenly struck him. The patch of darkened skin resembled a burn mark the size of a thumb print, similar in size and shape to another mark he had seen.

Without thought, Rixs's finger unconsciously pressed his own chest. He had the same mark.

FIFTY-ONE

Syersi walked through the orchards knowing exactly where she wanted to go. Isslewood's vastness made it easy to feel as though she was the lone human walking the earth, though her detail was never too far away. The walks helped clear her mind and ease her soul — but they also reminded her of *him*.

The coronation was only ten days old. She had taken newfound responsibility for her people and dug into her role of Empress. There was much she needed to learn.

Prince Tangorio had been a welcome distraction during the three days of celebration. His mesmerizing dark eyes and easy smile kept Syersi charmed and saved her from slumping into melancholy for a man who had tossed her love aside and disappeared without giving a second thought to her feelings or desires.

An illness had rendered Tangorio slightly weak, but he still managed to drag the fledgling Empress to every vendor that had something to sell, including a young, paralyzed man who sold jewelry of excellent workmanship. Then there were competitions to cheer, and performances to enjoy. She had remembered a particular performer who seemed to pop up wherever she went, his amber eyes peered through chestnut hair to watch her.

Even with Tangorio's grandiose presence which caught everyone's attention, men and women alike, there were times when he looked tired. Even so, the too handsome man kept to her side, and often took liberties of holding her hand, even though she pulled away. This never affected his confidence. He had no sense of rejection.

"You will find, beautiful Empress, that I do not give up so easily," Tangorio had crooned.

He had come to Gnomera with two hundred soldiers, in addition to his personal detail. They were led by the luscious Shield named Geiselle, a Sanguinary that had come from the Janjene land realm. Syersi wondered if Tangorio took liberties with the dark-skinned beauty that might have extended beyond the boundaries of Prince and Shield.

The second woman, Torrah, was a Sanicle Talent, and like the Shield, never strayed far from Tangorio's side. It was not common knowledge that she had the healer's gift, but Tangorio had told Syersi, then fished for information about the Talents who surrounded her. He never received confirmation – Syersi would never be naïve enough to divulge the secrets of her Intimus.

As Commandant, Orris was allowed to walk at Syersi's side, but as Shield, he was forced to walk behind her, and she was happy to keep him there. In her mind, he was lucky not to spend the rest of his life in lockup for ignorantly assisting Moganar in stealing Syersi away from Isslewood. She would hold her grudge forever if she wanted.

By the time Syersi arrived at her destination, her dress was damp with sweat. Her favorite stream was just ahead, and she squinted at the tall male who stood at its bank, his back toward her. The beat of her heart skipped. Rixsander had returned! Then the man turned around and waved. Syersi's shoulders sank.

"Empress Syersi, do you mind if I join you?" Tangorio called as he ambled over, his walk full of power. Geiselle and Torrah followed behind. He took Syersi's hand when he reached her, and without permission, pressed her knuckles to his lips.

Syersi stared past Tangorio to the majestic Gneiss Curtain and the burst of colors lining the base of the mountains. She had come to this place for the quiet solitude it offered. Tangorio was intruding.

Boldly, she replied, "You may stay, but only if you do not speak to me. You must remain silent."

Raising his eyebrows, Tangorio cocked his head to one side and flashed her a mischievous grin. "I am especially good with silence. Let's leave our entourages here while you and I sit near the water. Alone. And in silence."

Though she tried not to smile at his comment, the crook of her mouth could not be contained. Hoping he had missed her grin, she hurriedly turned away and walked to the stream's bank. The rock Syersi had claimed as her own when Rixs first brought her to this place, welcomed her to sit.

Orris scowled. He had been left behind with the unimportant people while Tangorio charmed Syersi by the stream's edge. He looked cautiously at Geiselle and wondered if she was discontented at being left behind. It appeared she was unaffected, nor did she seem bothered by Tangorio's affections toward Syersi, rather, she kept vigilance over Tangorio with a face blank of expression.

"I have never seen so many odd colors in all my life! It is fascinating!" Tangorio mused. "And this spot ... it is truly enchanting. I can see why you come here."

"Shhh," she pressed. "Silence, remember?"

It *was* Syersi's favorite place, but only because Rixsander had showed it to her. It seemed wrong that Tangorio sat where *he* should have sat. He had trained her here. Syersi had cursed him in this place. But they had laughed here too.

"Oh, yes! Forgive me." Tangorio pressed a finger to his lips. "Silence."

"You forget ..." she was saying when an involuntary chill tingled up her spine and silenced her words.

With neck strained, her blue eyes scanned the rocks and cliffs of the Gneiss Curtain. The lavender rock sparkled so bright under the sun it overpowered her ability to see. Anything could have hidden among the cliffs. She twisted in the opposite direction and studied the landscape with its hues of blues, reds and purples.

A frown creased Syersi's flawless complexion as she squinted into the hills and trees. Someone was watching. The pebbles rippling over her flesh bore witness of it.

"What is it, beautiful lady?"

She did not answer.

Orris noticed her behavior and rushed to her. "Lady Syersi, what is wrong? Has the Prince offended you?" His eyes lit up with the prospect of punching the heir of Tangrah.

"Hold your fist, Orris," she replied while her eyes still searched. "Prince Tangorio has been kind and respectable. I ..." she paused and visibly shuddered. Unseen eyes sent a chill all the way to her toes.

Could it be the Shade? Brown hair came to her mind. He had disappeared after she had stabbed him. When Rangus went in search of the body, it was gone. He stayed close to Syersi after Rixs left Isslewood. Without Rixs's talent, the Absolute's keen sense of smell became invaluable to her protection.

She scrutinized the brown hair around her. Orris, Tangorio, two of her guards that stood near Geiselle. She thought of Bronan and a few of the other men that had abducted her. There were so many with brown hair. How would she ever be safe?

"I need to return to the great house," she said, her voice quivering.

Snubbing proprieties as only Tangorio could, he swept Syersi into his arms.

"Put her down!" Orris demanded.

The Prince ignored the Commandant and carried Syersi to his Sanicle. "The Empress is unwell!" he exclaimed. "See to her."

"No!" Syersi cried. "I only need to lie down and rest. I do not need a healer."

Hesitating a moment, Tangorio narrowed his rich brown eyes. "Fine," he conceded. Then without warning, he hefted her onto his horse and swung up behind her.

"What are you doing?" Orris grabbed the reins which instantly earned a reaction from the female Sanguinary.

Geiselle grabbed his neck with long sharp nails, and though he choked under her grip, he managed to pull his dagger. In less time than he could blink, the Sanguinary yanked the dagger from Orris's grasp and pushed its point just behind his ear. Syersi's detail ran to the Commandant's aid, but Geiselle responded by pulling the dagger's tip down his skin. Blood beaded along the cut.

"Enough!" Syersi ordered, her voice fierce and bold.

Tangorio jerked his head. Geiselle obeyed and dropped Orris's dagger then blew him a kiss. Her red eyes blazed over his body.

Orris snarled as he pressed his palm against his blood-smeared neck. Geiselle grinned.

"Be civil! All of you!" Syersi ordered. She leaned back into the heir of Tangrah and asked, "I beg you, take me home."

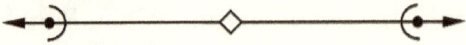

Chadgerwin stood next to the ornately carved bedframe with hands clasped behind his back. On display, a rich cache of scars swirled around his muscular arms. "I am sorry, Empress Syersi," he hummed as only Chadgerwin could.

The large bed swallowed her body like an insignificant morsal of bread. Curled on her side, she tipped her head upward and blinked at the Counselor, then chastised, "You dare call me *Empress Syersi*? Having wiped my wee baby's bottom, I would think formalities are unnecessary, Chadgerwin."

A dark hand gently stroked her hair. "Old habits break grudgingly, Syersi."

She nuzzled into his hand and closed her eyes. For an instant she wished that it was Rixsander who ran a gentle hand over her head, but he had abandoned her. Even knowing their lives were linked, he chose to leave. It was the worst insult. The man had rejected her love, and unfortunately, there was no way she could reclaim her heart to set him free.

"I always thought when I fell in love, I would be loved in return," Syersi mumbled softly. "It never occurred to me that my love would be tossed aside like unwanted table scraps. It never occurred to me that the man I loved would despise me."

"He is a fool," the Counselor whispered.

He thought to Soothe her broken heart but decided against it. Soothe was a temporary fix and things like broken hearts did not need temporary fixing. Syersi had to learn to conquer this mountain on her own, but to make himself feel better, Chadgerwin toyed with the idea of sending a party after Rixs just to have him whipped all over again. Maybe thirty lashes, or perhaps forty would make the Counselor feel better.

"I saw the way he looked at you, my dear," he said. "An old man like me knows that look. There was much more to his feelings than he admitted. He may yet return. I do not see how he can stay away."

"And that is the worst of it," she said with a sigh. "He is unwelcome if he returns because he must. I want him to return because he wants me."

As the days passed, the young Empress immersed herself into the affairs of Gnomera. Even while she kept busy, she was haunted by unseen eyes. She was convinced that the Shade, who had failed to abduct her, was toying with her as revenge for the wound she had inflicted.

The gates were never left open. Entrance or exit to Isslewood only occurred in the mornings and at midday when Rangus was on hand to smell everyone and everything. The gates remained closed when the Absolute was gone. Even so, Syersi worried.

Stop torturing yourself, Syersi. It is all in your mind. She kept herself busy. When her empirical duties did not take up her time, Syersi engaged in what had become her favorite amusement – fighting. Each day she trained with anyone who would teach her.

Tangorio frequently offered his services. He hung around Syersi like one of her pendants hanging from a chain. And he was soft. Where Pravin, Orris, Rangus and even Geiselle, demanded much of the Empress during their training sessions, Tangorio was easy on her.

Pivot, twist, thrust, and slice. If perspiration did not drench her clothing, she practiced harder or trained again with someone else. It brought her a sense of security. It brought her joy. It fueled memories of Rixs.

He had been the first to train her, insisting on it when everyone else, including the Governing Council was against the First Daughter undertaking such an unladylike activity. Fighting was for soldiers and warriors, not princesses and ladies. Training would never be as sweet as it could have been had the young man who stole her heart chosen to stay. They could have danced.

Syersi sat on the swing tied to the branches of the old knobby oak that grew between the great house and the lake. Unblinking, tear-filled eyes stared over the still water as she rocked herself back and forth, her hands gripping the fat ropes. Even the sky had felt her heartache and clouded over in solidarity with her gloom.

Again, she felt it.

Wiping her wet cheeks, her blue eyes searched the surrounding area. Except for her detail, two guards that hovered close by, Syersi was alone.

"Oh, Rixsander," she mumbled to herself. "If you only knew... I miss you. And not because I need the protection of a Denier Cri. I miss you because you demanded more of me. Demanded that I be a better person. Demanded that I never give up." She took a breath. "And you made me laugh. You were a true friend."

In that moment, a wayward gust of air wisped her hair away from her face to lay along her back. She looked around for the absent breeze and shivered.

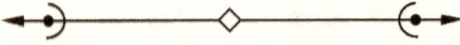

Unseen, a worn and weary Rixs stood back and regarded her as she rocked in the swing. Learning to cope with the Talents had kept him plenty ill, but over the long and dreary days, he had watched Tangorio dally with his Source then eye her hungrily when she was not watching.

It was ironic that the very powers which were to make Rixs invincible, instead made him powerless, helpless as a newborn babe. He had burned with fever and had no strength because food would not stay in his stomach. The Talents were uncooperative and temperamental.

He had remembered falling to the floor in one of the remote wings of the great house as he searched for a safe place to stay. For days he had been too ill to move.

The memories of how he had survived those early days were

unclear. There were dreams of running after prey, and he wondered if they were more than dreams. Rixs had kept his distance from Syersi until he was certain he had managed control over the Talents – especially the Sanguinary.

It had been difficult to watch Syersi and Tangorio at the stream. His life depended on her safety, so he had kept watch from a distance. He watched Tangorio call on her frequently, and it left Rixs with a sour taste in his mouth, but he had been the one to walk away – or let her think he had walked away, so he had no right to be jealous.

A Shade still stalked the countryside and Tangorio was trying to win Syersi's hand. Rixs wanted to grip his throat and squeeze until his eyeballs popped out of his head. Then he wanted to do the same to Chadgerwin and Rangus for being careless with Syersi's protection.

A full moon had made a complete rotation before Rixs noticed parts of him disappearing. Another full moon had come and gone before he had a little trust in his ability to Shade himself. The first time he had dared to get close to Syersi, she sat on her swing and mumbled into the air.

Without thought his finger brushed through her silky soft hair. He wanted to hate her, yet her tears softened his Sanguinary heart and a Shade's finger caressed her hair. Syersi could not have known it, but she had nearly broke Rixs's resolve to stay away.

FIFTY-TWO

The cavern yawned wide to swallow the Empress whole. It was more frightening than she remembered. Without the one person that made Syersi feel completely safe, the only time she could bring herself to go there was in her dreams.

Several nights her dreams allowed her to walk the darkness, standing firm against the black shadows that blanketed everything, even her breath. It was easier to find courage in sleep, and since the night held only small increments of fitful rest, she willed herself to dream of the dark place far below the records chamber, because even if she was lost and alone, Rixsander always found her there. And he always walked her back to the light.

Night after night, Rixs sat on Syersi's window ledge and watched her sleep. Her dreams took her away and he did not know where she went, but the whimpers and thrashes told him it was somewhere that frightened her.

Troubled by her restlessness when her dreams should have brought her peace, Rixs practiced his newly manifesting Talent. Soothe was as tricky as Shade. He could not be sure if he was effective, but this latest time he tried, her whimpers settled into a peaceful hum.

He always held himself to the shadows of her chamber, afraid that if he got too close, the temptation to stroke her soft cheek, or place a light kiss on her forehead would overpower him. His resolve to stay away was weakening, and the Talents were unpredictable, but he was not yet ready to be discovered.

Syersi stood in the black cavern. As expected, Rixsander appeared to pull her out of the gloom, only this time, the man of her dreams did not leave her at the light's edge as he normally did. In this dream, he escorted Syersi to her chamber and tucked her into bed.

The images were muted, the color dull, but it seemed so real. The Empress tried to talk to him, but her words only came out as garbled noises. He made no effort to speak. He only watched her from the edge of her bed with that crooked smile she loved and those mesmerizing green eyes, now flecked with tidbits of fire. And ... there was a touch.

Syersi shot up with a small yelp, her eyes as big as the moon hung low in a starless sky, but there was nothing. The door opened with a loud click and a guard rushed in with his hand on the hilt of his sword.

"My Empress!" he called. "Is everything all right?"

"It is nothing," she assured him. "Only a dream."

He refused to leave until every corner was inspected and he confirmed the balcony was clear.

The next day, Syersi kept to her bed. She refused the company of the ever-present Tangorio, who had finally pulled up his tents outside Tower Wall, and took up the grandest living arrangement available in Ormolu. A season had already passed, and it became obvious he had no intention of leaving Gnomera any time soon, particularly Isslewood.

In a fitful rage, Syersi cursed The Powers for leading her to the Pax Valley stranger the day she found him at Trifalls. Then she cursed Rixsander for having been born.

Sleep did not come to her at night, so she wandered the halls of the great house with Orris close on her heels. When the man ignored her threats to stop talking to her, she gave him a taste of what Rixsander had been subjected to as Shield. Syersi threw the Commandant into lockup. The next night, Orris kept his mouth shut.

Since the nights held no rest, the Empress napped on the

floating terrace by day.

Her naps took her to the top of the mysterious Gneiss Curtain where she could look out over the entire world. It was on the other side of the world that Rixsander waved to her, his smile brilliant. If she could have only stretched her fingers far enough to touch him, but then her eyes would snap open to a bright sun making her sweat.

She was losing her mind.

Chadgerwin had discouraged her from leaving Isslewood, but she needed a change of scenery. "I am going to ride into Ormolu," she announced, prepared to face her first real test against the Intimus.

"It is too dangerous!" Rangus snarled. "Have you forgotten a Shade still roams the land? You cannot leave Isslewood!"

"Watch me, Sanguinary!" she growled right back, and rode Juju out the main gate with no one to stop her.

"That girl thinks she's in charge," he grumbled to no one, then chased after her. Another fifty guards followed behind him.

The excursion was uneventful. There was no excitement to be found anywhere in Ormolu, so an exhausted Syersi returned to Isslewood, but her mission had been accomplished. She had tested her authority and ability to leave Isslewood without being challenged. Nobody stopped her. Completely exhausted, nothing could keep her from her soft, warm bed – except Mazzlin.

"Eat this meal!" the Guardian cried. She carried meat and soup on a sparkling tray. "I will not leave until you have finished it all. By The Powers! You look like death! If Prince Tangorio were to see you right now …"

"If he could see me at this precise moment, he would tell me that I am the most *beautiful* woman in all the world!" Syersi interrupted. "He wants my empire, Mazzy! The way I look makes little difference to him!"

After she had eaten, and the Guardian finally left, sleep found Syersi. Her dreams took her to a golden field where the grasses swayed to a musical breeze. She looked down at her body to find a silky dress whipping restlessly about her ankles. In the distance, a bed under a blue cherry tree called to her.

She walked to it and laid her head against the cherry blossoms that piled into a pillow. The bed was soft and warm, and in her dream, sleep took her almost immediately.

The ground crunched. Then it crunched again. Syersi opened her eyes to dancing emeralds.

Rixs sat over her, his features soft and concerned as he stared at her face. His brows narrowed as he fixed his sight on the hollow of her cheeks and the dark circles under her eyes.

Syersi gasped and sat up to a darkened, empty bed chamber. She rubbed trembling hands over her face then looked around the silent room, halfway expecting to see the man of her dreams standing in the corner or sitting in the window.

The stone floor was chilly against her feet as she slipped out of the bed and padded across the room, grasping her chest and holding back tears that testified of the hole in her heart. She looked out the window and stared into the dark. A subtle warmth fell over her and coaxed her back to her blankets. Sleep claimed her once again.

On the following day, the Governing Council had been assembled and claimed Syersi's time. A corrupt viceroy who had been stealing from his people needed to be ousted from power. Refugees caught up in the war between the land realms of Waukee and Kelmar were starving. A plan to provide relief was underway and she was involved in all the details.

The once proud and condescending First Daughter, now an Empress with a little more humility and wisdom, had even walked among her wamps. The new recruits would one day be Gnomera's next generation of combat forces. Their starry-eyed stares were clear indications that they were quite enraptured with their Empress.

Syersi had dutifully claimed her title, and Chadgerwin was quite proud of her yet worried over the twinkle that no longer danced in her eyes. Her willful nature had been quelled. He had never wanted that. He had wanted the spontaneous and rebellious girl to learn prudence and exercise good judgment, but he had loved the mischievous twinkle in her eyes that had faded with all that had happened to her.

At the end of the day, the Counselor tried to take the evening meal with the Empress, but she declined his company. Mazzlin attempted to wheedle an invitation to eat with her, but that too was met without success.

Syersi slumped against her bed, not bothering to trouble herself with a meal or changing into a sleeping gown. She crawled under the covers and yearned for shorter days and longer nights, because every night held the promise that she would find the man who now consumed her thoughts.

A misty image sat next to her in silence. Syersi batted her lashes, trying to determine if she still slept. Seeing Rixsander was no surprise. Her dreams tirelessly sought after him.

He sat over her with a partial smile illuminated on his face. A shadowed finger gently pushed a wayward lock of hair from her forehead. Then he stood to leave, like he always left.

As was typical in her dreams, she tried to reach out, and as per usual, her body would not cooperate. Walking never got her anywhere. Her legs jerked slightly, and when she reached for him, a finger twitched.

As if leaving her was painful, the object of her thoughts stalled above her, then bent down and brushed his lips ever so lightly over hers. Tingles fanned across her skin. She wanted it to be real. It felt … real.

Syersi shot up in bed. Dawn approached and a hint of light touched her chambers. It was enough to see that she was alone.

"No!" she cried, falling back onto her pillows, the noises of a waking world humming against the early morning. It had been another dream.

Syersi willed herself to fall back to sleep hoping to pick up where the dream had left off. She flipped herself restlessly from one side to the other. The memory of the phantom kiss kindled her resolve to find sleep … until she flung her arm across the bed and felt the prick of something sharp.

"Ouch!" Syersi blustered and propped herself up. The offender stretched across the pillow next to her. Her dark eyelashes fluttered.

An object rested on the pillow. She hesitantly reached out with eyes wide in wonder. It was a pendant on a chain.

Syersi touched the chain, an exquisite piece of workmanship. It was crafted with small golden links, and attached to it long spindly thorns shaped from gold formed an elongated oval cage. A spectacular blue sapphire polished and shaped in the form of a small delicate bud dangled within. The necklace was elegant and beautiful.

Never had she seen one before, but Syersi recognized it immediately. Pixee's Solitude.

Snatching up the pendant, her eyes immediately searched around her chamber. She ran to her balcony, her eyes surveying the nearby trees, and scanning the grounds of the courtyard below.

There was only one person that knew the meaning of this flower, and its significance to her. She held the pendant tightly against her heart and pressed her fingers to her still tingling lips.

It was *his* favorite flower. He had said so himself. He had described it to her in such detail, there was no doubt in her mind what it looked like, or what it meant. He had dubbed her Pixee, because she reminded him of the beautiful flower that could draw blood, and he had only called her by that name when they were alone. No one else knew about it. This necklace was a message for *her*.

It had not been a dream. Rixsander had been in her chamber. He had kissed her. And he had left her a message loud and clear. He never left Isslewood. He was watching, and to remind her that he was nearby, Rixsander had left her a token.

It was a powerful message. He had not left her even if her eyes could not see him. She did not understand why he kept hidden, but it was enough that he had given her a sign that held meaning. It gave her hope that he would visit her in her dreams, and then one day, when he was ready, he would return to her. The kiss he had left told her he would.

With necklace in hand, Syersi stood at the edge of the balcony, and scanned her blue eyes over the trees and courtyard. Somehow, she knew Rixsander was watching, so she sent him a message in return.

Pink lips pressed against the pendant then she blew the kiss into the early morning breeze.

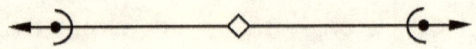

Thank you for reading.
K. Severe

If you enjoyed this story, please take a few moments to return to the book's product page and leave a review now. They are very appreciated, and every one helps draw more readers to books they might also like.

Just scroll down to the stars and immediately below the "Review this product" section, click on the gray box that reads, "Write a customer review."

Thank you in advance!

To sign up to receive Kim Severe's new release alerts and newsletter, visit www.kimsevere.com.

PRONUNCIATION GUIDE

Bravura: Brah-VOO-rah
Chadgerwin: CHAD-jur-win
Cliessa: KLEE-es-sah
Denier Cri: dah-NEER KREE
Fogle: FO-guhl
Gneiss: NEESE
Gnomera: no-Mare-ah
Hobb: HAHB
Intimus: IN-ti-mus
Isslewood: ISS-el-wood
Lothorius: loe-THOR-ee-us
Mazzlin: MAZZ-lin
Moganar: MOE-gan-ar
Moniere: mon-YARE
Ormolu: ORE-moe-loo
Orris: ORE-ris
Pravin: PRAY-vin
Rangus: RANG-gus
Rhages: RAY-jez
Rixsander: riks-SAN-dur
Sanicle: SAN-i-kul
Saggacious   sah-GAY-sheus
Syersi: see-UR-see
Tangorio: tan-GORE-ee-oh
Tangrah: tan-GRAW
Wamp: WAWMP

ACKNOWLEDGEMENTS

By the Powers! It's done! What started out as a diversion when tragedy struck became an escape to another place when I needed somewhere else to go. There is no agenda here – no deep life meaning. It's just a story that brought a smile to my face when I needed something to smile about, and I hope that by sharing, it brings a smile to you as well.

The journey has been a long one and a lot of people played a part. Thank you, Jackson, for being my first honest critic. You were one of the first to tell me I had a story worth fighting for. Hugs to Alicia, Alan, Camille, Jeni, and Hayley who were brave enough to wade through some rough drafts to give an initial thumbs up on a place called Isslewood. A big thanks to Samantha, Jena, Megan, and Tony who supplied a final keen read and a double thumbs-up. Rocky, you are the man! Thanks for polishing the final copy, and Karen thanks for getting the book ready for the world to see.

Kelli Ann, you are my Shield! From book cover inspiration to advising and guiding. When I couldn't see the next step, you were there to give me a nudge. I'd still be scratching my head if I didn't have you in my corner! XO.

Of course, where would I be without my family? You pulled out the pompoms when I needed it but kept me focused on what was important. I love each and every one of you! XOXO! To my partner in mischief, you must really love me to endure all the dribble about Syersi and Rixs, and to hear it repeated over and over. What a champ!
And finally, I have to thank a certain son who probably knew this story better than I did. You drove me crazy when I wasn't writing, reminding me that if I piddled around the story would never get done. Your relentless prodding kept the flame lit.

To those of you who took the time to read this story, thank you – from the very deep recesses of my heart – thank you. Whether you liked it or not, I express my gratitude for giving this fledgling author a chance. I can only get better from here! May the Powers bless you!

ABOUT THE AUTHOR

KIM SEVERE is a professional logistician with an affection for daydreaming. As an only child in a military household, growing up could get lonely, but thanks to a vivid imagination, there was always an amazing adventure to take, and extraordinary characters to meet. Years later, little has changed – only now, while she is in her own head, she's sipping on a smoothie.

If you would like to receive new release alerts from Kim, please visit her website at http://www.kimsevere.com where you can sign up for her newsletter.